Nobody's Child

Anne Baker

headline

First published in 1994
by HEADLINE BOOK PUBLISHING

First published in paperback in 1995
by HEADLINE BOOK PUBLISHING

24

ISBN 978-0-7472-4603-9

Typeset by CBS, Felixstowe, Suffolk

Printed and bound in Great Britain by
Clays Ltd, St Ives plc

HEADLINE BOOK PUBLISHING
A division of Hodder Headline PLC
338 Euston Road
London NW1 3BH

Nobody's Child

Book One

1920-1923

BOOK ONE

Chapter One

22 September 1920

'Thank God you're here!' Hannah Mortimer flung herself at her husband and clung to him, as much to give comfort as to gain it.

'I saw the doctor's pony and trap outside.' Matthew was breathless from running up the front steps. 'Has she . . .?'

Hannah's throat felt tight. The hours of waiting had awakened painful memories. She choked: 'Dorothy's had a baby girl.'

'Then it's all over?' He straightened up; she could see relief spreading across his face. 'Dorothy's all right?'

'No!'

Twice as anxious now, Matt's grey eyes fastened on hers.

'It was twins. Both girls. One has died.'

'Twins! Her mother was a twin.' His adam's apple moved slowly. 'I wish they'd both died.' His voice was harsh.

'Matt! You can't mean that.'

'I do, it would solve the other problem.'

'Just listen.' Hannah's gaze went to the sitting-room ceiling. The oil lamp hanging there swayed as a heavy footfall thudded against the floor above. Then a man's voice barked some urgent instruction.

'What's going on?' Matthew demanded.

She still held him close enough to feel his heart pounding; it made her own jerk faster. Clearly something terrible must be happening to Dorothy. 'I don't know.'

'Then we'll find out.' He pulled away.

'I sat with her all morning, but they asked me to go. Matt,

3

I'm frightened for her. It's taking too long.'

She watched him balance his bowler on the newel post, then slowly climb the stairs to knock on the bedroom door.

Most of the furniture had been pushed out on to the landing; even the carpet square had been taken up in the interests of hygiene. As they both waited for the answer that didn't come, Hannah studied their reflection in the wardrobe mirror.

The agonies of anxiety over the last months had put years on Matt and thinned his brown hair into a monk's rim. His paunch sagged large and low; he looked haggard, bewildered by events. It made her ache with sympathy.

In the dim landing light, her crimson dress was a splash of colour floating about her, softening her large patrician features and glossy dark hair. She'd never liked her height or her Roman nose and high cheek bones; in the half light they looked less strong. She was nine years younger than Matt, thirty-one. Today, when she'd spent less time on her hair, wisps were escaping from the large insecure bun on top of her head, making the age difference seem greater. The worry had made her lose weight so that now she looked girlishly slender.

Seeing herself like this, it was hard to believe Dorothy's trouble had left so little mark on her. She knew she'd taken it more painfully to heart than Matt. But, of course, the marks were there, they just weren't visible.

The thin whimper of the newborn came from inside the room. Matt was all Mortimer and none of them was used to being kept waiting. He pushed the door open.

The unexpected sight of so much blood left Hannah gasping for air. She felt Matt recoil, his horrified exclamation underlining his shock. The midwife turned round. Her white apron and navy dress were splashed with huge scarlet stains. The heavy odour of blood assailed her nostrils, caught in her throat.

Very little furniture remained apart from the double mahogany bed. The foot of that had been raised on two stools and the pillows tossed off to the floor. Hannah barely

4

recognised Matt's much loved seventeen-year-old daughter. Her lacy nightdress was blood-sodden and sticking to her.

Hannah gulped, hardly daring to take another look. Dorothy was lying flat and motionless in a knot of twisted and stained bedclothes. Blood had collected in a pool and was dripping down to the floorboards.

The doctor, his face stiff with tension and anxiety, was bending over her, rubbing her abdomen. His shirt and even his chin were smeared with blood too. Hannah watched Matthew's hand-made black Oxfords step into the pool. Her mouth had opened to warn him but she was too late; he was not the first to tramp stains across the floor. She shivered with fear. Impossible not to feel touched by this crisis. The chaotic mess before them was screaming catastrophe.

'Is she . . .?'

But no, she could see Dorothy was breathing, though her eyes were closed and they seemed to have sunk deeper into their sockets. Her youth had gone. She was as old and haggard as Matt, and her skin was grey and waxy and sweating.

'What's happening?' Matt demanded.

'Third stage bleeding,' the doctor said laconically. 'I think she'll be all right now.'

'Think? Aren't you sure?' Matthew's own panic made him sharp. Hannah closed her eyes. Her friend Clarissa Bender had recommended this man, but . . .

'We've got to be certain,' Matt said. 'What about another opinion?' That was pure Mortimer. They all thought their money could buy them out of every difficulty.

'I'm sure. It's stopping now.' The doctor's voice was weary, but he managed to instil some authority into it. 'Bleeding like this is an emergency we can't foresee. It doesn't allow time for other opinions. I'd have been only too glad of help a few minutes ago, I can tell you – retained placenta – but it's out now.' His face was shiny with sweat.

'She's lost so much blood.' Fear was sharp in Matt's voice. Hannah felt him brush past for a closer look.

'It looks more than it is, and it's stopping. I've every reason

5

to believe your daughter will be all right.'

'She looks deathly pale.' There was even blood in her long blonde hair, matting it together.

'Clinical shock. Give her an hour or two and she'll look better.'

The front bedroom was hot and the windows misting up. Hannah thought it a cold house, rather cramped and comfortless, but an ideal safe hiding place in Dorothy's hour of need. The fire had been kept roaring up the chimney all day, and now the grate was filled with brightly glowing orange coals. She could see the sweat breaking out on Matt's forehead. Would they really be able to keep such momentous happenings a secret?

'A lovely baby girl.' The midwife, cap awry, sounded falsely bright. Hannah watched Matt force himself to look at the tiny baby to which Dorothy had just given birth. It was lying beside her on the big bed, and had kicked its way out of the bath towel in which it had been wrapped. Its tiny, perfectly formed body was blotchy with blood and vernix.

A bath towel parcel, ominously still, lay on the tiled wash stand; the toilet trappings having been pushed back to make room. Hannah had to drag her gaze away.

The midwife was picking up the live infant.

'A strong baby, nearly six pounds, a good weight for a twin. The other was tiny, didn't stand a chance.' She re-tucked the towel round the living child, then held her out.

Hannah almost snatched her. Dark blue eyes stared up into hers, tiny lips sucked and blew. She felt a surge of love and wonder and was suddenly alight with longing.

She pushed back the towel to see all of her again. The infant was plump, beautifully rounded, perfect. Hannah cuddled her closer, captivated by the tiny waving fists.

'No!' Matt barked. She jumped, taken by surprise. 'Put her down. Don't do that!'

The strength of his anger frightened her. Shocked, she pushed the bundle towards the midwife and backed away, holding her arms behind her, feeling for all the world like a

6

naughty child caught doing something she shouldn't.

'I'll bathe her first,' the midwife said. 'You're right, she's not ready for visitors yet.'

'We none of us are,' the doctor muttered wryly.

For years, Hannah had been looking forward to the time when she could hold a child in her arms. Matt's first wife had already given him Dorothy and Gregory, but he'd married Hannah to beget more heirs. He'd said there was nothing he wanted more than to perpetuate the Mortimer family name, but the babies hadn't come though the doctors had told her there was no reason why she should not conceive.

'It can't possibly be my fault,' Matt had blustered. He had been married to Emma for five years, and had wanted more sons then. But Hannah had been unable to persuade him to consult a doctor for help. Too embarrassing – not the sort of thing he did, apparently.

Hannah recovered sooner than Matthew. She could see him shaking, and there was no mistaking the condemnatory air of both doctor and nurse. She put her hand on his arm drawing him away, protective as always. 'We've found out what we wanted to know.'

After one more look at Dorothy, he moved slowly to the door.

'Shall I send a maid to help you tidy up?' Hannah asked the midwife briskly. 'Find some clean sheets?'

She caught Matt up in the hall and helped him off with his overcoat; he seemed dazed. In the plain square sitting-room he settled himself in the only comfortable armchair while she poured him a stiff brandy.

Once she'd been his secretary, and though she'd been his wife for ten years, sometimes it seemed their relationship had hardly changed. There were days when she seemed to have been promoted rather than married. Her range of duties had been extended a little, but it was still her job to make life as smooth as possible for Matthew. She kept a social diary for him though there was hardly anything to write in it.

Before she'd met any of the Mortimers, Hannah had been

7

well aware of the reputation of Sir Hugo Mortimer, Matt's father. It was said he was one of the richest and most powerful men in England after managing to rise from being a penniless lad in Liverpool to become the owner of a fleet of tugs plying their trade in the ports of Liverpool and Birkenhead.

She knew he'd gone on to invest his fortune in other businesses with what seemed a Midas touch; that he'd given one fortune away to help the poor, and another to safeguard the power of those who shared his political views. Matt told her the war had brought him new opportunities to make money and now, in late middle age, his wealth was legendary.

'He gave me the company,' Matt had told her shortly after they were married. 'He bought it for me as a twenty-fifth birthday present. It had already been trading for a hundred years as A. A. Evans Limited.'

'That was generous.' Hannah had been surprised.

'I was already married with a family. I think he wanted me off his back. He believes very firmly that every man should be independent and earn his own living.'

When the Great War came, Matt volunteered to fight. He said: 'One way of getting my own back on Father. He'll have to look after the toffee factory for me while I'm away.'

Even after the Great War had been over for two years, Matt said he didn't feel he'd settled back to running the factory. He'd found the war in France traumatic, though he'd had a desk job behind the lines.

Hannah could see by this time that Matt didn't have his father's interest in money, nor his energy and talent for earning it.

He was academic by nature and had evaded his father's attempts to interest him in business long enough to go to university and gain a first in archaeology. He had a real passion for the ancient world. His father called it his hobby.

Matt's idea of a rewarding career would have been to work on a dig in Egypt, Mesopotamia, Knossos, or Athens. The one thing he really wanted was to read more widely in his chosen subject, and study it further. Because he had to run a factory, he was deprived of the time to do it.

Hannah couldn't understand now why none of this had been obvious before she married him. But he'd seemed an important man then. She'd imagined he'd follow in his father's footsteps and had expected him to be in the public eye, alert to every opportunity for adding to his fortune.

Instead she found Matt a retiring bookish person; selfish, set in his ways and hide-bound in his habits. His home was an untidy muddle of books and papers, which he instructed the servants to leave untouched.

Now he stirred. 'Poor Dorothy, she's had a bad time.'

Hannah was afraid the shock of seeing his daughter lying newly delivered would never leave either of them.

'Of course,' he added, 'it's different for you, less worrying. She isn't your own child.'

Hannah knew the hurt was unintentional, but would the worries bite deeper if Dorothy had been her own child? She didn't think so.

There was a good reason why it slashed at her peace of mind, though Matt knew nothing about that. During the long summer months alone with Dorothy, heightened emotions had led her to speak of things best left unsaid.

It had left her on a knife edge, and longing more than ever for her own child.

'I've done my best for Dorothy,' she said now.

'It was a good idea to bring her here. Good of your friend to let us rent this place.'

'Dorothy was very put off when she found Clarissa's mother-in-law had died in this house shortly before we came. Though it was in our room, not hers. She says the place is like a prison.'

'Poor Dorothy.'

She'd always known Matt loved his daughter dearly. He'd had a picture of his children in a silver frame on his desk. Years ago, he'd said: 'They need a mother, especially Dorothy.'

It had jarred that he didn't mention his need for a wife, but Hannah had been very much in love and touched at the thought of his motherless children. At the time, Dorothy was only seven and Gregory eight.

When she'd first come face to face with them, she'd thought their good manners and polite ways delightful. Gregory was home after a first term at prep school, already self-possessed. Dorothy had put her flower-like face up to be kissed and Hannah had been bowled over. In a white lace dress and with golden ringlets, the child looked utterly charming.

After fifteen minutes, Matt had rung for Nanny to take them away, and had taken Hannah out to the theatre. She foresaw no difficulties; it never occurred to her they might not accept her in place of their mother.

Greg was back at school when they returned from honeymoon. Dorothy ran downstairs to greet them and Matt swung her up into his arms, raining kisses on her cheek.

'Hannah is your mother now,' he said, drawing her closer. 'You can call her Mama.'

'She's not really my mother.' Dorothy had tried to pull away, glaring at Hannah from under her lashes. 'I don't want . . .'

'Don't be silly,' Matt said, keeping a firm grip on her arm. 'Of course you must.' Suddenly she was clinging to him, burying her face in his coat. Matt had prised her fingers loose and set her on her feet. 'Come on now, kiss your new mama.'

'We'll be friends,' Hannah had tried to comfort her. 'We need to get to know each other.'

Dorothy had immediately turned mutinous and scowling. 'I don't like . . .'

'Of course you do,' Matt had flared impatiently.

Hannah had put her arms round Dorothy to show that she could love her too. Prickly and resentful, the child had elbowed herself free.

To start with Hannah had thought it only a matter of time

10

before Dorothy accepted her, and she tried very hard. Dorothy never addressed her as Mama if they were alone; only, and with reluctance, if Matt was present.

Perhaps if she'd had Dorothy with her all the time she would have been able to wear down her sullen resentment. But she went to stay with her grandparents frequently, and during the war when Matt had been in France, her grandmother had insisted Dorothy stay with her.

The great Sir Hugo had seemed fond of his grandchildren too. In the school holidays Gregory liked to run at his grandfather's heels, and enjoyed nothing better than being taken to visit the factories he owned.

'Isn't he a distraction to you?' Hannah had asked Hugo at lunch one day. She got on better with him than with Eunice, his wife, as he did his best to include her in family affairs. He came to Oakridge to discuss Matt's business affairs with her. Hannah had known more about the factory then than she did now Matt was back.

'I am not,' Greg had piped up with the confidence of a twelve year old. 'When Grandpa goes in a meeting, somebody takes me round the factory and teaches me all about it. I know all about pickles and margarine, and candle making and brewing.'

Hugo had smiled. 'At my age I sometimes need distractions.'

'When I grow up I shall be like Grandpa and own lots of businesses and make lots of money.'

'Father's given up on me,' Matt had said. 'He's pushing the younger generation.'

The trouble was, Emma and Matthew had been doting parents who had wanted a large family. Hannah thought they'd been too indulgent. Gregory had grown up with a determination to have his own way in everything, and an offensively arrogant belief that he was always right. Dorothy, as their only daughter, was even more precious, a gift to nurture. She had the true Mortimer beauty with blue eyes and fair hair. Both children had grown up thinking they could have anything they wanted.

Hannah had not found the early years of her marriage easy, and knew now that she should not have stayed in the background and allowed her mother-in-law so free a hand in bringing up Matt's children. Matt had wanted Dorothy to go to school but Eunice had been shocked at the idea; she thought a governess more suitable.

During the ten years in which the children were growing up, Hannah had never managed to reach them. It made her feel a failure. As Matt said, everybody else found them perfectly charming.

When Dorothy reached the age for coming out, Eunice gave parties for her and introduced her into a level of society that would not have accepted her so readily had she not had the connection to Sir Hugo.

Lady Mortimer was soon trying to manipulate her into what she called a 'successful' marriage. She'd drawn up a list of suitors and introduced Dorothy to most of them. A distant relative of her own family called Franklin Flower seemed the most interested.

'She's little more than a child yet,' Hannah had protested to Matt. 'Silly to want to marry her off so young.'

'We all marry young in our family.'

'Surely it's more important for her to be happy? To marry someone who loves her?'

'Better if she marries in her own class,' he'd answered. 'She'll have more to be happy about afterwards.' That had bruised Hannah a little, and made her wonder if Matt had regrets about marrying her.

But Dorothy's pregnancy had changed all that and was definitely not something Matt wanted his mother to know about. She had strong views about public morals and even chaired a moral welfare committee.

'We can't possibly tell her, and what will Franklin Flower think?'

Hannah had sighed. Clearly it wouldn't increase his ardour.

'I mean, what a blot on the Mortimer name! You know what the newspapers are like about Father. He's always doing

12

something that gets him on the front page. We would all be so shamed.

'And Mother will be furious after all the trouble she's taken to groom Dorothy. No decent man will look at her if this gets out. What sort of life can she look forward to now? She won't be accepted by society. It'll ruin her. No, we must keep it quiet at all costs.'

'But what about the baby?'

'You'll have to find it a home elsewhere. It's been done before.'

'Do you think we'll get away with it?'

'Dorothy isn't the first, others have,' Matt had snapped.

Hannah felt that as another painful stab. She turned away so Matt would not see the hurt on her face. She'd never told him she'd gone through all this herself. How could she when Lady Mortimer spoke of the need to uphold moral standards in the lower classes? Hannah had then spent months worrying that her arrangements for Dorothy's baby weren't good enough.

Now Matt tried to comfort her. 'We knew it wouldn't be easy, but the worst is over.'

She shuddered, afraid the worst was yet to come.

Hannah wished the baby hadn't started crying then, just when she was pulling herself together. It made it impossible to blot the idea out of her mind. She was used to pushing her own needs into the background, but she'd been on fire with longing since she'd felt the weight of the child in her arms. She had to tell him.

'Matt, I'd like to keep the baby.' The words came out in a rush though she was trying to keep cool-headed. Footsteps sounded overhead. Matt stared into the dying coals. Giving the child away would be like tearing herself in two. She got up to refill his glass.

The injustice of it all had been boiling up inside her for months. How could fate be so unkind as to deprive her of the child she wanted so much, yet send one to Dorothy for whom it spelt disaster?

13

'I know, Hannah.' Matt's voice was gentle. 'I'm sorry.' Even his eyes were kindly. For once he was thinking of her feelings.

'We could say she was my child. We could bring her up as though she was.' Tension held her rigid. 'Once Dorothy sees the baby, she won't be able to part with her. She'll want to see her grow up too. What could be better?'

'It isn't possible, Hannah. You must see that.'

'Why?' she moaned.

'We've been married for ten years and there hasn't been the first sign of conception. Then you and Dorothy leave home for months and come back with a baby you say is yours. Who's going to believe that? Surely your baby would be born at home, with every attention paid to you? For Dorothy's sake, there must be no mention of any baby. It would be too easy for everyone to jump to the right conclusion.'

Hannah sighed. She'd been a fool to hope he'd agree. It was hurtful too, to have her wishes brushed aside for Dorothy's sake. Always it was Dorothy, Dorothy, Dorothy.

'No, the baby must stay here if we're to get away with this. Stick to our original plan, it's the only way.'

He was on his feet pacing to the window, no longer able to sit still. He peered out. Rain threatened, the autumn afternoon was drawing in.

'Here's our landlady coming to call.' His impatience was obvious. 'What a time to choose!'

'Clarissa has been good to us,' said Hannah, getting to her feet to look. 'She's bringing flowers. She must have heard I'd sent for Dr Moore.'

'He's not leaving?' Matt asked, as heavy footsteps sounded on the stairs.

'Must mean Dorothy's all right if he's going.'

Matt went to the door to see. Hannah heard the doctor say: 'I'm leaving the patient in Sister Thomas's capable hands. She'll send for me if she needs me, otherwise I'll be in tomorrow.'

Clarissa Bender's dumpy figure was climbing out of her

14

trap. She tied the pony's bridle to the gatepost. She was wearing a warm woollen dress of restrained plaid with a brown shawl round her shoulders. Her clothes were chosen for warmth and practicality.

Hannah reflected that Mortimer clothes were always the opposite. They placed emphasis on elegance and high fashion, practicality came bottom of their needs.

The doctor had a few words with Clarissa before untethering his own pony. Hannah went to meet her friend as she came to the front door. The sharp bitter scent of chrysanthemums was filling the hall.

'A girl, I hear, and Dorothy's all right.' Clarissa's face radiated tranquillity and contentment, as well it might. Hannah had long envied her the three sons that had appeared at regular two-year intervals. Then, last year, she had had a baby daughter, Lucy.

'It's over and all is well.'

Hannah buried her face in the flowers before ringing for a maid to take them away and bring some tea. For her, the new baby's presence dominated everything else. Impossible not to be continually aware of her. Footsteps continued to sound overhead. Her cries could still be heard.

Matt was ill at ease. 'Can you take the child away, Clarissa?'

Hannah's heart lurched. Although she'd helped arrange it, she wasn't happy that the infant was going to Maisie O'Malley in the gatehouse. Matt thought the arrangement ideal because her husband worked here on the farm belonging to Clarissa's husband. The only other woman to offer was the village postmistress. Clarissa had not thought highly of either.

'So soon?' Hannah asked hesitantly.

'The sooner the better. Dorothy hardly knows what's happened yet. I want it out of here before she does. More painful once she gets attached.'

'Perhaps that's wise,' Clarissa said slowly. 'What do you think, Hannah?'

She managed to choke out: 'Yes.'

15

Matt said: 'None of us can forget what's happened 'til the baby's gone.'

'Probably you'll all get a better night's sleep without her,' Clarissa agreed. 'I'll take her now.'

'I'll come with you,' Hannah hurried to say. Clarissa had already taken her and Dorothy to see the woman and the house where she lived. It was, in effect, a tied cottage on the farm.

'I'll ring for the midwife to bring the child down.' For once Matt got to his feet to do it. Hannah felt sick.

The midwife, in clean dress and apron, brought down the oak cradle that Hannah had provided. The infant was bathed and freshly powdered. Clarissa lifted her out with practised ease.

'She's lovely!' Her head was covered with feathery tendrils of white hair which caused Hannah's stomach to contract with love.

Then Clarissa was wrapping her up warmly and putting her back in her crib, calling for another blanket to go right over the top to shield her from the dank outside air.

'I've given her a drink of glucose and water.' The midwife was pursing her lips in disapproval of what they were going to do.

Hannah was aware of stumbling out to the trap behind Clarissa and the cradle. On the short journey to the gatehouse, barely three hundred yards, the infant made soft snuffling noises at her feet, smacking its lips and sucking on the blanket. Hannah watched mesmerised as Clarissa's capable brown hands looped her pony's bridle through what had once been the main gates to Yarrow Hall.

From the outside, the gatehouse was an attractive stone cottage with a steeply pitched slate roof and a good deal of decorative woodwork very much in need of a coat of paint. Nettles and dock leaves flourished in its flower beds.

There was a pretty porch but the front door opened straight into the untidy living-room. Two toddlers played on the stone-flagged floor, while a younger sibling slept on a heap of old blankets in the corner. It had seemed cleaner and more respectable when she'd last seen it, and the children had been neatly dressed.

The woman had seemed cleaner too. Today her hair hung loose in greasy strands and her apron was stained.

'I want twenty-five guineas a year for her keep,' she demanded, her hands on her hips.

Hannah felt in her handbag for her cheque book, and pushed back the clutter on the table a few inches so she could write. Suddenly she was gripped with panic. She couldn't write a cheque with the name Mortimer on it. Not when they'd been so careful all these months. What had she been thinking of?

Maisie O'Malley was eyeing her with sullen suspicion. 'Cheques are no good to me.'

Hannah breathed again and counted out six guineas. 'That's all I have in cash. I'll bring the rest tomorrow.'

'I don't think you should have it all at once, Maisie,' Clarissa said in her bossy way. 'Why don't you let me keep it and pay it over in monthly instalments? Much the best.'

Hannah thought she was going to refuse. Filled with resentment that negotiations like this had to be made, she pulled the blanket off the crib. Two bright blue eyes stared balefully up into hers.

'I've got to have real money.'

'I'll give you cash. That's no problem.'

'All right,' Maisie said grudgingly. It was hurtful then to see her dirt-engrained hands pick up the baby. 'Why, she's pretty! A bonny baby. What's her name?'

Hannah choked on another wave of guilt. 'It's barely two hours . . . We haven't had time to think yet.'

'I could call her Gertie, after the one I lost two years ago?'

'Mercy me, no!'

'Mercy? That's a plain name. Why not something pretty?'

Hannah almost smiled. 'Call her Elizabeth.' She'd intended to call her own daughter that, it had been her mother's name. But that made her feel guilty again. There should be nothing

17

to connect them with this child.

'Elizabeth? That's pretty enough, though it's a bit long.' Maisie smiled, showing a row of bad teeth.

'I'll walk home,' Hannah told Clarissa when they got outside. 'I need a breath of fresh air.'

By the next morning, the carpet square had been replaced in the front bedroom, dressing-table and chairs were brought back, and the room had lost its nightmare quality. Dorothy lay back against a tower of pillows, her golden hair clean and fresh about her shoulders. With colour back in her cheeks, she was a young girl again.

Matt had arranged to take two weeks off from the office. He sat all day in the sitting-room reading about Woolley's archaeological finds at Ur of the Chaldees in Mesopotamia.

Hannah hoped now that Dorothy would quickly gather her strength and they might return home together. As Matt said, if they could put Yarrow behind them, they'd all feel better.

Dorothy behaved as if she was resting a sprained ankle. She was light-hearted, wanting to try on her pretty clothes again.

Hannah felt a sense of loss she couldn't throw off, but the baby wasn't mentioned again in her hearing. As far as Matt and Dorothy were concerned, it might never have been born. On the last day, when the maids were packing up, she gave in to her need and wandered down to the gatehouse.

It had been built close against the eight-foot wall that surrounded the park, and was overshadowed by the gateposts, two tall oblong pillars each topped with a vicious lion rampant above a coat of arms. Now dead leaves were rotting between the lion's feet and greyish-green lichen blotched their stone backs. Both lions had lost some of their fangs; one had lost the paw it raised to attack, the other its tail.

The once elegant cast iron gates stood rusting and permanently open, one at a drunken angle. Moss and rank grass grew up the centre of the drive. A quarter of a mile away, surrounded by the great oaks of the park, Hannah could see Yarrow Hall Farm. From here, it still looked an elegant house. It was built of grey stone under a blue slate roof, long and low, with many windows all with small Georgian panes.

Once it had been Yarrow Hall, the home of a country squire. Sometime last century the family had dwindled to a spinster who had lived to a ripe old age and done nothing to keep the fabric of the house in good repair. The large herd of dairy shorthorns grazing in the park showed how it had come down in the world.

As she approached the gatehouse, Hannah could hear two babies crying. The sound led her through the open door and into the living-room. The crib was on the floor and seemed a mass of writhing limbs that made it rock from its own volition.

'Hey, what's the matter?' she asked. At the sound of her voice the feet stopped kicking, the cradle creaked more slowly. It was only when she stood over it that Hannah realised there were two babies inside. The larger, a whey-faced infant of five months, looked up from the pillow. She was shocked to find Elizabeth had been placed at its feet, with her head hard against the bottom. The bedding had all been kicked off. Legs and arms began jerking together like marionettes as both started to howl again.

Hannah gathered Elizabeth eagerly into her arms. Little spikes of hair, damp with sweat, curled against her hot face. She was as wet as a sponge and smelled none too sweet.

'What's the matter then, love?'

Elizabeth's mouth snapped shut. She was shuddering with pent up fury. Two round blue eyes stared up accusingly. Guilt and pity brought tears to Hannah's eyes.

'Maisie,' she shouted. 'Maisie, are you there?' The fire had gone out and the room was cold. Dirty dishes and uneaten food covered the table. She was suddenly angry. So much love and sympathy was being expended on the mother while this poor mite was dirty, hungry and ill cared for.

'Mrs O'Malley, come and change this child. She's in need of food and attention.'

Maisie almost fell down the narrow stairs, smelling none too sweet herself. She flung herself down on a chair, snatched Elizabeth up and heaved a stringy breast out of her crumpled blouse. Hannah was repelled to see the infant latch on to the brown nipple as though it were life itself. The rhythmic sound of sucking and swallowing filled the room.

'What are you doing?' Hannah was aghast, believing such customs had been lost over the years. She had provided bottles and humanised Trufood for the baby.

'Wet nursing. She likes it, you can see. It's quicker too. My Charlie's sick. He's got fever.'

Hannah felt the vomit rise in her throat and rushed outside. What a place to leave a baby! It was downright dangerous. But for Dorothy's sake it had to be done.

Chapter Two

2 October 1920

The autumn sun, mellow and golden, shone into the dining-room at Yarrow Hall Farm. Clarissa Bender poured herself a second cup of tea and edged her chair over until she could feel the sun on her face.

The remains of family breakfast were on the table, and the scent of bacon still hung in the air. Leo, her husband, had already gone out about his business on the farm, and she'd sent the boys upstairs so that Myfanwy could get them ready for school. Clarissa savoured these few moments of tranquillity in the morning, using them to make her plans for the rest of the day.

The crab apples were at their best, and it was a wonderful morning to go out and pick them. This afternoon, she'd make the crab apple preserve Leo loved so much. It always gave her satisfaction to see her larder shelves fill up at this time of the year.

'I didn't realise for a long time just how domesticated you were,' Leo had said with his wry laugh over breakfast. 'Nobody else would hire a cook and then do all the cooking herself.'

'Not all! Anyway, I enjoy it.' She pulled a face. Mrs Tatler, known as Tatty, described herself as a cook-general and had plenty of other chores to take care of.

'You enjoy nurse-maiding the children too.'

'Well, of course, I want to be with them as much as I can.' Clarissa knew it was a necessity. Sixteen-year-old Myfanwy acted as dairy-maid as well as nanny. She had butter to make three times a week, milk to separate after each milking, and countless utensils to scald daily.

'You make sure Myfanwy isn't idle.' He laughed again. 'You organise us all.'

'It's not hard.'

'You're not doing too much?'

'Of course not. Think of the economy. We manage with a quarter of the servants your mother used to have.'

Clarissa wanted to bite out her tongue. She should never have used the word 'economy'. It always wiped the smile from his face.

'If only you didn't have such big ideas about this house,' he complained.

'Why not? Your family has lived in it for the last fifty years.'

'And never quite managed to get it in good repair.'

'I'm happy to do a lot of the work on it myself.'

'You can't put a new roof on, Clarissa. And no, I can't get the farm workers to do it. We have neither the skills nor the time. Living in this house is a gross extravagance. It costs more to keep the rain out than it would to build a new one. If I had my way, we'd move to the dower house.'

Clarissa pulled a face. The dower house had been built long enough ago to be draughty and inconvenient, yet not so long as to have the elegant proportions of the main house. Leo stirred his tea crossly. 'It's soundly constructed, and should be plenty big enough. Your friends are moving out today, aren't they?'

'Yes.'

'I expect that's why you wanted them there in the first place. If they're renting it, we can't move in.'

The other worry surfaced in Clarissa's mind. 'I suppose it is all right to let them leave the baby with Maisie O'Malley?'

'Between them and their conscience, I'd say. She's had four and three are still living. Not a bad average.'

'Leo!'

'They're pushing some of the responsibility for it on to

22

you, but I've no doubt you'll cope.'

'I expect they'll come more often now. To see how the baby's getting on.'

'I don't.' Leo pulled a wry face. 'Less often. They won't want to have anything to do with it, easy to see that.'

Clarissa frowned. 'I can't imagine any mother handing her baby over, wanting it out of sight and hearing as soon as possible.'

'That's what I mean. That girl won't come back. Probably won't want to see you in Birkenhead either. They'll all be afraid you'll let something drop, and her dark secret will be out.'

Clarissa frowned again. Why hadn't that occurred to her before he'd suggested it? 'I shall miss Hannah if that happens.'

'Do think about the dower house, Clarissa. They had the whole place painted and papered in the spring. It won't look so good if it stays empty over the winter.'

She shook her head, rushing to protest: 'But I love it here. This is a wonderful rambling old house, I couldn't bear to tear myself away.' She had refurbished much of it with her own hands.

'I know, but it would be sensible. We'd have money for school fees and other things.' Leo had let the door bang behind him, shattering the domestic peace.

Clarissa climbed the stairs slowly, pausing at a landing window. She loved to look out over Leo's kingdom. From here she could see for twenty miles over a patchwork of rolling fields and woods and streams on the lower slopes of the Clwydian Range. It lay tranquil and beautiful in the morning sun. Behind the house, the land was wild and high, moorland and mountain.

Leo's forebears had been yeoman farmers for generations, and when in the last century Yarrow came on the market, it seemed a prize that enhanced their status. His great-grandfather had struggled to buy it and was fiercely determined it should stay in the family. To do this and safeguard against its ever being split up, the house and estate were entailed on the eldest son in succeeding generations.

Leo had inherited Yarrow Hall Farm with four hundred good acres. Like his father and grandfather, he was proud of it. He was a thrifty farmer who saw the first drop in land values as an opportunity to expand. He now owned five hundred acres, but land values had continued to fall, and his investment no longer seemed a wise one.

Clarissa ran up the last flight of stairs. On the attic floor above the six bedrooms, there had always been a nursery, a playroom and schoolroom as well as quarters for the servants. Leo didn't realise how much comfort all this space provided. She didn't keep the children confined up here; the boys were often out playing about the farm.

In the nursery bathroom Myfanwy had just lifted baby Lucy from her bath, and at the same time was overseeing the boys as they cleaned their teeth.

Clarissa took her towel-wrapped daughter from her and sat on the white wood chair to dry her. Perhaps Leo was right. Nothing short of gutting would improve this bathroom. The enamel had worn off the bath which had been installed when Queen Victoria was a girl. It was bitterly cold in winter too, right up under the roof. To install central heating was out of the question. Even to mention any of this would only remind Leo that they needed to renew several window frames, as well as the dreaded roof.

With the baby chuckling and rolling on the towel, Clarissa tried to see if there was any sign of a first tooth. She tickled one baby foot to make her open her mouth, and Lucy gave such a lovely throaty chuckle that Clarissa found herself doing it again for the pleasure of hearing her laugh.

Four-year-old Nicholas came crowding close, his playful smile letting her know he wanted to join in the fun. She watched his chubby child's fingers running up the soles of the kicking baby feet until child and baby were bubbling over with chuckles and she was laughing herself.

How any mother could hire a nanny to do this and cut herself off from her own children she couldn't understand.

She snatched an opportunity to slide Lucy's vest over her head.

Having Myfanwy was quite different; it meant, as mother, Clarissa was still in control. She liked to have her children playing about her feet in the sitting-room or kitchen. But if she wanted to concentrate on cooking or dressmaking, then there was somebody to take the children out for an airing.

She hated to see them reach school age. She wanted to keep them with her, enjoying their company. School had come already for Jonathon and Hal. Usually she took them herself.

'Hurry up,' she told them. 'It's time we were on our way.'

She hurried them downstairs, both dark-haired and serious, clutching their books, smart in their school uniforms. Nick tried to keep up. He liked to come along for the ride and pretend he too was going to school. Clarissa smiled when she saw he had a couple of old painting books tucked under his arm to mimic his older brothers. As a mother she couldn't admit she had a favourite child, but she found Nicholas very endearing.

He was unlike his older brothers both in appearance and character. He was more sturdily built, with paler tow-coloured hair and freckles; wide-eyed and innocent, and he chattered away non-stop. Leo said he couldn't keep him away from the animals.

Leo always saw that the pony was put between the shafts of the governess cart and waiting for her. He was leading it round to the front door as she came out.

'Think about it, Clarissa,' he said, as he handed her the reins and lifted Nick in. 'Have a good look round when you go to say goodbye to your friend. It's not a bad house. Good enough for the Mortimers anyway.'

'Only in their hour of need,' she answered tartly. Leo was smiling, trying to be gently persuasive.

Clarissa bit back the words: 'Hannah wouldn't want to spend the rest of her life there.' She hated to hurt Leo's feelings, and knew he saw it as a personal failure that they had to count every penny. His father had died in 1916 and his mother had struggled to run the farm until Leo had returned from France. He'd taken it over at the end of the war, and farming incomes had fallen every year since. He was barely making enough to meet his family's needs.

Why couldn't he understand that the pleasures of living in the gracious old house more than made up for the discomforts? But, of course, there was still the problem of school fees, a problem that would grow.

It was a wonderful morning, mild and sunny. A good day for Hannah to travel home. Except that in a car, good weather wasn't so vital. Once Clarissa had been envious of Hannah. Marriage into the Mortimer family had seemed such incredible good fortune.

'She'll be rich,' she'd said to Leo. 'No money worries for Hannah in future.'

They'd all read newspaper articles about Sir Hugo's business exploits and huge gifts to the poor.

'Sir Hugo's a legend in his own lifetime. Hannah says he speaks of Lloyd George and Bonar Law as though they're friends.'

'Perhaps they are. Can you see Hannah amongst the rich and high born as a society hostess?'

'No.'

'And it wouldn't suit you, Clarissa.'

She was beginning to think the marriage didn't suit Hannah either. All summer she'd seen her wilting under the strain of coping with Dorothy.

'The girl's bored stiff, that's her trouble,' Clarissa had said. She'd tried to entertain them by taking them shopping and for rides in her pony and trap. She'd tried to interest the girl in sewing and knitting for the coming infant, but Dorothy disliked handicrafts. She'd failed to interest her in either cooking or gardening. Dorothy had refused to go for walks or even sit outside in the sun. She seemed permanently prickly with everybody.

'What does she do with herself all day?' Clarissa had asked Hannah.

'As little as possible. She says she reads.'

Clarissa had kept them both provided with books. One wet afternoon, Dorothy had played simple card games with Jonathon and Hal and all had seemed to enjoy it. But the next time she'd taken the boys, Dorothy had been uninterested.

She'd stopped taking Nicholas with her because Dorothy couldn't hide her dislike of the very young. She didn't like his endless questions, nor his habit of pushing story books on her knee and asking to have one read. And she wouldn't stay in the same room for more than five minutes with baby Lucy.

'If it hadn't been for you, Clarissa, I'd have gone out of my mind,' Hannah had told her gratefully.

'You're trying too hard. You'd feel better if you came up to the farm more and left her alone.'

Hannah gave a wry smile. 'Daren't desert my post a second time. Anyway, it would be taking advantage of you. I shall keep trying.'

Only a few days before the baby had been born, she'd gone down to the dower house to find Hannah in the garden, deheading dead roses in a frenzied state.

'I thought I was better equipped to help Dorothy than anybody else. I wanted us to be friends and thought this was my chance.'

'What's happened?'

'Clary, I've told her. I've said too much. It's a stupid thing I've done.'

She'd caught at Hannah's waving hands to comfort her. 'She'll understand.'

'To think I half welcomed these months of waiting! I thought they'd bring us closer.'

Clarissa had drawn Hannah to the seat under the apple tree, and made her sit down. 'When you married Matt, you said you were going to put your trouble behind you. Forget the past.'

'Said it perhaps, but found I couldn't. Being with Dorothy has brought it all back. I told her I understood the grief and guilt she was living through. I thought it would help if we talked about it . . .'

'Dorothy doesn't take things to heart as you do. What did she say?'

'I couldn't get through to her. Her mouth was set in that obstinate line.'

Clarissa had put her own handkerchief in Hannah's hand, and watched her scrub her eyes angrily.

'I told her of the awful regrets I'd had after parting with my own baby. How hardly a day goes by even now when I don't think of Alice: wondering how she's getting on and if she's happy. She'll be thirteen next birthday.'

Hannah's anguish was very moving.

'Surely it must have helped her to know she wasn't the only one?'

'Dorothy gave one of those wild laughs of hers. "You too, Hannah?" she said. "I never dreamed my perfect Mama could have had the same fall from grace." She went on shaking with laughter. I didn't intend to tell anyone but you, Clary.'

'You did tell her that Matt doesn't know?'

'Yes. "Don't drop any hints to him," I said. "Please be on your guard. I've kept quiet too long to let him know now."'

'And she promised?'

'Yes, but I'm still afraid. I thought we'd be closer if I told her, but we aren't. Clary, I'm scared she'll tell him!'

Clarissa knew it had added another layer of tension when Hannah was already brimming over with anxiety over Dorothy's baby.

But even before this summer, Hannah had not seemed as happy as she had expected. Every spring Clarissa went to spend a week with her at their house in Birkenhead. Though she looked forward to Hannah's company and the big shops, she thought the Mortimers' house less impressive than Yarrow Hall Farm, and there seemed a distance between

28

Hannah and Matt she couldn't understand.

This year, her visit had been later because the Mortimers had been away in Bath. Hannah had met her off the train and nobody could have failed to notice her nerve-racked state.

Hannah didn't think herself a beauty, and in the accepted sense perhaps she wasn't – big-boned with large dark eyes and a Roman nose – but her looks were striking. Taller than most women, she now dressed with plain elegance. In a crowd, she never went unnoticed. Clarissa remembered with awful clarity first hearing of Dorothy's plight.

Hannah had asked for a tray of tea to be brought as soon as she'd got Clarissa into her sitting-room.

'You've got to help me, Clary,' she'd said as soon as the door closed behind the maid.

'Of course.' Clarissa waited for more but had to prompt: 'Is it Matt?'

'No. Oh God, it's a long story – it's Dorothy.'

At that time, it was a year since Clarissa had seen Dorothy. Then, she'd been straight out of the school room, a dainty girl with chocolate box beauty who always sat in the same chair in the drawing-room from where she could see her own reflection in a mirror.

Clarissa had watched her preen, taking little interest in anything else. 'She's a pretty girl, Hannah.'

'And doesn't she know it! A selfish little madam.' There was bitterness in Hannah's sharp criticism of her step-daughter. 'Her father spoils her, and as for her grandparents . . .'

Clarissa had been a little taken aback.

'And she's pregnant,' Hannah added.

The silence dragged out. 'Terrible for the Mortimers,' managed Clarissa, knowing she gaped as though she didn't believe a word.

'They don't know. And they mustn't. Eunice does what she calls "good work that can't be mentioned". She belongs to a group that's trying to change men's behaviour. Teach them more self-control. She's helping to uphold moral standards and stamp out prostitution. Matt is out of his mind with worry. He blames me, you see.'

'Why should he?'

'He said it was my duty to see Dorothy was properly chaperoned.' Now Hannah sat staring into space.

Clarissa swallowed. 'How dreadful! How can I help?'

'We need a bolt hole. That house where your mother-in-law lived . . .'

Clarissa relaxed. Nothing could be easier. They needed a tenant anyway. 'I'd love to have you living there, you know that. No problem.'

'Nobody must know who we are.' Hannah's voice was urgent. 'And I've another favour to ask of you. We won't be able to bring the baby back here, not ever. Can you find a home for it? Perhaps one of your estate workers?'

'Farm workers. It's a farm, Hannah.'

'Yes, well, I thought if you had a couple who couldn't have a child of their own, and wanted . . .'

'We only have three cottages.' Clarissa knew she flushed. 'That'll be the hardest part. One family is too old, we employ their sons.'

'What about the other two?'

'They both have children. Leo says they're breeding like rabbits.'

Hannah looked crestfallen.

'There's an orphanage not far away.'

'What do you suggest, that we abandon the baby on its doorstep?'

'Hannah!' It was not like her friend to snap so sharply.

'We'd expect to pay to have the child fostered.'

'Look, you'll be on the spot yourself all summer. We'll see to that then.'

'But you think it's possible? Might there be a family in your village?'

'I don't know. Perhaps.'

'I'll have to find somewhere.' Clarissa saw Hannah shiver then say in a rush of desperation: 'We're all dreading it.

Dorothy's scared stiff. I'll want to bring her to Yarrow before anything shows . . .'

'Of course. The house is empty now. Any time.' Curiosity drove her to ask: 'The father . . .?'

Hannah sighed. 'The Mortimers know the Tolmans. I didn't think they'd object to Lancelyn . . .'

'But they did?'

'Lady Mortimer sets great store by social success. She wants Dorothy to marry well.'

Hannah was silent for a moment, and then burst out: 'I'm a Mortimer by marriage only, and Matt's second wife. She's always kept me on the edge of family affairs, and let me know she thinks Matt chose unwisely the second time.'

Clarissa nodded. She hadn't realised it was quite as bad as that, but she'd sensed some of it.

'Tell me.'

Hannah was slow to start. It was a tale of failure, on her part as well as Dorothy's. She poured more tea for them both, fussed with the biscuits.

'Come on,' Clarissa urged.

'Matt doesn't enjoy the parties his mother gives. What pleasure he gets comes from watching Dorothy enjoy herself. After her first dinner party, he was as proud of her as his mother. Dorothy loved her first dance, and I was as pleased as he was to see she had plenty of partners.

'A few months later, at another dance, I knew Matt had hardly taken his eyes off her. She seemed to be enjoying herself even more. Full of vitality, she was twirling round the floor in a dress of pale blue satin, laughing up into the face of her partner.

'"Who is he?" Matt asked me. "She's been dancing with him all evening."

'"Lancelyn Tolman," I told him.'

'I know him,' Clarissa said. 'Isn't he Edith Tolman's cousin?'

'Yes, and I introduced them. He seemed a likeable fellow – a handsome young army lieutenant in full dress uniform.

31

From the moment Dorothy met him, she had eyes for no one else.

'Lady Mortimer thought him most unsuitable. It wasn't the Tolman family she objected to – they were well-connected. But Lancelyn was the youngest of five sons, and his prospects of inheriting anything were nil. He was about to depart with a local regiment on a tour of duty in India.

'Lady Mortimer said she'd enquired into his character and circumstances, and that he had a terrible reputation. His only interests were women and wild parties, drinking and cards.

'I tried to tell Matt his mother disliked him because she hadn't chosen him herself.

'"If Dorothy loves him," I said, "if she truly loves him, she'll be happy. Like us."'

Hannah paused. It had roused doubts she hadn't had before. Was Matt happy after all?

'Matt and I had our first serious row about Lancelyn Tolman. Dorothy couldn't hide her love for him. She was suddenly radiant and bubbling with happiness.

'Lady Mortimer had already arranged an introduction to Franklin Flower, years older than her and rather a sobersides. He'd already made one fortune, and had expectations of inheriting another. Mr Flower had shown considerable interest, but Dorothy laughed and said she found Lancelyn Tolman more to her taste.

'It tore Matt apart to disappoint her. He loved her and wanted her happiness above everything else, yet his mother convinced him he had to stand firm on this. He explained it as gently as he could to Dorothy. I can see her now, gazing up at him with hurt in her eyes, like an animal at bay. He told her she must forget Tolman for her own good.

'Then, urged on by his mother, Matt had a totally embarrassing interview with Tolman himself. He forbade him to come anywhere near the house, or make further contact with Dorothy. We expected that to be the end of the matter. It wasn't.

'Dorothy said she couldn't put him out of her mind, that

32

she loved him and he her. Matt had been conditioned to indulge her whims. Dorothy expected to get her way this time. We both knew Tolman was writing to her. We saw the letters arriving with the mail several times a week.

'Dorothy acted as though she didn't believe the British Army would insist on Tolman's departure with his regiment. "The war's over now," she said incredulously. "There must be plenty of men who'd like to go in his place."

'She spoke of an early wedding, as if only the timing was still to be decided.

'Matt stood firm and said a wedding as important as Dorothy's couldn't be rushed. And until she settled for a more suitable groom, it wasn't going to take place at all.

'We were all glad to see the regiment leave. I said: "She'll get over it," quite confident that two years' separation would solve the problem, but Dorothy continued to mope. The weeks passed and there was nothing we could do to cheer her up. The change in her was unbelievable. She even talked of travelling to India to marry him out there.'

'Good lord!' Clarissa commented.

'Matt was appalled too. "Dorothy," he said, taking both her hands in his, "you must accept that we'll never give our consent for this marriage." She stared silently back at him in frightened anguish.

'After that she no longer talked of Tolman, but she didn't pick up. Lady Mortimer was making plans to have her presented at Court and do the season and thought a holiday first might do her good. She goes to Bath every year in the early spring and suggested we all go with her.

'Matt got out of it by saying he'd too much work on, but he booked rooms for Dorothy and me. We were to stay for three weeks. He said he'd join us for the last few days.

'Franklin Flower was there and Lady Mortimer thought meeting him again would take Dorothy's mind off the unfortunate affair.

'Most mornings, we used to meet in the Pump Room.' Hannah swallowed hard; she'd relived this countless times. It was a nightmare. 'Lady Mortimer liked to take the waters. She thought they did her good. Disgusting taste, one mouthful was enough for me. Dorothy and I had coffee.

'I was embarrassed to find Edith Tolman in Bath too, with her mother and sister, though I've always liked her personally. Of course Dorothy was drawn to them. They were relaying snippets of news about Lancelyn, even bringing letters from him for her to read. I warned her to make her interest less obvious when her grandmother was with us. It gave her more reason to blame me, saying they were my friends.'

Hannah paused. Just to talk about that dreadful day sickened her.

'Dorothy kept turning round from our table to watch the door. It was as obvious to Eunice as it was to me that she was waiting for the Tolmans to come in. This morning they did not.

'The string quartet was playing a Strauss waltz when an acquaintance of Eunice Mortimer's paused to speak to her. "Have you heard? Such a tragedy for Mary Tolman – her son's been killed in India. They're having to return home in a hurry. Packing now, I believe."

'Dorothy croaked: "Not Lancelyn?"

'"Some skirmish with the natives. He proved himself a hero after all. An honourable death."

'I couldn't breathe, couldn't take my eyes from Eunice's face. She actually smiled, clearly thinking it a suitable end for a young man who didn't fit into her plans.

'The next instant I felt the table cloth moving beneath my elbow. Dorothy slumped off her chair in a dead faint, dragging it with her. I was too slow to save her. The crash of shattering china drew every eye in the room. Dorothy was lying on the floor in the middle of it, with coffee dregs staining her lavender dress. We were all crunching in the spilled brown sugar.

'Franklin Flower saw it happen from the doorway. He was just coming in. He was very helpful, calling a cab and seeing us back to our hotel, even helping Dorothy up to her room. I told him she was rather given to swooning as her chest had always been delicate.

'Dorothy was cross once we were alone and said I wasn't to fuss. She wept for the rest of the day. For the next week she refused to eat and wouldn't leave her room. She spent all day lying on her bed and all night walking the floor. She looked ill and seemed to be losing weight. I felt at the end of my tether.

'It was a relief when Matt said he'd come a day or two earlier than he'd intended. He took one look at the pair of us and called a doctor to prescribe for us both.

'Matt was dressing after having a bath when the doctor came up to our suite. I took him to Dorothy's room and he asked me to stay while he examined her. I thought him very young. Gradually, Dorothy's terrible trouble dawned on me from the questions he asked and the very reluctant answers she gave. I didn't want to believe it. The room began to eddy round me and my legs felt shaky as I followed him out.

'By then Matt was hovering on the other side of the door. "What's your diagnosis?" he asked in his bombastic way. "What do you advise to improve Dorothy's health?"

'"There doesn't seem to be too much the matter, her pregnancy's progressing normally. Of course, she's in her fifth month and beginning to find it a bit of a trial."

'I could see Matt shaking, barely able to control himself, impatient then to get rid of the doctor. It was awful, Clary. I can see the doctor now, the light reflecting off his glasses, soberly advising on the importance of a good diet. Matt bundled him out so fast, he never did examine me. I can't understand why I hadn't guessed months earlier. Matt turned on me then in a ferocious rage.

'"It was your job to chaperone her," he said, his face puce. But what good was anger when the man was already dead? "You neglected your duty. Dorothy is ruined."

'I went to pieces at the thought of what my mother-in-law would say, and lost my temper. In the middle of this terrible row, there was a knock at the door. Matt was in full flood too and we ignored it.

'It enraged Matt more when the knock came again. He tore across the room and jerked the door open. Franklin Flower was standing in the corridor, nursing a large bouquet.

'I froze, wondering how long he had been there and how much he might have heard. Matt let his mouth fall open in horror.

'"Sorry to disturb you at this time of night," our visitor said. "I saw the doctor call and wanted to find out how Dorothy was."

'"Settled for the night. Sleeping draught." Matt sounded as though he was choking.

'I managed to say Bath didn't suit Dorothy's delicate chest and that we were returning home early. "Her mother died of TB, you know."'

'Surely that would worry him?' Clarissa's face was aghast.

'Not so much as the truth. Next morning two letters were delivered by special messenger, both from Franklin Flower. One was addressed to Matt asking formally for Dorothy's hand in marriage. The other was for Dorothy, expressing his love.

'They brought Matt the first ray of hope. He said if we planned carefully, perhaps Dorothy's reputation could be saved. We must get her away from his mother as soon as possible.

'Dorothy didn't care one way or the other now, and was persuaded that her best chance of happiness was to fall in with her father's wishes.

'He dictated Dorothy's acceptance to Franklin Flower, saying I was taking her to Switzerland for a few months as the doctor recommended, to see if the mountain air would benefit her cough. He even invented a cousin for me living near Geneva, so that it would seem more natural for us to go there.

'We had such soul-searching about whether we dared tell Gregory. In the end Matt decided to do so, because he wanted him to go to Geneva to post letters and cards from

Dorothy, both to Franklin Flower and her grandparents. Such a complicated tissue of lies, Clary, but for Dorothy's sake, Matt insists we have to go through with it.'

Chapter Three

2 October 1920

The pony slowed as the gates to Yarrow came in sight. Impatiently Clarissa flicked the reins, sorry now she'd gone to the shops after dropping the boys at school. She wanted to say goodbye to Hannah before she left. She was worried about her.

As soon as she'd turned in to the drive, she saw Hannah running headlong away from the gatehouse.

'Wait a minute,' she called.

Hannah turned round looking distraught. There were scarlet blotches on her cheeks. She was panting when the pony pulled up beside her.

'What's the matter?' Clarissa asked. 'Come on, get in. It's not far, but . . .'

'No, no,' Hannah said, but she climbed the steps at the back of the trap and sank down beside Clarissa.

'I'm worried stiff. Leaving a newborn baby there! She isn't being properly looked after. Maisie's too tied up with her own children and they're sick with some sort of fever. What if Elizabeth catches it?'

Clarissa shivered. 'What do you want to do?'

'What *can* we do now? Matt would be furious if I suggested taking the babe with us. Dorothy would dissolve in tears.'

Clarissa thought Hannah didn't look far from tears herself.

'Has Maisie called the doctor?'

Hannah shook her head silently.

'Let's go and see.' Clarissa turned the trap round by

heading the pony across the grass. At the gates she jumped down and looped the reins through the ironwork. The door was wide open. She could hear a baby crying, and somewhere upstairs a toddler sobbing.

Maisie was feeding Elizabeth at her own breast, which she held with fingers engrained with black from her coal fire. The grate was full of cold cinders. Her fire went out for lack of tending it as frequently as for lack of coal in the shed. Clarissa suddenly noticed that baby Joey occupied the oak cradle Hannah had provided.

'There's nowhere else,' Maisie was muttering. 'Wanted to keep him away from the others. You know . . .'

'Quite right, Maisie, but you must find a drawer or something to put him in. This cradle is for Elizabeth. Only Elizabeth, all right?' The baby was sucking hungrily. Clarissa hoped Maisie had enough milk for two.

'Yes,' she agreed sulkily.

Clarissa had always known Maisie lived in a fog of confusion, that she was the sort of women who starts to prepare a meal but leaves the potatoes half peeled and forgotten when a child cries. Meals arrived late on Maisie's table, if at all. Food could be stewed to ribbons if forgotten, or under-cooked if preparations had started late.

She was the sort of woman who starts six jobs at once and never finishes any of them. Damp nappies were draped over the fireguard to dry, though the fire was out. More were soaking in a bucket in the middle of the room. Dirty dishes from the last meal were still on the table together with a half-eaten joint of boiled bacon. Chaos ruled in this house, with things left where they were last used.

''Course I haven't sent for the doctor.' Maisie was defensive, when asked. 'He'll want paying, won't he?'

'Shall I have a look? See what I think?' Clarissa had been a nurse before she married Leo.

'You might as well, since you're here,' said Maisie ungraciously.

Clarissa was conscious of Hannah peering round the

doorway, as though afraid to come in. She ran upstairs, guided by the sound of an infant snivelling. Thick curtains were pulled across the small window. In the gloom she could just make out a double bed and a cot, and that there wasn't a lot of space to walk between. Two tiny bodies tossed and writhed amongst rags of bedclothes.

She pulled back the curtains to see better and caught her breath. The first child had a marked and angry rash. She put a tentative hand on his forehead; he felt on fire. His nose was running, his eyes puffy and crusted, and his lips dry and sore. He looked very sick. The other, a girl, didn't look much different, except that there was no rash yet. Clarissa felt her spirits plummet as she went downstairs.

'How long have they been ill, Maisie?'

'I had a terrible night with them. They wouldn't sleep.'

'How long?'

Hannah came over the step to hear what was said.

'Our Charlie, about five days. He's proper poorly. Peggy went down a couple of days later.'

'I'll ask Dr Moore to call,' Clarissa said. She'd have to come back later when Hannah had gone. She took her arm and led her away. It was warmer out in the sun than it was inside that kitchen. She closed the door behind them.

'I've heard scarlet fever is rife in the Council school.'

'That's not where Jonathon and Hal . . .?'

'No.'

'Will Elizabeth catch it?'

'I don't know.' Clarissa was trying to think. 'Has Dorothy had it?'

'Yes, when she was about ten.'

'Perhaps not. Elizabeth might have immunity from her mother.'

'How can we make sure? Will the doctor know?'

'There's no way to be sure.'

'I'm so glad you're on the spot to keep an eye on Elizabeth,' Hannah said. 'Such a comfort.' Clarissa felt lips peck at her cheek. Hannah seemed more harassed than ever.

41

As she reined in the pony in front of the dower house, Matt came down the steps.

'We've been waiting for you, Hannah. Where've you been?'

He was all bonhomie and relieved smiles, looking as though an enormous weight had been lifted from his shoulders. His soft ring of hair lifted in the breeze as he removed his hat. Dorothy, pouting prettily, was all ready to climb into the rear seat of the Di Dion. She couldn't be driven away quickly enough.

Clarissa raised her hand in farewell, reflecting that Leo had been right about who would have to take responsibility for the child. She went slowly into the house, to ring the doctor. It was a blessing the Mortimers had had the phone put in.

Dorothy was in high spirits all the way home, bouncing about on the back seat, unable to sit still. She kept exclaiming with delight as the wild countryside of Wales gave way to the richer farmland of the Wirral. Matt seemed amused, but it irked Hannah to see Dorothy behaving as if she'd just been released from prison. Such obvious rejoicing seemed out of place.

'Pull yourself together, Hannah.' Matt lifted his eyes from the road to examine her. 'What's the matter?'

She shook her head silently. How could she explain? Leaving the baby behind was like tearing herself in two. She said: 'A bad conscience is a terrible thing to live with.'

Matt smiled. 'If Dorothy can do it, why can't you?'

Hannah tried. She was looking forward to being home again. Though she'd loved the tranquillity of the countryside at Yarrow, Dorothy had made the months she'd spent there emotionally fraught. She, too, had felt herself in exile.

Dorothy was whooping with joy as she recognised familiar landmarks. Once on Prenton Ridge, Hannah caught glimpses of the Mersey sparkling in the autumn sun. The tide was full in, shipping scudded up and down. In the distance, the Liverpool waterfront was hazy. Nearer at hand, she kept catching glimpses of houses half hidden in the autumn foliage. This was Prenton, this was home.

Oakridge had been a gift from Matt's parents to mark his first marriage. He had designed it himself for what he supposed his needs would be, and the building of it had not been finished until 1904. The large gardens needed a lot of upkeep but the trees and hedges had now matured and provided privacy. Hannah had thought it very grand when she first saw it.

She'd admired the vast and gracious drawing-room, but hadn't known then it was only used when there were guests. Matt had based his plans on his father's house, and only discovered later that he disliked pomp and ceremony and that a simpler life-style suited him. The rooms he used most were his study and a small sitting-room overlooking the back garden. There were eight bedrooms to accommodate the large family he hadn't managed to conceive.

Oakridge had been Hannah's home for the past ten years, but she saw it with fresh eyes now. It was Mortimer routine to have the house painted and papered inside and out every other year. Furniture and fittings were replaced at the first sign of wear. Heating, plumbing and other fitments were kept up to date. It was a smart and comfortable home, though Lady Mortimer described it as a suburban villa because it was in a road with other houses.

Hannah stood for a moment noting the difference autumn made in the front garden. Matt was making sure the maid took the suitcases to the right rooms when a taxi drew in to the drive behind his car, crunching on the gravel. Greg climbed out.

Dorothy had gone inside to tear from room to room in her excitement at being back. Now she came rushing out to greet her brother rapturously. Hannah thought him both taller and broader since she'd seen him last. He was almost nineteen now and grown into a very presentable young man.

'Hello, Mother.' Greg always managed to instil a hint of mockery in his voice when he called her 'Mother'. 'We all seem to be arriving at the same moment. Dad, have you got a guinea to pay for my taxi?'

43

'Haven't you?' Hannah watched Matt's gaze level with Greg's. His extravagance was a cause of explosive family rows.

'No.'

'Good God,' Matt said irritably. 'You've spent a prodigious amount on your holiday. Didn't you receive that hundred pounds you wired for?'

'Dad, you wanted me to go.' Greg's face flushed. 'The whole thing was your idea. Surely I'm allowed some enjoyment out of it?'

'You can't possibly have spent all that!'

'Well, I have.'

'I'll see to the taxi,' Hannah said quickly. She had to maintain peace in the house today. Greg strode indoors without bothering to thank her. The rest of the family followed him into the hall.

'What a lovely tan you've got.' Hannah gave a nervous shiver. She and Dorothy looked pale by comparison though they were supposed to have stayed in Switzerland much longer.

Greg had the same fair colouring as his sister, and his features were very like hers too. He had the same sensual self-indulgent mouth. He was handsome, except that his chin was already lax with dissipation. Hannah was used to seeing his bright blue eyes continually searching for pleasure; now they fastened on her aggressively.

'Wonderful weather,' he said. 'I had a good time. The scenery was magnificent, you don't know what you missed.'

'Tell us all about it, Greg. Every detail,' Dorothy urged. 'What you did and saw, what you ate, and what the weather was like. And we'd all better listen carefully and be ready to say the same things if we're asked.'

Matt led the way to the sunny cretonne-filled sitting-room at the back and closed the door. For the next hour they went over the story they were all to tell. That Gregory had holidayed in France, but spent a week with his step-mother and sister in Geneva before escorting them home. It sickened Hannah.

There seemed no end to the lies.

Then Dorothy telephoned her grandmother to let her know they were all home again. Matt spoke to her too. It came as something of a shock to Hannah to find he'd invited her to dinner that very evening.

'I was rather pushed into it,' he admitted. 'Franklin Flower is spending a few days with them and naturally he wants to see Dorothy again. Father won't be coming. He's going to some business dinner.'

Hannah was not pleased, she felt she needed more time to prepare herself.

'Nonsense!' Matt snapped. 'You've got to face them sometime. I couldn't put them off, it's the last night of Franklin's visit. Come on, Hannah, it's meant to be a celebration. You mustn't look so harassed. Everything's under control. The Lady Mother can't wait to welcome you back.'

'Welcome Dorothy back,' Hannah corrected. She had no heart for any of it.

'Wasn't that always our aim? All you have to do is behave as though you've had a long holiday. Show relief that Dorothy's health is so much better.'

Hugo Mortimer had been trying to work at his desk all afternoon. He felt restless and rather tetchy. For the umpteenth time he leaned back in his chair and lifted his eyes to his study window. The well-kept gardens of Ince Hall were laid out below him, tranquil in the autumn sun. Beyond was a wood of chestnut trees. The leaves, darkening at this time of the year, cut off the view in all directions, giving privacy and peace to his home. But nothing could soothe him today.

His eye came to rest on Dorothy's letter. He couldn't revive the warm glow of anticipation he'd felt at first that Hannah and Dorothy were coming home, he'd been waiting too long. He felt a simmering of impatience; he'd expected them home days ago. The letter had brought Eunice here to Birkenhead to see them. For once he'd been more than willing to fall in with her wishes.

45

He reached for it and unfolded it again. Dorothy had not written many letters while she'd been away because she was still using notepaper she'd taken with her. He held it to the light, confirming it was Birmingham Bond. He'd owned the company for a few years. Sold it at a good profit and it was still doing well. With hindsight perhaps it was one he should have kept.

Dorothy was very vague about the date of their return and Eunice had taken it on herself to organise Franklin Flower's visit without knowing exactly when Matt's family would be back. And Matt had acted very strangely, disappearing without saying where he was going.

Hugo read the letter through again though there was not a word about Hannah in it. Not the merest snippet of news of her.

At breakfast, he'd argued with Franklin Flower about the Cotton Exchange though Franklin knew far more about how it ran than he did.

'Hugo, you're very liverish this morning,' Eunice had complained.

'I'm not.' Hugo thought she was far quicker to take offence and unnecessarily sour. 'It's the waiting and not knowing exactly when they'll be here. Why did Dorothy have to be so vague? It isn't as though boats and trains don't run to a timetable these days.'

Irritation boiled within him. As a house guest Franklin was wearing him down. Hugo couldn't see that Dorothy could possibly be happy with him. Such a dull old stick. He himself was making excuses to absent himself from meals so he didn't have to endure too much of Franklin's company.

He stood up, stretching his shoulders to loosen them. There were times when he felt hemmed in by the woods that surrounded his home. Ince Hall was a long, low two-storey building and his study was on the upper floor. A previous owner must have felt hemmed in too, because a tower-like cupola had been built over this room, and a circular staircase wound up from one corner.

As he climbed the steep narrow stairs, he could feel the temperature rising. The cupola was built of white wood and glass, an eight-sided construction with a bench all the way round. He thought of it as a summer house on the roof instead of in the garden. Hugo opened a window so he could breathe and sank down to enjoy the view.

This was the only part of the house from which he could see over the woods. Now he could see cattle grazing on the lush pastures that curved down to the Mere. It seemed idyllically rural, yet on a warm autumn day like this there was no mistaking the industrial haze in the sky. Unseen but very close was Bromborough Pool and the big margarine and candle factories. Also unseen but close was the great soap factory belonging to William Hesketh Lever.

The haze was thicker downriver, over the ports of Liverpool and Birkenhead where so many industries were being carried on. He'd had a hand in many of them over the years; sugar refining, flour milling, the huge tobacco factories, tanneries, breweries, ship building and ship repairing, and the making of matches, jams, sweets, chocolates and biscuits.

Hugo took a deep breath. He liked coming up here; the haze was enough to remind him what he'd worked for. Merseyside was an exciting place to be.

Once he'd been keen to retire and do the things other people wanted to do. He'd thought he wanted to travel and see more of the world, but he'd soon got that out of his system.

He'd sold off many of the businesses he'd owned to reduce his work load, but it had given him a vast sum of money to manage. He was still very careful to get the best possible return on his capital.

He had a few directorships, and a seat on several Boards. Come to that, he still owned three companies. He was still earning a lot of money, doing what he'd done all his life, but in a somewhat different way.

Below him, he heard the door of his study bang back.

'They're home,' Eunice called up. He knew he was safe

from her company here, she could no longer pull herself up the steep winding stairs. 'Are you up there again, Hugo?'

'Yes.' He felt himself stiffen with hostility. It was his automatic reaction to the sound of her voice these days. Eunice was always trying to lock horns with him.

'Dorothy has telephoned. She's very well and wants to see us all. Matt went down to meet them. We're invited to dinner tonight.'

Hugo felt a stab of irritation that he hadn't foreseen such an invitation.

'I told them you had another engagement, but that Franklin and I will go.'

Hugo felt she'd won yet another round. 'How is Hannah?'

'She's all right, I think.'

He said carefully: 'Tell them I may pop in to see them after dinner. If I can get away soon enough.'

Hannah thought Dorothy had put on weight as a result of her pregnancy and the very lazy summer. It suited her; her rosy apple cheeks were rounded, she looked the picture of health. The euphoria she'd felt at leaving Yarrow was with her still. A smile playing about her lips, she laughed at the mildest hint of humour. She seemed to have only one worry.

'Surely, Daddy, Grandma will think it odd that I wear a dress she's seen before? If we'd really spent months in Geneva and travelled through France, both Mother and I would have lots of new clothes.'

Hannah thought Dorothy's pink silk party dress suited her, she filled out the bodice better now.

'There's nothing we can do about that,' Matt snapped. 'Perhaps tomorrow.' The look he shot in Hannah's direction told her he wished her worries were as trite.

'One last hurdle and we'll be out of the wood,' he said. 'You mustn't make the Lady Mother suspicious, nor Franklin Flower neither.'

Hannah hurried to the kitchen. If she could busy herself with preparations she might push her misgivings to the back of her mind. She did very little entertaining, because Matt preferred his own company to that of others, so normally only family members were asked to the house.

The housekeeper had been with Matt since before they were married, and Hannah found everything well organised, and preparations in hand for a family dinner to welcome her home.

Two guests would not prove difficult. She ordered an extra course so that nobody need go hungry. Even the dining table was already extended and set with their best china. She picked some flowers from the garden to put in a silver bowl in the centre. Nothing else was needed. Hannah grew more nervous as the time of their arrival approached.

They all heard the chauffeur-driven Lagonda pull up in front of the house. Hannah went to open the door. Franklin Flower raised Dorothy's hand to his lips. Her mother-in-law bustled in ahead.

Eunice Mortimer was short and stout. Hannah topped her by a good seven inches and was able to look down on her white hair which she combed up into a pile of fluffy curls on top of her head to add inches. Hannah could see her pink scalp showing through.

'You don't look well, Hannah,' she said, kissing her cheek in greeting. That sent another trickle of fear running down her spine. She knew she didn't look right, she shouldn't have worn black. It had suited her mood when she was dressing.

'A bit of a headache. Haven't got over the long journey yet.'

Eunice Mortimer's blue eyes surveyed her coldly. Her own shot silk dress was elegant, though it enhanced her girth. She was bunion-footed so her shoes were wide and looked too plain for the rest of her outfit.

Knowing his mother's fondness for chocolate, Matt had asked Greg to buy a large box of Swiss chocolates from a speciality shop in Geneva, and now Dorothy presented it prettily. In its authentic wrappings, it provided just the right note to substantiate the story they'd fabricated.

'So kind of you to invite me at such notice.' Franklin Flower was a staid bachelor bordering on middle age. He had prominent teeth which he half hid with an overhanging moustache. 'I do appreciate the opportunity to see Dorothy again.'

Hannah eyed him anxiously. Matt said he was thirty-six, five years older than she was herself. He had delightful manners and a very prosperous business. He seemed clever, but clearly not clever enough to see through Dorothy's pouting prettiness to the silly selfish creature within. Hannah couldn't understand what he saw in so young a girl, but he seemed enchanted and couldn't keep his earnest eyes away from her. Dorothy sparkled, chattering to him, full of vitality.

Matt looked quietly pleased that all was going according to plan, so Hannah told herself she must relax. Dorothy was holding centre stage and behaving wonderfully well and Greg was backing her up.

But Hannah couldn't stop her heart thumping sickeningly as she looked up the candle-lit table and toasted Dorothy's renewed health in champagne. The contrast between this house and the untidy gatehouse could not have been greater. Everything was being lavished on Dorothy, while that poor mite had to rely on Maisie O'Malley's good nature. Elizabeth was being deprived not only of worldly goods but of the love of her rightful family. She was, after all, Matt's grand-daughter.

'I think we've done it,' he whispered to her in the hall when dinner was over and he was fetching some special brandy he'd recommended to Franklin. Hannah had come out to fetch the chocolates from Switzerland that Eunice wanted to try straight away.

'Not a hint of disbelief from either of them. Thank goodness it's over and we can put it behind us.'

'It isn't quite,' Hannah reminded him sharply. 'There's still your father.'

It had taken Hannah some time to realise that Matt's parents were in a permanent state of conflict. Both tried to hide it when in the company of other people, but always

50

under the surface Hannah could feel waves of antipathy between them. There were times of relative peace but it took only a spark to have them grappling again.

It caused polarity throughout the family. Because Eunice didn't accept her, she saw herself siding with Hugo. Only Dorothy had a foot in both camps.

'Your father's asked us to tea tomorrow, he wants to see for himself how much Dorothy's health has improved. Your mother's sending her car for us.'

'He'll have heard it all from Franklin Flower before you get there,' Matt said easily.

'But he's so alert and he questions everything.' She liked Sir Hugo. To her, he'd always been friendly and outgoing. Always understanding if she had problems and ready to offer help. On the other hand, he was more perceptive than his wife and would be the first to spot any holes in their stories.

'He won't question anything.'

'He could pick up on some detail and we'd give the game away before we knew where it was leading us.' Hannah wasn't convinced. It still seemed a hurdle she had to jump.

Later on she saw Matt stifle a yawn. She was hoping their guests would go home so she might go to bed when she heard another car draw up in front of the house, followed a few minutes later by a ring on the doorbell. Dinner was over, even the coffee pot was empty. She was wondering who might be calling at this hour when Polly showed Sir Hugo into the drawing-room.

He was a giant of a man, over six foot tall, sprightly, slim and light on his feet. She felt the atmosphere change. The relaxed somnolence evaporated, they were all wide awake again instantly.

Dorothy leapt to her feet to greet him. Hannah got up more slowly. His beard tickled as he kissed her. She knew he was aware of it from the smile that lit up his face.

Nature had given him a strong chin but his small beard, more a growth of hair along the line of his jaw, strengthened it, making him appear really determined. He had thick wavy

51

silvery hair but his beard had a golden tinge, retaining some of its original colour.

'My business was over earlier than I'd expected, so I thought I'd pop in to see Dorothy. You look well enough, you rogue. Giving us all a fright like that.' His voice resounded round the room.

'I'm quite well again, Grandpa, thank you.'

'A glass of brandy, Hugo?' Hannah asked. 'Or coffee?' She could see Polly hovering by the door, still holding his black cape and top hat, waiting to see if he would accept a drink.

Now in his sixtieth year, Hugo Mortimer's manner made him seem much younger. He had the bright blue eyes of a seafarer.

'A glass of brandy would be excellent, Hannah.'

He turned back to the cape Polly was holding and produced two packages from it. Like the showman he was, he offered one to Dorothy.

'You weren't here on your birthday so I kept your gift 'til now.'

She screeched with delight when she unwrapped a pearl necklace and insisted Franklin Flower fasten it round her neck.

With a nervous jerk, Hannah found Hugo's bright blue eyes watching her.

'You weren't here on your birthday either.' The other package was put gently in her hand. It was larger than Dorothy's.

'It's kind of you to think of me,' she was saying, formally polite, as she unwrapped the fancy paper.

She gave a gasp. A necklace of large emeralds joined with diamonds sparkled up at her from a bed of black velvet.

'It's absolutely beautiful. Hugo, it's gorgeous! I hardly know what to say. It's a very extravagant gift.' She went over and kissed his cheek. 'Thank you.'

'Kept within the family, gifts are never an extravagance,' he said. 'How are you, Hannah?'

'I've been telling her she looks peaky,' Eunice put in.

'Just the long journey home,' she said.

Hugo was fastening the emeralds round her neck with cold clumsy fingers. She could see him in the mirror studying her reflection but his gaze was kindly. She had no need to fear anything from him. The emeralds flashed, bringing life to her black dress. Already she felt better.

'You mustn't let Matt book you on long train journeys, no need these days. Old-fashioned. Had a wonderful trip a week or two back. You must try it, Hannah. I flew from Le Bourget in to Croydon.

'Wonderful experience. A biplane; a converted Avro reconnaissance warplane. Just room for two passengers. The pilot sat outside in the cockpit and spoke to us on the intercom telephone. It took only two hours, though the pilot estimated two and a half. Sixty miles an hour we did.

'It's a commercial service now, Matt. You'd enjoy it. We flew at four thousand feet and could see the terrible devastation of war laid out below us. It's all still there – the trenches, the shell craters, gun emplacements and abandoned tanks.'

'Father, I've seen all I need of the trenches. I was there, remember?'

'Such a smooth and easy journey, except for landing. We did come down with a bump on the grass. That's the travel of the future. I thoroughly recommend it.'

Hugo fascinated Hannah as he did most people. He could spar with Eunice and yet be genial and expansive to other people only moments later. He always seemed to be in the grip of some new enthusiasm. In some ways he seemed younger than Matt.

Hugo Mortimer sipped his brandy and made a conscious effort to keep his eyes away from Hannah. The five long months she'd been away had dragged. He'd been eager to see her again and could stay away no longer. But he had to be careful not to betray his feelings.

Hannah had a magic that drew him like a magnet. There

were mauve shadows beneath her dark eyes tonight, adding to her haunting beauty, and an air of tension about her he'd never noticed before.

He felt a terrible urge to press her hand and sympathise. He surmised that her stay in Switzerland had not been pleasant, she was saying little about it. Dorothy had made no secret that they did not get on. Perhaps concern for Dorothy's health had been a worry to her? There were lines of sadness about her mouth.

He remembered the first time he'd seen her. Matt had brought her to tea one afternoon and announced: 'This is Hannah. My secretary for two years and soon to be my wife.'

'A very unsuitable position for a lady,' Eunice had snorted in a pretended aside, but loud enough to carry to Hannah's ears.

In the days before the war it was unusual for women like Hannah to go into business. He'd thought her a more interesting person because she had.

Hugo admired large women. He'd thought her stunningly attractive, but she'd been so shy she'd scarcely opened her mouth. He'd talked about himself to put her at her ease. Garbled on about some flour mill he was interested in at the time. Something in her dark eyes had drawn him to her from that day.

He'd told himself he was being ridiculous. The girl was in love with Matt, must be if she intended to marry him. Or could there be two like Eunice?

He didn't see her often and Hannah gave him no reason to hope. If she seemed to expect anything from him, it could only be family affection, friendship. Nothing more.

Hugo had told himself many times he ought to keep away from her, but because she was his daughter-in-law that was impossible. If she had not been, he'd have felt free to follow up this unbidden urge.

He knew now that unrequited passion burns ever more strongly. He'd held himself firmly in check and had made no advances towards Hannah. Contenting himself with a kiss on

54

each cheek when he met her, though her perfume could intoxicate him.

The trouble was that while he craved for her, he could not be enthusiastic about others. Seeing her again had made him feel calmer, though he dared not let himself think of Lavinia with whom he'd spent the early part of the evening. She'd caused a terrible scene; bad for his blood pressure and for his mental equilibrium.

'Do bring Dorothy to tea tomorrow as arranged,' he said. Hannah's luminous dark eyes looked at him with cool affection. He liked to think he could sense passion simmering below the surface.

'This has been a scant half hour and I've heard nothing about your stay in Switzerland, or how you managed to restore Dorothy to health.'

He thought she shied off nervously at that, but Dorothy said: 'Of course we'll come, Grandpa.'

The emeralds were shown off to perfection above Hannah's breasts. The diamonds rose and fell with her breathing, sparking multicoloured lights.

She was smiling a little to herself and running her fingers over the stones. He was glad he'd given her pleasure.

Chapter Four

Hannah felt stiff with tension. Matt's eyes kept meeting hers; she knew he was afraid she'd let something slip. Even Dorothy was beginning to look tired. She rang for another pot of coffee. They must all stay alert.

Hugo had put his feet on a footstool and stretched out on the chair. He was swirling his brandy round the glass. It was a habit of his to lie back like this in the late evening and talk.

One Christmas, years ago when she'd first married Matt, he'd been lying on that very chair. His eyes had followed her all day, through all the parlour games they'd played with the children. She'd wondered about him, how he'd come to be so rich. Then, when they were all tired and the nursery maid had taken Dorothy away to see her into bed, Hannah had plucked up courage to ask.

'Everybody says you're one of the richest men in England now, but you didn't come from a wealthy family. How did you do it? It must be very hard to get started.'

She knew by then that Hugo didn't feel he had to hide anything. He expected people to take him as he was, and if they didn't like it, he didn't care.

He'd laughed. 'Everybody wants to know that.'

'I don't,' Eunice had said sharply. 'I wish you'd stop telling these stories.'

'Your mother-in-law,' he'd smiled at Hannah, 'would prefer me to say I'd inherited a fortune and been educated at Eton. Actually, I ran away to sea when I was thirteen.'

'Hugo! I do wish you'd stop telling such ridiculous stories.'

'Why did you want to leave home?' Hannah persisted.

'My mother died when I was four and my father married again. He was captain of a Baltimore-built schooner called the *Iphigenia*. He said he wanted to provide me with a mother because he spent so much time at sea.

'I didn't like being left in her care. I think she hated me.'

'An unhappy childhood?'

'Yes. As a lad I spent a lot of time at the Pierhead watching the ships on the Mersey. Many of our neighbours were seafarers. One day I attracted more of my step-mother's ill temper than usual and decided to leave. To go to sea seemed the logical step.

'I shipped as cabin boy on the *Flying Fox*, a brig of a hundred and forty tons, belonging to a Liverpool merchant firm.'

'When would that have been?' Hannah's interest had been hooked immediately.

'Eighteen seventy-three. We were bound for the oil rivers. That's the West Coast of Africa.'

'Didn't they have steam ships by then?'

'Yes, but steam ships were highly thought of; faster and safer, they had no difficulty getting a crew. There were still plenty of wooden sailing ships like the *Flying Fox*, though, glad of boys like me. We carried two or three passengers, missionaries mostly, and trade goods . . .'

'What are those?' Greg had been about ten at the time. Hannah could see him now, seated at his grandfather's feet, hanging on to every word he said.

'Salt for a start. It was cheap in Liverpool and always in demand on the West Coast. Almost every vessel carried the weight of its registered tonnage in salt. We also carried cheap Manchester cottons, beads, Dane guns, gin, buckets and bowls – anything the natives might like to have. Trade goods were used by everybody, whether they had come to trade or not. Missionaries used them to barter for their own needs such as food, or to build a house or a church.' Hugo rubbed his beard thoughtfully. Hannah could see his mind was still on those faraway days.

'Go on, Grandpa,' Greg had begged impatiently. 'I want to hear all about it.'

'Our agent stayed out there and bartered the trade goods for palm oil which we brought home to Liverpool. I did two round trips, but when we arrived off Calabar for the third time we found there'd been an epidemic of yellow fever from which seven men out of eleven had died. They were needing replacements, so I volunteered.'

'Weren't you afraid you'd catch it?' Greg's eyes were wide with horror.

'Terrified. The captain spelled out the risks. The yellow fever epidemic was over, but I might just as easily meet my end from dysentery or malaria or the countless other fevers that raged there.'

'And still you decided to stay?'

'As a boy I'd already been tempted by advertisements in Liverpool newspapers. Every so often I'd come across one that read: "Young men wanted, eighteen to twenty-five years, as book-keepers in West Africa. A few hours' work a day in pleasant surroundings, unlimited shooting and fishing and fine tropical scenery with a boat and crew at your disposal. Free food and quarters. Salary to commence: seventy pounds."

'The crew knew of these jobs, and a few were tempted. I heard them discussing it. We all had the chance to see what it was like before we signed up. We thought we knew the drawbacks.

'We knew the attractions too. We'd all heard of men, other Liverpudlians, who had done it and come home with vast fortunes. The Holt brothers, Alfred and John, for instance. They managed it because they had strong constitutions. Strong enough to withstand the dreadful diseases. If I could survive there for three years, I knew I could come home with enough money to set myself up for life.

'The agent offered me eighty pounds a year if I'd join him, but I had to sign on for three years. Promotion was rapid, the deadly climate saw to that. By the last year I was earning three hundred pounds and that was good money then.'

Hannah shuddered. 'But no fortune, Hugo. You were risking your health. In fact, you were risking your life.'

'Yes, but without money life was very hard in those days. If we wanted to eat, we had to work. And the food was poor and monotonous. I'd already found that being a cabin boy provided food and shelter but not much more. I decided it was worth the risk.'

Hannah shook her head in amazement. 'But I still don't see how you made the money.'

'Companies relied on their agents to do their best with the capital entrusted to them and did not insist on detailed accounts. We were told they wanted a reasonable profit, and if they got it no questions would be asked. Policing would cost more than it saved. Salaries were based on the assumption that men would trade on their own account.

'Some made six thousand a year as well as fortunes for their company. A hundred pounds laid out in beads and coloured cloth brought thousands in return. Some took back ten or fifteen thousand after three years. I was determined to bring back as much as I could for myself.'

'How much did you bring back?' Greg had hardly been able to get the words out.

'Nearly twenty thousand.' Hannah heard the satisfaction in his voice.

'Is that a lot?' Greg's blue eyes had been so eager.

'It was then.'

'It is now.' Hannah had smiled.

'I want to go as soon as I'm thirteen.'

'Hugo, for goodness' sake!' Eunice Mortimer had been aghast. 'Look what you're doing, you're putting ideas into the child's head. You'll have him running away next.'

'You're too late, Greg. The world has changed, it's no longer possible to do what I did. And for every man who brought a fortune home, many went under, defeated by disease and by the terrible climate.'

'But what did you have to do, Grandpa?'

'The job was to bargain the trade goods for palm oil.

That's what the merchants of Liverpool wanted. We would also send back small amounts of gold, copra, rubber – anything that could be sold at a profit. Grey parrots were popular as pets and brought good prices in England. We sent any we could get.

'There was great competition to buy the palm oil. There were agents from Australia and America as well as from all over England. We all had to send back a full cargo on every ship. The price we had to pay rose and fell with supply and demand, but the price in England rose and fell too. Sometimes the only way to get the oil was to pay over the odds or to give big advances which could result in bad debts. Many gambled on a rise when a fall took place. It was bad for the nerves. Anxious men suffered. The tougher ones amongst us regarded it as a grand game.' Hugo pulled himself up a little in his chair, and his blue seafaring eyes twinkled at her. Hannah got up to refill his glass.

'So where did you go to buy it?' Greg wanted to know. Hannah watched Hugo ruffle his yellow hair and knew he thought the boy promised well for the future, that he might succeed where Matt had failed.

'The oil markets were miles away up in the interior of the country. Places that had never been explored.'

'Then, Grandpa, you couldn't go.'

'Greg,' Matt had interrupted, 'it's time you went to bed. It's getting late and Grandpa's tired.'

Hannah was afraid the antipathy between Matt and his father was becoming more obvious. Hugo was in full flood and clearly enjoying himself. He ignored Matt now.

'No, we had to rely on native middlemen to get it for us, and the hardest part was to decide which of them could be trusted. It was the custom to advance them goods to pay for the oil. Advances to the value of three or four thousand were common, and we had to wait months for them to bring the oil back . . .

'We had to keep our wits about us to avoid the trade tricks. They would mix sand and copper with gold dust, pour lead

61

into elephant tusks to make them heavier, add water, mud and chopped plantain suckers to palm oil to increase its bulk, or nail a piece of wood inside the cask to cut down its internal capacity.'

'So you stayed on the coast and waited for them to bring it? Which town did you live in?'

'Along the coast, the only port for thousands of miles is Lagos. We traders lived on old ships, bought cheap because they were ready for the breaker's yard. There were lots of them moored along the banks of the Niger River and in the delta creeks of the Cross River at that time. The *Lord Raglan* was sunk in shallow water just a little further up. Once she'd carried troops to the Crimea.

'The agents made themselves as comfortable as possible and ran the ships like any other. The one belonging to my firm was called the *Prince Igor*. Once she had been a proud passenger liner plying the Baltic. By my time she was anchored in a swift current and looked like Noah's Ark.

'She'd been dismasted and a roof of thatch had been built over her decks. Later it was replaced with corrugated iron. The hulk was then a permanent office, store and dwelling place for the agent and his assistants.' Hugo's voice was full of nostalgia.

'A ladder as wide as a staircase reached to the water's edge. All was clean and well scrubbed. We took visitors up to the sheltered cool of the upper deck which was our living hall. Matting blinds could be lowered from the roof to shade us from the sun. Madeira wickerwork chairs and sofas and hammocks were everywhere.

'The spacious old saloon was the trading shop where we spread out our goods. It still showed remnants of its former glory, solid mahogany tables and heavy gilt mouldings, but the fine gold had faded to dull yellow.

'We were all up at daybreak, because that's the coolest part of the day to work. Long canoes laden with palm oil and paddled by twenty to thirty naked boys came downriver, and there were always a few lying close to the ship discharging their cargo. We boiled the palm oil and ran it into casks on the bank, and when a ship arrived from England, she had only to discharge stores and trade goods and load up with the palm oil that we'd collected.

'The chiefs who brought the oil selected goods in return for their produce. At ten in the morning, a gong sounded for breakfast. The market was cleared of customers and the chiefs were invited up to the quarter deck for breakfast.

'It taught me all I needed to know about business, Greg. We had to have the trade goods they wanted, otherwise the chiefs would exchange their oil with those who had. Politeness was very important, and paying them what they were due to the last farthing. We had to deal honestly with them, and never take unfair advantage, or they wouldn't trade again.

'When I came home I went into shipping, but I dabbled in most of the industries carried on in and around Liverpool. Sugar and flour milling, for instance. Conditions change, Greg, sometimes one thing is more profitable than another. I sold at the right moment too. That's why I don't have a big business empire now like William Hesketh Lever. He's made a fortune out of West Africa too.'

'Did he want the palm oil, Grandpa?'

'Yes, but he leased land and planted his own oil palms so the sort of trading I knew has gone for ever.'

'You're a self-made man, Grandpa.' Greg was sitting with his arms wrapped round his knees, enchanted.

'And proud of it, though your grandmother doesn't like my saying so. She thinks there's more status to having money handed down through the family.'

'It's more a question of breeding,' Eunice had said through tight lips.

'Tell us some more, Grandpa.'

'The only thing I can tell you now, Greg, is that it really is time you went to bed.'

Hannah could understand how his disappointment in Matt had made him encourage Greg. Hugo had wanted him to follow in his footsteps and it seemed likely at that time his hopes would be fulfilled.

Franklin was beginning to fidget. 'It's getting rather late.'

'Lovely, Dorothy, to see you so much recovered,' Eunice said, accepting more coffee from Hannah.

Hugo knew she'd never notice that Franklin looked tired and wanted to go. Not that it was all that late, it just proved he was too set in his ways to marry a girl as young as Dorothy.

Eunice clattered down her cup. 'We've been working out, haven't we, Franklin, that we are related?'

'Distantly.' He stifled a yawn.

'Tenth cousins, we said?'

'Twelfth.'

Eunice was keen on her family connections. She kept in touch with them all. Inviting them to her house and visiting theirs. Hugo didn't care for any of them.

He'd met her father first. He'd been approached by him on a business venture soon after he'd returned from the Coast.

At the time, Hugo had been seeking an older man of some stature to act as a figurehead to his fledgling company, to give it respectability. He'd bought several tug boats and lighters and was contracting their services to the great shipping lines using the ports of Liverpool and Birkenhead. Sir Cecil Schofield, the incumbent of a hereditary baronetcy, seemed exactly the sort of person Hugo was looking for. Sir Cecil's head was bald, a pink dome rising through a curtain of crinkly hair that stuck out like puff balls of spun silver about his ears. He wore spats of grey boxcloth when in town. Hugo appointed him a director, without duties.

Sir Cecil had gone out of his way to be friendly. He'd taken Hugo to his home and introduced him to his wife, whom Hugo had found rather formidable, and his daughter Eunice, who had a bewitching, fragile beauty.

Hugo knew he'd come back to Merseyside hungry for everything. The only white woman he'd seen for years was the wife of a missionary, and she'd died within three months of arriving. He had all the appetites of youth, but his were sharper than most because they'd gone unsatisfied for so long.

He'd wanted a good time and white women seemed an exotic and very desirable species. But he wasn't the sort who played about; he went for what he wanted most. His intentions were entirely honourable: enduring love and marriage. Eunice was blonde and pretty, and for a young lady of rank made more of the running than he'd expected. Hugo thought no other girl he'd met could hold a candle to her.

As a father Sir Cecil was indulgent, spoiling Eunice with every luxury. Hugo felt flattered that he was receiving friendship from one and love from the other.

After living a communal bachelor existence aboard the old *Prince Igor* out on the Coast, the Schofields' home amazed him and the style in which they lived was a revelation.

Cecil Schofield's whole philosophy of life was getting the best of everything for himself and his family. Clothes from London and the Continent for his wife and daughter. A country estate of many acres with a magnificent house and a home farm. Hugo found he had a troop of servants providing splendid hospitality, antique furniture, delicious food and fine wines.

He kept a stable of magnificent horses for family use, and Hugo didn't know how many carriages he saw. In addition, he was shown round Schofield's bloodstock stables and taken racing at Haydock to see them in action.

In those days Hugo had gone about everything with volcanic energy. He was working hard to increase the profits from his tugs and seeking further opportunities to increase his wealth.

Eunice had drunk rather more wine than was good for her on the evening she'd said: 'I like you, Hugo, and I think you're good fun, but Father thinks you're rather bumptious. He says you show off outrageously.'

Hugo had been taken aback, but after thinking it over conceded that perhaps Sir Cecil was right. He'd been barely twenty years of age but he'd considered himself the equal of any man, confident he'd increase the fortune he'd brought home.

He knew he'd been on his best behaviour whenever he'd been with Sir Cecil. He'd been very careful to show him respect. He wanted to be on good terms because he was hoping to marry his daughter.

'Nobody spends years on the Coast and comes out unscathed,' he'd said, feeling hurt. He'd not felt totally at ease with Sir Cecil who was so much older, but he'd received more attention and kindness from him than he'd expected.

Cecil Schofield was a man who had travelled widely and in the greatest possible comfort. Hugo had thought him a sophisticate, a man with wide interests. He'd listened to his opinions expecting to learn a great deal, but what he said about money and business didn't always make sense.

Hugo was more interested in what Eunice thought of him. Her rounded cheeks had dimples when she smiled, her hair was pale gold and she wore it in a graceful Grecian knot. She also had deep blue eyes and a habit of giggling behind her hand. She could make him tingle with desire; he found her totally captivating. It didn't take him long to get round to asking if she'd marry him.

He'd known she'd say yes – the wholehearted way she kissed had told him that much. She also said her father would expect to be asked formally for his permission, and nothing must be taken for granted until that had been given.

Hugo felt nervous about this, especially since he'd heard Sir Cecil found him bumptious. He was steeling himself to do it when Lady Schofield invited him to dinner.

'Just a family occasion,' she'd said, in her sugar sweet manner. 'Not a dinner party.'

Hugo wondered then if it had been arranged just to give him the opportunity. He knew he'd have to do it sometime during the evening. As it happened, Sir Cecil was coming downstairs as the parlour maid let him in. Hugo decided he would get it over with as soon as possible, so he might then relax.

'Good evening, Sir Cecil. I wonder if I might have a word in private?'

He was led into the library, the doors were closed carefully, and Sir Cecil stood before him, elegant in his dinner jacket and black tie. They dressed every evening, even if there were no guests. All the proprieties were observed in this household.

Hugo thought he'd put the question with total clarity.

'May I have your permission to marry Eunice?' He'd gone on to say a lot more about loving her and wanting to take care of her, and the plans he had for buying a suitable house.

Sir Cecil was quite expansive about marriage generally, but Hugo found himself in the drawing-room with the rest of the family, still unsure whether or not he'd been given permission.

The atmosphere was very affable, so he decided by the time they were going into the dining-room that the permission he'd asked for must have been granted. Certainly it hadn't been refused.

He whispered to Eunice that all was well, expecting their forthcoming engagement to be openly discussed over the meal.

Eunice was in high spirits, very talkative, dimpling at him across the table, but she gave no acknowledgement that their marriage could now take place. Twice he tried to bring the subject up himself, but first her mother sidetracked the conversation to the old Queen's health and then Eunice herself turned it to rose growing. Sir Cecil's main interest seemed to be a race horse called Lady of the Night.

Hugo felt bewildered by their reticence. Surely Eunice's engagement must be of paramount interest to them all? He began to suspect collusion. That meant Eunice . . .

At about ten-thirty the ladies got up from the table. Usually they went to the drawing-room for coffee and the men joined them later. Tonight it was made clear to Hugo that they were going up to bed, leaving him to finish his port with Sir Cecil.

Hugo was surprised and disappointed, but careful not to

overstay his welcome, he'd stood up shortly afterwards to take his leave.

'Don't rush off,' Sir Cecil had said. 'I'd like to talk to you.'

Alarm bells began to ring in Hugo's head then. He was afraid he'd misread the situation. Was he about to be told he wasn't good enough for Eunice?

With glasses refilled, Sir Cecil started on a discourse about two very desirable mares that had caught his fancy. One called Havana Queen had won every race for which she had been entered last season. Somewhat bemused, Hugo tried to humour him.

'Is it possible to make money on horses like that?'

'With a real winner, yes. Very much so. There's the pleasure, too, of seeing it romp home.'

'If it *does* romp home. What about stabling expenses?' Hugo felt ignorant about horses, he'd never even ridden one until recently.

'Heavy.' Sir Cecil's puff balls of white hair nodded. 'Horses like this need the best of everything. But I can provide it. Stable lads to exercise them, a trainer, everything. At five thousand guineas the pair, they're a bargain, I can tell you.'

'Good lord!' Hugo couldn't imagine anybody spending money like that on a couple of horses.

'I'll cut you in, old chap, you can't go wrong. You'll soon get your money back.'

Hugo jerked with shock. A small wave of port came over the lip of his glass. His heart was thumping wildly. He had to ask: 'Are you serious?'

'Yes. A wonderful opportunity.'

He licked the wine from his hand. A certain eagerness in the other's manner was screaming a warning. 'No, thank you.'

Sir Cecil's affronted blue eyes stared into his.

'Against the security of this house then? You could hardly refuse a chance like that?'

Hugo was on fire with embarrassment. It was the last thing he'd expected.

Was Schofield asking for a loan or did he really want him to take a share in these horses? He decided at that moment he didn't want to do either. But did his marriage to Eunice depend on whether he did? He dared not ask.

'What do you say to that?'

Hugo felt he was being edged towards a black hole. He gulped at his port. He'd finish it quickly so he could go. He wasn't going to be blackmailed into anything.

'I think I'd better stick to what I know. I'd be out of my depth with horses.'

'Absolute blue chip opportunity, my boy.'

'Then this time next year you'll thank me for leaving all the profits to you.'

Again the blue eyes held his. 'The horses need a bit of input. Had a bad year. Run of bad luck. It goes like this sometimes. Not enough have been first past the winning post recently.'

Hugo blenched. 'Wouldn't it make more sense to sell off those that are losing?'

'You don't understand, one's luck can change overnight. Besides, I get fond of them.'

He'd assumed Schofield had unlimited wealth. There was evidence all round him of high spending. He'd heard over the meal that the dinner service had been specially commissioned by an earl in 1790. There was enough plate for three families displayed on the sideboard. Everything was of the highest quality.

If Schofield sold the pictures on the walls of this room they would surely bring him the sum for which he was asking? He'd spent with a free hand in the past. Why then, if he was short of funds, didn't he sell some of these possessions?

'When you go racing, to have a horse of your own running makes all the difference.'

'You're trying to mix business with pleasure.' Hugo knew he sounded fifty years older than Sir Cecil. 'It rarely works.'

69

'Two thousand then? I really must have that much. Running costs, you know.'

Hugo's head was swimming. He was paying this man good money to have his name on his company notepaper, believing it would enhance his business. In fact it could do him more harm than good. The man was mad.

'I'm looking for ways to earn money,' he said coldly. 'Not spend it.'

He couldn't stay here. Couldn't stand any more of this. Hugo pulled himself to his feet and strode blindly to the door.

'Thank you for your hospitality,' he said curtly. 'Good night.'

His mind raced. He was far too angry and upset to sleep when he got to bed. He spent most of the night worrying, afraid that Schofield financed his life-style by preying on unworldly youths such as himself. He was even more worried about Eunice. It seemed she was part of the deal he'd been offered. He began to wonder whether she'd set out to entrap him. He certainly felt she was not all she'd seemed. He felt they'd deliberately set out to defraud him and he'd been taken in. He'd only grown suspicious because they'd asked too much, too quickly.

Towards morning he came to a conclusion. He'd be unwise, nay foolish, to marry into the family.

Hugo was out of bed at first light, determined to make closer enquiries into Schofield's affairs. He knew he'd taken far too much on trust.

He'd spent the day in his office but been unable to work. He'd stared at the wall opposite in an agony of indecision. Logic told him he was doing the right thing and must not change his mind. His heart led him to believe otherwise.

He couldn't get Eunice out of his mind. He saw her at the piano, her blonde Grecian knot swaying gracefully to the waltz she played. He saw her raising her wine glass to her lips, her eyes smiling at him across the dinner table.

On the third day he received a letter from her.

Dearest Hugo,

Please do call and see me again. Tea time on Sunday would be convenient because Father will be out.

He says his enquiries about you have uncovered things that in his opinion would make you an unsuitable husband.

I can't believe you mean never to see me again. I love you. Do please come, so we can talk about it.

Your,

Eunice

It made him feel heady and altered everything. He'd known all along it was too late to cut himself off from Eunice. He loved her and wanted her and she felt the same.

He could not stay away from her. On Sunday Eunice, looking distressed and tearful, received him with her mother in their drawing-room.

As she poured tea from a silver pot, the formidable Lady Schofield said: 'I do feel there's been some misunderstanding. Poor Eunice has been very upset.'

'So have I,' said Hugo, accepting a cucumber sandwich.

'Of course, I don't know exactly what passed between you and Cecil, but I'm sure you both got it wrong.'

Hugo dared not say the words 'blackmail' or 'extortion' in this very elegant room. Perhaps he had misunderstood?

'Cecil has Eunice's best interests at heart, but perhaps he acted too hastily. We do hope you'll be able to forget what happened and start again.'

Hugo munched silently, realising he was receiving a formal apology. It didn't quite remove the ice from the pit of his stomach. He'd been going through agonies all week.

But Eunice had cheered up. After tea she suggested they walk in the grounds. He went round the rose garden with her clinging to his arm and holding up her yellow silk dress far enough to show her yellow shoes.

'It wasn't exactly a misunderstanding, was it?' he asked.

'Mother says . . .'

'You were all in it together. You had it planned. Your father asked me for money, you know.'

'Oh, no!' She laughed. 'No, Hugo, you must have misunderstood.'

'I feel I was set up.'

'He probably wanted to know if you had enough money to support me. Isn't that what a father's supposed to ask?'

'It was nothing like that,' he protested. 'Why did you go to bed so early that night?'

'Oh, that was arranged so that you could tell him privately about your finances.'

Hugo wanted to believe her. Perhaps it wasn't collusion?

'Nothing else was planned.' Her eyes were wide with innocence. 'Of course, I wasn't there, I don't know exactly what he said, but I'm sure he'd never ask you for money. Why should he? If we love each other, surely that's all that matters? And I do love you, Hugo.'

He felt more certain of Eunice, even when he discovered Schofield was considered a rogue and a profligate spender. That his town house was rented, and his country estate mortgaged to the hilt already. That he owed a small fortune on his racing establishment and that he had huge gambling debts.

Hugo extricated himself as quickly as possible from the business dealings he'd had with Eunice's father.

Chapter Five

Hugo shivered in the night air out on the step as he watched Birtwhistle, his chauffeur, swing on the cranking handle until the Lagonda fired. He held open the back door himself for Eunice and Franklin to climb in.

Dorothy and Hannah had come out on the steps to see them off. He kissed Dorothy and that meant it was all right for him to kiss Hannah too.

She smiled. 'You're very generous, Hugo, and I love the emeralds.'

He had to turn away quickly and get in his Buick, a much less showy vehicle. They were both waving as he moved off in the wake of the Lagonda.

Hannah tantalised him. He'd told himself last month it was his own imagination that tantalised. He knew now it was not and he would never be free of it.

Already they'd left the suburbs of Prenton and Bebington behind, and he was driving through lush country. Raby Mere was surrounded by large farms with open fields – a rural oasis. He drove past Raby Hall, dipped down to the Mere itself where the ducks rippled the surface in the moonlight. The road narrowed and began to wind up through leafy chestnut trees.

His house was about halfway between Raby Hall and Poulton Hall. Built in a three-acre clearing in the trees, it was more secluded than either. Birtwhistle was already opening the rear door of the Lagonda when Hugo pulled up behind. He'd leave him to garage the Buick tonight.

Ince Hall was built of red sandstone and partly clad with

creeper, the great orangery windows glinting in the moonlight. Fortunately it wasn't too near the Mere itself because that had become a popular beauty spot, attracting crowds on sunny weekends to rent the skiffs and rowing boats by the hour. He'd planted more trees on the lower fields when he'd first bought the place, screening it off more securely.

'A night cap, Franklin?'

'No, thank you, I've had more than enough for one night. Bed is what I need now. I do thank you both for your hospitality.'

Hugo smiled. He'd not have asked if he'd thought it likely Franklin would accept. Franklin was old before his time, set in his ways, and Dorothy was such a child still – he was far too old for her. Hugo couldn't understand the attraction; couldn't understand why Eunice encouraged such a match.

He was pouring a last brandy for himself in the library when she came in and closed the door carefully.

'What on earth made you give emeralds like that to Hannah?' She was at her most shrewish. Her antagonism made him respond in kind.

'Didn't you like them?'

'Of course I liked them! Far too good for her. They looked more expensive than the pearls you gave Dorothy.'

'They were. Pearls are more suitable for a young girl.' Dorothy couldn't carry off emeralds like that, not yet. Probably not ever, he thought.

'You overdid it. You made far too much fuss of Hannah.'

That made him catch his breath, but Eunice knew there were other women in his life, he'd told her straight out there would have to be. She couldn't be thinking that Hannah might be one of them?

'I feel sorry for her,' he said. 'She wants a family and it doesn't come.'

Eunice clicked her tongue with exasperation. She'd heard all that before and was not to be sidetracked. 'Expensive gifts of jewellery like that should only be accepted from a husband.'

'What about Dorothy's pearls?'

'They are not so expensive. Anyway, she is a blood relation. Hannah is not.'

'Still a relation.' He never would understand Eunice. He'd been twenty when they married, and head over heels in love. Eunice was a year older. It hadn't taken him long to discover it was the biggest mistake he'd ever made.

He put it down to the impatience of youth. He couldn't wait, couldn't believe she wasn't all she seemed. He'd been bowled over by her beauty and her pretty clothes. But they had nothing in common, nothing to share.

'They're both family, Eunice,' he said more gently.

She had never taken to Hannah. 'Great strapping woman,' she'd said. 'Lower-middle-class.' Hannah's father had been a solicitor running his own small practice that dealt with humdrum conveyancing work. 'I can't think what came over Matt.'

Hugo sighed. It was almost the only thing his son had done of which he did approve. He envied him Hannah.

'Keep your hands off her, Hugo.' Eunice's voice was suddenly more waspish. 'Hannah's too close to home. If that ever got out, I don't know what I'd say to the other members of the moral welfare committee.'

He blazed up. 'I've never laid a finger on Hannah. I think you and your snooping moral welfare committee have all got filthy minds, Eunice. Prurient minds. Poking your noses into other people's business. Looking for dirt where there isn't any.'

'Somebody has to look after poor fallen girls . . .'

'Nobody has fallen further than you!'

There was no doubt in his mind now about what she and her parents had set out to do. They'd believed they could part him from his money without Eunice having to marry him. He knew they saw him as no great match. Money was necessary, but they wanted social status too and at the time he didn't have any.

He believed that when he refused to give her father money, she'd seen marriage as the only way to get it, and deliberately set out to trap him into it. She'd shown a wildly passionate nature at the time and a cold disinterest in him since. He heard she'd had a previous suitor who had pleased both her and her parents more, except that he'd been almost penniless. With hindsight, he could see he'd been chosen because he was better able to provide.

'I'm well regarded by society now, Hugo. You know that.' Her blue eyes regarded him belligerently.

'Because you hide what you are. I should have had the sense to divorce you years ago.'

He'd thought long and hard about it, been on the point of doing it. Even talked of it to Eunice. There had been a hundred fresh starts over the years. All had failed. Hundreds of disappointments. Hundreds of quarrelsome rows. Now they spent more time apart, it suited them better that way.

'Don't start nagging about divorce again, Hugo.'

'Go to bed,' he said coldly.

Matthew was born later in the year they married, and the year after that Cecil Schofield was made bankrupt. It was a five-day wonder. He owed more than any other bankrupt in the last two decades.

Eunice saw it as a terrible disgrace. Hugo was quite sure she'd known it was coming, but afterwards she'd convinced herself it had never happened.

The passing years had made him realise she was a silly woman. As an adult she couldn't deny herself anything. She had a good appetite and a sweet tooth, and soon lost her figure in pillows of fat. Hard to believe, looking at her now, that she'd once been a very pretty girl. Still, forty years had passed and time played havoc with a woman's beauty.

Eunice wanted the world to stand still. She wanted to keep the traditions and privileges she'd enjoyed in Queen Victoria's time. She hated the servant shortage and the erosion of class differences the Great War had brought. She still did everything she could to enhance her own status in the world and naturally she wanted a husband she would not be ashamed of. Hugo's social status had improved with the years.

Looking back, they had each gained just enough from the union to keep it going. Like her father, Eunice was a profligate spender and could not control money. He provided that.

He'd been young and had wanted all the trappings of wealth. She had found Ince Hall for him, and chosen the furniture. She had style. She sent him to the right tailors, and above all she had the right contacts and knew the right people to point him in the right direction. He would have found it more difficult to expand and build on his first business if it had not been for Eunice.

Hannah thought Dorothy had gained confidence overnight. She wasn't at all worried about talking to Grandpa about her stay in Switzerland.

'For heaven's sake,' she said to her step-mother as they sat in the back of the Lagonda that Eunice had sent over to fetch them, 'Grandma has already accepted everything we've said. Why should he not believe us? You're a bag of nerves, that's your problem.'

Raby Mere was deserted as they drove through. The rowing-boats were lined up on the edge of the crystal clear water. There were no customers at the Mill House Tea Gardens although it was sunny. It was a weekday and most people were at work.

Eunice pecked her cheek as usual when she arrived, and Hannah saw her eyes fix on the emeralds she was wearing.

'Did I give you to understand it was a party? Emeralds like those are better kept for evening, dear. They give the appearance of being a little over-dressed for tea in the garden.' Her smile was superior, her tone condescending.

Hannah's fingers felt for her emeralds defensively. She wore them on a plain dress of dark green linen that came high at the neck.

'I wanted to wear them, but Matt and I hardly ever go out in the evening.'

'I'm glad you have.' Hugo came to her rescue. 'It gives me pleasure to see them.'

'Come on outside,' Eunice said coldly, leading the way into the garden. A table had been set up under the trees.

'I see Dorothy is wearing her pearls, too,' Hugo added.

'Pearls are correct for day time, Hugo.' Eunice was frostier than ever. 'Even you should have noticed that by now.'

'Let's hear about Switzerland instead,' he said, rubbing his hands. 'You've told me nothing about it yet.'

Dorothy started recounting the same facts in identical words to those she'd used last night when she'd told her grandmother. She even sounded a little bored with it all.

Would Eunice notice? Hannah dared not look at her. Instead, she found Hugo studying her intently. She tried to smile at him, and instil a little enthusiasm into her manner as she talked of the mountains and lakes she'd never seen. But Hugo wouldn't be surprised if she sounded flat, he'd think it was because Eunice had needled her about the emeralds.

Tea was barely finished when Eunice invited Dorothy indoors to see a sable cape she meant to give her. Hannah wasn't asked to accompany them. She continued to sip her tea. Hugo got up to refill their cups.

'You mustn't mind what Eunice says,' he said gently.

'No. No, I don't.' She didn't know what made her add: 'It isn't that.'

She froze in panic, knowing she'd invited a question she mustn't answer.

'I know,' he murmured.

That made it worse. Her heart was pounding like an engine in her chest.

'I do understand and sympathise. I can see you're on edge, Hannah.'

She raised her eyes to his face in disbelief, feeling drained. What was he getting at?

'Eunice and I have been through it too. You'd like a family, wouldn't you? And it doesn't come.'

'Yes.' She could breathe again. It wasn't what she'd expected. 'Oh, yes.'

'Eunice would say such things are not to be spoken of, but

78

within the family, like this, it might be of some comfort to you. Few know there are downsides to marrying into the Mortimer family.'

He got up and cut himself another slice of cake. Offered one to her. She shook her head.

She moistened her lips. 'You did have Matt.'

'We both wanted more children.'

'Eunice?'

'Hope faded and she was bitterly disappointed. She went through hell because she couldn't. I sense you feel the same.'

'Yes, I think of little else,' she admitted.

'Perhaps, Hannah, you feel it more because you've been denied even one child. Perhaps Matt feels it less because he already has two.'

'Yes,' she said. 'But why us?'

Hugo shook his head. 'We asked ourselves that. It seems a normal desire: to have a child, to be a parent. But when it can't be fulfilled, it brings the most desperate anguish.'

'I found it hard to believe I wouldn't . . .' Hannah swallowed. She couldn't tell Hugo she'd found it hard because she'd already had a child and proved she could.

'But now?' he asked.

'It's a goal I can't achieve. I tell myself it's just a basic biological drive. But, yes, it fills me with anger and frustration that I can't have what I want.'

'Eunice found it unendurable.'

'But we have to endure. Matt is against adoption.'

'Eunice never wanted to adopt, but she took over Greg and Dorothy. They were an outlet for her maternal instinct. I'm afraid that upset you too.'

'I couldn't get close to them.'

'But isn't that why? Eunice was already acting as their mother.'

'Perhaps.'

'You do understand, the problem most probably lies with Matt?'

'He doesn't think so.'

'I have a problem with fertility, I was told it was hereditary. It isn't easy for a man to accept. I found it hard. Makes me feel less of a man. Brings feelings of inadequacy.'

'Hugo, I can't believe you ever had feelings of inadequacy.' She didn't quite hide her smile.

'We all have feelings like that. The difference is, I put them firmly behind me.'

'Thank you for telling me,' she said. His hand rested on her shoulder, imparting warmth. She felt close to him.

Hannah looked round her home and rejoiced that she was back where she had electricity and a decent hot water system. She wrote a letter of thanks to her friend Clarissa, asking how Maisie was managing and whether the infant thrived. She was missing Clary's company. She felt unsettled and weighed down with guilt.

It didn't help to see Dorothy throw herself into a round of shopping and social engagements. She was exuberantly high-spirited, and her chocolate box beauty blossomed.

'Grandma wants to bring me out next summer,' she said. 'But Franklin doesn't want to delay our wedding. He says he's waited long enough.'

'Give yourself time,' Hannah advised. 'You'll feel better if . . .'

'I'm over all that,' she said scornfully.

Hannah found it frightening to see Dorothy reacting in exactly the same way she had before. Now the birth of her baby was behind her, Dorothy was prepared to pretend for the rest of her life that it hadn't happened. Hadn't Hannah tried that too?

She shuddered again. For her it hadn't been possible. Her thoughts went often to the child she'd had. She felt a throbbing need to know how she was growing up. She expected Dorothy to feel the same and wanted to stop her making the same mistake.

'You're still too close to it. It must be a raw wound and there's no hurry.'

Hannah was afraid Matt was pushing Dorothy into this marriage. He wanted it because it would end his responsibility for her. 'Don't be pushed . . .'

'I won't be pushed ever again. All that's over and done with. Like you, I've put it behind me. It's what you did, after all – marry someone else on the rebound.'

That made Hannah anxious. She didn't want anyone else to overhear such remarks.

'I was in love with your father,' she managed, and then worried that she'd used the past tense.

Dorothy kept referring to what she'd told her in confidence and it made Hannah shiver. She was afraid her step-daughter would do it in Matt's hearing, and he'd ask what she meant.

At supper last night, she'd taken Dorothy to task for saying she'd be home for lunch then not returning.

'If you telephone when you change your mind, it would save Cook a lot of trouble.'

'Sorry,' Dorothy said lightly. 'I have my faults, I know, but then we both have. You and I make the same mistakes, Hannah, you should understand.'

She'd felt the heat rush to her cheeks. The girl was openly goading her. She was thankful to find Matt engrossed in some discussion with Greg, but was afraid she'd have to tell him before Dorothy did. It was the only way she could put an end to it.

She received a reply from Clarissa:

Dear Hannah,

I do wish you'd been here to share things as they happened, but I've good news and bad.

First the good news. I'm totally thrilled to tell you I've managed to rent the dower house again. Such luck! It seems Dr Moore has elderly and ailing parents living down in Kent and wants them closer. He's moving them in this week. Leo was keen that we should live there and, of course, this has stopped him dead in his

81

tracks. He was afraid we wouldn't manage without the rent.

Maisie reports that the infant Elizabeth is putting on weight and is always hungry. She sleeps well between feeds and is giving no trouble.

Now comes the bad part. I was right about Maisie's children having scarlet fever. Dr Moore sent the two older ones to the fever hospital to reduce the chance of spreading it to the others. Tragically, the eldest, Charlie, died last week. We were all terribly upset. Now Maisie's youngest child Joey has gone down with it. He's only five months old, but he's big and strong for his age, while Charlie was small and always puny. We all have high hopes he'll pull through. Maisie is bereft, poor soul.

I'm afraid the Parry children, our cowman's family, have caught it too. Dr Moore has forbidden me to go near any of them, in case I bring it back to Lucy and the boys.

I do miss not having you here for long gossipy sessions.

Your friend,
Clarissa

Hannah sat back appalled. She should never have left Elizabeth in that terrible place. What attention would she be getting from Maisie now? She'd barely coped when things were normal. She felt tears prickling in her eyes and told herself she must talk to Matt.

After a time, she got up and went to the bathroom to slap cold water against her face. In the mirror her face looked pale. She had such large strong features, so why wasn't she strong enough to cope with Matt? She was always finding out too late she'd done the wrong thing.

'I don't understand you, Hannah, you did so much to help Dorothy,' he'd said that evening when they were going to bed. 'But now we've got her through with reputation intact,

82

you're endangering everything by being miserable and depressed.'

'It's the baby.'

'I know that, but you must see it would be quite impossible to bring it here.'

'It haunts me, Matt.'

'It's all over. Put it behind you. Why should it bother you more than it does Dorothy?'

Hannah shuddered, knowing the answer to that.

Matt was never generous with his sympathy. He was rather an aloof, self-sufficient man, wrapped up in his own needs, and his pressing concern now was to put his family affairs back into the peaceful rut they'd been in before Dorothy's troubles. Hannah knew she had his ear, he wanted to soothe her back to normality.

Now was the moment to tell him. She had to do it because Dorothy meant to let it slip out before much longer. Hannah wanted to hear Matt say he understood, and surely he must after this?

She forced herself to go on: 'Is she going to tell Franklin Flower?'

'Of course not!'

'Do you think that's wise?'

'Fortunately for Dorothy, I think he's fairly innocent about women. I've heard it said Franklin's more interested in making money than making love. He's put off marriage 'til he's thirty-six, and Mother's failed to discover any previous women in his life. I hope he'll never know.'

'I meant,' Hannah said, determined to keep to the point, 'that it changes a girl's thinking. She may not be able to forget the baby.'

'Dorothy showed no interest in her babies. She wanted no funeral for the dead one, and since it was stillborn we managed to get away without.'

'But in time . . .'

'If she changes her mind and decides she wants a family, then she can once she's married.'

'That's what I thought when you married me,' she dared.

Matt sighed noisily. 'I only wish we could, Hannah. I know you're disappointed.'

'But keeping Franklin in ignorance?' She'd really pondered on that.

'What he doesn't know, he won't worry about.'

'I thought that once,' she dared again. 'But later she might feel a need to talk about it. She might want to get it off her mind.'

'Hannah, the baby was never on Dorothy's mind. Why delve so deeply into the psychology of it? If Dorothy wants to tell him at some time in the future, she can. Far better to do it when the marriage is *fait accompli* and they've both settled down.'

'Wouldn't it destroy his trust?' She knew she sounded agonised. She was rigid with tension.

'How would I know? You're taking it all too hard.'

Hannah closed her eyes, she had to force herself to go on. 'No, I'm not, Matt. You see, it happened to me.'

The silence seemed to throb in her ears. As it lengthened she had to look. He understood now.

She knew she'd never forget Matt's face at that moment: his mouth gaped, shock glazed his eyes. He'd frozen with his pyjama jacket half on.

'You mean you . . .?' He was choking.

Suddenly she turned away, horrified at what she'd done. She'd wanted it off her chest. Now she was frightened.

'Yes, I had a baby.'

Matt's grasp was rough on her arm, swinging her back to face him. She dared to meet his gaze.

'I was seventeen, like Dorothy.'

'But why didn't you tell me?' It was his turn to agonise.

She found it an effort to stay calm. 'For the same reasons Dorothy won't tell Franklin Flower. You said it was best.'

'Not for us.' His face flushed with anger. 'The man . . . Who was he?'

'You said before, it was better not to know.'

84

Hannah knew she was breaking down. She could feel tears prickling in her eyes. She'd imagined herself telling Matt a hundred times, and none of them had been like this. She'd expected him to put his arms round her, to be loving and forgiving.

'I've got to know now,' he said bitterly. 'You can't just leave me hanging in space, wondering about it, imagining the worst.'

Hannah swallowed. 'For me, nothing could have been worse. The nuns took me in six weeks before my baby was due and kept me for six weeks afterwards. There were seven other girls in the same situation. They let us all know we were fallen women.'

'Who was the father? I've a right to know.'

Hannah's mouth was dry, her voice not much more than a whisper. 'He was older than me, worked in the same firm.'

'You weren't his secretary?' He sounded aghast.

'No, he was a salesman.'

'Good God, Hannah! This is a bit hard to take. You're my wife! What did he sell?'

'Office stationery.' She was petrified. This was going all wrong.

'Go on,' he ordered.

'I suppose you'd call him the office Romeo. He was playing the field but I didn't realise that at the time. I was over-innocent at seventeen. I loved him, I thought he loved me. Once he found out about the baby he didn't want to know. Dropped me like a stone.'

'A tawdry tale, isn't it?' The sneer in his voice stabbed hurtfully.

'Yes. At least Dorothy can tell herself things might have been different if Lancelyn Tolman had lived.'

'To hell with Lancelyn Tolman! I don't know how you could keep quiet all these years.'

'I wanted to tell you, was on the point of doing it many times. I didn't dare, 'til you encouraged Dorothy to do the same. That made me think you'd understand.'

'I understand all right. I just can't stomach it.' Matt was bristling, pushing up his monk's rim of fine brown hair.

'You said for Dorothy it was the best thing . . .'

'Best for Dorothy and best for you! Not best for me.' He was seething with half-suppressed rage. 'I mean, how can I trust you after this?'

'It was years ago, Matt. Before I knew you.'

'You recovered well. What raised your expectations? You married up.'

'You sound like your mother.'

He sighed noisily. 'I expect you still think of him, compare me with him?' Hannah turned away sickened, there was to be no sympathy from Matt after all.

'I often think of my baby. I signed her away. She went for adoption. She'll be nearly thirteen now. I do hope she never finds herself in the same awful situation.'

'So that's what drove you to tell me?' He was spoiling for a fight. Hannah pressed her fingers to her lips. She mustn't say any more, she was making matters worse.

'I knew the baby was playing on your mind. Now I know why your conscience is heavy. This alters everything. You disgust me, Hannah.'

She heard him run downstairs. The front door slammed, reverberating through the house. Tears were welling up, stinging her eyes. Telling Matt had driven a further wedge between them and deepened her misery. It was yet another mistake.

Chapter Six

Hannah found it hard to settle back into her old life at Oakridge. Too much had happened. Things seemed to have changed for ever.

'I'm going to marry Franklin,' Dorothy announced a day or so later at dinner. 'The date's set for May Day. Grandma says she can present me at Court after I'm married.'

Matt indulged her with a big cheque to buy a trousseau of beautiful clothes.

Eunice spoke of arranging a sumptuous wedding for her grand-daughter and launched into a round of entertaining. Hannah found, as the bride's step-mother, she was included in much of it. She saw more of Hugo; sometimes they spent most of the occasion talking together.

'For her, everything's possible again,' Hannah said to Matt when dinner was over and the children gone.

'Don't sound so depressed,' he said. 'What's the matter with you now?'

Hannah knew it would do no good to mention her need for a child once again. She didn't have to.

Matt's grey eyes flashed at her aggressively. 'You only feel like this because of the baby you had. It's playing on your mind.' He turned impatiently back to his book.

'It makes me feel thwarted and useless because I haven't a child to care for.'

'You could try caring more about me,' he said sharply.

'I do care, Matt.' She met his gaze steadily. She wasn't functioning properly as a wife and they both knew it. 'If not a child, perhaps a job? Could I help in the factory?'

'What's the point of that, Hannah? You couldn't do anything but office work.' His voice was full of impatience.

'I could learn, like Greg.' She hoped they weren't going to end up like his parents, in a state of permanent domestic combat.

'No, your job is to run this house. Look, I'm just as frustrated as you are. Do you think I like slaving in that factory week in and week out? You wouldn't like it.'

Hannah had heard all Matt's dissatisfactions many times over. He felt archaeologists were now uncovering the secrets of ancient civilisations at a breathtaking pace. He longed to be there with them on the digs, sharing the fascination.

'Perhaps I'll take a holiday, go to Ur of the Chaldees. Perhaps I'll write to Leonard Woolley and ask if I can give a hand for a week or so. Do Greg good to manage the factory for a while.'

'He's keen.' Hannah sighed. 'He needs to show his grandfather how well he can cope.'

'Perhaps after the wedding,' said Matt, because Dorothy's wedding preparations were building up. 'The Lady Mother's making a tremendous fuss about it.'

Hannah smiled. She had married Matt in the register office in Birkenhead. Matt had told her his mother had arranged his first wedding. It had been a tremendous ordeal and he didn't propose to go through anything like that again.

He hadn't told his parents they'd set the day until a week beforehand. They'd been invited because he didn't want to offend them, but Eunice let it be known she hardly classed it as a wedding.

Dorothy's wedding was to be very different. The national newspapers billed it as the country wedding of the year. Grand-daughter of Sir Hugo Mortimer marries. There were photographs and articles in the society magazines.

Hannah now knew what she herself had missed. It was a very extravagant affair with six bridesmaids in pink and two pages in white satin. The guest list was enormous. The church was filled with flowers and a full choir sang. Dorothy looked absolutely charming in a dress of ivory silk.

Hugo had bought a new car, an Isotta-Fraschini sporting tourer, because Eunice said the bride must have something more elegant than his Buick to take her to church. Eunice liked it because of the glamour surrounding other owners.

'Such a lot of important people own one,' she told Hannah. 'Rudolph Valentino and Jack Dempsey, the Aga Khan and the Pope. Even royalty. Foreign royalty, of course.'

The reception was held at Ince Hall, and as it was a sunny afternoon the guests spilled out on to the lawn. The wedding cake had five tiers.

Hugo was at her side for a lot of the day, introducing her to guests she didn't know. Hannah had deliberately chosen a green dress to show off his emeralds again. He'd noticed them, she knew, though he didn't mention them.

When Dorothy and Franklin had driven off for their honeymoon and the guests were beginning to leave, Hugo led her off to see his garden in which he took a great interest. He managed it as he did his businesses; by deciding what he wanted grown and exactly where it was to be planted, and then delegating all the work to others.

He was interested in fruit growing, and at the right season Hannah had admired the great bowls of strawberries and raspberries, peaches and nectarines. He was keen on roses too, and the first buds were just coming on his bushes. 'Everything is early in my garden,' he told her. 'It's very sheltered amongst all these trees.'

They were returning to the house the back way, passing what had once been the stables.

'I've given up on horses, never did take to them. Cars are the thing now.' They paused in the open doorway. In the dim light of the old building Hannah could see four cars lined up inside. All were highly waxed. She recognised Eunice's Lagonda, and the Buick he usually drove.

'Your new car made a big impression.' She admired its elegant lines, open-topped with an extra windscreen to protect passengers in the rear seat. Already the running boards had

89

been swept free of confetti and the body work repolished.

'Six-litre engine,' he said.

'Total luxury, absolutely fabulous.'

'Eunice is planning to take it over.'

'I wish I could drive.'

'Would you like to learn? My chauffeur could teach you.'

Hannah felt overcome. 'I'd love to,' she said. 'I didn't mean . . .'

'You'd be able to get about more. It's a good idea.'

'Would I be able to? Is it difficult?'

'Nothing to it. You could learn on the Buick.'

'What if I prang it?' Hannah followed him over to the vehicle

'I don't suppose you will.' Hugo was smiling. 'Anyway, as long as you don't damage yourself, I won't mind.' He opened the driver's door for her to see the instruments. Hannah was about to climb in when she was aware of wild movements on the back seat.

It took her a moment to realise Greg was there with his arms round a girl whose legs were the most visible part of her. They'd shrunk down almost to the floor to avoid being seen.

Hugo stepped backwards in alarm but recovered quickly. 'Get out, Greg,' he said calmly.

'Just admiring your car, Grandpa.' His face was scarlet as he got out, pulling the girl by the hand. She'd dragged her hat off the seat behind her and was covering her face with it. With an embarrassed giggle, she pulled down the skirt of her crumpled blue dress.

'Greg, it might be wise to fasten your flies before you meet someone else.'

Hannah gasped, but sure enough the buttons could be seen gaping on Greg's striped morning trousers. He was complying hurriedly.

'What would your grandmother say if she knew?' Hugo called after him. 'She'd be very shocked.'

As they disappeared out into the garden Hannah found Hugo grinning down at her.

'Hot-blooded,' she said. 'He's young.'

'I'm afraid he's a fool. Not so much because of this . . . but he's too intent on having a good time. He's never going to achieve anything. I had high hopes for Greg.' He sighed. 'But they won't come to anything.'

Hugo couldn't make up his mind. It was so unlike him to dither that it bothered him more. He sipped his sherry and let his eyes wander across the cards and holly on Hannah's drawing-room mantelpiece. It was the Sunday before Christmas and he and Eunice had been invited to supper.

It was a meal with a purpose rather than a social occasion. Greg had become engaged.

What was the girl's name? Hilary, yes, that was it. She'd been here drinking sherry a few minutes ago. Greg had taken her home, she lived just round the corner. Eunice didn't want her to hear what was said. It was a family matter and she wasn't family yet.

A nice enough girl, polite, no great beauty, but Hugo found youth itself attractive. Graceful legs and showing more of them than seemed decent in a skimpy blue skirt that made Eunice's eyebrows go up, and a powder blue cloche that covered all but a few tendrils of dark hair against her cheeks.

When Greg had first introduced the girl and spoken of marriage, Eunice had said: 'It's all very well for a girl to marry young, but a man needs more maturity.'

Not sure what to make of that, Hugo had said: 'You married me when I was twenty. Greg's the same age.'

'A man needs to find his feet first,' she corrected. 'Marriage can't take place on a shoe-string.'

He might have known she'd meant money.

'It's time you did something for him, Hugo.'

He sighed, wanting to put off making decisions for Greg. He'd thought twenty-one quite early enough.

'Necessary to do it now, if he's to marry.'

And in spite of his misgivings tonight's dinner had been arranged.

Hugo's eyes seemed to find their way to Hannah even when he meant to keep them away. She was wearing a red dinner dress that fell loosely to her hips. Eunice didn't approve of the strange modern fashions.

'Matt's found a new lease of life since the news from Egypt broke last month,' Hannah told him. 'He scours the newspapers daily to see what else they've found.'

Hugo had never seen Matt in such a state of animation before. His eyes glistened, his usually sallow cheeks were flushed.

'Such a wonderfully exciting find for Howard Carter! To clear sixteen steps and see a sealed door with the name of Tutankhamen on it.'

His face was radiant. 'He's found unbelievable treasures.'

'Absolutely priceless treasures,' Eunice put in, patting the fluffy white curls on the top of her head. Even she had read of them.

'Gilt couches, their ends in the form of fabulous golden beasts, great gilt snakes, bouquets of gilt flowers, inlaid caskets, alabaster vases, some beautifully carved,' Matt listed. 'I'd love to see them all.'

'I wish Greg would come back,' Hannah worried, looking at her watch. 'Everything's cooked. I don't want it to spoil.'

'It won't hurt for a few minutes,' Eunice consoled easily, getting up on painful feet to help herself to more sherry.

Hugo knew she'd be the first to complain if she didn't have adequate help in the house. Now she made light of the fact that Matt's housekeeper had retired, and the woman hired to replace her had departed in high dudgeon after less than a month because Matt had upset her.

Hannah had said it wouldn't do her any harm to do more in the house herself, that she could manage well enough. She came now to refill his glass.

'Can you imagine what it means to find a tomb like that?' Matt's eyes still blazed at him. 'I would give my back teeth . . .'

The news was firing half England with enthusiasm for Egyptology. Hugo felt touched by it himself.

Matt was passionate. 'I'd give anything to have been in the Valley of the Kings last month.'

He might have been there, thought Hugo, if I'd not given him a business to run. Or he'd be with Woolley and Mallowan in Mesopotamia, or Evans in Knossos. Of course, he'd still have wanted to be with Carter since his find had eclipsed all others, but he'd have been happier in any sweltering dusty country on a dig.

'I'd give anything to go there now.'

The glance Matt cast in his direction made Hugo more guilt-stricken. He sighed. His motives had been the best but with hindsight . . . His money had not enriched Matt's life. Quite the opposite.

Hannah murmured: 'They say excavation and cataloguing will take Carter ten years.'

Hugo studied her large features and high cheek bones and asked himself if she was trying to tell him he must let Matt go?

'It's taken Leonard Woolley ten years in Ur of the Chaldees,' Matt said. 'I'm thinking of writing to Howard Carter to see if I might visit the tomb.'

'I hear he's inundated with important people all wanting to do that,' Hugo said sourly. 'Photographers and writers . . .'

'But I'm an archaeologist, Father, I'll be useful.'

They all heard the front door slam. 'Greg's here at last.' Hannah got up with a jerk. 'I'll see about dishing up.'

Greg came in. He reminded Hugo of Eunice's father. He was better-looking than Matt had ever been, or he himself for that matter, and didn't appear to lack maturity.

Hugo cleared his throat, wanting to get it all sorted out, but Hannah was calling them to the table. The dining-room was reached through double mahogany doors that matched those leading from the drawing-room. The silver and crystal sparkled in the candlelight, there were white flowers on the starched white cloth. Hannah's one remaining maid waited to serve the meal.

'Such good news about Dorothy.' Eunice tucked into the

salmon. 'It'll be lovely to have a new baby in the family.'

It was Hannah's turn to flush. Hugo could see envy there, and anxiety too.

'Dorothy's very lucky,' she said, and Matt nodded agreement.

Hugo had to stifle a chuckle. Howard Carter had up-staged Dorothy's announcement so far as her father was concerned.

'About Greg,' Eunice reminded him. Her eyes were steely with determination. He could see her pink scalp shining through her thin hair. 'We've come here to settle what you'll do to help. Aren't you going to get on with it?'

Hannah's eyes were twinkling with sympathy. He said: 'So, Greg, you want to follow your sister's example, get married and have a family?'

'Get married anyway,' he mumbled.

'Traditionally the time when the family gives a helping hand. And you'll be twenty next month?'

'You're luckier than I was there, Greg,' his father put in. 'I had to wait until I was twenty-five.'

Hugo took heart; delaying the gift had not helped Matt.

'You were a full-time student still at university at Greg's age,' he pointed out. 'It wouldn't have been appropriate.'

It was no good expecting him to make God-like decisions for the family when he knew now he'd made the wrong one for Matt. 'What do you want me to do for you?'

Greg was chewing as though roast lamb was the most important thing in his life. Hugo knew he'd embarrassed him, but what was momentary embarrassment compared with the freedom to choose his own way of life?

'It's very kind of you to help me, Grandpa. Getting married is very expensive.'

'I've had something in mind for you for several years,' he said. 'A company making margarine.' He saw Greg's face stiffen. 'But it doesn't have to be that,' he added hastily.

'Father, I think you ought to know,' Matt was pale now

94

and rather subdued, 'I want to get away from Evans's for a while. I've been showing Greg how to run things. I want him to take over from me.'

Hugo let the breath out of his lungs slowly and gave thanks that Matt had finally made up his mind. It had taken him far too long.

'You'll be off to Egypt, I take it?'

'If Howard Carter will have me.'

Hugo began to relax. 'What are your plans, Greg? You have no ambitions to dig up some desert looking for pots?'

He laughed. 'You know I haven't, Grandpa. My ambition is to do exactly what you've done.'

'And he's going to start by running Evans's for me,' Matt confirmed.

Hugo laid down his knife and fork. Greg wasn't going to do exactly what he'd done. He'd started to make real money by the time he was Greg's age.

'You're sure that's what you want, Greg?'

'Yes, I'm sure I could do it.'

Hugo forked meat into his mouth. 'What about this margarine factory? I've had it for years. I bring in the oil from West Africa. It's a growing business, will grow bigger. People have to eat and it's cheaper than butter.'

Greg was hesitant. 'I feel I should give all my attention to Evans's while Dad's away.'

'It might be too much for him,' Matt agreed. 'Trying to run two businesses at once.'

'Two, too much?' Hugo's voice resounded round the room. He couldn't believe it! Even now Matt didn't realise the scale on which he operated.

'I've run over twenty at one time. It isn't difficult. The margarine factory virtually runs itself, but if you don't want it, Greg, I know I can sell it. In fact, I was approached not so long ago.

'What you don't realise, Matt, or you, Greg, is that I don't get myself bogged down with the day to day running of any business. You can hire a good manager to do that for you.

95

What I do is control overall strategy. Make sure they all function efficiently and at the height of profitability.'

'Do you think I should put in a manager then?' Matt was unusually hesitant.

'You've just told me you have. Greg's going to manage it, isn't he? You could have promoted somebody else years ago, if you'd wanted more time away. I want you to do things in your own way.'

He hadn't seen Evans's accounts since he'd handed them back at the end of the war. His opinion had not been asked on any point since. He was fairly certain the company was less profitable now.

All Matt's energy went on prehistoric antiquities, and Greg didn't seem to have energy for anything.

'So what you really want, Greg, is money to buy a house and help support a wife?'

'Yes please, Grandpa.' He sounded grateful at last.

Hugo had already worked out the value of the margarine works. Now he mentioned a sum, roughly half, which he was prepared to make over to Greg.

The lad's beautiful blue eyes practically came out on stalks. His gratitude doubled.

'Now you can name the day,' Hugo said dryly. He was afraid there was more Schofield in Greg than Mortimer. He didn't even realise what he'd turned down.

Hugo told himself it was ridiculous to feel let down. It was his own fault and his alone. He should have chosen more wisely when he'd chosen his wife. He'd never stopped to think then that the Schofield traits could have a stronger hold in their family than those he'd contributed.

The clock in the hall struck three. Hannah Mortimer tossed in bed for the tenth time, waiting hopelessly for sleep to come again. As usual, Matt was snoring. He always slept like a log. In the silvery half light she could see the pile of new summer shirts he'd left balanced on his tallboy.

He'd bought them for his forthcoming trip to Egypt. He'd

written to Howard Carter and was going to see Tutankhamen's tomb for himself.

Matt had taken her to Mesopotamia once and she'd enjoyed it. His knowledge and enthusiasm had spilled over to fire her own. But this time he hadn't asked her to go with him and seemed to assume she wouldn't want to. Yet she felt a greater interest in the antiquities being discovered in Egypt because there had been so much about them in the press. It drove home to her just how wide the rift between them had become.

Matt seemed to be withdrawing even further from her. She no longer knew what he was thinking or feeling. More and more they were going their separate ways. His interest in archaeology was the only thing that brought him to life.

She knew now she should never have told him about her baby. Things had not been the same between them since, and any mention of Elizabeth shortened his temper too.

'She's thriving,' Hannah had told him. 'Clarissa says she's got a good appetite and is eating solid foods now.'

'That's normal, isn't it? I'd rather not know.'

'I like to have news of her.'

'It's unhealthy, Hannah, following every step of her progress. You'd do better to forget her.'

She knew it was a terrible mistake to say: 'Clarissa says she's a beautiful baby. A swan amongst ducklings in Maisie's brood. If I were to see her now . . .'

Matt had turned on her in anger.

'You can't go anywhere near Yarrow again.'

'I can't leave all the responsibility . . .'

'You'll only cause trouble for Dorothy. Clarissa will cope. Come on now, see sense. Say you'll stay out of the way?'

Grudgingly she had. To refuse would only have alienated Matt further.

'The less you have to do with your friend the better, after this.'

Hannah sighed and pummelled her pillow. Dorothy's downfall was still crushing her, although everybody else seemed to have put it behind them. What it had given her was

97

this terrible longing for Elizabeth, the baby she couldn't have.

The whole year had been an emotional purge that left less in her life, and she saw all too clearly that future years would be exactly the same unless she did something about it. She must try to get closer to Matt. Surely he'd welcome it? He must have this empty feeling too.

The next thing she knew, Polly the maid was opening the curtains. Hannah struggled to open her eyes in the grey morning light. She knew she'd made up her mind to do something, but for the moment it was gone like a forgotten dream.

Matt was already out of bed and pouring himself a cup of morning tea on the tray put down by her bed. She felt sleep-sodden and had to force herself to sit up.

'Matt, can I come to Egypt with you?'

As he turned from the window, she saw a flicker of surprise on his face, then something else. Yes, it could only be reluctance.

'Are you sure you want to? I expect to spend a lot of time working in the tomb.'

She made herself say: 'I did enjoy it last time.'

'That was different, Hannah. We visited the big museums and travelled a little, saw several different sites. This time I'll be staying in the Valley of the Kings. You'd soon get bored.'

'I don't think so. There'll be other wives there, surely?'

'I don't know. I'm expecting to stay a long time. A year perhaps. I want to get involved. Do real archaeological work.'

Hannah felt she wasn't making much progress. 'Couldn't I help? There must be something useful I could do?'

'I think it would be better if you stayed here. I won't have time to entertain you.' He went to the bathroom and banged the door. She heard his bath running.

Entertain her indeed! She poured herself a cup of tea, knowing Matt wasn't prepared to give an inch. She felt rejected; she was being pushed to the sidelines and there seemed no way back.

She went downstairs for breakfast some five minutes after

Matt. Before she opened the dining-room door she could hear his voice raised in argument. It made her feel worse. Greg faced her across the table with mutinously flushed cheeks.

'Good morning, Greg. What's the matter?'

Matt looked thoroughly exasperated. 'He wants to go to Deauville now, that's what's the matter.'

He swung on Greg again. 'You agreed. You said you'd run the factory so I could go to Egypt. Haven't I been handing everything over to you? I've been planning it for weeks and you know it.'

'I'll do what you want, Dad.' There was a whining note in Greg's voice. 'I just want to get away for a few days.'

'A few days! Why go all that distance then? I was hoping to go next week.'

'You haven't got your tickets yet?'

'It's just as well I haven't, isn't it?'

Polly was bringing in scrambled eggs and hot toast for them. Nobody spoke until she'd placed a plate before each of them and gone.

'Why do you have to go now?' Matt spluttered. 'I can't believe it. Why now, for God's sake?'

'Hilary and I broke it off last night. I'm a bit churned up.'

Hannah's fork fell back on to her plate with a clatter. 'Greg, I am sorry . . .'

'I need a bit of a break, Dad, that's all.'

'What happened?' Hannah asked.

Greg turned on her balefully. He was powerfully good-looking, and now his grandfather had settled a large sum of money on him, it seemed no bride could ask for more. He must be the ultimate catch.

'Hilary seemed a nice girl.'

'We changed our minds. All right?' His tone was aggressive.

She assumed Greg was more polite to his girl friends than he was to her. 'Does that mean you'll be staying on here?'

'Of course it does. I've just said, haven't I, it's all off.'

'I understand you're upset, Greg,' she said stiffly. 'I'm just asking whether you intend to go ahead and buy the house?'

'No. What's the point?'

'I'm sure you're right. You'll be more comfortable here with us.'

His blue Schofield eyes continued to glower at her. He might appear to have every blessing the world could give but he certainly wasn't happy. He turned to his father.

'Of course I'll manage the factory for you. I've said I would, haven't I? But you've never mentioned any dates. I assumed there was plenty of time for me to have a few days off first.'

Hannah stifled a sigh. It seemed neither of them was particularly interested in the business. She hoped it would continue to provide for their needs.

Book Two

1924-1934

Chapter Seven

22 September 1924

Clarissa Bender looked round her drawing-room with satisfaction at what she'd achieved. She'd scoured sale rooms and second-hand shops until she'd found just the right furniture to suit it. The Turkish carpet square had been on the floor when they moved in, but she'd had it beaten and scrubbed regularly, until the colours had come up bright and clear.

She paused at the window looking out across what had once been the park. It was a blowy day of fitful sunshine and scudding clouds. Brown leaves were swirling everywhere. This year they were falling early; already some of the great oaks had bare branches.

The signs of autumn saddened her because the room could not be used much over the winter months. The charming Adam-style grate did not throw out enough warmth. Even now she could detect a faint smell of damp underlying that of wood smoke.

She pulled up a chair to the escritoire and took out a sheet of notepaper. In large script she wrote: '22 September 1924'. She stopped, pen poised. It rankled that the bonds of friendship she'd felt for Hannah Mortimer had slackened.

She'd found it hurtful not to be invited to Dorothy's wedding. To know nothing about it until the pictures appeared in the newspapers under the heading of 'Wedding of the Year'. Leo said it was understandable that Dorothy would not want to see her on her wedding day. Not when she was the one person who knew her shameful secret.

Dorothy had two daughters now. Children the Mortimers could be proud of. Not surprising that even Hannah should no longer hanker after Elizabeth.

'Dear Hannah,' she wrote. 'Thank you for your letter enclosing the cheque. I continue to dole out your money for Elizabeth's keep every month. Maisie would never be able to manage one lump sum.'

She put down the pen and sighed. Everything had changed since that arrangement had been agreed. Only four short years and yet . . .

It wounded her feelings more that Hannah had not invited her to stay ever again, and though she had asked her and Matt for a weekend, Hannah had written back to say Matt had problems at work and couldn't get away just then. They used to come once or twice a year and Matt had said he enjoyed fishing in their river.

She plucked Hannah's letter out of its envelope to re-read. 'Do let me know how Elizabeth is getting on,' she'd written. It seemed she only pretended an interest.

'Your friend Hannah takes advantage of you,' Leo had said.

'She's not like that,' Clarissa had protested then. Perhaps circumstances had made her so? But if Hannah felt no guilt at Lizzie's situation, Clarissa certainly did.

She had never rated Maisie O'Malley highly as a foster parent. She'd known from the beginning Maisie wanted the money more than she wanted the child. The postmistress would have been a worse choice. Last year, she'd done a midnight flit with post office money. Whether or not she would have taken the child with her, had she been looking after her, was academic.

The trouble was, Maisie had just had another son. She'd barely muddled through with Peggy and Joey. Now with baby Patrick to care for as well, she'd have no energy left to attend to a foster child.

Clarissa despaired of the O'Malleys. Maisie and Seamus were turning out to be feckless parents. Even worse, the gatehouse was dirty and overcrowded and Clarissa suspected Maisie favoured her own at Lizzie's expense. Nobody called her Elizabeth here. She was known as Lizzie O'Malley.

All the O'Malley children were ill cared for and half wild, Lizzie was no exception, but Clarissa couldn't write that. If Hannah still thought about the child, there was no point in giving her good reason to be anxious.

She wrote: 'I'm pleased to report Elizabeth is in good health and is a lively child, bursting with energy and curiosity about everything.'

Clarissa strongly believed her own children needed others of the same age to play with, and living in the country there was not a lot of choice. She hadn't discouraged her boys from playing with the children of the farm workers, and welcomed them if they brought them into the house.

But Lizzie was the only one who knocked on the kitchen door and asked straight out if she might come in to play. Clarissa found it strange that she seemed to have more in common with Nick than she did with Lucy. She invented games that they played together, though Lizzie also loved every toy they had.

She would have encouraged Lizzie to come more often if she hadn't been so attached to the whey-faced Joey O'Malley, and had him so often in tow. He was an impudent little imp and none of them found him attractive.

Clarissa took up her pen again. 'Elizabeth is growing prettier with feathery white hair, big mischievous blue eyes and a lovely wide smile.'

She paused. Lizzie was pretty when she was clean. It was easy enough to wipe unsavoury smears of food and mud from her face, but usually her hair and clothes were in need of a wash too.

Tatty, Clarissa's cook-general, was very taken with her. Clarissa had heard her say countless times: 'Lizzie's favourite,' as she put slices of cake and syrup tart on one side for her. Many times she'd seen her seated at the kitchen table tucking in to hot meals.

'Such a thin little scrap. I don't think she gets enough to eat from Maisie.'

'Lizzie knows what to do about it,' Clarissa had said dryly. From time to time she was guilty of giving her biscuits and chocolate herself. She had dread misgivings about Lizzie all the same.

Leo had seen her taking eggs from the hen houses with Joey O'Malley running behind with a dish to put them in.

'Mam sent us,' Joey had announced brazenly. 'She told us to bring eight. Three for Dad and one each for the rest of us.'

Although he was five months Lizzie's senior he was even smaller and thinner, with legs like spindles. He'd been a weakling since he'd had the bout of scarlet fever shortly after Lizzie was born.

'Uncle Seamus needs three because he's big and he has to work very hard for you,' Lizzie said with round innocent eyes.

Leo had been about to claim his eggs back.

'Mam said you wouldn't stop Lizzie taking them.' Joey had been indignant. 'She says you won't mind her having them.' So Leo had allowed them to keep the eggs.

Clarissa was concerned that Lizzie was being primed by Maisie to steal. She'd seen her take peaches from the green house and heard accounts of marrows disappearing from the garden. One day she'd taken the child aside and explained about ownership, saying Lizzie must ask permission before she took anything that didn't belong to her.

The little minx had asked there and then for another eight eggs, saying Maisie had nothing for their dinner that day. There was no guile about the child, she was just an innocent four year old. Clarissa knew she should never have agreed, she'd taught Lizzie nothing.

Maisie and her family were a bad influence on the child, but it wasn't easy to write about these things to Hannah.

Clarissa sighed again. Because there was nowhere else Lizzie could go, she'd even toyed with the idea of bringing her into her own home. Leo had been against it. He said she had already infiltrated the kitchen and the playroom and he didn't want to see more of her, and anyway, she was settled with Maisie and it would be cruel to pluck her away from poor Joey.

'I do miss the long gossipy sessions we used to have,' wrote Clarissa. 'Couldn't you fit in a long weekend here sometime? I'd love to see you.'

It might make it easier if Hannah could see Lizzie for herself. She sealed the letter into an envelope and went briskly to the kitchen.

Mondays were always busy with washing and churning to be done, so Clarissa was in the habit of preparing lunch on Mondays. Tatty saw to peeling the vegetables, of course, and there was usually cold meat left over from the Sunday joint. What she liked doing was making a good substantial pudding to compensate. Leo had a hearty appetite.

The kitchens at Yarrow Hall Farm were immense. A warren of store rooms, sculleries, pantries and dairies, and one big room heated by an Aga where the cooking took place. Today the windows ran with moisture. The room opposite was fitted with a deep brown sink topped by a single cold tap and was used for laundry. Every Monday, a fire was lit under the big boiler in the corner to heat the water and boil the whites. The steam got everywhere.

As she rolled out the pastry, Clarissa was aware of Lizzie's alert blue eyes watching every move she made. Two grubby fists clutched the edge of the table, her chin just cleared it.

'Blackberry pie? That sounds lovely. I wish I could make things like that. Will I be able to when I'm bigger?'

'Yes, I'm sure you will.'

'Why are you stretching it out?'

'To cover this plate.'

'But you've done it once. Are you making two pies?'

'No, a base and a lid.'

'Tatty.' Lizzie turned as the woman bustled in from the laundry, her hands white and wrinkled from long immersion in water. 'Can you make blackberry pie?'

'Yes, of course,' Clarissa answered for her.

'I don't think Auntie Maisie can.' The child was frowning.

'She could if she wanted to,' Tatty sniffed on her way out again.

Clarissa expertly slashed the overhanging pastry from the plate. 'Come on, if you gather up these trimmings you can practise now.'

'Can I? I'd love to.'

'Better wash your hands first.' The rinse Lizzie gave them was perfunctory. 'Bring the footstool so you can reach.' Clarissa floured the marble slab in readiness.

Lizzie found the rolling pin unwieldy. 'Am I doing it right?'

'Don't thump it. More like this.'

'My pastry's got creases in it. Yours was smooth.'

'You must roll them out.'

Clarissa had to smile, the child was so full of enthusiasm it was impossible not to be drawn to her. She shot a disapproving glance at Joey O'Malley, asleep in the old basket chair by the Aga.

'Joey won't sleep tonight.'

'He didn't sleep last night,' Lizzie said. 'Uncle Seamus was after him with his belt.'

'Why?' Clarissa knew her voice was sharper. She'd heard rumours about Seamus belting his children with a heavy hand.

'Joey didn't bring in any sticks for morning.' Lizzie was concentrating on rolling out the pastry, the tip of her tongue gripped between milk teeth.

'Oh!' It seemed harsh punishment for such an offence from a four year old.

'It's our Joey's job, you see,' Lizzie said earnestly. 'To collect sticks to light fires. There's plenty in the park, Uncle Seamus said he was lazy. Joey's supposed to bring them in before they're needed, to make sure they're dry. But he didn't and the sticks ran out. Joey said Aunt Maisie used too many. He's got marks on his back from the belt.'

Clarissa asked faintly: 'Do you have a job?'

'We all have. Peggy washes and changes the baby. She's

going to feed it too, when it learns to eat food.'

Leo said Clarissa should not allow Lizzie free access to their kitchen. At first she'd come alone, waiting until Tatty welcomed her with meals and cups of broth, and only then introducing Joey to the same largesse. Clarissa found it hard to believe any child could be so devious as to think out a strategy like that. She had always begged for little titbits to take to Joey.

'Poor Joey is hungry,' she'd say to Tatty, and little offerings of cake and biscuits would be handed over to him too. Now Joey frequently drowsed in the basket chair while Lizzie followed Tatty from pantry to scullery and back, chattering all the time.

'What job has Maisie given you?'

'I collect the milk every morning.' There was a touch of pride in her voice.

Clarissa caught her breath. 'From our dairy?' She knew that up to now Leo had allowed his workers all the milk they wanted after the cream had been taken off for butter making. But now he was arranging to sell fresh milk instead and he was worried his farm workers would resent being cut down to a couple of pints daily. He said the O'Malleys got through a gallon most days.

'I take our biggest jug,' Lizzie said. 'Sometimes I go twice and we have milk puddings. And it's my job to fill up the sauce bottle for Peggy.'

'What sauce bottle?' She felt mystified.

'An Okay sauce bottle. Peggy takes milk to school in it.'

'Yes, of course,' Clarissa said absently.

Lizzie let the kitchen door slam behind her and Joey. Slowly they crossed the yard, each carrying a pastry man on an outstretched palm.

Now that Yarrow Hall had become a working farm, the centre of activity had moved from the front of the house to the back. What had once been rose garden and shrubberies had become the farm yard. Barns, cow sheds and stables had been put up; implement sheds and chicken houses had been added.

Lizzie nibbled. 'I made that 'specially for you. Mine's still warm.'

'Pastry looks a bit grey.' Joey picked off the currants that represented eyes. 'Tastes all right, though. Do you want all of yours?'

'Yes, you've got your share.'

'Mrs Bender lets you do anything you want,' he said enviously. 'Go upstairs to play with Lucy and Nick sometimes.'

'She showed me how to make pastry. She likes me a lot.'

'How do you know?'

'I feel it, she gives me a warm feeling.'

'She doesn't like me,' Joey said resentfully. 'I suppose you like her?'

'Yes, she's kind.'

'Do you like her better than me?'

'I like you best,' Lizzie said. 'You know that.'

'Yes,' he said gruffly. 'You and me are twins.'

'Not real twins.'

'Better than real twins.'

'Mrs Bender feels sorry for me. Tatty and Myfanwy are sorry for me too.'

'Everybody calls me Poor Joey, so it stands to reason they should be sorrier for me. But she doesn't let me do what I want, just you. You're different from the rest of us. She'll let you do anything.'

'Not absolutely everything.' Lizzie crammed pastry into her mouth. Washing was fluttering above them on two long lines.

'That's Lucy's best frock. The one with birds on it. I wish I could have a dress like that.'

'You could take it,' Joey said. 'Mrs Bender wouldn't stop you.'

'I think she would, but I'd love it.'

'Go on, take it. It's the only way. Shall I let the prop down?' He was already doing it. The line of washing descended, but

110

she still couldn't reach the frock.

Lizzie glanced guiltily back to the house, but the kitchen windows were running with moisture. Nobody would see her take it. Joey gripped her round the thighs and tried to hoist her the few inches she needed. She pulled on the bottom of the garment but could not reach up to the pegs, Joey just hadn't the strength to lift her high enough. She collapsed back on the ground and they both doubled up in a fit of the giggles.

'I know,' she said, 'something to stand on. Over there, look.' A pile of logs had been brought to the yard and were waiting to be split ready for the Aga. They chose a piece of tree trunk and together rolled it into position. Joey pulled on the hem, and now she could reach high enough. Seconds later the frock and two pegs were in her hand.

'What are you two up to?' a deep voice bellowed at them.

Joey was off like a rabbit. Lizzie turned to run but two strong arms enclosed her and jerked her up. She found Mr Bender's angry face only inches from her own. Shocked, she hid her face against his shoulder.

'What's this you've taken, you little imp?' She was wriggling, trying to get down on her feet; his arms were a vice-like grip. 'Who said you could take Lucy's dress? It is Lucy's, isn't it?'

Lizzie was filled with shame.

'Nobody gave you permission, did they? Come on, you can put it back. It's still wet.'

She was struggling hard, but couldn't escape his arms.

'Come on, peg it out properly.'

Lizzie opened her mouth and howled with fright. She could barely see the line for tears. Mr Bender had such authority she dared not refuse.

'Caught you out, didn't I?'

He was holding her up to do it. Reluctantly she did as he ordered.

'That's better, apart from the dreadful noise. Stop it this minute or I'll give you good reason to cry.'

111

Almost before Lizzie realised his intention he'd put one foot on the log they'd rolled under the line, and tossed her over his knee. She felt his hand deliver a powerful wallop to her bottom. She howled louder, struggled harder.

'Don't ever take anything unless you have permission. Not anything,' he was saying sternly. 'Do you hear?'

Lizzie was ready to promise anything to stop the heavy handed whacking she was getting. Suddenly something launched itself at Leo Bender. She felt him lurch under the impact and his grip on her relaxed.

'Come on,' Joey hissed urgently, and he was towing her out of the yard as fast as he could go. Her buttocks were stinging, they hurt more as she tried to run. She heard Mr Bender shout angrily: 'Clarissa, see what your little protégée is up to now?'

Joey let her pause to get her breath back when they reached the corner of an outhouse.

It added to the indignity to see Clarissa come to the kitchen door, concern on her face.

'What is it, Leo?'

'Someone has to teach her a lesson. She helps herself to everything we have. Nothing's safe.'

'Poor Lizzie.' Joey's arm went around her shoulders and pulled her close. She burst into noisy tears, but they were tears of relief and gratitude. Joey was the one person who understood how she felt.

'I dropped my pastry man,' she lamented. 'The hens are fighting over it. Just look!'

Hannah remembered studying the embossed invitation for 5 August 1927 before enclosing it in her letter to Matt. She'd wondered then whether he'd come because he'd already been home this year in June and it didn't give him much time to make arrangements. Greg had given them no inkling then.

The years seemed to be passing so quickly. She'd grown used to Matt's absence in Egypt. He'd said he much preferred working there to being at home and running Evans's.

Now Hannah shuffled on the hard pew, half mesmerised by the familiar words.

'Gregory, wilt thou have this woman to thy wedded wife, to live together . . .?'

Seated in the pew in front, Eunice's plump shoulders were ramrod stiff with disapproval. Not disapproval of Matt, though she thought he should have come, but disapproval of the bride.

'Throwing himself away!' She'd been outraged when first told of Greg's intention. 'It'll never last.'

Dulcie Wentworth was eight years older than Greg, the widow of a photographer with a five-year-old daughter. That was bad enough. What Eunice couldn't stomach was that Dulcie had been his housekeeper.

Hannah assumed Dulcie had found him easier to live with than she had. She'd had a row with Greg because he'd gone away without telling her when she'd had meals prepared for him. He'd come home three days later and said he'd been in Doncaster at a race meeting.

She'd already eaten her dinner that night, and he'd had the gall to complain because there was nothing prepared for him.

She'd said: 'I'm not going to be treated in this way, Greg. You'll have to show more consideration. Either you tell me in advance what your movements are going to be, or you'll have to leave Oakridge.'

He'd moved his things out the following week and she hadn't been invited to see his new quarters.

Dulcie's daughter Fay was fidgeting in the aisle, dressed in a blue bridesmaid's dress she seemed to find uncomfortable. Now she was scratching her arm. Dorothy's two little girls, similarly dressed, behaved with greater decorum.

Hannah studied the bride's back view: elegant cream oyster satin veiled in masses of fine net with a train that dragged the floor. An up to the minute wedding gown that looked scant and loose and straight from the front, and showed the bride's knees.

Greg's handsome shoulders towered over hers. They made

113

a lovely couple, and at least he'd managed to get Dulcie to the altar. Greg had been formally engaged three times before and each time the bride-to-be had changed her mind before the wedding.

The ceremony was coming to an end. While the bride and groom were signing the register in the vestry, Hannah noticed that the church had grown dark though it was midday. As the bride came down the aisle on her new husband's arm and Purcell's Trumpet Voluntary was being performed with great verve on the organ, lightning flashed and a tremendous rumble of thunder drowned it out.

The bride's little daughter disgraced herself, screaming and clinging on to her mother's dress. After the next clap of thunder, Eunice's voice carried clearly up the church, praising Franklin's daughters for not making such a silly show of themselves.

Hugo lifted his top hat from the seat where he'd used it to gain space between himself and Eunice. Hannah saw the look of disdain he gave Eunice as he stood back to let her go out ahead of him. Hannah went to scoop the frightened Fay into her arms to comfort her, but she wouldn't stop pulling her mother's dress into unsightly creases, and showing more of the bridal legs than was seemly.

It seemed Heaven disapproved of this marriage too. Outside the rain was coming down in sheets. The official photographer, together with several press photographers, braved it to snap two or three times at the bride and groom in the church door, while the guests crowded the porch behind them.

Then Hugo was summoning the cars to come as close as possible. Once Fay had been despatched with the bride and groom in the same Isotta-Fraschini sporting tourer that had been bought for Dorothy's wedding, all formality went. Umbrellas were produced and guests were crowded into cars as quickly as possible to get them out of the wet.

Eunice had agreed to arrange the reception but she wasn't making anything like the fuss she'd made for Dorothy. The guest list was much smaller.

A marquee had been erected on the lawn. The ladies with satin slippers and open shoes got their feet damp crossing the grass. Hannah felt Hugo take her arm and run her across under an umbrella, huddling close to keep her dry.

For the last few years, her only contact with the Mortimer family had been through him. He asked her to family gatherings at Ince at Christmas and for his birthday. Every few months he would take her out to lunch.

She knew he was spending more time alone at Ince while Eunice stayed in London. She had invited him to an occasional meal at Oakridge but always with other people.

'To play host for you while Matt is away,' he'd suggested, his blue eyes twinkling down at her.

'To help the conversation along, Hugo.' He was good at that. Always friendly but very proper.

'I enjoy coming to your home,' he'd said one night when he was leaving. Occasionally, he'd drop in unannounced at tea time and spend an hour or so with her. Hannah thought of him as a friend.

The champagne flowed, the feast was excellent, and the wedding cake had five tiers again. But the tent was dank and the light pale mud-coloured as it came through the canvas. The drumming of rain was only too audible.

Franklin Flower, his prominent teeth showing below his moustache, towed a little girl by each hand while Dorothy whirled through the guests oblivious to her family.

Hugo was full of gossip as always. 'Would you say Dorothy was cooling towards Franklin?'

'She's cool towards everybody.'

'And did you notice,' he chuckled, 'Eunice didn't kiss the bride.'

'But you did, twice, to make up.' Hannah smiled. 'So perhaps the bride didn't notice.'

She'd felt even closer to Hugo since the General Strike last year. Throughout the nine-day crisis, he'd come to Oakridge many times. He'd been very worried, not only about the national situation but also about his own factories which had been brought to a standstill by lack of coal and other supplies.

'Thank you, Hannah,' he'd said when it was over. 'For listening to my fears and outpourings. You helped keep me sane.' She felt she'd learned a good deal about the economic and industrial troubles the country had gone through since the end of the Great War.

The Mortimer connections began making for the greater comfort of the house as soon as they'd eaten their fill of the buffet and the speeches had been given. The dubious comfort of the marquee was being left to the bride's friends and relatives.

'Let's go,' Hugo said, picking up their glasses and a full bottle of champagne from the table. 'It's stopped raining at last.'

The house seemed full of people too. He led her up to his study.

'What's up here?' Hannah peered up the circular stairs to the cupola.

'Let's go up and I'll show you. Here, you carry the bottle.'

The stairs were steep and narrow and winding. Hannah marvelled at the ease with which Hugo climbed up.

When she reached the top and was able to see over the trees she gasped with pleasure at the view spread out below. It was late afternoon, the sky had cleared and the first watery shafts of sunlight were coming through.

She could see for miles, out over Bromborough docks, and downriver to the Liverpool skyline.

'Have a look through my telescope. You can see the people on the landing stage.'

Hannah trained his telescope on the Liverpool shore. The atmosphere had been washed clear of smoke and haze. Every detail, every street, every house, seemed to stand out with utmost clarity. She could even see raindrops sparkling on the distant roofs.

'I love it when it's clear like this,' Hugo said, and bent closer to show her how to adjust his instrument to suit her eyes.

116

His thick white hair brushed her arm. Hannah felt a tingle of desire. She straightened up surprised, shocked at herself.

He noticed and smiled at her. 'The Cathedral looks wonderful, they say it's almost finished now.'

She felt something pass between them, a yearning, a thrill, and realised she'd loved Hugo for a long time. A pall of guilt followed quickly. He was, after all, her father-in-law.

Chapter Eight

10 September 1929
Lizzie could not remember a time when Joey didn't have bouts of illness.

She was always the first to know when he took bad. She would hear his breathing rasp in the night, or a cough would make him hack for hour after hour. If illness started in the day she would hear the first hoarse note in his voice, or feel the heat from his body when he started a fever.

It always scared her to see him wilt before her eyes. Auntie Maisie talked of his sister Gertie and brother Charlie who had already gone to Heaven after being taken ill. She was afraid she might lose Joey in the same way.

That night, she woke feeling stiff with anxiety. It was pitch dark. Peggy's head pressed heavily into her shoulder but she was still asleep. Sharing a single bed, Lizzie often felt squashed. She tried to edge further away without wakening her.

Uncle Seamus's heavy tread sounded from the next bedroom; his voice came, rough with anger though he kept it low. It was only when she heard the thin whimper that she remembered there was another new baby.

'Thank goodness it's a girl this time,' Maisie had grunted. 'They're more help about the house. Patrick and Georgie are nothing but hard work.' Georgie was well under two and still needed napkins.

'Babies, so they are,' Seamus had muttered. 'Time to grow, that's all they need.' The recent birth had put him on edge, but now it was safely over.

'Boys are nothing but trouble. Look at our Joey.'

119

It came again then, the half-suppressed croak, and she knew what had wakened her, knew why she'd been filled with sudden dread. She raised herself up on her elbow.

'Are you all right, Joey?' She couldn't see him, couldn't even see the sagging curtain that shut off the boys' double bed from her and Peggy. There were only two bedrooms in the gatehouse and Joey's parents occupied the other with the latest baby.

'Yes,' he answered, but he sounded wheezy. She knew he was ill. She was always conscious of the bond between them. Joey was the person she felt nearest to in all the world.

She flopped back on her pillow. She was sure he had some sort of special power. Joey had quick darting eyes that left the casual observer with the feeling there was something odd about them. They were extraordinary eyes, alert and intelligent. It had taken her a long time to realise that they were not the same colour. It wasn't that one was bright blue and the other dark brown, the depth of colour was about equal. The right one was the colour of strong tea, the left slate blue, and both were marbled with deeper shades.

'I've seen a dog with ill-matched eyes,' she'd heard Uncle Seamus brood. 'But never a human being.'

'At least they're straight,' Maisie was apt to snap, 'and he sees well enough with them.'

'I put it down to mixed blood.' Seamus was of pure Irish stock, while Maisie had the olive complexion and dark brown eyes of her gypsy ancestors, though she described herself as English. Joey had her colouring but his foxy features came from his father.

Lizzie slid out of bed and drew the curtains at the window to let in a little light. The only other piece of furniture, apart from a couple of upright chairs, was a chest of drawers. She lifted the pink curtain round the boys' bed. Joey's eyes sparkled feverishly up at her.

'I could do with a drink,' he said hoarsely. Beside him Patrick slept with his arms round little Georgie, who had been

120

put out of the cot in his parents' bedroom to make room for the latest baby.

She went quietly downstairs and filled a jug from the bucket of drinking water they kept in the scullery, took a mug off the shelf and went back upstairs.

Poor Joey. He felt on fire when she touched his forehead. He drained the mug without stopping, gulping it down noisily. It made her heart turn over in dread. She refilled it and he drank that too.

'I'll be all right now,' he said, collapsing back on his pillow.

Joey felt fuzzy when he heard the clock downstairs strike twelve. His bed was shrouded with rose-tinted gloom, but he knew it was broad daylight that filtered through the curtain dividing the room. He struggled to sit up. It was cold and he felt clammy with perspiration.

There was no other sound; the house seemed to die when Dad went to work and his brothers and sisters went to school. His head throbbed and he felt as though he was suffocating. He wanted to take deep breaths but a pain stabbed through his chest every time he did so. His mouth was dry. He craved another drink, but the jug was empty. He wanted Lizzie to come home and comfort him. He felt alone, abandoned and unwanted, but the hours stretched ahead empty and uncomfortable until she would return.

'Mam?' His voice sounded weak and puny. There was no answer. Joey shivered and let himself fall back on his pillows. Nobody but Lizzie took much notice when he failed to get up for school. He was sick so often.

'Mam?' he called again. She must be here somewhere. He felt she didn't care whether he got better or not. This time he heard her stir in the next room.

'What d'yer want, Joey?'

'A drink. Aren't you getting up?'

'Not yet.'

'It's dinner time.'

'Get up yourself, Joey.'

Perhaps he would, he had to have a drink. He was tired of lying here and the sheets had come loose. He sat up and put his feet on the floor. Instantly he was shivering, cold seemed to invade his bones. He'd been cold last night and put his pullover on over his pyjamas. He always slept in his vest. It wouldn't make him much warmer if he replaced his pyjama jacket with his shirt, and he didn't feel up to it anyway.

Downstairs the front door slammed and quick footsteps came running. He knew it was Lizzie before she flicked up the curtain and came to sit on his bed. He felt his spirits rise as clean cold air wafted in with her.

'I've come home to get you some dinner.' She was out of breath. 'Ran all the way. Are you feeling better?'

He nodded, tried to smile.

'Poor Joey.' Her arms went round his shoulders. 'You do look poorly.' Her face against his was cold, her eyes sparkled and her cheeks were rosy. 'Where's Auntie Maisie?'

'Still in bed.'

'Fire's gone out again. It'll take me a few minutes but I'll find you something to eat.'

'A drink,' he gasped.

It was always Lizzie who looked after him when he was sick. She knew what to do. She refilled his water jug and brought up warm water in an enamel bowl so he could wash. Found him a clean pair of flannel pyjamas. Wrapped him in the eiderdown off her bed, while she made his. Then brought him a bowl of warm bread and milk. He heard her next door talking to Mam.

'Our Joey's sick. You must have known he was dying for a drink. How can you lie there doing nothing?'

'I'm lying in myself. I've got to be careful, haven't I? I don't want the new baby to catch his cold.'

'It's more than a cold. Don't you care about Joey?'

'Of course I care.'

'The doctor would give him medicine to make him better.'

'He came last month to our Joey and now he's sent a bill. He's been here since seeing to me. And he said he'd look

122

in again at the end of the week.'

'Our Joey's feeling awful now. He can't wait 'til the end of the week.'

'We can't afford the doctor all the time.'

'I'm going to ask him to come.'

Joey wanted to cry with relief. He'd never felt this bad before. This morning he'd tried to ask Patrick for more water, but he hadn't been able to get the words out. Lizzie had brought him mugs of tea without being asked.

'Don't you dare!'

'Joey needs him.'

'You'll have to get Mrs Bender to pay for him then. We can't, not with all the expense of the new baby.'

Lizzie was hovering by his bed when he opened his eyes again.

'I've got to go back to school. Will you be all right?'

'I feel a bit better.'

She paused, looking at him doubtfully. 'All the same, I'd feel better about you if the doctor came.' He knew she'd never asked him to come before, not without his mother's agreement.

As Lizzie came out of the house she was just in time to see the doctor's new Morris Cowley swish through the gates and turn towards the dower house. It made up her mind for her. She ran after it, but he'd gone inside by the time she got there. She marched up the front steps and rang the bell.

'Hello, Lizzie.' He'd got no further than the hall and was still wearing his overcoat when he opened the door. 'What brings you here?'

'I saw you come. I know you can make people well again.'

'Not always.'

'I want you to make our Joey well.'

'Joey? Did your Aunt Maisie send you?' Lizzie hung her head in misery.

'That means she didn't,' he pressed.

'She didn't,' she admitted. 'She says Joey's just got a cold,

123

but he's really poorly. It frightens me to see him like this.'

'What frightens you exactly?'

'The difference in him. He's weak like a kitten. Can't do anything. When he's well, he's strong.'

'Joey will never be as strong as you. He was very poorly when he was a baby. So ill we didn't expect him to . . .' She knew he was biting the word back. Knew he thought Joey was a puny weakling.

'But he is strong,' she assured him. 'Strong in mind anyway. Strong enough to boss everybody and make us do what he wants. He always gets his own way. He can even make Auntie Maisie do what he wants. That's strong, isn't it?'

'A different sort of strength, Lizzie. Not physical. Illness makes no difference.'

'It does,' she said earnestly. 'Joey can't do anything today. Can't even think straight. He's sweating and shivering and got a pain when he breathes.'

'Right then. I'll pop in and see him as I pass,' the doctor promised gravely. His hand was resting on her shoulder. It was a gesture she recognised. So many grown ups tried to show kindliness and support that way. Her teacher at school, for instance, though she gave extra homework too.

'You did right to come and tell me, Lizzie. If you are ever sick, I'd want to know too. If you can't come and tell me, send Joey or Peggy.'

'Yes, Doctor.' She knew there was something about her that made him show an interest in her welfare.

'Is Joey in bed?'

''Course he is.'

'Is that why you aren't at school today?'

'I am, I'm going back now. I came home at dinner time to see how he was.'

'Then you'd better run all the way,' he said. 'You're late already.'

Lizzie ran until she got a stitch in her side. She hadn't explained it properly to the doctor even now.

She should have said that when Joey was well he seemed to

have a rod of iron for a backbone. He knew how to avoid doing what he didn't want to do and he dared to do those things which teachers and parents forbade. Rules and regulations were for others to keep, not Joey. He had lots of energy, and lots of brilliant ideas, and nobody was more fun.

But when he was sick all that magic went. He lay in bed, a wan ghost of himself. He couldn't even get his mother to fetch him a drink of water.

Every evening, after she'd got the children to bed, Clarissa and Leo ate supper together in the dining-room. By then the day's work was done and they could relax. Tonight they were later than usual because he'd started to harvest the hay. Everyone on the farm had worked late into the evening. Clarissa knew he was tired out.

'The sheep are pushing through the hedge to the dower house garden again,' he worried. 'I'm afraid I'll have the doctor asking when I'm going to do something about it.'

'Tell him you can't spare anybody for hedging at the moment.'

Hay harvest was an anxious time for Leo. From the moment he gave the order to cut, it was essential to have dry weather, otherwise it could be ruined. He was always edgy until the crop was safely in the barn.

'I saw the doctor this afternoon outside the gatehouse.'

'Did he mention the sheep? They've made a mess of the flower beds.'

'No. He said he was sending Joey O'Malley to hospital. He's quite poorly. Pneumonia.' Clarissa helped herself to another slice of bread. 'He said Lizzie begged him to go and see Joey. He'd called in to see Maisie and the new baby earlier in the morning and she never mentioned Joey was even off school.'

'Typical! Seamus O'Malley's been a thorn in my flesh for years. A trouble maker. I'd have sacked him long ago if you hadn't billeted your protégée on him.'

'Not my protégée,' Clarissa objected. 'And she's not

125

billeted. They're bringing her up as their own. Maisie's told everyone her sister died in childbirth. Lizzie's been there all her life, everyone accepts that.'

'Seamus didn't turn up for work again today.'

'You should have sent someone down to get him.'

Leo liked to think of himself as a tough and practical manager, but Clarissa knew he usually deferred to her wishes. Lucy could persuade him to do anything she wanted.

'I did. That meant I was two hands short for the first hour. He had a mammoth hangover when he did turn up.'

'Still wetting the baby's head?'

'Goodness knows why.' Leo sounded exasperated. 'He openly said he had too many before she was born.'

Clarissa saw the O'Malley family in her mind's eye. The deaths of Gertie and Charlie left Peggy as the eldest, now a lanky eleven year old, and Joey coming next in age, at nine. He'd been known as Poor Joey since infancy, when he'd been so ill with scarlet fever.

All the O'Malley tribe suffered from permanently dripping noses, but Poor Joey caught every infection that came to the village, severe or otherwise.

Recent years had added two toddlers, Patrick and Georgie, of four years and twenty months respectively. She'd resented each arrival because it made Lizzie's position more difficult. Now there was the new baby, to be called Flora.

All were whey-faced and whippet thin with mousey hair. All on spindly legs ending in heavy boots. The boots were smaller versions of those their father wore to work. Stiff unlined leather, laced tight over the ankles, steel-tipped and with studs in their soles. No child could ever wear them out. They grew into them and out again and the boots were handed down to the next in age.

'He's been standing about all day. Done virtually nothing except set a bad example to the others. In the middle of haymaking it doesn't help.' Leo blinked angrily.

'Sounds as though you should never have taken him on,' she replied shortly.

'Hard to get rid of him now. Though I can't see they'd be much worse off if I did. Seamus probably drinks all his wages anyway. There's that empty cottage up on the hill he could rent.'

'It's a long way for the children to go to school.'

'Even further for Seamus to get to the pub. Maisie might be grateful.'

'You wouldn't, Leo! They'd have nothing but the money Hannah sends for Lizzie's keep. Seamus would never get another job. Everybody knows what he's like.'

'You mean he won't find another fool like me,' Leo said grimly.

It was early September a year later, and a chill afternoon for the time of year. Maisie had shut all the children out of the gatehouse, her patience worn thin by the long school holidays. Flora had been hanging on to Lizzie's hand, but Joey was ten and thought her too much of a baby to come with them. He'd persuaded her to play ball with Georgie and Patrick.

Now Joey was up a tree in Bender's orchard, picking the biggest apples he could reach and dropping them gently. Lizzie stood below, holding out the skirt of her dress to catch them.

'That's enough,' she called softly. 'The bag's nearly full.'

'There's plenty more good ones here.'

Lizzie was anxious, she was keeping look-out too. 'I think I can hear someone coming.'

'I can't.' Two more apples thudded into her skirt.

'It's all right for you. You're hidden by the leaves, nobody would see you up there.'

'I won't be a minute.'

'There is someone coming! Mr Bender's crossing the yard. He'll see us in a minute. I'm going.'

She caught the last apple he threw down, snatched up the full carrier bag and started to run. Behind her she heard the soft thud as Joey jumped. He was pounding after her, catching her up, taking the heavy bag from her grasp and racing ahead.

Now that he was growing older, Joey was at last getting stronger.

He turned out of the orchard and showed a clean pair of heels up the lane. It was a long straight stretch, but he'd turned the corner before Mr Bender had a chance to see him. Lizzie ran on, trying to reach the same bend where the hedge would hide her. She was within twenty yards when what she was dreading happened.

'Lizzie!' Mr Bender called angrily. 'What are you doing?'

She stopped running. She could hear his long stride gaining on her in any case. 'Nothing, Mr Bender,' she gasped.

'You've been taking my apples.'

'No! No, I haven't,' she denied.

'Lizzie! You've got one in your hand.'

It slid from her fingers as she stared at it. She'd forgotten she was still holding it.

'And I saw you come out of the orchard. When you're caught, Lizzie, you only make matters worse when you tell fibs. You know you shouldn't take them. You deserve to be punished.'

Lizzie was quaking and glad to hear Joey coming back to support her.

'We only took one each, honest, Mr Bender. We were hungry. And it wasn't Lizzie's fault, I made her come with me.'

'I might have known you were at it too, Joey O'Malley. I'm going to speak to your father. It's got to stop.' He kicked at the apple on the lane, shattering it to pieces, and turned abruptly on his heel.

'Rotten luck,' Joey whispered when he was out of ear shot. 'He was going down to the water meadow. There's a sick cow down there. Still, he didn't see the rest of the apples.'

Lizzie was touchy. 'If you'd come down straight away, when I first heard him, we'd have been all right.'

'Come on, Liz, we've still got the apples.' He retrieved the bag he'd hidden from the other side of the hedge. 'Let's go to the stables.'

128

They often went to the stables. It was a place of refuge where they could escape from Maisie. In the summer, the horses spent their days out in the fields and they had it to themselves. In winter, it was warm and dry and the horses were an added attraction.

Last year, Leo Bender had caught them feeding extra oats to the horses and put the stable out of bounds to them, but that only served to increase the attraction. There was a hay loft above, reached by a ladder, where they knew they could hide if they heard someone coming.

Only five horses were kept at Yarrow now; two large shire horses to pull farm machinery, the pony that pulled Clarissa's trap, a hunter that Leo rode to hounds, and Dando, the pony the Bender children shared.

Their pace slackened. The stable door was wide open and they could see Nicholas Bender curry combing Dando, a small broad-backed pony. Nick came to the door as they approached.

'What was all that shouting?'

'Your father's cross with Lizzie again,' Joey said. 'He was nasty to her.'

'Why?' Nick was a squarely built lad of fourteen with tousled hair, golden brown eyes and a smile that lit up his face. He had the same high clear colour in his cheeks his father had. 'You been up to something, Lizzie?'

'No,' Joey said. 'Nothing at all. I won't let him speak to Lizzie like that. She's a princess, you know. Her father's a king and he's searching for her. She's been lost for years.'

Nick laughed. 'That's baby talk. Lizzie's no princess and you'll never convince anybody she is. What's that you've got?'

'Apples.' Lizzie took a large bite. 'Do you want one?'

In times past more horses had been kept at Yarrow, and one of the empty stalls was now used to store straw for bedding. Lizzie threw herself down on it, and pulled Joey down beside her.

'Are they from our orchard?' Nick selected one from the

bag, while Lizzie burrowed into the straw to make a place to hide it.

"Course they are.'

'Mother says we mustn't pick them yet. They aren't ripe.'

'They're ripe. They taste ripe, don't they?'

'Your mother doesn't mind Lizzie taking them,' Joey said. 'She likes her. Lets her do anything she wants.'

'Well, you know why,' Nick said.

Lizzie felt mystified.

'Of course, I just told you,' Joey said. 'Because Lizzie is a princess who was kidnapped from her palace and given to me. Your mother knows this, but your dad doesn't. Like we read in that book, Lizzie. I told you you were someone special.'

'What nonsense. You are silly.' Nick offered an apple to Dando.

'It was your book once,' Lizzie reminded him. 'You read it, didn't you?'

'Fairy tales, that's all those are. I know who you are. I heard Dad talking about you only last night. He calls you Mum's protégée.'

'What's that?' Joey demanded suspiciously.

'Someone she's taking care of. Someone she wants to protect.'

'But why should she?' Joey wanted to know.

'You really don't know who she is?'

'No,' Lizzie said. 'Uncle Seamus calls me the cuckoo in the nest.'

Nick threw back his head and hooted with laughter.

'Mam says she's my cousin,' Joey volunteered.

'She can't be. Why would my dad and mum fuss like this if she was?'

'Who am I then?' Lizzie demanded.

'I don't believe her either. I think her mother was a very important person. A queen or something,' Joey said.

'Now you're being stupid again. I think her mother is a friend of my mother's,' Nick said importantly. 'In fact, I know she is.'

'But who?' Lizzie gasped.

She and Joey had mulled over this question endlessly. Joey kept coming up with different answers, each more exotic than the last. She no longer knew what to believe.

'Mum is always going on about her friend Hannah. I'm sure it's her.'

'Hannah?' Lizzie tried the name. 'Are you sure? Auntie Maisie says her name was Bessie. And that she was her sister.'

'That's just to cover up.'

'Cover what up?'

'I don't know exactly. Something dreadful happened and your mother had to leave you here.'

'She didn't want me.' Lizzie felt a shiver run down her spine.

'I want you,' Joey said. 'You're my twin.'

'Is my mother rich?' she asked in a small voice.

'I think so.' Nick pulled a paper bag from his pocket. 'Richer than us. Have one of my humbugs?'

'What's she like, this Hannah?' Joey asked, stuffing a sweet in his mouth.

'I don't remember much about her,' Nick admitted. 'But she was here once. Used to live in the dower house. She must be someone important or my dad would sack yours. The only reason he lets you O'Malleys stay is so Mum can keep an eye on Lizzie.'

'I thought Mrs Bender liked me,' Lizzie was saying sadly, when she caught Nick's eye. 'Though not, of course, as much as she likes you and Lucy.'

'She likes Jonathon and Hal more than me. And my dad does.'

'She's sorry for me,' Lizzie said. 'That's all.'

'Only because your mother left you with us, and we're too poor to look after you properly,' Joey said. 'Lizzie should be as rich as you are, Nick.'

'We aren't rich,' he said with a grin. 'Dad's always on at us about being more careful with money.'

'But you've got a pony,' Joey said.

'I've grown too big for Dando, but my dad won't get me another. He says he can't afford it.'

'There's Shandy and Caspar.'

'I'm forbidden to ride Caspar, he's too big for me. Not until I'm older.'

'But you go to boarding school instead of the one in the village. Even Lucy goes to school in Colwyn Bay.'

'That's not being rich.'

'It's not being poor either.' Lizzie rounded on him. 'It was a horrible thing my mother did. Every child should live with its own mother and father.'

'I bet she's sorry now. When I'm grown up, I'll find her for you,' Joey said, his eyes blazing.

'I might be able to do it sooner.' Nick took another apple. 'My mother gets letters from her. She knows where she is.'

'Would you?' Lizzie laughed excitedly. 'I do wish you would. Find out everything you can about her, please, Nick.'

'Well, I think I could get her name and address for you.'

'I'd love to find her,' Lizzie enthused. 'I'd love to know what she's like. Is she beautiful?'

He shook his head. 'I don't remember that either.'

'But you must remember something,' Lizzie protested. 'If she was really here.'

'She was, honest.'

'If Nick can get her name and address, we'll go and find her one day,' Joey said. 'I'll help you get your own back. We'll make her sorry for what she did.'

'How?' Lizzie asked.

'I don't know yet. We'll think of something when we're grown up. I'll make us rich first. Rich people can do anything.'

'You're back in cloud cuckoo land,' Nick said. 'I wish you'd grow up. I'll look after Lizzie, and there won't be any nonsense like that.'

Lizzie had always had the feeling of not quite belonging anywhere.

At home in the gatehouse, Auntie Maisie made it plain she

came last in order of importance. At dinner time, if there wasn't enough food to go round, which often happened, she was always the one to go short. She would be given bread and jam when the other children had plates of stew put in front of them.

Auntie Maisie would look at her with cold eyes and say: 'You can always go up to the farm. Tell them you're hungry and they'll give you something.'

And nothing annoyed her more than seeing Joey fork his helping in half and push the plate between them so they could share it. But he always did, and took half her bread and jam in exchange.

'You need feeding up, Joey,' Maisie would scold angrily. 'You aren't strong, not like Lizzie. It won't hurt her.'

Sometimes it seemed Auntie Maisie resented having to feed her at all. Lizzie felt an outsider in the midst of the O'Malley family.

It was true she never failed to get something to eat in the kitchen at Yarrow Farm. Tatty seemed to like her, and even if visitors were expected for a meal and Tatty was busy, she would still find time to cut a piece of cake for Lizzie.

If there were only routine family meals to prepare, Tatty welcomed her and let her help.

'You've got a light hand with pastry, Lizzie,' she'd say. 'All you need is practice, and one day you could become a cook like me.'

Yesterday, she'd gone to see Tatty and found Lucy in the kitchen with her.

'You're just in time,' she'd said. 'I'm going to show Lucy how to make a sponge cake. You can make one too if you like?'

'Yes, please. I love making cakes, don't you, Lucy?'

'No, I wanted to go into town with Mama, but she wouldn't take me.'

'Your mama's gone to the dentist, Lucy.'

'I don't like you looking after me, and I don't like cooking.'

'You've never tried it, Miss Hoity Toity,' Tatty said. 'Your

133

mama's a good cook. You could be too, if you wanted.'

'I don't,' Lucy told her crossly. 'I want to choose material for a new party dress.'

'Can you sew your own dresses?' Lizzie asked, her eyes wide with awe. 'Would you show me how?'

'My mother does it, silly,' Lucy sniffed. 'I just tell her what I want.'

'But she'd teach you if you asked her?'

'She is teaching me but I can't do it by myself, not yet.'

'I wonder if she'd teach me?'

'Why don't you ask your own mother and leave mine alone? You're always here, wanting something.'

Lizzie felt Tatty's floury hand rest on her shoulder for a moment.

'Lucy, you are a cross patch this morning. I thought you'd like Lizzie to keep you company.'

'Well, I don't. I hate her. My mother keeps making me sort through my things so she can give my toys and clothes to *her*, and she's always trailing after Nick, wanting him to play. She battens on all of us, even you. I wish she'd stay away from us.'

'Lucy, you're being very naughty.' Tatty's voice was angry now. 'I want you to say you're sorry to Lizzie.'

Lucy abandoned her cake-making to stand with her back to the fire, legs apart, glaring at her. 'Won't then!'

Lizzie took a deep shuddering breath, appalled at what she'd heard. 'I'm going,' she choked, already halfway to the door. It was cuttingly hurtful because everything Lucy said was true.

Mrs Bender was always kind to her. Sometimes she ran the bath for Lizzie up in the nursery and helped her wash her hair. She had such lovely big warm towels. Peggy and Joey hadn't even seen a bath like that and didn't know how lovely it could make you feel.

Mrs Bender would bring her a whole set of clean clothes. She'd always known they'd been Lucy's once, but she thought Mrs Bender gave them to her when Lucy had grown out of them. Last time, she'd gone home wearing a blue dress and feeling very smart.

'That would do for our Peg,' Maisie had said, feeling the good wool worsted between her fingers as soon as Lizzie was through the gatehouse door. 'You've plenty of things to wear without that.'

Lizzie didn't want to part with it but she'd done so, because it was true Peggy hadn't had anything new for ages. Already she was taller than Peggy, so there was no problem with the fit.

Once the underwear she was given went into Maisie's wash, Lizzie couldn't rely on getting it back again. Like everything else, there was never enough to go round. Even Joey wore Lucy's vests because Maisie said they would keep him warmer than any she could buy and if he was warm he wouldn't be ill. Lizzie was glad to give anything to Joey, particularly if it would prevent him catching another chill.

Sometimes, Lizzie thought the greatest possible luxury would be to know where she did truly belong. Everybody else seemed to know and take that for granted. She didn't belong at Yarrow Hall Farm either. Lucy hated her and everybody else felt sorry for her.

She ran down the drive, angrily rubbing blinding tears from her eyes. Promising herself that when she grew up she would go and find her real mother. Find where she truly belonged.

Chapter Nine

17 December 1930
Seamus O'Malley twirled the three rabbits triumphantly. It was such a dark night he could barely see their outlines now he'd turned the lantern out, but they felt plump and heavy. Shooting them was the only thing he'd enjoyed doing for days. His life seemed one long stretch of hard labour.

He was striding out at a comfortable pace now he was nearly home. It was a pleasure after moving with quiet stealth for so long. He'd almost reached his own front door when a shadow detached itself from the dense black square that was the gatehouse.

A torch snapped on and his heart missed a beat. His shot gun slipped from under his arm and clattered on the frozen ground as he found himself standing in a pool of light. It glinted off the brass tops of the cartridges still in his belt. He tried to hide the rabbits behind him.

'It's no good denying it this time, O'Malley. I've caught you red handed.' Leo Bender's voice was full of indignation. Seamus could feel himself shaking.

'This is blatant poaching and if there's ever a next time, I'll have you charged. I could have rung for Constable Watkins to meet me here now. Really I don't know why I didn't. Do you think I'm both blind and deaf? I saw your light down in my water meadow.'

Seamus swallowed, his mouth dry. He'd thought he was being careful. Maisie had been at him to get rabbits all last week, but he'd waited for the wind to change direction so that it carried the sound of his shots away from Yarrow Hall. The boss must have been out spying, there was no way he could see the water meadow from his house.

He felt fluttery with guilt. ''Tis just for the pot, Boss, so it is. The bairns are hungry. They've got to be fed.'

'Not on my game. I won't warn you again.' The light reflected up into Leo Bender's face, his high colour heightened by anger. 'I knew it was you last month. No other poacher would leave his spent cartridges on the field for me to find.'

Seamus felt an icy ball in his stomach. He always picked them up, he must have missed one.

'I will not have you shooting over my land, is that clear? The shooting rights are strictly for my use.'

'Yes, Boss.' Seamus writhed with frustration. It was all very well for Leo Bender. Shooting was a sport to which he invited his relatives and friends, a pleasure to be guarded jealously. He thought he was being generous because he gave most of what he shot to his tenants and workers, but Maisie wasn't happy with his occasional largesse. And his kids were hungry now.

The fact that there was an abundance of rabbits and woodpigeon at Yarrow, and even an occasional pheasant to be had, made it worse. Leo Bender would hardly miss what Seamus took, but in future he would have to go further afield and shoot over land belonging to neighbouring farmers.

'You'd better hand those rabbits over, hadn't you?'

Seamus was outraged and would have liked to refuse. He'd been looking forward to having a pan of rabbit stew tomorrow, and he'd planned to get on his bike and go straight down to the Madryn Arms. If he could interest the landlord in the third, he'd take the price in beer.

Feeling powerless, he watched Leo Bender stride off up the drive swinging his rabbits until the dark swallowed him up.

He swore loudly. It meant he'd wasted three cartridges when only minutes ago he'd been congratulating himself on making every shot count. Another wave of frustration washed through him. Why did he get so little from life? There was no justice. Everything was so much easier for the likes of Leo Bender.

Seamus O'Malley had grown up in Killarney in a three-roomed bothy, the ninth child in a family of ten. His father, a devout Catholic, farmed nine acres of hill and kept a cow, ten sheep and a few chickens. Times were hard and he had to add to his income where he could. He helped on other farms, did a little building work and sometimes sailed as an extra hand on a local fishing boat. What he earned was never enough, but he was very proud of his children and what they had been able to achieve.

By the time he was half grown, Seamus was tired of hearing how well they were all doing. He had two brothers in the priesthood, another was rising through the ranks of the executive civil service in London, and a fourth teaching in Dublin. His eldest sister was a nurse, two more taught in the local convent and the other was a novice in a contemplative order. He was afraid he would never achieve the equal of that.

At school his teachers said he was lazy and regularly pointed out that he was failing to achieve the standard set by his siblings. But he knew that when the time came, he too would have to leave home to earn a living.

He couldn't imagine his father ever boasting about him. He had complained too often.

There had been O'Malley relatives living in Liverpool since the potato famines of the last century, and young Seamus was sent to them in the hope that he would settle into city life.

He hated the teeming city streets and loathed working in the cigarette factory where his cousins found him a job. He couldn't abide being shut indoors without fresh air. He'd had to get out into the country where he could breathe. He couldn't settle to navvying on the railway cuttings or working on the docks. He survived as a ferry boat hand for only three months.

Farm work seemed to suit him best and he'd tried eight different farms before he'd ended up in a tied cottage at

Yarrow on thirty shillings a week.

At first this was officially augmented by an occasional sack of potatoes and a limitless supply of skimmed milk, which would only be fed to the calves if they didn't drink it. But now Leo Bender was selling liquid milk, Seamus was rationed to two free pints a day. Maisie was very bitter about it.

With his growing family to feed, Seamus had had to put his mind to other ways of adding to his income. He found pleasure and profit in poaching river trout from Leo Bender's best pools. He wasn't fond of fish himself, but the landlord would serve him a few pints of best bitter in exchange for his catch. He raided the Benders' orchard for apples and plums, their green house for tomatoes, their fields for vegetables. He also visited their hen house for eggs and an occasional cockerel.

But he desperately needed something in the pantry now. He hated mid-winter with its long dark nights and bitterly cold days sharpening everyone's appetite. He especially hated Christmas. It brought feasting to many people, but he could provide little extra. He didn't like to think of the Christmas trade bringing opportunities for others to earn more money.

Every year Leo Bender fattened geese and turkeys in their hundreds, and his flock of capons was the biggest for miles around. He sold them to butchers all over the county and they were sold in shops as far away as Manchester.

Seamus had been doing his best all week to avoid the long sessions of plucking and dressing poultry. He loathed being in the barn, hardly able to breathe for down and feathers floating in the air. Every time the door was opened, they swirled up into his nose and throat again.

Because he'd complained, he'd been given the job of screwing their necks and cutting their throats, and though it was done outdoors, he liked it even less.

Half joking, he'd already asked Maisie if she'd prefer a goose or a turkey for Christmas. He'd spent many hours trying to work out how he might help himself to one.

But he hadn't had five minutes alone with the birds all week, and was unlikely to have because the Benders brought in casual labour to help at this time of the year.

When the birds were weighed and dressed he had to help carry them into the house, where they had a special store room for them. He tramped backwards and forwards until both legs and arms ached, laying them out on shelves and trestles while Tatty grumbled at the mud he brought in to the kitchen passage, and Mrs Bender kept a check on numbers and made up orders. Once delivered there, they were beyond his reach. Mutinously, he kicked out at a stone. It wouldn't be easy.

Most shops wanted a small number of birds with their feathers left on. These were displayed outside, hanging up by their feet, though once inside the housewife preferred to take home a bird with the job completed. Seamus had been told to pick out the birds with the best plumage for this, and now they were hanging up in the barn.

He propped his gun against his front door and made up his mind. This would be the best time to take one. Leo Bender was safely at home with his wife, no doubt complaining about Seamus taking the rabbits. Everybody else had only finished work an hour or so ago and they'd all been exhausted. It had been after nine when the boss had let them all go home.

It served him right if he lost a good bird. He had it coming. He'd take a turkey, more on it than a goose and he had a lot of mouths to feed. He wouldn't even wait for Christmas Day. He'd get it into the oven tonight.

With a bit of luck he'd be on the same job again tomorrow and could replace the one he took so that the figures would work out right. There were so many, he couldn't believe Leo Bender would notice, but if so, he'd think he'd got his count wrong.

Seamus kept to the grass verge on the drive where his footfall would not be heard. He could find his way to the barn blindfold. The bolt was on the outside of the door so he had no problem getting in. The atmosphere was heavy with down and the smell of raw birds. It was an effort not to cough.

He didn't want to use his lantern, there was no knowing

who might see the light, but it was very dark inside. He'd tied the birds by their feet and hung them in pairs. Now he felt along the rail for the twenty-pound turkey cock he remembered. He was half tempted to take the turkey hen as well, but one would more than fill his oven.

He hesitated. Would he be able to sell one? Not tonight, it was too late now and he didn't want to keep evidence of this theft in his house. He took the one that felt heaviest and tiptoed out.

He'd managed it, but the bird still had its feathers on and he couldn't risk having traces of those about his place either, in case Leo Bender should come looking.

He made his way down to the river. The going was harder in the dark, he didn't come this way so often. It was full and babbling noisily after the recent rains. Stooping on the bank he started to pluck the bird, carefully putting each handful of feathers into the swirling water. He could see them being swept downstream, and if he came back this way tomorrow he could check that nothing was left on the bank to give him away.

His back ached long before the job was finished and his fingers were sore because he'd already plucked for six hours this morning. He took his pen knife from his pocket and cleaned the bird too, getting rid of everything he didn't want. He even rinsed the cavities in the river, but by then his hands were frozen. Only the fact that he'd got even with Bender and got himself a good meal spurred him on to the finish.

His mood was exultant on the way home, though he was staggering with fatigue and every muscle ached. There were no lights now in Yarrow farmhouse nor any of the cottages. Nobody would be any the wiser.

When he got home at last and lit the oil lamp swinging from the open beam, the bird seemed enormous. He felt absolutely spent. It was all he could do to pull himself up the stairs. Going into the children's bedroom, he dragged the sleeping Joey to the edge of the bed.

'Come on, get yourself up, yer lazy good-for-nothing.' His

head was spinning. He felt light-headed he was so tired. 'There's a job you can do. Wake up, damn you, I want you downstairs!'

'Whassa time?' Joey gasped.

'Bejasus, what does the time matter?'

He went to the other side of the curtain, lifted Lizzie from her bed and stood her on her feet.

'Kindle the fire and get the turkey in the oven,' he said. 'There's a treat in store for you tomorrow, eh? Christmas is coming early this year, so it is.'

'Won't it wait 'til morning?' She was rubbing her eyes.

'Would I be waking you now if I wanted it to wait 'til morning? Get the kettle on and make me some tea too.'

Lizzie was wakened by the movement of the bed springs beneath her. She opened her eyes to find Peggy already dressing in the morning half light.

'Is it time?' This morning they had to be up early. Mrs Bender was taking Peggy into Talybont to catch the train.

Peggy nodded, her teeth clenched in misery.

'You'll like it, Peg, once you're used to it,' Lizzie consoled as she got out of bed too. There was hardly room for both to dress at once in the curtained off space. She knew Peggy had been dreading this day.

Lizzie's eyes went to the calendar that Mrs Bender had given her. It hung on a nail over the chest of drawers. Peggy had pencilled a heavy circle round 14 July 1932, and the dreaded day had come. On the floor was a large brown paper parcel, tied tightly with plenty of string. It contained all Peggy's worldly possessions. This morning she was leaving home.

Her mother had found her a job as a scullery maid in a boarding house for railway men in Crewe. Peggy had had her fourteenth birthday last week, and up until now she'd never spent a night away from the gatehouse.

Lizzie had been dreading it too. Time was passing so quickly. As the eldest girl, Peggy got them all up for school in the morning. Once Peggy went, Lizzie knew she would be expected to take over.

'Joey, are you awake? Come on, it's time.' As the eldest boy, he was expected to get the fire lit so that the kettle could be boiled for tea. Usually he got up first.

It was July but the morning was dark. There had been a thunderstorm in the night, and the trees, now in full leaf, still dripped moisture. School would break up next week, and Auntie Maisie had decided Peggy must get a job before other school leavers snapped them all up.

A thin wail came from the next bedroom, reminding Lizzie that there was yet another new baby. Auntie Maisie was lying in again. The infant had only been born three days ago and intermittent crying had broken their sleep ever since.

Lizzie sighed. The single bed she'd shared with Peggy had been exchanged for a double when the time had come to accommodate little Flora as well, but it seemed they wouldn't have it to themselves for long.

She hurried downstairs. Joey already had the fire blazing up with the kettle swinging on its chain. Lizzie set out mugs and bowls on the table, then ran up to the farm with a jug. Peggy had made porridge the night before and put it in the haybox to keep warm until morning. Now she was stirring it on the hob to bring it back to the boil.

Lizzie ran upstairs with breakfast for Auntie Maisie. Uncle Seamus was still asleep on the other side of the double bed and snoring heavily. She could smell the beer fumes as soon as she opened their bedroom door.

'Isn't Uncle Seamus going to work today?'

'Doesn't look like it.'

'Shouldn't we wake him?'

'Leave him be.'

'He should be milking by now. Mr Bender will be angry. I'll get some tea for him, shall I? We should wake him.'

'No, he'll turn nasty. Let him alone. With our Peggy going and all that . . .' Lizzie saw Aunt Maisie's mouth turn down in misery.

144

'She'll be all right once she's used to it.'

'I'm losing her, aren't I? I hate seeing her go, what mother wouldn't? I wish I could have found something better. I mean, what sort of a life is she going to have? Scullery maid! They'll work her from morning 'til night. I'd like to do more for her, but she's got to go and earn her own living. You can bring me another cup of tea.'

Lizzie pushed the other O'Malley children downstairs in front of her, tying Flora's apron strings as she went.

Peggy was wearing her best brown dress. To indicate that she'd left childhood behind, her meagre pigtails were pinned round her head for the first time. They barely met on top. Lizzie saw tears clouding her eyes.

'It'll be all right, Peg,' she comforted.

Peggy sniffed hard. 'It'll be your turn next.'

'Lizzie isn't going to be a scullery maid,' Joey said fiercely from between clenched teeth. 'And they're not sending us to different places. Me and Lizzie are staying together, whatever happens.'

'Mam says Lizzie could be joining me in two years.'

She turned cold at the thought and pushed the tea cup she'd refilled into Peggy's hand. 'Better take this up to Auntie Maisie and get your goodbyes said.'

It seemed only moments later that Lucy Bender, in smart school uniform, was knocking on the front door. Lucy was a weekly boarder and going back to school for the last week before her summer holiday. Lizzie could see the trap halted at the gate with Mrs Bender sitting bolt upright holding the reins.

She really felt for Peggy as she watched her push her arms into her coat, her mouth clamped into a straight line, her eyes glazed with the effort of holding back her tears.

'You'll have to stay off school to look after Mam for a few days,' she said as she kissed Lizzie's cheek.

They all crowded into the porch to watch her climb slowly into the trap, and waved until it turned into the road. Lizzie listened until the melancholy clop of Shandy's hoofs and the creak of wooden wheels faded in the distance.

'Come on, time to get ready for school,' she said briskly, mindful that she must take Peggy's place. Pen-y-Clip village school was only ten minutes' walk down the road. She spread plum jam thickly on thick bread, a double slice for each of them to eat at dinner time.

'I don't like staying home,' she said. 'Uncle Seamus is here if she wants anything.'

'He'll be mad if he has to do anything.' Joey hesitated. 'Tell you what, we'll both stay home. We stick together, don't we?'

Lizzie nodded, finding comfort in that.

The younger children had gone when a heavy footfall sounded overhead. Joey was biting into the last crust. Lizzie saw him freeze as the stairs creaked. They waited, hardly daring to breathe.

All the family was scared of Seamus. They had reason to know his temper could flare up in seconds and it was always more volatile the morning after he'd had a night on the beer. The latch lifted on the door at the bottom of the stairs and Seamus, bleary-eyed, slouched into the room.

He towered over them; his very size seemed threatening. His unshaven jaw had a mean line. He went straight to the teapot and emptied an inch of dregs into a clean cup.

'You,' he turned on Lizzie, 'make me some tea.'

She was on her feet when his face turned crimson. 'Yer stupid devils!' he spat. 'The fire's gone out, so it has. You've let it.'

For the first time Lizzie noticed there was nothing but white ash in the grate. The few small pieces of wood Joey had put on to get a quick blaze to boil the kettle had burned away.

'Never think of anyone but yourselves,' Seamus raged. At forty, he was a heavy man gone to seed with black hair and a high colour to his face. His dark eyes were cruel and calculating.

Physical work ought to have kept him lean, but his taste for beer had given him a large gut. In the summer he wore denim work trousers, and in the winter brown corduroys held up with the same leather belt. Seamus was proud of his belt. It

146

sported an ornate brass buckle with several brass bars.

'Sorry,' Joey said. 'There's more wood here.'

'It'll need paper and sticks again before that'll catch, any fool can see that. What yer thinking of, Joey?' He lifted the poker and raked until white ash rose in a cloud to mantelpiece height.

'I'll get the sticks.' Lizzie fled to the lean-to beyond the pantry where they were kept.

'Let me do it, Dad,' Joey said.

'I want a cup of tea,' Seamus bellowed. 'Everybody else has had one.'

'It won't take long,' Lizzie said, rushing to refill the kettle.

'Lazy good-for-nothing devils!'

Lizzie knew Joey wouldn't take much of this. 'You can talk,' he muttered mutinously, pushing dried moss and wood shavings into the grate, and laying sticks on top.

Lizzie froze as she saw Seamus raise the poker he still held in his hand. He seemed about to bring it down on Joey's shoulders.

The strength was draining from her knees as she gave a choking cry and rushed at him, knocking the poker from his grasp. It clattered on the flagged floor and rolled under the table.

He turned on her savagely. 'You little bitch! What do you think yer doing?' He was advancing, unfastening his belt, his face suddenly puce with rage. They'd all felt the buckle of his belt as he lashed out at them, Lizzie still had weals and scratches on her legs from the last time. Often it happened when they least expected it. She'd got into the habit of watching his hands, ready to run if they strayed near his belt.

She backed off but wasn't quick enough. He was pinning her against the scullery wall when she wanted to escape through the front door. She caught a glimpse of Joey behind him, a murderous look on his thin face. The belt buckle was spinning through the air. Lizzie turned her face away to protect it, sick with terror. She felt her hair flick in the draught it made.

147

'Run,' Joey was shouting. 'Run, Lizzie.'

She knew he'd launched himself at his father in order to free her. She saw Seamus stumble because he'd been caught off balance. He fell back against the table. His weight made it scrape eighteen inches across the flagstones. He went down like a felled tree, catching his head against the oil lamp, making it swing wildly from the beams. Then he slumped to the floor, pushing the table still further. He groaned, then lay still.

In the shocked silence, Lizzie met Joey's eyes, wide with consternation. One quite clearly tea-brown and the other slate-blue.

'Christ! He'll kill us,' he said, grabbing her hand and half dragging her out of the house. He headed up the drive towards the stables.

Lizzie raced with him until she gasped for breath. Fear spurred her on. The early-morning rain had eased to a light drizzle, but it was enough to soak her pinafore. Joey's face was running with moisture as he urged her up the ladder to the hay loft.

'Shandy will be brought back soon,' he whispered. 'We'll have to be quiet.'

'Uncle Seamus will belt into us,' she quaked.

'I won't let him hurt you.'

'It was an accident.' She clung to Joey's thin frame. 'Do you think he's dead?'

'No,' said Joey. 'Take more than that to kill him.'

'He's hurt bad though,' Lizzie worried. 'We shouldn't have run away and left him.' The pounding of her heart was gradually slowing as she got her breath back.

'Got to take care of ourselves,' Joey puffed. 'First rule in this life. If Dad wasn't hurt, he'd have murdered us.'

It was several hours before they plucked up courage to go home. They'd been watching and knew Seamus had not turned up for work. Filled with dread, Joey paused on the gatehouse step, his heart thudding like an engine.

148

'Go on,' Lizzie urged. She was so close behind him he could feel her breath on his neck. He pushed open the door and went into the living-room.

'Where've you two been?' Maisie was belligerent. 'Thought you'd gone for good.'

The table was back in its usual position. A fire blazed in the grate, the kettle sang on its chain. His mother was in the old chair rocking furiously, with the new baby gripped tightly to her shoulder.

'Where's me dad?' Joey couldn't lift his eyes from the floor where he'd last seen him stretched out.

'Fighting him, were you?'

'No.' Joey was indignant. 'He went for me.'

'Well, you've done for him this time.'

'Where is he?' He felt cold with fear.

'Gone to hospital. Doctor thinks he's broke his leg.'

He met Lizzie's horror-stricken gaze. 'Serve him right,' he blustered. 'It was his fault.'

'So what are we all going to live on now? If his leg is broke, your dad won't be earning for months. It costs too, being in hospital.'

Joey swallowed hard.

'Mr Bender might turn us out too.'

'He won't,' Lizzie comforted.

''Course he won't. Won't put Lizzie out of house and home.'

'He'll be paying your dad's wages to someone else. It stands to reason he'll have to get other help. And where's he going to live?'

'Needn't be here.' Joey felt a ball of agony in his stomach.

'We've all got to eat, and a new baby only three days old.'

'I'll see we don't starve,' Joey said, putting on a show of confidence he didn't feel.

'A good job our Peggy's gone. One less mouth to feed.'

'We'll be all right, Mam. I've told you, I'll see to it. It won't be hard.'

She hooted with forced laughter. 'Yer young fool, of course it'll be hard!'

'You'll be glad to have him out of the way. See if you aren't.' His mother's dark gypsy eyes stared into his helplessly.

'You're the eldest now, Joey. Twelve, aren't yer? You'll have to get food for us.'

'I've said I will, haven't I?'

'We'll all help,' Lizzie echoed.

The days were passing, the food they had was gradually being used up. Joey began to worry. He knew the money in his mother's purse was being used up too as she sent Lizzie to buy smaller and smaller amounts of bread and tea in the village shop.

Chapter Ten

28 July 1932

Joey had no idea how to go about earning money but he knew he could follow his father's example, perhaps even refine his ideas on how to fill the larder.

When the food was all gone, he and Lizzie did what they always had: waited until the day's work on the farm was finished and Mr Bender was safely back in his own house.

Then, equipped with garden fork and a sack, they went to his potato fields. He grew potatoes for the market, but it was early in the season and they were very small. Joey started digging in the middle of a row, well away from the gate. It took several plants to provide enough for a few days. Lizzie buried the tops, carefully smoothing the soil over them and transplanting a weed or two to make it seem that was all that had ever grown there.

Then they went on to a smaller field in which Leo Bender had sown a row or two each of onions, carrots, lettuce, beetroot, peas and runner beans for his own use.

'There's so much,' Lizzie breathed.

'More than one family could possibly eat.'

'We'll help them. Just look at this spinach.'

'We don't want any of that,' Joey said. 'Can't stand the stuff.'

They were picking stick beans and neither noticed Nick until he spoke.

'Caught you red handed this time!' Nick was now sixteen and as tall as a full-grown man. He grinned as he opened the gate. 'When Dad complains about you helping yourselves,

Mum tries to tell him he's imagining it.'

'He hasn't sent you?' Lizzie asked anxiously.

'Tatty sent me to get some parsley.'

'You won't say you've seen us?'

''Course not, only make Dad worse. He's already mad at you.'

'Parsley's up the other end,' Joey said slowly. 'Would you like to see my new ferret?'

'It's lovely,' Lizzie added.

'Is it just a pet?'

'No, it's for catching rabbits.'

'Where d'you get it?'

'Bought it from a lad at school. It bit him and his hand went septic, so his mam made him get rid of it. His family was sick of rabbit anyway.'

'Does it really catch them?'

'Yes.'

'How many have you caught?'

'I only got it today. I thought I'd try it tonight.'

'Bet you won't catch anything.'

'Bet you I will. Billy says it's guaranteed. Come and see.'

'You're just a couple of kids,' Nick said loftily. 'You wouldn't know what to do.'

'We do then. Come and see.'

'I might for a little while. Hang on a minute while I pop this parsley in to Tatty.'

'Isn't it your supper time?' Lizzie asked.

'I've had it. Guests for dinner tonight, so I had mine in the kitchen with Tatty.'

They went on to the gatehouse where Lizzie went inside to put the vegetables in the pantry. Maisie straightened up guiltily when she caught sight of Nick hovering in the doorway.

'What's he doing here?' Her manner was anything but welcoming.

'Can I come in? I've come to see Joey's ferret.' Nick peered in.

'Of course,' Lizzie said. 'I'm always in your house.'

Maisie retreated to the fire. 'It's a vicious thing, Joey, and it'll need feeding. Don't know why you want to bring it here.'

'It's out in the back,' he said awkwardly, leading the way. Outside in what had once been a garden, a cold water tap had been fitted against the perimeter wall. Alongside it, a rabbit hutch was raised on four bricks.

'Have to be careful in case it nips me,' Joey said. 'I'll get the sacks.'

'The Parrys used to have a ferret. Harry used to put it inside his coat.'

'He wouldn't put this one there.' While Joey held the sack at the ready, Lizzie cautiously opened the door of the cage. The ferret, an attractive bundle of honey-coloured fur, crouched at the back and she had to push a stick through the wire netting to urge it forward.

'That's it. Got it.' Joey swiftly closed the sack and slung it over his shoulder.

'I hardly saw it,' Nick complained.

'It's not for looking at. You'll see what it can do. Bring a couple more sacks, Lizzie. Do you know a good burrow?'

'No,' Nick said.

'You said we could try the one in the park again,' Lizzie said.

'You're sure your dad's in the house?'

'Certain.'

Joey led the way in guilty rushes, trying Red Indian-style to keep cover between them and Yarrow Hall.

'We ought to wait 'til it's darker,' he worried. 'Don't want to be seen.'

'It takes ages to get dark at this time of the year. And I get into trouble if I stay out late.'

Joey straightened up in surprise. 'We stay out as late as we like.'

'Come on, let's get on with it,' Nick said impatiently. 'Dad will be having a bath now, getting ready for his visitors. Are you having me on about this ferret?'

'No. I saw Harry Parry's ferret catch rabbits in this burrow,

153

but it was a long time ago. I think there's more here now.'

'What are you doing?'

'Have to block up all the exits but two before we do anything. Help kick this soil back in, Nick, and over there too. Then Lizzie will put the ferret down the burrow and we'll catch the rabbits when it chases them out.'

Already they could hear a snarling and scurrying underground and the grass seemed to tremble.

'Here they come,' Lizzie screamed excitedly as she ran to join the others at the outlet. The first rabbit burst out and into Joey's sack an instant later, surprising all of them.

'Another sack!' Joey screamed, forgetting the need for caution as he grappled to tie the top of the gyrating sack. They weren't fast enough. The second rabbit escaped from the burrow before either Nick or Lizzie had the second sack in position. Nick went careering after it, screaming with delight. The fever of the chase was on him, but the rabbit was gone in an instant.

Lizzie caught the next, and Joey was tying the sack on another when Nick came back. 'Gosh, this is good fun.'

Two more escaped from the burrow because they weren't quick enough, but Nick caught two in the last sack, while Joey netted his ferret again.

'That's all then,' he said regretfully when it was quiet again.

Joey then stunned the rabbits he'd caught by banging each sack in turn against a tree trunk.

'Good, a big buck rabbit. Not old,' he enthused. Taking out a piece of string he tied it to a low branch so it hung upside down. Then, taking out his penknife, he flicked up the blade and slit its throat.

'Good lord!' Nick stopped dead in his tracks. 'That's a bit savage, isn't it?'

'Kindest way.' Joey was dealing with the second in the same way. 'Can't eat them 'til they're dead.'

'Are you going to eat them?'

'One of them. We might be able to sell the others. Three

154

good bucks. Good for roasting.'

'I think it's cruel,' Nick said.

'No more cruel than shooting them,' Lizzie defended.

'Better eating this way.' Joey grinned. 'They aren't full of lead shot. These two you caught, Nick, are not much good. One's an old doe, and the other is just a baby. Be all right in a stew.'

Joey felt a glow of satisfaction. He'd learned all there was to know about ferrets from Harry Parry, and the ferret he'd got for himself was a good one. They'd not be short of rabbits for the pot. He'd also proved he could do something better than Nick Bender.

'It's no good being jealous of Nick,' Lizzie had said to him more than once.

'Hard not to be. He's given everything he wants, isn't he? A bike and a pony.'

'Nick's all right. He lets you ride his bike.'

'He lets you ride his pony.'

'I like Nick,' Lizzie said. 'So do you, really.'

'He treats us like a couple of kids,' Joey sniffed. 'Thinks he knows more than we do.'

'He ought to, he's nearly grown up.'

Now, Joey gloried in being able to teach Nick Bender how to rabbit. Especially as he wasn't showing much aptitude. 'You aren't very practical,' he said, putting two rabbits in one sack.

'Nick's kind to animals, too gentle for this,' Lizzie said.

'He'd do it if he had to. You eat rabbit, don't you, up at your house?'

'Yes, sometimes. There's blood all over that sack,' Nick said in disgust.

'Have to wash them in the river tomorrow,' Joey told him. 'It always happens.'

'What you doing now?'

'Skinning this one, because we'll be eating it. Dad showed me how.'

'Gosh, there's lots of things you can do,' Nick said with

admiration. 'It's all a bit messy though.'

'Are you coming with us to the village? To see if we can sell the other two?'

'What, now?' Nick asked.

'Better while they're fresh. It's not late. We'll go as far as the shop and the pub.'

'Come with us,' Lizzie urged.

Joey wanted Nick to come with them too. He and Lizzie could be treated with suspicion in the village. Nick would lend an aura of respectability to what they were going to do. Also Joey was leading this expedition. It was good to have sixteen-year-old Nick towering over him yet feel he was in charge.

Pen-y-Clip was a straggling row of houses and cottages only ten minutes' walk down the road. Beyond that was an untidy collection of pens and yards and a large building with a corrugated iron roof, where the weekly sales of sheep, pigs and cattle took place. Amongst the cottages were the school, the Salem Chapel, and the Madryn Arms.

The village shop and post office had closed for the night several hours earlier, but Joey hammered on the door until the postmaster came in his shirt sleeves to loosen the bolts.

'We've got rabbits to sell,' Joey told him. 'Good big bucks. Plenty of eating on them.'

'How much?'

'Ninepence each.'

'You're a bit pricey, son.'

'Sixpence to you then? They're both young, should roast well.'

'Been out poaching, have you?'

'Of course not,' Nick said indignantly. 'Caught on our land.'

'I'll have that one then.' The postmaster pulled a fistful of coins out of his pocket and picked out six pennies.

Joey had already noticed the publican had come to the door of the Madryn Arms.

'Want a rabbit, Mr Jones?' he called as he ran across the road to him. The others followed. A car was slowing down to avoid them.

'Oh dear,' Nick said, grimacing. 'Those people are coming to our house for dinner. Hope they didn't see the rabbit.'

'Sold them both,' Joey was enthusing. 'A whole shilling. I only gave two shillings for the ferret and his hutch. It's going to be a good earner.'

The vehicle had stopped a short distance along the road. A voice called back: 'Do you want a lift home, Nicholas?'

Nick muttered under his breath, 'Hope they don't tell my dad about this,' before breaking into a run.

'Can we have a lift too?' Joey shouted after him. But the car moved off as soon as Nick was on the back seat.

Nick Bender went slowly downstairs to the dining-room. He didn't know why he spent all term looking forward to the school holidays. They always turned out to be a disappointment.

The scent of bacon and the sound of his father's voice met him at the door. He knew his parents watched him warily as he pulled out his chair and sat down. Things had been difficult at home for some time. He'd heard them discussing him in the kitchen.

'Did you have to be so brutal about it?' his mother had complained. 'He was so keen.'

'Too keen,' his father had said gruffly. 'Always behind me asking questions. "What type of oats do you sow, Dad? What's your yield? How many tons to the acre?" And he wants to try his hand at everything.'

'All he ever wanted was to help about the farm. I think you should let him. Give him something to do.'

'The farm will be Jonathon's one day, Clarissa. You know it's entailed. It's kinder not to let Nick believe he can play any part in it.'

'But to stop him going to Agricultural College? He'd set his mind on it.'

'You know Yarrow is mine only because I was the eldest son. It's soured things between me and my brother all our lives. He would have made a good farmer too, maybe better than I am. He's always been so envious. I don't want that to happen to Nick. There's no way we could afford to get him another farm, and what future would he have farming for someone else?'

'Nick isn't the sort to be envious. He's such a kind-hearted, sensitive boy.'

'He's young enough to develop other interests.'

'But he doesn't know what he wants now.'

At the beginning of the holidays, Nick always felt less at ease here than he did at school. His father was as strict as any master, and the rules were no fewer than at school, just different. Here in the country nothing much seemed to happen.

'You're late, Nick,' his father said.

'Sorry, Dad.' He reached across for the teapot. All the others had reached the toast stage.

'Tatty's keeping your breakfast warm in the oven,' his mother said, an impatient note in her voice. 'Run and get it, dear.'

His egg yolk was solid. He wasn't hungry anyway.

'I didn't want to say anything in front of the Apleys last night, Nick, but I do think you should have more sense. Selling rabbits in the village like that.'

'They weren't my rabbits. I was just there.'

'Damn it, I know that.'

'Sorry, Dad.'

'What do you see in those O'Malley children?'

'Joey's got a new ferret. I wanted to see it work. Gosh, it did well.'

'I wish you'd keep away from them. They're always up to some mischief.'

'I have to have somebody to talk to.' He missed the perpetual companionship of the boys at school. 'I'm not used to being by myself so much.'

158

'You've got your own family.'

'Jon and Hal don't want me tagging on, and Lucy hasn't broken up yet. Anyway, she's too young and only interested in dolls.'

'The O'Malleys are even younger.' His father's face condemned him.

'True.' He shrugged his shoulders. 'But Lizzie doesn't seem so childish. She's not so wrapped up in toys and dresses.'

And part of the attraction for him was that the O'Malleys gave him a glimpse of a different way of life. One where meal times were not important. They had a freedom he did not. Scruffy twelve-year-old Joey was in charge of his life, a provider of meals for his family, just like an adult. While Nick, at sixteen, was still being treated like a child.

'Perhaps you could invite your friend Johnson to come for a week?' his mother suggested.

'He's gone with his family to France. Isn't he lucky?'

His father stared silently back at him. He'd explained often enough that summer was his busiest time so they could never go away. Nick knew there would be no holiday trip. 'If you won't let me help on the farm, and you don't like me rabbiting with the O'Malleys, it doesn't leave me much to do.'

'Since you seem to have time on your hands,' his father said shortly, 'I suggest you give some thought to what you want from life. Buck up your ideas. How are you going to earn a living?'

'I'd like to work with horses, Dad. I've told you.'

'I'm afraid, Nick dear,' there was an edge to his mother's gentle voice, 'working with horses poses the same problems as farming. A riding school would require a big investment and we can't help you with it.'

Nick took a gulp of tea. They'd been through all this before. He had been putting his mind to it and was eager now to try his latest idea on them.

'I wouldn't mind being a stable manager for a racehorse owner or something like that.'

'There's not much cash in that,' his father said shortly.

'You might as well aim to be a farm manager, Nick,' Clarissa said. 'Your father is afraid you'll end up as a groom or a farm labourer.'

'Why can't you make up your mind about what you want? Set yourself goals like Jonathon and Hal?' Dad was irritable.

'I've never needed to make up my mind. I've always known I wanted to do farm work. Or if not that, work with animals.'

'We've been through all that, Nick, a dozen times. For you it isn't possible. We want you to have a decent career.'

Nick studied his two brothers from under his lashes. One day Jonathon would inherit Yarrow. He'd not been pressured to make any choice. He'd wanted to become a vet and practise until Father retired. He'd already sat his finals and was awaiting the outcome with every confidence. Hal was a medical student, and hadn't thought of being anything other than a doctor from the time he was at school.

'Have you thought about being a vet like Jonathon?' His mother was smiling at him again. It wasn't the first time this had been put to him. He dismissed the idea again. He couldn't explain why, but he just didn't think he could.

'You mustn't drift, Nick.' That made him blink hard. Dad thought more highly of his brothers.

'Why don't you go out for a ride on Dando?' his mother suggested.

'Mother!' He instilled as much scorn into his voice as he dared. 'My feet practically touch the ground when I sit on her.'

He'd adored Dando once, but he'd grown out of her. She'd been bought for Jonathon and they'd all learned to ride her in turn. If she had a fault, it was that her back was so broad it was difficult for a small child to get his legs across it. With her thick-set hindquarters and stocky legs, she had the shapeliness of a bed.

As soon as he went into her field, Dando would amble over and put her soft damp muzzle against his hand, and if she found that empty, would try to push into his pocket for the carrot or apple he usually took her. She had a rough coat, a flowing mane and big benign eyes, and was of a cross breed that owed something to the Welsh cob.

Nick thought of her with affection. She was so placid that at times she seemed to be sleep walking. Very safe for a child's first mount, but not an exciting ride once the first skills had been mastered. Mostly she strolled at snail's pace, but she could be persuaded to trot for short distances. A canter was more difficult to achieve and Nick had never seen her gallop.

'I forget you're growing up, Nick, and ride Shandy now. I won't be going out today.' Shandy was often between the shafts of his mother's trap, but he'd been allowed to ride her for some time.

'I've grown out of her too, Mother. I thought you were going to sell her and the trap?'

'Soon,' she said. 'When I get a car.'

'Could I ride Caspar, Dad?'

'I suppose you're big enough to manage him. You'd like that?'

'I'd love it, Dad.'

'All right.' Permission was given only grudgingly. 'Don't go off our own land for a week or so, until you get used to each other.'

Nick nodded. He and Caspar were not complete strangers. Caspar was a lightweight hunter of nearly fifteen hands. Once he'd been a very good jumper. Nick had ridden him over the last two holidays and found him a more exciting ride than Shandy. The fact that he hadn't had permission meant he'd had to head off the farm when his father's back was turned.

'Your father's thinking of buying another horse for himself.' He felt his mother's eyes watching him.

'Caspar's getting old,' his father said.

'Over twenty, isn't he?' Nick spoke with his mouth full. 'Not got a lot of energy for hunting now. You need a stronger horse, Dad.'

His father turned to his two brothers. 'What are you planning to do today?'

161

Jonathon could drive and had a car, so they didn't have to hang about the farm all the time. But they wouldn't take Nick. They thought him too young to trail behind them round pubs chatting up girls.

'Will I be allowed to ride the new horse?'

'No,' his father said shortly.

The new horse was huge, a seven-year-old gelding named Ambrose. He stood nearly eighteen hands and had bounce in his step and a glossy black coat. He came in a horsebox a few days later and was made twitchy by the experience.

Leo had decided it would be wise to stable him for a few days until he was used to his new surroundings. Nick soothed and settled him in, groomed him, gave him a feed of bran and oats, and brought Dando in to the next stall for company. He couldn't leave the new horse alone. He'd never handled such a fine animal before and he longed to ride him.

The next day was bright and sunny and it seemed a shame to keep Ambrose in the stable now he'd had time to calm down. His ears were pricking backwards and forwards and his eyes were bright. He looked alert and intelligent enough to cope with any difficulty he might encounter on the hunting field.

Nick watched his father lead him to the field and turn him out with the other horses.

'I'll saddle him this afternoon and try him out,' he said. 'Haven't time now, I want to take those calves to market.'

Nick had already seen Lizzie's fair head peeping through the hedge. Once his father was out of sight, she came running to get a better look. 'Isn't he a beauty?'

'Should be, he cost twenty-five guineas.'

'Whew!' Joey whistled. As usual he was not far behind. 'You could have had two horses for that.'

'I thought you said your dad wasn't rich?' Lizzie piped up.

'The farm's done a bit better over the last few years.' His father didn't like to admit he was getting more prosperous, but Nick had noticed other signs.

Joey's lopsided eyes smiled up at him. 'Just look at his muscles rippling. I bet he's wonderful to ride.'

'You couldn't ride him.'

''Course I could.'

'You're too small for a horse like Ambrose.'

'I can ride anything.'

'He can,' Lizzie confirmed.

'Who taught you?'

'You don't need lessons for things like that!' Joey's lip curled in contempt. 'I get on and do it. Have you had a go yet?'

'No,' Nick admitted, and felt again a pang of something near desire. He really wanted to.

He watched Ambrose's head go down to the grass. At breakfast his father had held forth at great length about his choice of this particular horse. He needed a strong heavyweight hunter with plenty of stamina because he himself was heavily built and getting heavier in middle age. He'd said he'd outgrown Caspar just as Nick had outgrown Dando and Shandy. And yet, he maintained, Ambrose was quite the wrong horse for Nick.

Nick didn't agree, because he was almost as tall as Dad now. Okay, he'd be a little overhorsed, but that was no reason to forbid him to mount. And Joey O'Malley was stones lighter than he was.

'I know I can. Want me to show you?' Joey took a home-made head collar of frayed rope from his pocket.

'Joey can ride that old black cow you've got,' Lizzie said. She wore her hair in plaits like the other O'Malley girls, but hers were really long and thick.

'You'll never even catch him. He's still a bit skittish.'

'Catch anything with a few oats, I bet you.'

Nick grinned. 'Why not?' He'd seen his mother settling down to some dressmaking and the window of her sewing room faced the other way. 'Wouldn't mind having a go myself. Lizzie, be a good girl and make sure my father's gone. Then go and distract Tatty. She'll tell on us if she knows.'

'Nick! I don't want to be left out. You and Joey are going to have all the fun.'

'I'll make it up to you some other time,' he promised.

'Now,' she bargained. 'I want to come too.'

'All right then.' All Nick wanted to do was to ride.

'Where are you going?'

'Out on the common. Daren't go past the house.'

Ambrose was easy to catch. Nick rattled a few oats in the bucket and the horse came over and put his head in it. Joey slid the head collar on and they had him.

Nick was surprised to find how good Joey was with horses. He soothed and stroked Ambrose, talked to him until he seemed as placid as Dando.

'Let's take him back to the stable to saddle him,' Nick said as he opened the gate.

When Ambrose came alongside, Joey shinned up the five bars and slid on to his back. Nick had seen him ride both Caspar and Dando bareback. The horse walked slowly up the lane and back to his stall in the stable.

'I told you I could,' Joey crowed as Nick was saddling up. 'Nothing skittish about him. A smashing horse.'

Nick agreed. It was a long pull up into the saddle, but he felt quite safe and in control once there. The next instant Joey was up behind him.

'A big enough load for him now,' he said into Nick's ear.

'You leave him to me,' Nick ordered as he turned Ambrose into the lane. As soon as they were out of sight of the house they rode up and down the road, waiting for Lizzie.

'Nobody saw you go,' she gasped as she came running up. 'My turn, Joey. I want to ride. I've got a stitch in my side now.'

'Come on then, up in front,' Nick said. Joey had to give her a leg up but she got there. She was grabbing handfuls of mane.

'Loosen up,' he said, 'Ambrose won't like that. I won't let you fall.' His arms, one each side of her waist, held her in

164

position. He could see over her shoulder, though the breeze fluttered wisps of white hair against his chin, tickling him, and sometimes the plaits rose and fell with the gait of the horse.

He put Ambrose through his paces, from walk to trot, and on to canter and gallop. They rode him together and separately. One or sometimes two running behind.

He tried him at a few fences. Ambrose sailed over with ease. Nick gloried in it. The sun was warm on his face and the breeze blustered. He felt on top of the world.

'Dad's wrong,' he said to Lizzie. ''Course I can manage him. He's no harder than Caspar. In fact, Caspar can be a bit obstinate at times.'

Nick was enjoying himself so much he forgot the time. It was his stomach that reminded him. He'd stayed out longer than he'd meant to and travelled further. Lunch time had come and gone. His euphoria vanished, leaving him cold and anxious.

He wanted Ambrose safely back in the field before his father came home. With Lizzie up in front, Joey kept shouting to him to slow down so he could keep up. They tried three up and Ambrose could still keep up a brisk canter. He slowed to a walk over the last mile, but when they dismounted in the stable and Nick pulled off the saddle, the horse was steaming and streaming with sweat.

They both helped him. Joey picked out Ambrose's hooves while Lizzie used the sweat scraper and Nick rubbed him down. Once they had a light blanket on, they led him back to the field.

'I'd like to take the blanket off,' Nick worried. 'Don't want Dad to see it.'

'Why don't you then?'

'He needs it on while he cools down. Can't risk him catching a chill. Another ten minutes. He ought to have a feed of bran and oats too.'

'Surely your dad will go in the house first? He'll want his dinner.'

'We'll get him a bran mash,' Nick decided. 'He can have

165

that and we'll take off the blanket, so there'll be nothing to show . . .'

They were walking back up the lane to the field when Nick heard footsteps behind them.

'It's Dad!' His heart thudded with panic. All three took to their heels along the grass verges.

'I'll grab the blanket,' Joey panted.

'No,' Nick hissed. 'Clear off. And Lizzie, take this bucket of bran mash with you.' He leaned on the gate, trying to look as though he'd been there for an hour, but he was holding his breath until Lizzie turned the corner and was out of sight. It seemed only seconds before his father joined him.

'Hello, Nick. You've got a blanket on Ambrose?'

'Yes.' He was afraid his voice squeaked with guilt.

'Were the flies bothering him?'

Nick felt paralysed. He didn't disagree.

'No trouble catching him?'

'No, Dad.'

'Good. Tatty says you haven't been in for lunch.'

'Wasn't hungry.' His stomach gurgled a protest. To cover the noise he said: 'Have you had yours?'

'Of course. She's keeping yours hot if you want it.'

'I'm not hungry.' Guilt made him stifle his appetite. He couldn't leave the horse now.

'Thought I'd make time for a ride. Put Ambrose through his paces. Why don't you saddle Caspar and come with me?'

He blamed himself. Nick knew he ought to tell his father that the horse needed rest and food. He tried to work out how many hours of vigorous exercise Ambrose had already had today. He was worried stiff, but Dad had been impressed with the horse's stamina. Perhaps he'd be all right?

He didn't feel at all like another ride. Another fear was growing: that the horse would still be sweating when the blanket was removed.

Ambrose was difficult to catch. Nick had to fetch some oats before they managed it. There was a sudden short shower, so although Ambrose's blanket was wet it didn't

166

occur to his father that it was sweat. He had to dry Ambrose off before he could be saddled.

His father rode ahead, ramrod straight in the saddle, classically correct in his horsemanship. Nick felt taut with tension as he re-trod the route he and Ambrose had travelled earlier. Ambrose seemed all right though Nick thought there could be less bounce in his step than there had been.

Out on the common where the ground was firm and level, his father urged Ambrose into a gallop. Nick was careful to keep Caspar well behind.

Ambrose cleared a couple of ditches satisfactorily and his father put him at a low wall.

'He's good,' his father called to him as Nick sailed over on Caspar. He sounded pleased with his new horse.

Nick told himself to ease up, it was going to be all right. The horse had stamina, hadn't it? They cantered on. He noticed Caspar had no trouble keeping up. He seemed quite frisky. Nick wished he didn't feel so famished and exhausted.

He felt the rain in his face again and moments later it was coming down heavily. He felt Caspar slide but he regained his footing and carried on.

'Take care, the grass is slippery now it's wet,' he called. 'And where it's muddy it's worse.' His father's back was still ramrod straight in the saddle.

'Have we gone far enough, Dad? We're going to get soaked.' It seemed enough of an excuse to return. But his father had set Ambrose at a gorse thicket that provided a wider obstacle.

Nick decided he was going round it, he was spent. He was concentrating on the rhythm of Caspar's stride at the time and couldn't believe he was seeing Ambrose slip and flounder. He knew he let out a scream as his father was being thrown off.

It all happened so quickly. He reined Caspar to a sudden halt. Slid down to the ground.

'You all right, Dad?' He knew he sounded terrified, but his father was getting stiffly to his feet. He was splattered with

167

mud, his face screwing with pain.

Nick stood transfixed with guilt, both hands pressed to his mouth. The rain was driving in his face. 'What happened?'

'The horse!' His father was shouting. 'See to the horse.' Ambrose was still floundering on the ground, churning it to mud, unable to get to his feet. 'Mind he doesn't kick you,' he warned.

Nick's mouth was dry. What had he done? This was cataclysmic. He caught hold of the bridle and tried to encourage the horse to his feet. Went closer, grasped his noseband and heaved. Ambrose was trying to push himself up on his forelegs but his back ones would not straighten under him.

His father pushed him out of the way. 'Come on,' he said to Ambrose. 'Up you come.' He achieved only an anguished neigh.

Nick was aghast. Ambrose's back legs would not take his weight. His father was running his hands over them, his face paper white.

'Could be broken, I suppose.' He was biting his lip, then gently feeling down the horse's backbone.

'Is it there?' Nick felt rigid with horror.

'I don't know.' His father was taking off his jacket and spreading it over the animal to keep him warm.

'Get the vet here as soon as you can,' his voice rasped out. It was Leo who caught Caspar's bridle and thrust Nick upwards into the saddle. 'Bring my gun too, just in case.'

The word 'gun' made Nick sick with anxiety. This was worse than anything he'd imagined. He felt on fire. What he'd done this morning must have contributed to the accident. He felt a desperate urge to get it off his conscience.

'Dad,' he said, blurting it out, 'I've already ridden him. I . . .'

'Get on with you, you're wasting time.'

He dug his heels into Caspar's ribs then and rode as hard as he could. It began to rain more persistently. The day took on a nightmare quality.

When he reached home he rode straight to the back door

yelling to his mother to ring for the vet. Then he shut himself in the downstairs lavatory to wipe the rain from his face and pull himself together.

He didn't want to go back, but his father's gun was still in its cupboard when he looked. Caspar had gone when he peered out in the yard.

'Jonathon said to tell you he'd taken him,' said Tatty. Nick started to walk, hardly able to drag one foot after the other. When eventually he got back to the scene of the accident, a crowd had gathered. Some of the farm workers, both his brothers who happened to be home. The vet, even Lizzie and Joey O'Malley. Nick daren't look them in the eye.

'Broken his back.' The words he'd dreaded. He wanted to put his hands over his ears, to shut it all out.

He was aware of Joey edging close on one side and of Lizzie snuggling against him on the other, her fair skin wet with rain. Then the onlookers were backing off. He saw his father raising the gun, his face rigid with anguish.

Ambrose, his sleek black coat smeared with mud, was weaker now but still making futile efforts to stand.

The shot when it came reverberated through Nick's head.

Lizzie was feeling for his hand, Joey was clinging to him, he shook them both off. He knew that if he didn't he'd disgrace himself. The beautiful horse lay still at last.

Everybody was turning away, going home. Nick followed blindly.

'Let's go to the stable,' Joey whispered.

Nick shook his head and wished they'd go away. He never wanted to go to the stable again. Never wanted to see another horse.

'How much did you say it cost? The horse?'

'Shut up.'

'How much? Tell me.' There was no shaking Joey O'Malley off.

Nick felt ill. The adults ahead were moving at funereal pace and he didn't want them to hear. 'Twenty-five guineas,' he muttered.

'Shooting it just like that! I can't believe anybody would shoot twenty-five guineas' worth.'

'Don't you understand? He wasn't worth anything. He'd broken his back. We helped to do it, Joey. All of us.'

'You didn't tell him?' He saw the tip of Joey's tongue moisten his lips.

'I tried, but I don't think . . . I ought to.'

'Don't be daft! He thinks it's his own fault.' Joey forced a laugh. 'Don't you dare. He'd half kill us.'

'He was riding it himself,' Lizzie protested. 'Better if he doesn't know.'

'He doesn't mind wasting twenty-five guineas.' Joey's strange eyes glittered up at Nick. 'He shot it without turning a hair.'

'He minds terribly,' Nick said through clenched teeth. 'See how stern he is.'

'He's talking to the vet as though nothing terrible has happened. He must be rich to spend that sort of money on a horse in the first place.'

'It caught his eye. It was an extravagance. A rare indulgence, if you like,' Nick said miserably.

'That's what I mean,' Joey said. 'Then to shoot it the very next day . . . that's being really rich. One day I'm going to have money like that.'

'Don't be stupid.' Nick felt crushed and could take no more from Joey. 'When you're fourteen, your dad will find you a place as a farm boy. You'll be a farm labourer just like him. A tied cottage and thirty shillings a week.'

'I'll ask Mr Bender to take you on here.' Lizzie let go of Nick's arm and rushed to support Joey. 'He took on Harry Parry.'

'He won't take me.' Joey shook his head. 'He thinks I'm not strong enough, and I get sick too often, and he doesn't like my dad. Anyway, I want to work in a big city. That's where you can get rich, isn't it, Nick?'

Lizzie sighed. 'I don't know how you'll do it.'

'I'll do it somehow. Other people do.'

'Not people like you.' Nick was exhausted. He'd no more patience with Joey; he was boasting like the silly child he was.

'I'll do it, Lizzie,' Joey vowed. 'I'll work 'til I drop. I'm going to do it for you. We're going to be rich one day.'

Book Three

1934-1936

Chapter Eleven

2 May 1934

Last night, Matt had arrived home for a month's leave from Egypt, and to Hannah it felt like having a stranger in the house. The month stretched ahead uncomfortably.

As she went downstairs behind him, the morning sun was streaming through the stained glass windows, filling the hall with prisms of coloured light. The post came plopping through the letter box. Matt stooped to pick it up.

Usually Hannah ate her breakfast with Edna in the kitchen. This morning, a white cloth had been spread on the table in the dining-room. Matt was already pulling out a chair to sit down.

In the kitchen there was a smell of burned toast and Edna looked harassed because of the change in routine. She'd made both tea and coffee and set them out on a tray. Hannah carried it in.

'Letter for you,' Matt said from behind the morning paper. She poured him a cup of tea before reaching for the envelope by her plate.

'You told Greg I was coming home?'

'Yes, I said you'd see him in the office this morning. You will be going in?'

'Of course.'

Hannah started to read her letter.

'Is he going to pick me up? Run me in to the office?'

'I told him there was no need. Hugo's sent a car here for you to use while you're home.'

'You said Dorothy and Franklin would be coming

to Mother's for dinner tonight?'

'Yes, she's asked us all.'

'Have you seen her new baby?' Dorothy's family was growing. Hannah never ceased to marvel that Dorothy had taken to motherhood after all. She had given birth to a fourth daughter, Patience, two months earlier.

'Yes, I went up with Hugo. Your mother stayed with her for a week or two. Matt, this letter's from Clarissa Bender. I want you to listen to what she says.'

With bad grace he let his newspaper fall back on his plate. Even his hands were deeply tanned. He was scowling at her.

'"Leo and I have a favour we want to ask,"' read Hannah. '"Our third son, Nicholas, is having difficulty settling to a career. He's very interested in farming, but Leo sees no future in it for him. He's not academic and doesn't want to study further.

'"He rejects most suggestions we make out of hand, but says he would be interested in running a business. Would Matt be good enough to take him under his wing? Find him a job in Evans's and see if he can make a go of it?

'"We really are at our wits' end with him. We articled him to Leo's cousin who is a London solicitor, but he threw that over and came home."'

Matt was frowning. She knew the letter must resurrect bad memories for him. 'Lucky for Clarissa you happen to be home.'

'I suppose we should feel indebted to her,' he said grimly.

'Matt, we owe the Benders any favour they care to ask. This seems little enough.'

'I don't like the idea. Nick might remember Dorothy being there.'

'He was only four years old. He wouldn't have known what was happening, and even if he did, he's unlikely to remember. It was all kept very quiet and it was fourteen years ago.'

'But we don't want any rumours.'

'Matt, he hardly saw her. Dorothy didn't take to Clary's children. She had to keep them away from the dower house.'

'I don't suppose we can refuse. How old is he now?'

'Clarissa says eighteen.'

'I suppose we can slot him in somewhere. I'll have a word with Greg when I go in this morning.'

'She wants him to learn how to run a business.'

'Yes, I suppose Greg could arrange that.'

'Greg will remember Dorothy's stay at Yarrow. You'll have to warn him not to mention it to Nick.'

'Of course I'll do that.'

'Nick could stay with us for a few days until he finds lodgings for himself,' Hannah said. 'It would be easier once he's here. I'll write back and say so.'

'I don't want him living here while I'm home,' Matt retorted.

Hannah took a deep breath. 'Clarissa will want him to start soon.'

'There's no desperate hurry. A month won't make much difference. I wish we didn't have to do it at all.'

Hannah was cross with him, but it mollified her somewhat to hear him compliment Edna on the eggs and bacon.

Once Matt had driven off to the office, the house settled back to something like normality. Hannah started her letter to Clarissa.

Matt had made her promise to have as little contact as possible with the Benders. Now all that would change. Nick would know Elizabeth, he'd be able to tell her all about the girl. She felt quite excited at the prospect of his coming.

Hannah was relieved when Matt's leave came to an end. She was looking forward to getting back into her own routine again.

Weeks ago, she had written to Clarissa: 'Why don't you come with Nick and see him into digs? I'd love to see you again.'

Hannah had been disappointed when her friend had replied that it was a busy time of the year for Leo and she didn't feel she could desert him at the moment.

177

Two days after Matt sailed for Alexandria, Nick was due to arrive by train. At Woodside Station, six feet of youth straightened up over his suitcases.

'It's very kind of you to take me in like this, Mrs Mortimer.' His handshake was bruising. He had soft golden brown eyes and a smile that lit up his whole face. There were still a few boyish freckles across his nose. Hannah thought him recognisably like Clarissa.

She felt pleased to have him, and enquired about his parents. They were both well.

Nick chattered on, telling her Jonathon was now in a veterinary practice in Yorkshire and waiting for an opportunity to move nearer to home. Hal was working as a houseman in a London hospital and Lucy was in a boarding school in Colwyn Bay. He hadn't seen much of any of them recently.

Hannah wanted news of Elizabeth, but she decided to wait for the right opportunity to ask, in case he should wonder why.

She showed him to the room prepared for his use, and tried to make him feel welcome. 'I've asked Greg to call in to meet you on his way home.'

Greg came and they seemed to get on amicably. Nick was asking all sorts of questions about Evans's. She thought he sounded interested, and he seemed to know a good deal about Matt's business already.

When Greg went, Nick began talking about Yarrow. She liked his friendly manner and thought Clarissa should be proud of him.

They were in the dining-room having supper when he said: 'Do you remember Lizzie O'Malley?'

'Yes.' She guessed immediately that he knew more of Dorothy's business than she'd supposed.

'Mother asked me to be sure to tell you about her.'

Hannah was disconcerted. 'Has something happened?'

'Maisie's arranging for her to go to a boarding house in Crewe as a scullery maid.'

178

Her stomach muscles contracted in alarm. 'Good gracious! Already?'

'She'll be fourteen in September. All Maisie's children go into service after their fourteenth birthday. She has so many, she can't keep them all at home, and anyway they have to earn their own living.'

'But as a scullery maid?'

'Peggy, her own daughter, has been doing the job for two years. She's to be promoted to housemaid or something, and Maisie's planning to send Lizzie to take her place. She thinks it's a good opportunity. And having Peggy there should make it easier for Lizzie.'

She thought Nick was talking too quickly.

'Mother thought you'd want to know. Obviously, she couldn't just let it happen.' His eyes met Hannah's apologetically, as though afraid his mother had presumed too much.

Oh God! Why had she not thought of this? Hannah crashed her knife and fork down on her plate. She'd just kept sending the pittance for her keep, expecting things to stay the same for ever. Elizabeth was growing up and she hadn't considered what that would mean.

'Surely that's not what she wants? To be a scullery maid?'

'She accepts it. She doesn't expect to have any choice. It's already happened to Peggy, you see.'

Hannah felt cold with shock. 'But Elizabeth could do better for herself?'

'She's quick to pick things up. Very quick.' Nick was frowning in concentration. 'Bright as a button. I can see her running that boarding house before very long.'

Not a great future for a Mortimer, Hannah thought bitterly. She blamed herself. 'Not much of a life for the girl.'

What a fool she'd been! All those years ago, she'd let Matt persuade her to forget Lizzie. She should have done much more.

'I hate to think of Lizzie having a life of drudgery,' Nick went on earnestly.

He was making her feel even more guilty. She tried to think.

'What would be the best thing for her? How can we help her?'

'A few more years at school would be the best thing,' Nick answered briskly. 'Boarding school.'

Hannah looked at him with fresh eyes. 'Is that what your mother says?'

'It's what I say, but she agrees.'

Hannah wondered why she hadn't thought of that years ago? It would have got Lizzie away from Maisie O'Malley and given her a decent education. At the very least she and Matt should have seen to that. She warmed towards Nick, pleased that he seemed to like the girl.

She could pay the fees herself. Matt was generous with her dress allowance and never questioned what she spent on the house. He need never know, though she didn't think he'd object to boarding school.

She wrote to Clarissa the same evening and since she'd had more experience of boarding schools, asked her opinion as to which one they should approach.

What about Lucy's school? she suggested.

Clarissa wrote back:

Do come and see us. We need to discuss this, and talk it over with Lizzie. I still miss the gossipy sessions we used to have and a few days in the country would do you good.

I don't think Lucy's school would be the best choice for Lizzie. She and Lucy don't get on too well. Oddly enough, Nick seems to have more in common with her. I've sent for prospectuses from two different ones. If you come, we could arrange to go and see them together.

Of course Lizzie will want to know why you're willing to go to this trouble and expense for her. You'd better have your explanation ready before we do anything further.

The wisdom of that made Hannah think again.

Dorothy wouldn't want her to know. Apart from natural embarrassment, she'd kept Franklin Flower in ignorance and Lizzie now had four half-sisters.

Ridiculous to go to such lengths to cover it up fourteen years ago and now broadcast it. If she told Lizzie the truth, there was no knowing how far she'd spread it. She might even want to see her mother. Sir Hugo Mortimer's family was always news, and this could still seriously embarrass them all. Matt would be furious with her if she let the story out now. It could finish off her own marriage as well as Dorothy's.

But she'd wasted far too much time already. Hannah decided she would accept Clarissa's invitation.

Joey's fourteenth birthday had come at the end of April. As he had no job to go to, he was continuing to go to school until he had, or until school broke up for the summer holidays.

Lizzie was uneasy. Change was obviously coming, and not knowing what it would bring made it harder to bear. She knew it was weighing on Joey's mind too, though he pretended it did not. It made her wonder if all the talk of running away was just bravado, and in the end he'd go to a farm somewhere and she'd join Peggy in Crewe.

'We'll never see each other again if we let that happen,' he'd said. 'Our Peg has only been home once and it's getting on for two years since she went.'

'She's coming for a week in August.'

'When you're free to come home, you can guarantee it'll be harvest time and I won't be able to.'

They were walking home from school together a few weeks later. They'd reached the great iron gates of Yarrow Hall Farm, and the gatehouse came in view. Lizzie recognised the dogs circling the front door and snatched at Joey's arm.

'Mr Bender's here,' she breathed. 'Do you think he's come to take you on?'

She saw his newly prominent adam's apple move as he swallowed. Relief flickered and died in his lopsided eyes.

181

'He's probably come to see my dad.'

It was getting on for two years since Seamus had broken his leg, but he still used a stick to walk to the Madryn Arms. He had worked since, but never for more than a month or two at a time.

Maisie had been cleaning for the doctor's relatives in the dower house for over a year now. Just a few hours each morning to add to their income. Her employers had given her an old couch. All last week Seamus had taken time off work to lie on it.

'He says his leg aches if he stands on it for long, and farm work's hard. You know him, any excuse. He'll not want to hurry back.'

Joey took to his heels and burst into the living-room. Lizzie followed more slowly, allowing herself to hope.

'There you are.' Leo Bender was standing with his back to the empty grate. He beamed at Joey.

'Mr Bender's come to take you on.' His mother was all smiles, there was relief in her dark eyes too.

'Not permanently, I'm afraid, Joey. I can't do that, but with the hay harvest almost on us and your father still not fit to work, I'd like you to come as casual labour for a few weeks.'

'Yes, Mr Bender. That'll be a great help.'

Relief and joy exploded inside Lizzie's head. It put off the need for Joey to go elsewhere.

'If you get an offer of a permanent place, then of course you must take it.'

The next day, Miss Jones, their teacher at Pen-y-Clip school, gave him his leaving reference.

'It's not glowing, Joey, but I do my best to say something good about every child who passes through my school.' After she'd shaken his hand and wished him well for the future, and he'd said goodbye to his fellow pupils, he and Lizzie walked home from school together for the last time.

'Gives you a chance to finish school and me a chance to save some money,' Joey whispered afterwards.

182

'Some hope of that,' she retorted. 'Your mam will have it all off you.'

'No, she won't.' Joey's lips were set in a firm line. 'She needn't think I'm working instead of me dad. I'm not handing it all over.'

A week or two later, as Lizzie walked into the village on her way to school, she found housewives standing on their doorsteps gossiping instead of getting started on the day's work. They told her the village Post Office had been broken into during the night and several days' takings stolen.

Pen-y-Clip was a place where doors were always left open. Theft was unheard of in the village. Only the postmaster and the publican bothered to lock their doors at night and that hadn't stopped the thief.

Lizzie had a cold feeling in the pit of her stomach, and wondered whether Seamus could be responsible. She and Joey whispered about it at bedtime. Seamus seemed to have plenty of pipe tobacco in the following days and Maisie had butterscotch. They came to the conclusion it was more than likely.

Thursdays were the days Lizzie dreaded now. A busy cattle market was held in Pen-y-Clip every Thursday, and Seamus went regularly, hoping he'd hear of a farmer wanting to hire a young boy.

Farming remained depressed, but there was still a demand for school leavers in the district. They were strong and would work for a lower wage than their more experienced fathers.

When she came home from school on Thursdays, Lizzie expected to hear Seamus had succeeded. For three weeks on the run, she felt reprieved when she found he had not. Now, on the fourth, as soon as she closed the living-room door behind her she sensed the change. All the younger O'Malleys had arrived home before her and the atmosphere was unmistakably charged.

'You've found a place for Joey?' She could hardly get the words out.

183

'No.' Auntie Maisie's face was flushed. She was pacing round the small room. 'And hardly likely to after this.'

Uncle Seamus was lying on the couch, his bad leg stretched out in front of him. He looked spent, but roused himself sufficiently to spit out: 'They won't all have heard, so they won't. They come to the market from miles around.'

'Heard what?' Lizzie moistened her lips. 'What's happened?'

'You know the Post Office was broken into last week?' Maisie's eyes were round with horror. Lizzie nodded. 'Constable Watkins came here this morning. Dad's been down at the station all day. He's been charged.'

Lizzie's scalp crawled with horror. Seamus was good at talking his way out of trouble. Both she and Joey had expected him to get away with this even if he was guilty. He had a reputation for sailing close to the wind, but he'd never been in trouble with the police before.

'He searched the whole place. Looked in all my drawers and yours too.' Maisie was trying to sound indignant, but her sly smile betrayed her. 'But he found nothing.'

'Not a bloody penny of it,' Seamus said victoriously.

'I'm hungry,' little Flora complained.

Maisie had been too fraught all day to think of meals.

'I'll cook,' Lizzie said, but when she went to the larder it was almost empty. Seamus gave no sign that he had money. She found it hard to believe he'd eat bread and treacle for his supper if he had.

Afterwards she went up to see Tatty who let her make boiled bacon sandwiches for the children. She kept one for Joey when he came home though he was now fed with the other farm boys.

As he stood eating it at their bedroom window, he said: 'He's hidden the money somewhere, I'll bet my bottom dollar. Buried it perhaps?'

'Not in the garden,' Lizzie said. 'Soil hasn't been disturbed.' They looked down on it. Months ago cabbages had been planted but now they could hardly be seen for weeds.

'Under the water butt?' Joey hazarded. 'Under something.'

'There's a good side to this,' Lizzie murmured, leaning her forehead against the cool glass. 'Your mother's right. Who'll want to hire you now? If your father's proved to be a thief, they won't want you in case it turns out you've inherited his light fingers.'

Joey grinned. 'I'm going to sell my ferret all the same. If I have to leave, I might as well have the few bob for it. Might need it.'

But the fun had gone out of everything. Already they saw very little of each other. Joey was working until nine or ten at night in the hay harvest. He wasn't used to such hard work and was too exhausted to do anything but sleep when he came home.

The news came, just as Lizzie had expected, on a Thursday afternoon. She'd walked home from school with the three younger O'Malleys.

Seamus was rubbing his hands with satisfaction. 'Found a place for our Joey, I have.'

Lizzie had been untying Flora's bonnet. She straightened up, feeling as though the bottom had dropped out of her world. 'Where?'

'A farm called Pandy. Near Brithdir, eighteen miles or so from here, and higher in the hills.'

Lizzie's spirits fell. Eighteen miles was too far to walk.

'They want him to start on the first of July.' Maisie looked unusually cheerful. 'They'll be cutting their hay in the first spell of good weather after that.'

Lizzie was trembling. There was only one thing she could do. She ran straight up to the farm to tell Joey. She found him forking hay from on top of the cart to the top of the barn.

'We've nearly finished.'

'Last load, thank God!' His three fellow labourers were putting on a spurt now the end of the job was in sight.

'I hate the hay.' Joey had split his shirt up the back. His clothes were in rags. The huge shire horse between the shafts

185

shuffled restlessly, flicking its tail across its back to remove flies.

When Lizzie called the bad news up to him, his fellow workers jeered.

'Rotten luck, Joey! Who'd want to go through another bloody hay harvest this year?'

'It'd kill me!' He straightened up on his pike, his face running with perspiration.

For the first time Lizzie sensed his determination. She had the feeling he didn't intend to go quietly to Pandy. She walked home slowly, knowing big changes were on them now. Joey came home earlier than usual, as soon as milking finished.

'Come for a walk,' he said quietly, but threw himself down on the grass as soon as they'd put a few trees between them and the gatehouse. Lizzie sat with her back against an old oak.

'This is it,' he said. 'No putting it off any longer. I can pack your things along with mine. Everybody will think I'm going to Pandy. You'll say you're coming to the station to see me off and we'll both go to Birkenhead. How's that?'

'They'll expect me to go to school.'

'First of July is a Sunday, and I've got to be there the night before. We're in luck, we'll be leaving on a Saturday.'

'Why Birkenhead?'

'Isn't that what you want? Nick says it's where your mother is.'

Her stomach was churning with apprehension. 'Yes, where Nick is too.'

'We'll be all right.'

'Joey, you'll have to get a job. Look how long it's taken here, and it could take longer there. How will we manage?'

'Trust me, Lizzie. We'll manage. I'm going to make us rich.'

She was staring at him in disbelief, both hands pressing against her mouth.

'I've got palpitations, just thinking about it.'

'I know I can do it, but it might take a little time.'

She laughed then. She mustn't doubt Joey, he'd have it all worked out.

Joey went ahead with his preparations. Mrs Bender gave him a Sunday suit that Nick had grown out of and a blanket for his bed. The farm boys at Pandy slept over the stable and she'd heard he might need extra bedding. Somebody gave Maisie an old suitcase. One of the locks was broken but it could be tied with string and was easier to carry than a parcel.

Lizzie sorted through her own clothes and washed what she wanted to take. Joey wanted to pack them in his case, but she was afraid Maisie might see them there. She said they must stay in her drawer until the last moment. She was edgy and anxious.

Four miles beyond Pen-y-Clip was a somewhat larger village called Talybont. She and Joey walked there to consult time-tables at the railway station. His mother had given him money to buy his ticket to the farm. He brought it home to show her and announced that he was going to catch the afternoon train.

'We can catch a train in the opposite direction an hour later and change to the Birkenhead train at Ruabon. It's all working out,' he pointed out to Lizzie.

She woke early on Saturday morning in a lather of apprehension.

'Come on, get up,' Joey was whispering. 'Be quiet, we don't want to wake the others.'

Joey said they must be up first so they could cut jam sandwiches without anyone knowing. It would look suspicious, he thought, if he asked for food to take on an eighteen-mile journey.

Lizzie shivered as she pulled on her clothes and crept downstairs behind Joey. As soon as the fire burned up enough she put the half dozen eggs Joey had collected from the hen house last night in a pan to boil hard, all the time listening for sounds from the floor above.

Joey seemed calm as he packed the food into the pockets of a mackintosh that had once belonged to Nick. Lizzie couldn't

187

believe it was going to be as easy as he said it was.

During the morning she went up to the farm. Tatty had promised to make a cake for Joey to take with him. She showed Lizzie the fruit cake, already in a tin.

Clarissa Bender was in the kitchen too, making fairy cakes. She packed as many of her first batch round the fruit cake as the tin would take.

'Thank you,' Lizzie said. 'Joey's always hungry these days. He'll be pleased with these.'

'He's beginning to grow at last,' Tatty smiled. 'He's broadened out over the last few months.'

'I expect you'll miss him?' Mrs Bender was being kind.

Lizzie felt her heart jerk faster. She couldn't talk about missing him when she meant to go too. She said quickly: 'How's Nick? Does he like his new job?'

'I think so. We probably miss him more than he misses us. He says the changes aren't all for the better but he's probably settling down.'

'I'd like to write to him.' Lizzie could feel herself blushing. 'Would you mind?'

'I'll give you his address.' Mrs Bender smiled. 'He'd probably like to hear from you. Anyway, Lizzie, you'll be going yourself soon.'

'Yes.' She tried to ignore her pounding heart. Sooner than anyone supposed.

Maisie cooked them a good dinner, though Lizzie could hardly get hers down. Then the younger boys clamoured to walk to the station with Joey to see him off.

'Make them stay home, Mam,' Joey said as he kissed her goodbye. 'Lizzie will come and help me carry my things. I'd rather it was just her. You know how me and Lizzie are. We don't want them all hanging round us. It'll be hard to say goodbye to her.'

With her heart in her throat, Lizzie got herself ready and took one last look round the room she'd slept in all her life. Maisie was at the bottom of the stairs.

'You won't need that big coat today, Lizzie,' she said.

'You'll be too hot.' Lizzie opened her mouth in consternation, unable to speak. She couldn't possibly go without a coat.

'Mr Bender said the glass was falling.' Joey came to her aid, putting a hand on her sleeve and drawing her through the front door. 'He says the weather's breaking, it's going to rain and get much cooler.'

At last they were heading out through the ornate gates of Yarrow Hall. Lizzie turned to wave for the last time. As they walked through Pen-y-Clip several people wished Joey well and said goodbye. The postmaster's wife ran into the shop to get him a few boiled sweets to suck on the journey.

'Nice of her, considering what your dad's done,' Lizzie said. Miss Jones, the schoolmistress, waved from the school house window. It was a warm sunny afternoon and the walk to the station seemed long. Lizzie had to take off her coat and carry that too.

'We should be grateful it's a long way,' Joey reminded her. 'We don't want people waiting on the platform to see us off. With luck nobody we know will be there to see us getting on the wrong train.'

Talybont was a country halt with just two platforms, one used for trains going up the line, the other down. They watched the up train come through and two passengers get on.

'Burned my boats now,' Joey said as it pulled out. Then he gave Lizzie some money and steered her to the booking office to buy a ticket to Birkenhead.

'What about you?'

'I've already got a ticket. No point in throwing our money about.'

'Are we going to have enough?' Lizzie couldn't stop her anxieties showing. 'I mean, we'll have to eat . . .'

'We'll be able to eat. I didn't want to tell you until we'd left home, but I found the money Dad hid.'

'You mean – from the Post Office?' She only dared whisper the words after she'd made sure nobody else was within hearing.

'He buried it in a tobacco tin under the ferret cage. I searched the shed. I knew it had to be outside or Constable Watkins would have found it. I was afraid he'd hidden it in a hollow tree somewhere, or down a deserted rabbit burrow. That would have meant I couldn't have it, but someone might have come across it by accident.'

'How much?'

They crossed the bridge to the down platform. There were benches in the sun and a wooden shelter with seats inside. Lizzie felt conspicuous, and Joey didn't want to be recognised now. They went behind the shelter where they were less likely to be seen but there was only one person about and he was a railway employee raking the flower beds back to perfection.

'Dad only got eight pounds ten shillings,' Joey said. 'Well, that's all he's got left. Hardly enough, considering it put the police on his back and he's got to go to court over it.'

'But the ferret cage went last week. Weren't you afraid he'd check whether the money was still there?'

'I left it there 'til this morning. I cleaned out the cage before it went and dumped all the muck and straw on top. I was banking on him leaving it where it was until the whole business blows over. After all, he wouldn't want to spend money he couldn't account for now.'

Lizzie giggled nervously. 'I'd love to see his face when he finds it's gone.'

'I'd rather not! He owes us, Lizzie, and it'll give us a start.'

'But we have to be careful with it all the same.'

'Here's what we'll do if the ticket inspector comes round . . .'

It only served to put her on tenterhooks. 'I wish we'd bought two tickets. I wish your dad had got away with hundreds and we didn't have to do this.'

'Just be ready to slip me the ticket. That's all you'll have to do.'

The hour they had to wait dragged, but at last other people began to gather on the station. Lizzie was terrified they'd see someone they knew. Joey was biting his nails and every few minutes craning his neck in the hope of seeing the first plumes of smoke down the valley as the train approached. It came at last, sliding to a standstill in the station in a whoosh of escaping steam.

She'd never been on a train before but Joey had. Once Dr Moore had arranged for him to see a specialist in a Liverpool hospital. Seamus had taken him.

Lizzie was full of relief that they were on their way at last. The risk-taking began to be exciting; the sensation of speed was wonderful. She felt truly alive. Joey's eyes sparkled. Smuts were flying past the window and the taste of smoke was on Lizzie's tongue. She could see smoke trailing back as the engine curved round the valley.

They changed to the main line train. There were more passengers on this and they couldn't get a carriage to themselves. An elderly man was reading the *Manchester Guardian* in one window seat. Opposite him, a young mother nursed a shawl-wrapped baby on her lap and watched over a toddler who slept on the seat beside her.

'The ticket inspector's coming,' Joey was whispering out of the corner of his mouth. Suddenly Lizzie was stiff with nerves. From further up the corridor, she heard the call: 'Tickets, please.'

'You stay here, I'll move up the train. Be ready to slip me the ticket when I come back.'

Lizzie took the ticket from her pocket in readiness. She could see her hand shaking slightly as she waited.

Chapter Twelve

It took only seconds for the inspector to clip the tickets of the passengers in her carriage. As he left he slid the door across but it didn't quite click home. Lizzie, who was sitting closest to it, edged it back an inch or two with her foot, feeling a bag of nerves.

She must do her best for Joey, but what exactly?

She checked there was enough space to push her nearest hand through the door. Transferred the ticket to that hand. Checked that the other occupants of the carriage were not watching. The woman was looking out of the window at the flying scenery, the man reading. Lizzie crossed her knees so they would not be able to see her hand.

She didn't dare take her eyes from the corridor now as she watched for Joey.

Further down the train, she heard the inspector calling: 'Tickets, please,' and the sliding of doors as he closed them behind him.

Joey appeared silently as if from nowhere. She pushed the ticket at him and it was instantly snatched from her fingers. She craned forward to see what he did. He was opening a window further up the corridor, leaning out.

Then her stomach turned over as she saw the ticket inspector returning.

'Ticket please, sir,' he said to Joey. His tone was no longer polite, she knew he was suspicious. Joey must have passed him somehow.

'You've already punched it.' Joey's voice sounded unbelievably calm. She watched him fish the ticket out of his pocket, taking his time before handing it over. She was quaking, hardly daring to look.

'Right, thank you.' The inspector was giving it him back, returning down the corridor. The blood was pounding in Lizzie's head and she was sweating with relief. Joey had got away with it.

It was another ten minutes before he came back to sit opposite and his face was still pale.

They were coming into Birkenhead now. Terraces of smoke-blackened houses backed on to the line, Lizzie could see into countless back yards. It seemed dirtier and shabbier than Pen-y-Clip had ever done. The lines proliferated and snaked in all directions. The train was slowing.

They slid into a station with many platforms; she could see other trains waiting. She glimpsed a sign that read 'Birkenhead Woodside'. The air smelled different, smoke-laden and flat. A loud speaker blared out some message she couldn't grasp.

Lizzie had Joey's arm in a vice-like grip. She clutched the parcel under her other arm, dangling the cake tin by its string.

'Come on,' he urged, quickening his step. 'Keep up with the crowd. We've got to get through the gate in the thickest part of the crush.'

Lizzie went cold when she realised their tickets would be checked again.

Joey was holding them so it was just possible to see there were two, the valid one hiding the invalid. His knuckles showed white.

'Keep going whatever happens,' he whispered in her ear. 'Don't turn round.'

The crowd jostled them and they were borne through the gate as though on a tide. The tickets were snatched from Joey's grasp and not given another glance.

His pace speeded up. Lizzie's heart was in her mouth, but she ran with him until they came out of the station into a busy terminus.

'We managed it,' Joey crowed. 'Managed it very well.' The summer twilight was just deepening into night.

Lizzie stared about her. 'Are those what they call trams?'

'Must be. Even the buses look strange.'

'Where to now?' she asked.

Joey leaned against the station wall to get his breath back. Lizzie had never seen anything like the busy terminus in front of her. There were double decker buses coming and going, people streaming through the entrance to the ferries and others passing them to go into the railway station.

'Don't know. Couldn't think beyond getting here.'

They began to walk. It was uphill and Lizzie had never seen traffic like this. She hardly dared cross the road. A big hotel overlooked the terminus. The sign 'Woodside Hotel' was lit up. The lighted windows looked inviting.

'Where are we going to sleep?' Now she was calming down that seemed the most pressing problem.

'Not in there, we can't afford it. We'll find a room or something.'

'It's almost ten now.' Lizzie bit her lip. 'And we've no idea where to start looking.'

'I'll buy a newspaper. That'll tell us.'

Lizzie had heard the news vendor's raucous call, but had not understood the words until now. '*Liverpool Echo, Echo, Echo.*'

From the bar, a roar of ribald laughter rose above the babel of voices, and a waft of hot air from the dining-room carried the savoury scent of roasting beef.

'It's almost too dark to see small print.' Joey refolded the paper. 'And I'm hungry.'

'We can't eat here either.' For her own part, Lizzie felt irritable and exhausted. 'We've still got plenty of cake.'

They walked on up the hill, past shops that were now closed, until they came to a square of elegant buildings. A clock in a tower struck ten. There was a garden in the middle.

'Could we sleep in there?' Lizzie looked at the grass. 'It's a dry night.'

'No.' Joey pulled her along after one short glance. 'Too many people about. Too small and too many flower beds. Be all right if we could find a wood.'

'We'll never find a wood here, we're heading into town. There's more shops. I think we should get away from here, it's too busy.'

They stood undecided on the pavement. 'There's a bus coming,' Lizzie said. 'It says Rock Ferry on the front. That's where Nick's living now. Mrs Bender said it was on the outskirts of town.'

When it stopped almost in front of them to pick up passengers, Joey took her arm and hoisted his suitcase.

'Good idea,' he said. Lizzie followed him up the narrow stairs to the top deck.

The bus jerked forward. Joey paid their fares and asked the conductor to put them off in Rock Ferry. There were lights twinkling everywhere. Shops and houses lined the busy road which stretched ahead for what seemed miles. Lizzie felt mesmerised.

They only realised they'd gone too far when the bus turned into a bus shed and everybody stood up to get off.

'Where are we?' Lizzie asked.

'New Ferry. You can stay on the bus, it'll be going back in ten minutes.'

But Joey pulled at her arm. He'd seen a small cafe displaying boards with chalked prices they could afford. 'This is as good as anywhere,' he said, pausing to consider the menus they offered.

Lizzie waited restlessly. She wanted, more than anything else, to put her head down and sleep. She ached with exhaustion. The emotional effort of leaving home had left her drained.

New Ferry seemed a busy place too, though most of the shops were closed now even though it was Saturday night. Light spilled out on to the pavements, but there were fewer people about. Lizzie's arm ached with carrying her bundles and she thought with longing of the bed she'd shared with Flora. For the first time, she wanted to be back in the gatehouse.

'Perhaps there's a park. If there were shrubs to hide us . . .'

'Let's ask,' Lizzie yawned, and stopped an elderly man coming out of a pub to do so.

'Yes,' he told her, looking at her strangely. 'Just along there.' He pointed the way they must go.

'I can see a fish and chip shop,' Joey said. 'We'll get some to eat as we walk along. You'll feel better with something hot inside you.'

Lizzie agreed. Her mouth filled with saliva as she waited at the counter. She pulled at Joey's sleeve.

'Let's ask if they know where we can find a room.'

But he shook his head. 'Not here.'

The chips were delicious and she did feel better with food inside her. The park was only a short walk, but when they came to it, they found it had iron railings round and gates as big as those at Yarrow. They were firmly locked.

'We'll get in somewhere,' Joey said enthusiastically. 'This will be fine.' There was a handsome black and white building at the gates but it was all in darkness.

They kept on walking but here houses had been built between the pavement and the park. They came to a side street. It seemed to mark the end of the park in that direction. They turned into it.

'We've been walking for ages.' Lizzie hadn't meant to complain but she felt ready to lie down on the pavement.

The moon had come up and they could see a little more. There were fewer lights on in the houses, and those were mostly in the upper windows now.

'Everybody's going to bed,' Lizzie said as they trudged on.

'Here's an empty house,' Joey said suddenly. 'No curtains, look.'

'It'll be locked.' Lizzie let her bundles slide to the pavement to rest her arms. 'What are we going to do, Joey?'

'It has a big garden.'

Lizzie looked up and down the road. It was deserted. Joey had the front gate open.

'Let's see if we can get round the back. Walk on the grass,

so as not to make a noise. No point in letting the neighbours know we're here.'

The front door, when he tried it, wouldn't budge. The two massive Victorian bay windows on each side were too high to reach. The front garden was shut off from the back by a door set into a wall. That too was locked.

Joey set his suitcase against the door. 'I want a leg up. Might just be able to get a toe hold on the thumb latch and nip over the top. You stand there and I'll step on your shoulder.'

After one painful jerk, Joey was up and slithering down on the other side of the wall. A second later she heard the bolts being drawn and she was through.

Joey was trying the back of the house. 'I'd have to break a window to get in.'

'We'll be all right here.' Lizzie felt a little safer with the door securely bolted again. She told herself they couldn't be disturbed. 'As long as it doesn't rain.'

Then she saw the moonlight shining on the glass. 'There's a green house here.' She tried the door and it opened to her touch with just the slightest scrape on the uneven floor. Inside, the air was warm and musty.

'This is it,' she crowed. 'Won't matter if it does rain now.'

Joey pushed in behind her. She could just see him feeling his way round. 'Beds of soil, built up. Just like real beds and as dry as bone. Nothing's been planted. This house must have been empty for ages.'

'Everything's died off because it's not been watered.'

'Let's have that blanket. We can scoop out little hollows for our hip bones. This'll be a great place to camp.'

Lizzie had the string undone and the blanket out.

'Boots off,' Joey said. 'I'll find us each an extra pair of socks. Got to be comfortable.'

Lizzie could feel herself drifting off almost as soon as her head was down on the makeshift pillow. She tucked her coat under her chin. Somewhere in the distance a dog barked.

★ ★ ★

As Hannah packed her suitcase she thought of Clarissa; she was looking forward to seeing her again.

Silly to have been so grateful for what Clary had done and still let their friendship die. Almost die . . .

Perhaps, when she saw Elizabeth, she'd be reassured that what she'd done was not so very wrong? Matt had thought it all for the best. If the child had been happy . . .

The journey to Yarrow brought back memories. She'd forgotten how beautiful the Welsh countryside was. In Pen-y-Clip the years had changed only one thing: the road was Tarmacadamed now. Matt had complained how much the rutted earth track had jolted his Di Dion all those years ago. She slowed down as she came to the entrance to Yarrow Hall.

The gates themselves had been rehung but stood wide open. The lichen on the lions had been scraped off. The gatehouse seemed smaller. A little girl was standing at the open door wearing a torn and dirty dress several sizes too big for her. Hannah stopped the car. It was on the tip of her tongue to call to her and ask for Elizabeth.

She stopped herself in the nick of time. It would be more discreet to ask Clarissa. A boy who had been throwing stones up into a tree was running towards her. Both his elbows stuck out through the sleeves of a V-necked pullover which he wore without a shirt. The difference between these children and Dorothy's girls appalled her. She put the car in gear and moved off.

The ten-acre park was dotted with sheep and cattle, just as she remembered it. The dower house was just a roof seen through the trees as she drove up the drive.

Yarrow Hall Farm had been recently painted. It looked trim and more prosperous than it had. Clarissa met her at the door, bubbling a welcome as she kissed her cheek.

Clary had hardly changed at all except for the smile lines round her eyes. Leo's hand clasp was warm enough, though he seemed wary. He looked older and a little stouter.

They'd hardly got her as far as the sitting-room fire before she had to ask about Elizabeth.

'She's very well,' Clarissa said, her manner formal. The change made Hannah uneasy. 'We didn't know what to do for the best.'

'She doesn't know – about Dorothy?'

'No. She thinks Maisie is her aunt.'

Hannah pushed her dark hair from her forehead. 'I'm longing to see her but . . . It isn't going to be easy to explain why I'm interested in her.'

'No need to say anything yet,' Clarissa soothed. 'She often comes into our kitchen. I've asked Tatty to let us know next time she does. We'll go down and start doing something. She needn't know you have any special interest.'

'You think of everything,' said Hannah gratefully.

'She was up here this morning, but we probably won't see her again today.'

Hannah felt disappointed. 'I'll have to be patient a little longer then.'

'I'm afraid so. She said she was going to see Joey O'Malley off. His father's found him a job. A farm some distance from here. She'll miss Joey, they've been inseparable 'til now.'

Both Jonathon and Hal had come home, and for Hannah the evening passed pleasantly. They all wanted to hear about Nick though he'd been home for a weekend visit since going to Birkenhead. Leo thought he was settling in. Hannah was able to describe his lodgings. Clarissa was reassured because she'd chosen them for him. She told them all she could about his work and about Evans's toffee factory.

Next morning she and Clarissa sat in the garden and talked.

'I want Elizabeth to think boarding school is your idea,' Hannah said. 'Matt won't be happy with anything else. I'll help choose the school, I'll pay for it, but she mustn't connect the Mortimer name with it. I hate to ask more of you, but will you go along with that?'

'I suppose so.' Clarissa's face told her she'd found Lizzie a responsibility. One she didn't feel she'd discharged satisfactorily.

'She won't question it, will she? She knows you, Clary. Nick says you've been kind to her all her life.'

Clarissa sighed. 'I'll do it, of course. It's in Lizzie's best interests.'

'I'm afraid Matt and I have left far too much to you.'

'I'll have a word, when she next comes up.'

Hannah was anxious to see her plan put into action. 'Does she come every day?'

'It's Sunday, she always comes on Sunday mornings. She likes to help Tatty cook lunch. Tatty gives her food to take home for the other children.'

But lunch time came and went and nobody had seen Lizzie. It was Leo who brought them the news when he came in for his tea.

'Harry Parry says she's run away. That she went down to the station to see Joey off and never came back. They're all talking about it.'

'I'd better go down and talk to Maisie,' Clarissa said. 'What's she doing about it?'

Hannah was struggling for breath. She felt stiff with awful foreboding.

Lizzie was woken by a gentle tap-tap on the glass roof and, looking up, could see the yellow feet of birds splaying out as they walked. Beside her Joey was laughing.

'Funny to see them from underneath. Not a bad night's lodging, was it? Slept like a couple of tops.'

Lizzie laughed. The sun was streaming in, she felt better. 'Now it's daylight, I'm not sure I like all this glass. If someone came into the garden, we would be seen.'

'Who's likely to come?'

'It's all right for the odd night or two but not for the long term.'

'I can see an outside tap. We could have done a lot worse. This is high-class camping.'

'What are we going to do today?'

Joey got out the newspaper and started reading the adverts.

'Find us a room. What about some breakfast first?'

'We've got hard-boiled eggs left and some cake. I'm going to have a wash first under that tap.'

'All mod cons here.' He fluttered the pages open. 'There's plenty of places advertised. One room would be enough to start with until I get myself a job. Pity I can't look for work today.'

'You should,' she said.

'It's Sunday.'

'Why don't we see if we can find Nick Bender? I've got his address. Perhaps he'll help us get jobs in the same toffee factory.'

'That's a wonderful idea, Lizzie! Nick said your family owns it. We'd be well placed to get even with them then.'

'Never mind about getting even, what we have to have are jobs. I just want to be sure we can eat and have somewhere to live.'

'Oh, come on, Lizzie, we'll be all right. But it's a smashing idea. Where does he live?'

She'd put Nick's address in her coat pocket. 'He lives in Rock Ferry, we can get a bus. My legs are still stiff with all that walking last night.'

'Nonsense. It did us good to stretch our legs after sitting down in that train all afternoon.'

Joey looked through the newspaper, putting pencil ticks opposite the cheapest rooms.

Lizzie tidied up, shaking the blanket free of soil. 'Are we going to leave our things here?'

'I dunno.' Joey hesitated. 'Be terrible if someone came and saw them. We might get them pinched.'

From inside the glass house the garden seemed a tangle of green overgrowth. The grass was thigh-high and there were plenty of unpruned trees and shrubs with thick foliage.

Lizzie said: 'We could hide our stuff somewhere out there. There's a real tangle of bushes, nobody would notice a case under them. We could even bury it if you like. I don't want to lug it round.'

'If we can't get a room, we'll come back here tonight. It's not too bad, better than out in the park.'

It took a long time to get ready. They dug a hole under some flowering shrubs, using old slates they found, and covered their belongings with soil.

When Lizzie showed Nick's address to a man selling newspapers, they discovered they were not very far from Rock Ferry, but it took some time to find the right road.

Nick's lodging was in a substantial Victorian semi, set in a well-kept garden. The front door was as large and solid as that of a church and glistened with new black paint. They were let in and directed up to the fourth floor.

'Something like this would suit us fine,' Lizzie whispered as they climbed the stairs. The banister was polished mahogany. The carpet gave way to linoleum after the second floor.

'This would cost too much for us.'

Nick answered their knock.

'Hello, Nick.' Lizzie found it comforting to see his familiar brown eyes after so many strange faces. His mouth was open with surprise.

'I can't believe . . . What are you two doing here?'

'We've run away,' Lizzie said.

'What on earth for?' Alarm rang in his voice.

'I'm not working on any farm.' Joey sounded sullen.

'But Lizzie! What's made you come?'

'Maisie was getting ready to send me to Crewe.'

'No.' Nick seemed quite put out. 'I told you, Joey! I told you to tell her. That weekend I went home, you were milking at the time. My mother's sending for prospectuses of boarding schools, she's choosing one for you, Lizzie. Everything was coming right.'

'A boarding school?'

'Yes, like the one Lucy goes to.'

'She didn't say anything to me about it.' Lizzie frowned. 'And I was talking to her the morning we left.'

'For some reason she didn't want you to know yet. She was

very insistent that I say nothing to you, so I didn't, I told Joey. I knew you were worried about Crewe.'

Lizzie shivered. Doubts were crowding in on her. 'Joey, why didn't you say?'

'Schools like that cost money.' He was belligerent. 'Why would she do it? I don't believe it.'

'It's the gospel truth,' Nick said furiously. 'None of us wanted to see you packed off as a scullery maid. We wanted to help you.'

She could see Nick was upset. His eyes shone with honesty and Joey wouldn't look at her. 'It would have been far better, Lizzie, if you'd stayed where you were until she'd organised it.'

'We're staying together,' Joey snapped. 'That's what we agreed, didn't we?'

'Honestly, what a silly thing to do!' Nick blazed at him.

'I wanted us to be together. And Lizzie wanted to come, she said she did.'

'Yes, but if I'd known . . .' Lizzie put her hands to her face in an agony of doubt. 'Why didn't you tell me, Joey?'

'Joey, you must have known how much better it would be for Lizzie. How selfish can you get? You must go back, Lizzie.'

'No, you're spoiling everything. I want her here with me. She'll be perfectly all right.'

'Oh, Joey! You should have told me. I had a right to know.'

'Don't you start on me too. Everything was going well. I wish we'd never come near Nick.' Joey was angry and sullen. The frosty silence dragged on, then Nick seemed to give up and changed the subject.

'Where are you staying?'

'Well, we haven't got anywhere yet,' Lizzie said.

'You didn't sleep out?'

'Yes, but that was all right too, wasn't it, Lizzie?'

'I'll help you get somewhere.' Nick was tight-lipped with disapproval.

'What I really want help with is getting a job. I could find

204

us somewhere to live if I had money to pay for it.'

'You've no money?' Lizzie could see incredulity on Nick's face now. He seemed suddenly grown up. She was afraid he was going to grapple with Joey.

'Yes, we have.' Joey was only just in control of his temper. 'We're all right for money, it's jobs me and Lizzie need. Couldn't we come and work where you do?'

'I don't know about that.' Nick rubbed his chin thoughtfully. 'Though they are looking for a new office boy.'

'That would suit me down to the ground.' Joey's desperation made him eager. 'What would I have to do?'

'See to the post, make the tea. Run errands and help generally.'

'I could do that easily.'

'Yes, but it's not up to me. I don't decide who gets the job.'

'Who does? Couldn't you put in a good word for me?'

'The job was advertised in the newspapers a week or so back. We had a lot of applicants. School leavers, that's what we were asking for.'

'That's me,' said Joey earnestly. 'I know I could do it.'

'Please help him, Nick,' Lizzie said.

He sighed heavily. 'I did get the job of picking out the best three or four and sending for them. Mr Gleeson's going to interview them tomorrow morning.'

'Couldn't I come along too? Come on, fix it up for me, for old times' sake.'

'You're asking a lot.' Nick's face was tense.

'For Lizzie's sake. Please.'

'I don't know . . .'

'Go on,' Joey urged. 'What do I have to do?'

'You'll have to write a letter of application. Now, straight away.'

'Tell me what to say, and I'll do it.'

Nick got out his writing pad. 'Your letter will have to make you seem better than the others. What about your address?'

'We're in the back garden of a house in Stanley Road. What number is it, Lizzie?'

Nick shook his head in disbelief.

'Who's to know we're camping in the garden?'

'If a letter was posted there, would you get it?'

'Not if the postman puts it through the front door,' Lizzie said. She couldn't stop thinking about being sent to boarding school. She couldn't believe Joey wouldn't always do the best for her. Wasn't sure whether she could believe any of the story.

'You'd better put this address on it.' Nick pursed his mouth with reluctance. 'There are four more lodgers here.'

'Good idea, then you'll get any reply and be able to give it to me.'

'I hope Mr Gleeson doesn't remember that I live here too, and ask me about you.'

Joey had his pen poised. 'What shall I say?'

'Let me think.' Nick pondered a long time but the sentences came. 'Aged fourteen. Just left school.' Lizzie listened, knowing he was putting plenty of gilt on what Joey had achieved there.

'Start again,' Nick ordered when he read it through. 'A neater copy, in your best handwriting.'

'This is just like school,' Joey grumbled.

'It's worse,' Nick told him. 'They set even greater store on neat handwriting.'

'I'll take it in tomorrow morning and put it under the letters I've picked out. Yours will be the fifth, and he said three or four, but your letter's as good as any. Make sure you look smart, wear a tie. Have you got a suit?'

'Your mother gave me one of yours.'

'Show you know a bit about the firm. What we make, that sort of thing.'

'You'll have to tell us,' Lizzie said.

Nick reeled off a list.

'How much will they pay me?'

'Less than a pound a week.'

'That's not much. I'm surprised they go to all this trouble.'

'If you look alert and jump to it they might give you

206

another half-crown after six months. You might eventually be made a clerk.'

'It'll do, anything will do. At least it'll be regular.'

'You've still got to convince Mr Gleeson.'

'I can manage that. Me mam says I don't need to kiss the Blarney Stone.'

'Hah. You wait 'til you come face to face with him. Things may not go your way.'

Lizzie stirred herself. 'Bet it does. Joey always gets what he wants.'

Chapter Thirteen

1 July 1934

Lizzie felt uneasy. She could see Nick studying her, frowning, pushing his thick brown hair back off his forehead.

'Lizzie, come with me to see Mrs Mortimer this afternoon. She'll help you.'

'No, Lizzie,' Joey protested. 'They'll persuade you to go home. Then I'll be on my own.'

'My mother will be worried stiff, you going off like that. Did you leave a note?'

'No.'

'Lizzie's staying with me,' Joey said obstinately. 'She can always go back later, can't she?'

'They're trying to find a school for her. You don't want them to stop looking.'

'Lizzie'll write and tell your mother she still wants it,' Joey said. 'She'll go back later.'

She burst out: 'I wish you'd both stop arguing about me.'

'There's a train this afternoon, Lizzie. I'll take you to the station and then find a phone and ask my mother to meet you.'

'Why won't you take no for an answer?' Joey's rage spilled over. It made Lizzie want to reach out to him. She could sense his growing desperation. She knew she was his security, in the same way he was hers. Together they could do anything. Apart, she felt lost. Joey must feel the same.

Nick changed tack. 'What about your dinner? Where will you have that today?' Already there was a wonderful smell of cooking drifting upstairs.

'We'll go to a cafe or something. Leave us alone, can't you?'

'Why don't I go down and ask if my landlady has enough to feed you two?'

'How much will she charge?'

'It'll be on me. It's the least I can do.'

'Ask her,' said Joey, 'if she's got an empty room too.'

'I know she hasn't, but she might know of somewhere.'

'That'd be a help,' Lizzie said, and sat listening as Nick's footsteps squelched on the linoleum as he ran downstairs.

'Don't let him persuade you,' Joey said through clenched teeth. 'I need you, Lizzie. Haven't we always stuck together?'

She felt twisted in two. Nick, she knew, had her best interests at heart, but she couldn't imagine what that sort of school would be like.

'I'm not leaving you, don't worry.'

'You'd be on your own in a boarding school. We'd be apart for years. It would change you. It would never be the same for us after that.'

Lizzie shivered. Joey had always been the most important person in her life. All her hope, support and affection had come from him, she couldn't imagine being without him.

'You're in luck,' Nick said when he came back. Not only could they stay for dinner, but the landlady's cousin had a room she wanted to rent.

'She says it's not as good as this, but it'll be all right. She's asking twelve-and-sixpence a week.'

'Just for one room?' Joey asked. 'How can we afford that?'

'You get breakfast and evening meal as well.'

'For one?'

'Yes, for one. I want Lizzie to go home. My mother would never forgive me if I let you stay here, without anywhere to live.'

'No,' said Lizzie. 'I'm staying with Joey. I'll get a job too.'

'Me and Lizzie stick together. We're twins, aren't we?'

'That's childish nonsense and you know it. You're too

young, Lizzie. I don't like to think of you wandering about on the streets, it isn't safe.' Nick put the weight of his eighteen years behind his words. 'You're just a couple of kids, you don't know what you're doing.'

'It's no more difficult to manage here than it was at home. Our place wasn't like yours, you know,' Joey said fiercely.

'I do wish you'd stop fighting over me,' Lizzie said. 'I couldn't let Joey come on his own.'

While they were tucking into a good dinner, Joey looked up. 'Can you show me where I have to go tomorrow? I don't know where to find Evans's.'

'It's in Birkenhead, not far from Cammell Laird's. You have to walk under the railway bridge. I could take you on the bus to see the place.'

'Thanks,' Joey said. 'That would be a big help.'

Lizzie found herself on the top deck of a bus again.

'You can pick up the bus at the sheds in New Ferry,' Nick explained, as they walked down to the bus stop. They had to walk a short distance at the other end too.

'They've been making toffee here for over a hundred years,' Nick told them when the building came in sight.

'Looks like it,' Joey said, pulling a face.

Lizzie had seen pictures of old cotton mills in her school books that looked like this. It was a high gaunt building of smoke-blackened bricks, with iron bars on the small windows. The large sign which read 'Archibald Alfred Evans. Toffee Makers to the World' was crusted with dirt too. Lizzie thought it looked a depressing place. 'Do you like working here, Nick?'

'Not much.' A sweet, rather sickly smell of toffee hung about it and the adjoining streets.

'Why is it called Evans's if it belongs to the Mortimers?' Joey demanded. 'It doesn't make sense to me.'

Nick explained. 'Hugo Mortimer bought it from the Evans family as a going concern. He'd have lost trade if he'd changed the name.'

He hurried them back to the bus stop. 'I'm going up to

Prenton to see Mrs Mortimer now. I want you to come with me, Lizzie.'

'No.' Joey had a mulish look on his face. 'Leave her alone, can't you?'

'If I'm going to do something for you, Joey, you have to do something for me,' Nick said.

'I'm sorry I asked you to help. I'd have got a job on my own if I'd known.'

'Go ahead and try then. I'll have to go and see Mrs Mortimer by myself.' Nick was frowning. 'Lizzie, they'll be out of their minds at Yarrow. She'll let them know.'

A thought was pounding in her head. 'Is she my mother?' It had been on her mind since Nick had first mentioned her, that day in the stables at Yarrow. 'I do want to find my mother.'

'I'm not sure.'

'You said she was. A long time ago, you said she was.'

'I don't know, Lizzie. She's very kind, she'll want to help you.'

'Let's go, Joey.' Lizzie turned to him. 'If she's my mother, I want to know. You said you'd help me look for her. Isn't that why we both came to Birkenhead?'

'I don't want . . .'

'I won't go home and I won't stay with her,' Lizzie told him through clenched teeth. 'Now will you come?'

Joey gave in with very bad grace. He sulked on the seat behind them in the bus. Walked behind them dragging his feet when they got off.

The sight of Oakridge made Lizzie catch her breath in disbelief.

'Is this her home?' She let her eyes feast on its many windows, elegant porch.

'It's a mansion,' Joey added.

Lizzie hung back shyly when Nick rang the front door bell. A woman in a maid's uniform opened it. She knew Nick. Lizzie felt hope die when she heard her say Mrs Mortimer had gone away for a few days.

Nick's spirits seemed to droop. 'Would you mind if I used the telephone? I'd like to ring home and talk to my mother.'

Lizzie hung back. 'We'll go, Nick,' she said awkwardly. 'No point in us staying if she's not here.'

Joey was feeling for her hand, pulling her down the path. She could feel his relief that Nick had achieved nothing.

'Don't forget to do the necessary for tomorrow, Nick,' he called cheekily. 'I'll get there before ten.'

Nick asked the operator for the Yarrow number.

'Nick?' His mother sounded distraught. 'We've just discovered Lizzie O'Malley has disappeared. It seems she went to the station and . . .'

'She's here, Mother, in Birkenhead. That's what I'm ringing about. I've seen her and Joey, they came to my rooms this morning.'

'Is he there too? We were wondering . . . Maisie's certain he's gone to his farm job.'

'He's here, Mother, I've just said so.'

'Nick, you must persuade her to come back.'

'I can't. I've been trying to, but she wants to stay here. She's determined.'

'Tell her we're looking for a school.'

'I already have. I don't think she believes me.'

His mother sounded cross with him. 'You can't have tried very hard.' Nick shuffled his feet on the carpet and didn't answer. 'Is she all right? Does she look well?'

He thought of Lizzie. She had plaits fastened with elastic bands like all Maisie's girls. But while theirs were mousey and finger thin, Lizzie's hair was ash blonde and the plaits thick long ropes. She was almost as thin as the O'Malley children, but taller and stronger. She wore the same heavy boots and crumpled clothes and had the same air of vulnerability.

He'd grown used to seeing Lizzie about his home. He'd teased her as he did Lucy. He remembered her sitting watching him in the playroom when he'd been building his first crystal set, and the look of utter astonishment and pleasure on her face when he'd handed her the earphones and she'd heard her first broadcast. He'd larked about with her, he liked her. He was afraid she'd come to harm. Fourteen was far too young for her and Joey to be on their own.

'Make sure you stay in contact with her. Do you know her address?'

'I don't think she has one yet.'

'I blame the O'Malley lad. He's always up to some mischief.'

'He wants the job as office boy at Evans's.'

'What job?'

'Office boy.'

'Look, Nick, Mrs Mortimer's here. Hannah Mortimer. She says . . . Such a shock to find Lizzie gone.'

'I didn't know she was with you.'

'Just for a few days. She wants a word with you, hold on.'

Nick closed his eyes and waited. Hannah Mortimer's voice, when it came, had a note of urgency. She made him repeat every detail and asked more questions.

'Please don't lose contact with Elizabeth. I was looking forward so much to seeing her. I can't believe she's gone. That I'd have seen her if I'd stayed at home!'

He had to tell her they had no lodging yet.

'Ask Greg to make sure Joey O'Malley gets the job. Have you got that? They'll stay together, won't they? I'll be able to find Lizzie if you do that.'

'They'll stay together,' Nick said.

'Everything I try to do for the girl is always too little and too late,' Hannah mourned. 'I'll be home on Tuesday. I'll have a word with her then.'

Together Lizzie and Joey ran back to the bus stop, took one bus into town and then immediately caught another out to New Ferry again. Riding on the top of a double decker bus was a novelty they enjoyed. It bounced Joey back to his usual good temper.

They had a walk round but all the shops were closed.

214

They found the Labour Exchange.

'I'll get a job too,' Lizzie said cheerfully. 'This is the place for me to come tomorrow.'

The windows were covered with green paint so it was impossible to see in and she could see no jobs advertised.

'The important thing now is to find ourselves a room.' Joey took out the newspaper page he'd folded into his pocket. Lizzie put her head close to his, to study the ticks he'd made on it.

There were two rooms advertised to let in New Ferry. It took time, because they had to keep asking the way, and energy to find the addresses given. The first room was dark and dirty and one peep decided them against it. The second was a sunny and pleasant upstairs room overlooking a back garden.

Lizzie felt relief as soon as she saw it. She knew she'd feel more settled if she could get a roof over her head. 'I like this. It would suit us down to the ground.'

'They're asking too much,' Joey said crossly. 'No wonder they didn't put the rent in the paper.'

'We've got to get somewhere,' she said. 'Be reasonable, we can always move later if we find a cheaper place.'

'No, I said,' Joey barked, his face tight with tension.

Lizzie felt exhausted. They went into the park and sat on the grass.

'Sorry, but it was more than we could afford.' He stopped a Wall's ice cream tricycle and treated them to a penny Snowfruit each by way of consolation. The sky was growing more overcast and it was no longer warm enough to sit about. Soon there was drizzle in the air.

'Let's go back to the green house then.' Lizzie was trying hard not to complain. 'It's getting miserable here.'

Joey was reluctant. 'It would be safer to wait 'til after dark.'

'It won't be dark for hours and we'll be soaked. Even under this tree we're getting wet.'

'We don't want to be seen going in.' He insisted they walk across the top of the road first. They could see an old man

215

and a boy walking a dog, so they went on a few yards to give them time to get out of the way. There was a car parked outside one of the houses further down. Joey continued to hesitate.

'What if the owner comes out and sees us?' He was all for walking on.

'We'll have to risk it,' Lizzie said in a voice that brooked no argument. It was beginning to rain more heavily and she was worried the things they'd buried would get wet.

'The bushes will shelter them,' Joey insisted. 'But come on then, let's get in and out of sight as fast as we can.'

Even he was smiling with relief as he shot the bolts behind them on the door to the back garden.

'I don't think we've been seen. Did the curtains twitch opposite?'

'No.' Lizzie was relieved. 'We're in safe and sound.'

But in the overgrown garden, it was impossible to move from the path without getting wet. The shrubs and trees were in full leaf and dripping with moisture. The long grass made her stockings wet.

Lizzie felt cold drips down her neck as they dug up their belongings. Rain dripped off Joey's face, and worse, he was proved wrong about their belongings staying dry. The brown paper was disintegrating around the blanket and that was wet too.

They hurried with them to the green house. Lizzie pushed open the door expecting to feel the same airless warmth she'd felt the previous night. Instead it felt chill and damp. Drips were pattering down on to the soil where they'd slept the night before. A little pool was collecting in the hole she'd dug for her hip. It hadn't even occurred to her that the green house might not be water tight. For the first time she noticed several panes were cracked.

'Joey!'

He dropped the suitcase and put his arms around her, hugging her tight.

'This is awful! What are we going to do?'

'I don't know. Lizzie, I'm sorry. We should have had that room.'

'We've got plenty of money,' she said. 'Hardly spent any yet.'

'I wanted to keep it in case we need . . .'

'Isn't this a need? We'll never need anything more.'

'I'm sorry.' He kissed her cheek. 'I never thought.'

'What are you keeping the money for?'

'To make more. Lots of people could be rich if only they could put their hands on a few pounds to start off.'

'We have to live too, Joey.'

'We were all right last night. I didn't realise that if the weather broke . . .'

'Neither did I,' Lizzie admitted. 'I suppose it's a bit late to start looking now?'

'We need another newspaper.' Joey was untying his suitcase. 'Look, this corner isn't too bad and at least we know we won't be disturbed.'

'What are you doing?'

'There's a nail here, I'm going to hang up my suit and best shirt so they won't be creased tomorrow.'

Paving stones had been laid along the floor. They were hard and cold but at least they were dry. They decided to keep all their clothes on and roll themselves in the blanket. Lizzie clung to Joey's warm body for comfort. His arms held her tight.

'Are you sorry you said you'd stay with me?' he whispered, his breath warm against her cheek.

'No, we belong together. This is what we planned.'

'Nick was right, I shouldn't keep saying we're twins. We aren't any relation, Lizzie, though we've always been together.'

'Shared the same cradle.'

'We'll get married when we're properly grown up. That's what we'll do.'

'We always said we would.'

'Tomorrow we'll get a room,' Joey promised as they tried to settle down to sleep again. The rain splattered against the glass and the drips were only too audible.

By morning Lizzie felt dishevelled and damp. She would have liked a good wash, but the best she could do was to splash cold water on her face. She advised Joey to do the same. After all, it was important they both looked as though they'd spent a night in bed.

Joey dressed himself up in his suit and borrowed Lizzie's comb. He was thankful to find the rain had stopped, so he wouldn't get a soaking on the way.

Joey felt nervous as he took the bus down to Evans's. So much depended on his having this job. No other would be quite so good for his purpose. The factory looked even more forbidding this morning, against the dark sky.

Nick had told him that the other applicants would have received letters telling them all to come at ten o'clock for an interview. Joey hoped he wouldn't be asked to show his letter. If he was, he'd pretend he'd left it at home. Nick had said they would be seen on a first come, first in basis, so he planned to be early.

But because neither he nor Lizzie owned a watch, when he reached Evans's, he found the office staff still streaming in to work. He followed. A clock in the entrance hall told him it was an hour before the appointed time.

He was swept into a cloakroom by a crowd of men. Most seemed of a different breed to those he was used to. They were smartly dressed in suits and clearly knew each other. They juggled newspapers, umbrellas and brief cases while they hung hats and mackintoshes on pegs.

Joey was afraid one might ask him his business. He was afraid too that the man who was to interview him might be amongst them. Many were middle-aged. He shot into a cubicle and locked the door until the chorus of good mornings had died down and the silence told him he was alone.

Then, because there was hot water, soap and towels, he decided he might as well take his shirt off and wash properly. When he'd finished, he wrapped the soap in toilet paper and put it in his pocket to take back for Lizzie.

He checked again with the clock in the hall. He still had time to kill so he went out into the street again and walked briskly. There were other factories near by. He knew he was close to Cammell Laird's, he could hear hammering. He could hear a train. The whole area seemed to be filled with industries. Joey hated the high brick walls, the dirt, noise and smoke.

At what he judged might be quarter to ten, he went back through the front door and asked the receptionist for Mr Gleeson. He was the first interviewee to arrive.

They left him sitting in a corridor for a time. Joey tried to gear himself up, tried to remember all Nick had told him about the business. Another youth came to occupy the seat next to him. Joey studied him, trying to see reasons why he might be preferred. He decided there weren't any.

The waiting was making him nervous. At last a middle-aged secretary came to the door and summoned him in. In an adjoining office, he found himself facing Mr Gleeson's desk.

'Good morning, sir,' he said, and stood waiting to be asked to sit down. Those had been Nick's instructions. It took a moment for Mr Gleeson to look up. Black-framed glasses didn't hide the calculating look that came Joey's way. The man had a bulbous nose and flabby cheeks.

'Good morning.' He was shuffling through letters. Joey watched him extract the one he'd written and put it on top. 'It's Joseph O'Malley?'

'Yes, sir.' He was trying to smile and look relaxed as he was asked about his age and his school. It wasn't easy. He brought out his school reference.

He was asked why he'd come to Birkenhead to work, and why he'd chosen to apply to Evans's. Joey was keen to get the job, and tried to show it. He talked about treacle toffee being made here for a hundred years. It was easy to be enthusiastic about toffee. He'd seen it on sale in Pen-y-Clip but rarely had money to spare for it. He didn't doubt the other boys would show their enthusiasm for the product. He enquired what his duties would be and tried to show enthusiasm for them too.

Then he was sent back to wait in the corridor. Two other boys had arrived by now and were trying to find out what he'd been asked. He kept his mouth firmly shut. He was beginning to feel hopeful.

When he was called in again Mr Gleeson offered him the job. No need to force a smile now, he knew he was beaming. He'd got what he'd wanted.

On the way out he called in the same cloakroom, took down a roller towel, folded it neatly and buttoned his jacket over it. Not much point in taking soap back to Lizzie if she couldn't dry herself afterwards.

It was drizzling again so Lizzie waited for Joey in Woolworth's doorway which was almost opposite the bus sheds. She'd walked all round it twice and thought it a wonderful shop. She caught a glimpse of Joey as the bus turned in, and waved. Moments later he ran across the road to her, gripped her arm and pulled her into the shop.

'I've got it! I've got it!' he crowed. 'I've got the job.' He was euphoric, his strange eyes shone with success.

'Did you see any of the Mortimer family?'

He laughed aloud and shook his head.

'Didn't even see Nick. Only a Mr Gleeson who's in charge of personnel. A real old misery guts. Can't believe my luck, Lizzie.'

She felt a surge of relief that all was going according to plan.

'This is our chance, don't you see?' He took both her hands in his. 'We'll get our own back on them.'

'No,' she protested. 'We don't know the Mortimers. All you want is a job.'

There was a new intensity in his manner. 'I'll take everything I can from them. I want revenge and I want their money. They'll pay for what they did to you. I tell you, Lizzie, I'll wreak vengeance on them.'

She shivered. 'No. You won't be able to anyway. You're just the office boy.'

'I won't always be. You mark my words, I won't always be. There's nothing I can't do for you.'

'Joey, I don't want you to do anything but work. Let's just have a good time.'

'You should hate them, they abandoned you at birth. They're rich but they didn't care how poor you were. They didn't help you.'

Lizzie laughed nervously, a little shocked at Joey's vindictiveness. 'When are you starting?'

'Tomorrow. We've got to find somewhere to live before then.'

'I think I already have.' She felt put out by Joey's mood. 'Not far from here, not far from the greenhouse where we've left our things. There was a notice in the window about a room to let, so I knocked and asked to see it. It's not wonderful but it would do to start. Only four shillings a week. I said you'd have to see it before I said yes.'

'Let's go now then. The sooner we get somewhere, the better.'

Lizzie had never known him step out so briskly. As they came to the house, she said: 'This is the place.'

The gate had broken from its lower hinge and hung at a drunken angle. The garden was overgrown with rank grass. Tall trees and bushes dripped moisture from the recent shower.

It was another of the many substantial Victorian semi-detached villas in the district. It had been designed for the middle classes but over the years had come down in the world. The front door stood open, the paint was peeling off, adding to the general air of neglect. The bell didn't work. Lizzie hammered on a large brass knocker covered in verdigris.

An inner door with stained glass panels was snatched open by an unshaven man wearing braces over a soiled vest.

'What do you want?'

'I've brought my twin brother to see the room, Mr Redway,'

Lizzie said. 'You remember me?'

'Come in,' he grunted, and stood back to reveal a narrow hall with worn linoleum and peeling wallpaper.

'Don't think much of this,' Joey whispered when he turned his back.

The man threw open a door further down the passage. They were blinking in the sudden gloom. Lizzie could feel Joey crowding in behind her to see.

'Electric light,' the man said, snapping it on. 'Your own meter.' A single bare bulb swung from the centre of the ceiling.

There was a sitting-room grate set in dark green tiles in an oak surround. A kettle and three battered saucepans stood on the hearth. A stuffed Victorian couch and arm chair were pulled up close. There was a small table and a couple of dining chairs. The sagging double bed was pushed into a corner.

'Not bad,' Joey said in guarded tones.

'Everything you need.' Their guide picked his teeth in the doorway and waited.

Joey pulled back the curtains to let in more light. The sash window looked out on a wall of blackened brick some three feet away. This was a middle room, originally meant to be a dining-room, between the sitting-room to the front, and the morning-room and kitchen which overlooked the back garden.

'Not enough blankets on this bed.' Lizzie was separating the threadbare covers.

'I s'pose I could let you have an eiderdown.'

'What about dishes?'

'In the cupboard there. Use of bathroom upstairs, and you can wash up in the kitchen.'

'How many other people here?' Joey wanted to know.

'There's a married couple got the front room next door and the front bedroom above. And another in the room over yours. That's all apart from us.'

'We'll take it,' Joey said. 'Yes, Lizzie?'

222

'Yes,' she agreed. They had to get somewhere dry before tonight. She watched Joey pay. The man wanted two weeks' rent so that they'd always be a week in hand.

When they were alone, Joey inspected the contents of the cupboards.

'It'll do for a start,' he said. 'But I hope we won't be staying long.'

'At least we don't have to sneak in and out.' Lizzie felt filled with relief. 'We've a right to be here.'

'We're doing all right. We've somewhere to live and I've got a job.'

'I'll soon find a job too.'

When he'd looked down the columns of the newspaper he'd bought yesterday, Joey had said: 'It'll be easier for you to get a job than me.'

Lizzie had agreed. Mostly the jobs advertised were for women. It was only now after she'd studied them more closely that she realised those for which she could apply were mostly live-in domestic posts.

'They won't do,' Joey said with disgust when she pointed it out. 'You've come here to be with me. I don't want you living somewhere else. We'd never see each other.'

Lizzie would have liked to work in an office like Joey, but for that she needed to be able to type. Factory and shop work seemed harder to come by.

Later on that day, when they'd picked up their suitcase and parcels from the greenhouse and unpacked them in their room, they went out to buy food. A short walk past the park brought them to New Ferry Toll Bar.

Tolls had ceased to be paid in the last century and the toll cottage demolished to make room for a bank. It was now a busy cross roads and shopping centre with a small market.

They were waiting to buy sausages in a butcher's shop when Joey drew her attention to the notice in the window:

Help Wanted, young girl for general shop and household work

'Ask about it,' he urged. 'Only a short walk from our room. Handy for you.'

When she did, the man serving her in a bloodstained apron called upstairs for his wife.

While Lizzie waited, Joey whispered: 'I'll go home and start cooking the sausages.'

She found herself being led past a butcher's block where the carcass of a pig was half cut up. The smell of raw meat and blood was strong. Then she was climbing dark stairs to the living-room over the shop, and once upstairs delicious scents of roasting were filling the air, making saliva run in her mouth.

'I'm Mrs Edmonds.' The woman had a tough face and iron grey hair dragged into a tight bun. 'I hope you're a worker. We've no use for slackers here.'

Lizzie assured her she was. She heard that her duties would be to clean the living accommodation and help with the cooking. She peered round the door of a poky kitchen. Sounds and scents of roasting came from a black gas cooker on legs. Another huge joint of beef cooled on the drainboard.

'Cooked meats for the shop,' the woman explained. 'We slice it and sell it by the quarter. Pork too. And we make potted meats and faggots and refine lard and dripping. I usually put in a few roast potatoes for our own dinner at the same time. Your job will be to help with all this.'

'I've done quite a lot of cooking,' Lizzie assured her, though she'd never seen joints the size of these. 'Will I be serving in the shop too?'

'Perhaps, at the weekends when we're busy.' They were downstairs again in the room behind it. 'But it's more important that you keep this room clean. And I mean really clean, it has to be hygienic. You'll have to collect any bones and fat we can't use and pack them into boxes and paper bags ready to be taken away.'

Lizzie viewed the pile collecting in the corner and tried to smile.

'Fifteen shillings a week,' the woman said. 'Half day

Thursday and we stay open late on Saturdays. You can come on a week's trial.'

Lizzie agreed. She had to have a job and this was a firm offer, but she thought Joey had come off better than she had.

Still, if she didn't like it, she could keep looking, and if anything better came up she could give in her notice. This would be a start.

'Nine o'clock sharp tomorrow,' the woman said as she closed the door behind her.

Once outside again, Lizzie looked above the shop. 'Enoch Edmonds,' she read, 'Family Butcher since 1906.'

She ran home to Joey who'd got a fire going in the grate. It made their room seem cosy and cheerful.

Chapter Fourteen

3 July 1934

Joey felt less confident when the time came for him to start work. He dressed himself in Nick Bender's suit again, and polished his boots on a piece of newspaper.

He found himself sitting in the same corridor, and trying to fill in forms the forbidding secretary gave him. Then she summoned a youth called Stanley with pimply skin and a cheerful grin.

'Show Joey what's expected of him,' she said. 'And make sure he knows his way round the factory.'

The first place he was shown was a dark and airless room under the stairs, furnished with a hard chair and a table that almost filled it.

'Your bolt hole, otherwise called the mail room. You sort out what comes in and distribute it round the office and factory. You collect up all letters and memos, either for posting outside or taking to another department. That takes up a lot of your day.'

'I open the letters?'

'No, take them to the right department. Only open them if there's no clue on the envelope. It's a black mark if you open private mail.'

He followed Stanley, the office boy he was replacing, into a long hall furnished with rows and rows of desks. Joey thought Stanley over-full of himself now he'd been promoted to clerk.

'This is Joey, your new lackey,' he said, introducing him to superior young ladies with scarlet lacquered finger nails.

Their names and positions reeled off Stanley's tongue, and Joey thought he'd never remember them. They looked at him with cold disinterest and turned back to their typewriters. Offices for the managers opened off the hall on three sides. He was looking for Nick Bender's name on the doors but couldn't see it.

'Mr Bender?' Stanley said. 'Sits at that desk over there. He's just a trainee.' The desk was deserted and bare.

In the centre of the longest wall was an alcove furnished with two desks. Only one was occupied. Stanley said: 'Miss Peacock, Mr Mortimer's secretary.'

Miss Peacock had the wrong name. There was nothing showy about her middle-aged iron grey hair and pearl grey twin set. Rather she seemed to shrink into the background.

Two offices opened off the alcove. One was labelled 'Mr Matthew Mortimer'. Joey paused, feeling a shiver of trepidation. This was the reason he was here. To get even with the Mortimers.

'He's never here. Goes off to Egypt for a year at a time. Lucky old him. His son, Gregory Mortimer, is in charge here now. That's his room.' Stanley pointed to the door on the other side of the alcove.

'Come on. You don't get personal introductions to them. Any mail you deliver to the Peacock.'

Joey was moving away when the door swung open and a tall broad-shouldered man with handsome features came striding out. His blue eyes raked Joey arrogantly as he passed.

'That's him.' Stanley nudged his arm.

Joey couldn't move. His resemblance to Lizzie was notice-able. His Lizzie! It was true then, she was a Mortimer. He couldn't doubt it now, the family likeness was strong. Same fair colouring, though Greg's hair was pale yellow whereas Lizzie's was ash blonde. But in the face . . . Alike as two peas.

'Right skirt puller, isn't he?' Stanley said behind his hand. 'If he was a pauper, they'd still all be running.'

'The man who has everything,' Joey choked, feeling his

dislike for Greg growing. His shirt had been freshly ironed, his suit smarter than any Joey had seen. He couldn't drag his eyes away from Greg's white hands. Clean, manicured nails. Easy to see he'd never done a hand's turn in his life.

Joey turned to peer into the office Greg had left, feeling a little sick. Large and airy, with a distant view of the river. Polished parquet floor and a big desk and leather chair. He hadn't realised until now just what he was pitting his strength against.

'He's not much like his father but they say he's the spitting image of his grandfather.' Stanley was growing more communicative.

Joey knew how everybody spoke with bated breath of the great Sir Hugo Mortimer, one of the most successful men this century.

'He's expected to follow in his footsteps.'

'Lucky fellow.' Joey felt livid with envy. More than envy, a green purulent jealousy, a simmering anger that everything was so much easier for Greg Mortimer than it was for him. Greg had started with every advantage, but Joey was going to strip every penny from him. He'd vowed to Lizzie he would, and he was twice as determined now he'd seen him. And he wouldn't let Greg take Lizzie from him either. She was his. One day she'd be known as Elizabeth Mortimer, her rightful name, and he, Joey O'Malley, would restore her fortune to her.

Joey thought the office seemed alien enough, but the factory was a hell hole. It was the largest building he'd ever been in. Everything felt sticky. His boots stuck to the floor as he walked across it. He soon learned to keep his hands in his pockets. Even the handrails on the stairs felt tacky.

The sugar-crushing room was full of moving machinery the like of which he hadn't known existed, and the floor was gritty as well as sticky. In the boiling shop, great vats bubbled and spat, making sinister noises. He watched engrossed as toffee was tipped into great cooling trays, and operators

229

in white coats added something.

'What's that?' he asked.

'Rum. Only rum flavouring, of course, and there go the raisins.'

Conveyer belts snaked about, jerking the product from one process to another. The toffee went on to be rolled and stretched and kneaded. Finally, it was cut into small bars or bite-sized pieces and wrapped.

Machines crashed and clattered. Men tending them shouted to each other above the noise, making Joey want to put his hands over his ears. The whole place was hot and airless and so heavy with the scent of toffee and flavourings it caught at his throat.

He wondered desperately if he'd ever find his way round on his own. Yet despite everything he was fascinated. Money was being made here. Real money, in amounts that made its owner a rich man. It would not be hard to make toffee like that. Anyone could do it. Next time he went into the factory, he would study the machines they were using, carefully, one at a time.

When he was left to himself for a few moments, he went to an outside door to gulp deep lungfuls of fresh air. He was out on a loading bay which ran right along one side of the building. Beyond was a yard. A red van nosed its way in through the gates, gaudily advertising slabs of Evans's toffee on both sides. The driver, sharp-featured and thin, and only a few years older than Joey was himself, got out and swaggered towards him.

'Hello, you new in this madhouse?'

'Is it a madhouse?'

'You bet.'

'I'll soon get used to it,' Joey answered. To himself he vowed, very soon.

'The stuff they make's okay. Have you tried it?' A couple of wrapped toffees were pushed into his hand.

'Thanks.' He put them in his pocket. 'What's your name?'

'Bill Purley. I'm a salesman here. See you around, pal.'

He was the first person at Evans's to treat Joey like a human being. He watched Bill disappear through the door.

Minutes later, Stanley was shouting to him: 'Look lively, you. Come and give a hand when you're needed.' Joey stumbled after him to the stockrooms.

'Like I said,' Stanley sneered, 'if the stockmen want help loading the vans, you gotta do it. You're the dog's body.'

The stockman was indicating the boxes he wanted loading on to a hand-truck and checking them off his list. Joey estimated he was working twice as fast as Stanley and he still had time to study the contents: treacle toffee, toffee with nuts, vanilla fudge, Devon cream fudge. The varieties seemed endless. When the trolley was loaded to capacity, there remained one large package on the floor.

Bill Purley had been signing papers and giving them a hand too. It seemed it was his van they were loading.

'Bring that package down, mate,' he said to Joey. Stanley and the stockman manoeuvred the truck through the door.

'And this.' Bill Purley slid another box from the shelf and piled it on top of the one in his arms.

Joey felt heady with excitement. It was perfectly obvious what Bill was doing. He was using him to carry out a contraband box.

He watched Bill carefully, half expecting a conspiratorial wink. It didn't come. Bill was whistling tunelessly under his breath. Joey placed his two boxes into the van. The contents of the hand-truck were now being loaded. He'd recognised Bill as a likely soul mate the moment they met. Now it seemed he was like-minded about helping himself to his employer's goods.

Nick drove carefully. He'd bought himself an Austin Seven Chummy, third hand and already seven years old. The ride was bouncy and it wasn't all that easy to control on corners but owning it was giving him a boost.

He knew he'd been right to indulge himself with this car even though he'd had to do it on HP. His father would be

231

shocked if he knew, he'd have preferred to lend him the money himself, but Nick couldn't bring himself to ask for favours.

He hoped the car would do two things for him. It would anchor him to Evans's in a job he didn't like because he had to pay for it. He'd promised his parents he really would try to settle down this time.

It would also get him out of the town and into the countryside. Nick didn't think he was going to make a town dweller, not even to please Dad. He hadn't seen green fields for two months and today he was feasting his eyes on them. He'd ignored the main roads into Chester and driven through the lanes in between. Here he seemed to be a hundred miles from the nearest town. He knew Hugo Mortimer lived somewhere near. He'd met him at Hannah's house.

The road widened opposite a country pub which was closed. Nick pulled into the side and stopped. Having the car allowed him to take an interest in other people's farms by looking over their hedges.

The land was richer, more productive here, very different from Wales. There were hedges and not stone walls. More crops were grown, he could see wheat and barley. There was a lot of market gardening and many acres put down to potatoes. Now in mid-summer the grass was lush. He missed the sheep but there were plenty of cattle here.

His eye caught a movement behind the hedge of a nearby field. He got out of his car and stood on the bank for a better view. He could see a young lad with a child trying to deal with a cow which seemed to be in some difficulty. A childish treble carried across the field.

His interest aroused, Nick climbed the gate and crossed the field.

'Can I help?' he asked, peering over the far hedge at them. 'Is something the matter?' The figure he'd thought to belong to a lad was distinctly feminine now he was closer. She wore trousers tucked into Wellingtons and a pork pie hat over short brown hair.

232

'Yes, please. If you could help us get her back to the cowshed . . . There's a stile just there. My father . . . She's calving, you see.' A young girl in a print dress was helping her to jostle the cow along. 'She's been at it for hours, I'm a bit worried.'

The cow, an old shorthorn, was near exhaustion and could hardly walk.

'Your father would be better giving you a hand to get it in,' Nick said.

'He can't.' The girl's voice was agonised. 'Do you know anything about cows?'

He'd helped cows to calve many times at home. It could take the brute strength of several men.

'Come on,' he urged the animal. 'How far do we have to go?'

The little girl walked ahead, showing him the way. 'Dad said to leave it, it would calve on its own. It did last time.' He could see they were sisters.

'I'm afraid this time it won't,' Nick said gravely. 'There's some complication.' Once tethered in its stall the cow sank to the floor. He took off his Harris tweed jacket and rolled up his sleeves.

'I thought if we could get Clover in, then we could get Dad as far as the cowshed and he could tell me what to do.' The older girl seemed grateful that he was taking over.

Nick did what he'd done many times at home. 'The calf's still alive, I can feel it sucking at my fingers.' He was relieved to find it was a simple mispresentation. It didn't need much strength. He had it delivered within ten minutes. A strong bull calf. He pulled it up to the mother's head and after a few moments she began to lick it. Nick felt a glow of satisfaction. 'I haven't lost the knack.'

'Thank goodness.' The older girl was smiling at him. 'It's going to be all right. Thank you, I was so afraid . . .'

'Your father shouldn't have left her so long.'

'It's not his fault.' Her smile was gone. 'If we have a problem we call on our neighbour, but he's gone to visit his

233

wife in hospital. My mother's gone with him. We all thought Clover would be all right. Come into the house and meet Dad. You'll need a wash anyway.'

'How did you know what to do?' the smaller girl asked, picking up his coat and tie.

'My father's a farmer too.'

'A farm like this?'

'A little different,' he said. 'But we keep cows.'

'This is my sister Lorna, she's twelve. I'm Marion, by the way. Marion Dodge.'

The farm buildings were old and in need of repair. The farmhouse was in a similar state. As they went through the kitchen, Marion poked the fire into a blaze and lowered the kettle on to it. 'You must stay and have a cup of tea,' she said. 'I was so glad to see you coming to help.'

Lorna showed him where he might wash and found him a clean towel. Then she took him to the parlour to meet her father. Nick was brought up short at the sight of the wheelchair. He'd not expected that.

'Tossed by a bull,' the man said philosophically as he shook his hand. 'Neville Dodge.' He still looked relatively young. Nick understood only too well what a terrible handicap it must be to running a farm. 'I'm very grateful for your help. I'm afraid I'm in the wrong job now.'

'So am I,' Nick said expansively. He felt on home ground.

'We're trying to sell the farm.' Marion was a sturdy girl with a cheerful smile. About his own age, he thought. 'No buyer yet, though.'

'Marion's a great help,' her father said. 'I don't know what we'd do without her. I don't suppose you'd be interested in buying?'

'Couldn't afford it,' Nick said regretfully. 'But I'd like to help. Perhaps I could come again?' He explained his circumstances. 'I'm free at weekends, at a loose end really. I don't know many people in Birkenhead.'

'Our guardian angel must have sent you to Birch Hill,' its owner said. 'There's nothing we'd like more, is there, Marion?'

Her friendly brown eyes smiled at him. She was almost as tall as he was, with well-built shoulders. A country girl born and bred. Nick was pleased. He felt a friend like Marion was exactly what he needed.

Before Lizzie had even taken off her hat and coat the next morning, Mrs Edmonds said: 'You can start in the kitchen. First the washing up, then tidy round and mop the floor. There's a few clothes to rinse out and put on the line. Then dust and hoover the living-room and stairs.'

Lizzie was trying in vain to remove the blood stains from striped aprons when Mr Edmonds called upstairs.

'Come and scrub my chopping blocks and clean out this mincing machine. It's more important to have this room clean. We get inspectors round, you know.'

Before she was halfway through that, he called her to help in the shop. All day, the jobs she was asked to do piled up. Mrs Edmonds complained because she hadn't got round to hoovering the living-room.

She didn't sit down between nine in the morning and six at night except during her lunch hour, when she went home and made herself a sandwich in the dark room which felt colder than it did outside in the street. The following days were exactly the same. Lizzie decided the work was heavy.

Joey was usually home before her in the evenings and had the fire going and was cooking dinner on it by the time she got in. She was too tired to do more than doze in front of it for the rest of the evening. Joey said that perhaps she'd feel better when she got more used to the job. Lizzie doubted it. She knew that on Friday and Saturday nights she wouldn't finish work until after nine o'clock.

On Thursday, as she was leaving for her half day, she paused to look at a blue dress in the window of the shop next door. A dark-haired girl was locking up.

'Settling in your new job then?' she asked.

Lizzie pulled a face. 'Rather work in a dress shop like yours.'

'Not my shop, I'm the sales assistant.'

'I'm that, and the charwoman, washerwoman, cook and bottle washer as well.'

The girl laughed. 'I suppose you know you're the seventh girl the Edmondses have had this year?'

'No!'

'Nobody can stick them. I hear they're right old slave drivers.'

'I don't suppose there's a vacancy in your shop?' Lizzie asked hopefully.

'No, but they're looking for another cleaner at the pictures if you're interested?'

'At the cinema? Further along this road?'

'Yes, at the Lyceum.'

The blind was just coming down in the butcher's window. Lizzie dropped her voice. 'Anything would be better than this.'

'There's a matinee on a Thursday, so the manager will be there now. You could pop in and ask about it.'

Lizzie went slowly up the white marble steps, knowing she had to find herself a different job.

The girl in the pay desk seemed friendly. She called the gold-braided commissionaire to take Lizzie up to the manager's office. He let her pause in the foyer to study the stills of Shirley Temple and the posters advertising her film *Now and Forever*.

'On for the next three days,' he told her. 'Good film.'

She thought the manager friendly too. He said he needed somebody young and slim to get between the rows of seats and pick up all the cigarette packets and sweet wrappings that were dropped. It was morning work only, but he offered her the same wages she was getting from the Edmondses.

'I'll take it,' she said quickly, and agreed to start the following Monday.

'Make sure you get your money from the Edmondses,' Joey said, 'before you tell them where to put their job.'

'The offer was a week's trial to see if we suited each other,'

236

Lizzie told him. 'They don't suit me, so it's fair enough if I don't want to carry on.'

'They'll want you,' Joey said. 'Just make sure you get your money in your hand before you tell them.'

He suggested they go to see Shirley Temple that evening so she could get a better view of what she'd be cleaning.

As the usherette showed them to their seats, Lizzie whispered: 'I asked the manager if he ever had vacancies for usherettes. They see all the films. I think I'd like a job like that.'

'No, you wouldn't,' Joey said indignantly. 'I'd be home by myself every night. You wouldn't get home 'til midnight.'

'Of course I'd like it, just showing people to their seats, no cleaning,' she said. 'And the pay's better. Twenty-five shillings to start because it's evening work.'

'No, Lizzie, we'd hardly see each other.'

'I thought you'd want me to, when you heard about the wages?'

'No. Money isn't everything.'

'I thought it was to you.' Lizzie swallowed back her resentment. Joey was always telling her he thought her very special, but sometimes she wished he would allow her to make her own choices.

'No, definitely not an usherette. You'd even work weekends.'

'No need to argue about it, Joey. It's a cleaning job I've got, and it's mornings only,' Lizzie said as the curtains swished open and the lights dimmed.

'Good thing too. You'll have every afternoon to rest and you'll be able to have my tea ready by the time I get home.'

She made herself forget Joey's domineering ways. It was a rare treat to go to the pictures and she meant to enjoy it.

'We'll go as often as we want when we're rich,' he said on the way home. 'Every night if you want to. No need to be an usherette to see all the films then.'

Joey got off the bus in New Ferry and was walking back to his room when a red van overtook him and pulled into an adjoining street. He couldn't miss the slogan 'A.A. Evans, Toffee Makers to the World', nor the slabs of brightly wrapped toffee displayed on its sides. He recognised Bill Purley, the salesman, behind the wheel. Some twenty yards down, it pulled into the kerb and stopped.

'Hello,' Joey called. 'I didn't know you lived here.' He was surprised to see Bill's sharp features twist into a grimace. 'What's the matter?'

'Don't say anything at work about seeing me here,' he warned.

'Why not?'

Bill drew his finger across his throat in a dramatic gesture.

'You're not supposed to bring the van home? Of course I won't say anything.'

'See you don't,' he grinned.

'I won't. I'm not daft.' Joey thought for a moment. 'Any chance of a lift in the mornings?'

'You're not slow! All right, be here quarter to nine sharp. I'm not waiting for you.'

Joey went on more slowly, musing that perhaps one day, when he looked a bit older, Bill might be persuaded to teach him to drive that van.

Lizzie had a saucepan of stew simmering on the fire when he got in. Their room seemed more welcoming these days, brightened by a fire and the succulent scents of dinner. It made all the difference to his comfort that Lizzie didn't work in the afternoons.

'I love having every afternoon to myself,' she'd said. 'Plenty of time to shop and tidy up here, and then I go down to the river and walk along the shore. It's lovely on a breezy day and you'd never believe what's washed up by the tide.' Lizzie picked up anything burnable on the high water line. She always brought home a large bag full of wood, odd boots and rubber-soled plimsolls, enough to give them a fire all evening.

Joey's duties included making tea twice daily for the office staff. Tonight he brought out packages from his pockets and laid them on the table.

'Tea, sugar and biscuits,' he said. 'Don't buy any more, I think I can bring all we need.'

'You'll get caught, Joey. It's silly to lose your job for a few biscuits.'

'Silly to spend hard-earned cash on something we can get for nothing,' he retorted.

Previously, he'd brought toffee home for Lizzie. She'd looked at that suspiciously though factory workers were not barred from eating the product while they were making it. It was thought they soon grew tired of the taste.

'I'm very careful,' he said.

'It's not the point. You can't get rich by taking biscuits. Petty pilfering won't make the Mortimers poor. All it does is frighten me. If you're caught . . .'

'I'll have to think of something else,' he cut in. 'Get my hands on bigger amounts.'

'Joey, no. We're doing all right, aren't we?'

'Cleaning the picture house isn't much of a job.'

'I like it. Going along the rows picking up cigarette packets and toffee papers. You'd be surprised how many of Evans's I find. It's easy work, not a bad life.'

'It could be better.'

'We could make it better,' she said. 'We could go to see Nick again.'

'Whatever for?' He was bristling with irritation in an instant.

'He's a friend, and the only person we know in Birkenhead.'

'I see more than enough of him at work.'

'But I don't. He'll help me find my mother.'

'Lizzie, I'll help you find your mother, but one thing at a time. I need to think of a way to do it.'

'No, you don't. Nick would take me to see Mrs Mortimer. There'd be no harm in hearing what she has to say.'

'No, Lizzie.' He felt a jab of alarm.

'I'll go by myself then, one afternoon. I think I could find my way to her house. It was called Oakridge, wasn't it?'

'No! Don't you dare go near her!'

239

He saw her face grow pale with shock. Her mouth was open. His sudden flare up had shaken him too. He said more gently: 'I don't want you talking to her. She'll persuade you to leave me.'

'No, I won't leave you. We're having a good time here now, aren't we? But you've always said you'd help me do it. Wasn't that why we came to Birkenhead in the first place?'

'No,' he almost groaned. Just the thought of it brought the unknown closer, with cold feelings of loss and insecurity.

'It was. When we were children, you used to say my father was a king. That we'd find out all about my family. I thought you wanted to.'

'No.' Her blue Mortimer eyes were searching his face in dismay. He had to explain. 'It frightens me, Lizzie. I'm afraid I'll lose you.'

'No need to be frightened.' Her arms were round him, hugging him close.

'The Mortimers could change everything for us, I know it. I don't want anything changed. Not yet. You said you like being here, that we're all right as we are.'

'Yes, yes. Don't worry yourself, Joey. I don't like seeing you upset.'

'You promise, Lizzie, not to go near her? I don't want you going in the afternoon when I'm not about. Not yet.'

'I won't. I wouldn't go without telling you.'

'Promise then? One day we'll do it together, like I planned. Just be patient with me.'

'All right, I promise.'

That made him feel a bit better. He should have known he could depend on Lizzie. 'After all, they knew you were at Yarrow for fourteen years and never came near you.'

She said nothing for a long time. Then he heard her sigh: 'It would be fun to see Nick though.'

'No, we got what we wanted from him. We don't need him now.'

'You always said Nick was all right, that you liked him.'

'Not any more. He's one of them.'

240

Joey had been working for Evans's for almost a month. 'Everybody's very stuck up,' he said. 'They treat me as though I'm the lowest of the low. Nobody speaks to me, except to say "Joey, do this", "Joey, do that".'

'What sort of things do they ask you to do?'

'Take this to the foreman in the factory. Get me a cup of tea.'

'They just don't know you, Joey. It'll be different when you've been there a while.'

'It certainly will. I'll show them. I even have to call Nick "Mr Bender". And Mr Mortimer is the worst of the lot. I hate him.'

'I thought you said he was away?'

'Yes, he is. Greg Mortimer, I mean. He's really bossy.'

'Well, his father owns the business.'

'He's taken a dislike to me.'

'More likely, Joey, you've taken a dislike to him. Just relax. You'll feel different when you settle in.'

'It's a dirty, horrible place. They've been making a fortune in that building for over a hundred years. The windows are so high nobody can see out. It's unnatural.'

'Unnatural for you. You're used to being in the open air.'

'So are you.'

'When winter comes, perhaps we'll be glad to be indoors.'

Hannah drove home from Yarrow feeling depressed. She'd taken far too long to make firm plans for Elizabeth, and because of that she'd lost her again.

She rang Greg at the office the next morning.

'Did you give the job to Joey O'Malley?'

'Yes, he's started here. Gleeson thinks he might be all right, though I don't like the look of him myself.'

'Why not?'

'He looks sly and malevolent somehow.'

'I'll come in, Greg. I want to talk to him.'

As she got out of her car later on that morning, Hannah looked up at the old building. When she'd worked here all those years ago, she'd felt at ease in these long bare corridors but had rarely been here since her marriage.

In the alcove off the main hall she found Greg's secretary working at her old desk. Miss Peacock had been hired to replace her; Hannah remembered showing her round all those years ago. Leila Peacock looked older but she hadn't changed much. She still had a self-effacing manner, wore drab clothes and steel-rimmed spectacles.

Matt's office was not being used while he was away. Greg unlocked it for her and opened the window because already it smelled disused. The sweet sickly smell of boiling sugar she knew so well was soon rolling in. Hannah sat down at the bare desk and pulled the clean blotter towards her.

The tap on the door was polite. It opened immediately. A strange-looking lad stood nervously on the threshold.

'You wanted to see me, Mrs Mortimer?'

'Are you Joey O'Malley? Do come in and sit down.'

He edged further into the office but remained standing, holding on to the back of the chair she'd indicated as though seeking support. Hannah couldn't make out why his face should seem so lopsided.

'I've just come back from Yarrow.' She wasn't going to beat about the bush. 'I hear you've just come to Birkenhead and brought Elizabeth with you?'

'Yes,' he agreed.

'I want to find her.' His face had a cunning, rather foxy look. 'I want to help her.' He didn't answer. She assumed Matt's imperious manner.

'So where is she now?'

'She doesn't need help, Mrs Mortimer. She's perfectly all right.'

'Nevertheless, I and everybody at Yarrow would like to know where she is.' Hannah had the feeling in the pit of her stomach that she was going to fail again.

'She wouldn't want me to tell anybody.'

'Why on earth not?'

'She doesn't want to go back to Yarrow.'

242

'There's no need, it's up to her. I only want to speak to her, to make sure she's all right. To help her.'

'She has a job, thank you. She's managing perfectly well.'

'Is she living with you?'

His eyes were casting about as though for inspiration. She realised for the first time that they were not a pair. One was the colour of strong tea and the other of blue slate.

'No.'

Hannah wasn't sure that was the truth. His address would be on his records, she could check on that.

'She has a live-in job working for a couple of elderly ladies. She's safe and well. They're kind to her and she's happy there.'

Hannah's stomach muscles contracted. 'That's housework. Look, I've found a boarding school for her, St Hilda's. A few years there will make all the difference to her prospects.'

'Lizzie doesn't want to go to boarding school. She reckons she's had enough schooling. She thinks she's too old to start at another.'

'She's not fourteen yet!'

'That's the leaving age for the likes of us.'

Hannah felt another stab at that. She'd never liked Maisie O'Malley. She didn't trust her son. Didn't like him. She tried harder to persuade him.

'She'd never forgive me if I told you.' Joey had become defensive. 'She told me not to. She doesn't want people going round to see her. It might upset the people she works for. She just wants to be left alone.'

His lips came together in a firm line. Nothing Hannah could say would shake him.

She let him go. What was the use? She sat on at Matt's desk trying to think. Merseyside was a huge conurbation. It wouldn't be easy to find somebody who didn't want to be found.

Her last hope was that the girl would be at Joey's address. When Greg took out his records, she found he'd given Nick's address. Greg sent for Nick to come up.

He sat down in front of Hannah, his boyish freckles

making him look both honest and worried.

'I'm sure they're together but I've no idea where they're living,' he said. 'I've already had a go at Joey, but he's not saying. He thinks he's protecting Lizzie. Keeping her out of our clutches. I can't persuade him otherwise.'

Hannah believed him.

She went to have another word with Greg. He was losing patience both with her and Joey O'Malley.

'I'll tell him we have to know where our employees live. I'll get an address out of him. I won't stand any nonsense from him.'

He came back five minutes later waving a piece of paper at Hannah. 'Here you are. He's got a room at this address.' Greg was pleased with himself.

Stanley Road, New Ferry, she read. 'I'll call round now and see if Elizabeth is there.'

Hannah was full of hope. Joey O'Malley was pinned down at work. Even if the girl had got herself a job too, she could ask if she was living there and when she'd be at home.

She drove slowly along Stanley Road looking for the number he'd given. When she found it she got out, unable to believe her eyes. The house was untenanted and looked as though it had been for some time. The front garden was overgrown. She walked back, checking the house numbers. She had not made a mistake.

It filled Hannah with a boiling frustration.

'Perhaps it's as well,' Greg said crossly when she told him. 'Stop worrying about her. She's old enough to make her own way in life now, if that's what she wants. I'll give that little sod the sack. I'm not putting up with this sort of behaviour from an office boy.'

'No,' Hannah said. 'Don't do that.' She had the feeling that Nick was right. And if Lizzie was living with Joey O'Malley, it would create more problems for her if he didn't have a job.

Chapter Fifteen

5 July 1935

Joey felt fed up. He'd been office boy at Evans's for a year and was sick of spending every day trying hard to lift some cash, and finding he was only able to get his hands on small amounts.

Petty pilfering was possible, but he had no use for the stamps he handled, and Lizzie had turned strangely scrupulous and would no longer use the tea and sugar he took home.

'Remember how Mr Bender used to wallop me?' she'd flared at him angrily the last time he'd taken it.

'He never did anything worse than wallop. However many times you helped yourself, he let you carry on.'

'We were children. We knew he wouldn't. Mrs Bender would never have let him hand us over to the police. They accepted we had to eat. Joey, it's different here.'

He knew she was terrified he'd be caught, but he'd learned a thing or two in his time. He was very careful. He was saving money but the amount was growing far too slowly.

He knew the only answer was to find an accomplice who handled money. Joey would have much preferred to work on his own, but as he had to have a partner, he knew he wouldn't do much better than Bill Purley. He felt he could trust him, though of course he didn't intend to tell him more than he needed to know.

The trouble was, Bill didn't take him seriously enough.

'You're too young,' he said. 'Little more than a kid, hardly out of nappies. You want to run before you can walk.'

Joey felt more experienced than Bill. He and Lizzie were

already living on their own wits and surviving, while Bill still lived at home, protected and nurtured by his parents. Joey felt he'd served a long apprenticeship too. He thought his schemes through before doing anything, and made sure everything he did fitted into his general plan.

He looked across at Bill now as he concentrated on driving Evans's van along the New Chester Road on his way to work.

'Smashing new van.' Bill seemed to sense his gaze. 'The very latest Ford T. Handles like a dream.'

'What happens to the old ones?'

'They get sold off. Bargain prices if you want a van.'

'Could they still do the job?'

'Sure. Evans's sell them as soon as they get a bit shabby. They go cheap because they need a re-spray to get rid of the toffee adverts. Thinking of buying one?'

'Not yet, but I might. You go round all the sweet shops, you sell this stuff to the shopkeepers?'

'That's right. Newsagents mostly. Corner shops.'

'You give them a bill straight away? Do they pay you on the spot?'

'Yes.' Bill shot him a sly glance.

'Cash?'

'Usually. They have the takings in the till. Saves them banking it and then paying for the cheque.'

'Then you're well placed to make a little on the side,' Joey dared.

'I wouldn't do such a thing.' Bill's face broke into a sly grin of indignation.

'Of course not,' Joey agreed. 'But if you wanted to, it would be easy. All this stuff loaded in the van. Who's to know what happens to it all?'

'It's all sealed into them boxes and jars,' Bill said, jabbing a finger towards the rear. 'Can't open them without it being obvious. Then the shopkeepers refuse them, thinking they're getting short weight.'

'You need to deal in whole boxes. Only way to make anything worthwhile anyway.'

'Well, maybe I do once in a while,' Bill said confidentially. 'But there's a limit to what I can get hold of.'

'Depends who loads the van?' Joey guessed. Hadn't he seen it for himself? He'd also heard rumours that for a back-hander one of the stockmen would oblige.

'All down to paper work in the end,' Bill lamented. 'They've got it all tied up tight. I have to account for what's put on the van.'

'Only right and proper,' Joey said, sniffing appreciatively at the scents permeating through from the back; a real pot pourri of vanilla, almonds, caramel, butterscotch and fudge. Although he didn't like the stronger factory smells, he found the finished products more attractive than ever. Bill had helped him sample most of them.

He'd been trying to screw himself up to ask since he'd got into the van. He knew he would lose the chance if he didn't do it soon.

'I could help you with the paper work,' Joey offered. It was a relief to get it said openly. Bill laughed. It grated on his nerves. 'I can make it so they'll never know.'

'No. No, it can't be done.'

'It can, listen . . .'

After several minutes during which Joey outlined his plan, Bill was eyeing him differently. 'Would it really work?'

Joey didn't answer. Bill had to want to do it, really want to. They were waiting at the traffic lights at the bottom of Bedford Road when Bill added: 'Might be worth thinking about.'

'I've already thought about it,' Joey said. 'The deal's fifty-fifty.'

Bill's indignation boiled over. 'It'll mean extra work for me. Think of all the extra selling, and I'll still have to do a day's work for Evans's. Make them suspicious if I don't.'

'And I've been working out how to do it for weeks, even thinking of it in bed,' Joey snapped back. 'I'll be keeping their books straight so they won't find out.'

'I'll be taking all the risks . . .'

247

'We'll both be taking risks. Come off it, Bill, we could be on to a good thing.'

They covered the last half mile in silence, then Bill said: 'Okay, let's give it a go. See how we get on.'

Lizzie wedged a square of folded newspaper under the table leg to stop it wobbling, then set out the cracked dishes ready for their evening meal. She'd bought bloaters in the market and a crusty loaf.

The yellow flames roared in the grate, and the room was full of cheerful flickering light. Everything was ready for when Joey got home. Although it was summer, it had been a dull overcast day and the evening was chilly.

As she sat down to wait, Lizzie sighed with satisfaction. On the whole she'd enjoyed her first year in Birkenhead. If this was being grown up and independent, it beat being in the care of Seamus and Maisie.

She didn't mind that the lino was worn and that all their cooking had to be done on the open fire. They'd done much of it this way at the gatehouse, she was used to it. She and Joey could do exactly what they wanted, and didn't have to think of anyone but themselves. Being on their own had made them grow up fast. The last vestiges of childhood had dropped away during this year.

She heard something heavy being dragged across the ceiling. They could do with fewer people living in the house. Quarrels broke out quite often, in the kitchen or on the stairs. If Joey was out, she would stay here quietly until the shouting died down. She didn't like that part.

She was lucky in her job though. She quite enjoyed cleaning the cinema with either Irene or Mrs Pole. During the mornings, there were only the two of them in the empty echoing place. They shouted across to each other as they worked.

Mrs Pole suited her name, being tall and gaunt. She wore cross-over pinafores, tied her hair up in a bandana to work, and recounted an endless saga of her husband's failings.

When Irene was on, Lizzie shared the thrills and delights

her string of boyfriends gave her. None seemed to mean as much to Irene as Joey did to her, but she couldn't talk about that. Irene was a few years older, but didn't seem so.

They always started the morning's work on the balcony, one at each end of the back row. They pushed the litter forward under the seats, prodding with brooms in the confined space, wiping out ash trays and tossing the rubbish into huge containers. Then they hoovered down the aisles and went down to the auditorium. Lizzie even liked the scent of the heavy disinfectant they used. The first whiff of it transported her to a fantasy world.

They lingered over floor-mopping in the foyer, discussed the stills of the Hollywood greats that decorated the walls, and marvelled at the glamorous lives they must lead. The programme of forthcoming attractions was of prime interest. The cashier would allow them in free, except when they had a full house and a queue waiting outside. It was a much appreciated perk that went with the job. Lizzie took Joey to see every film. The programme changed twice-weekly.

Lizzie jumped up when she heard the front door slam and Joey's step in the hall. Joey was broadening out, looking more of a man. The girls at the cinema said his lopsided gaze was attractive. She certainly found him so. Everything had changed between her and Joey this year.

His face was cold against her own as he nuzzled her, kicking the door closed behind him. When he took off his coat, Lizzie went to balance the frying pan on the trivet and swing it into the flames.

'Happy, Lizzie? No regrets about coming?'

She shook her head.

'We're doing well now, just as I said we would.'

She turned from the fire, her cheeks scarlet from the blaze. 'You did say that one day you'd help me find my mother. We aren't doing much about that.'

She hankered to know more. It seemed she was letting the chance to do so slip through her fingers. It wouldn't be hard to get in touch with Hannah Mortimer, except that she'd promised not to. Poor Joey was terrified she'd be lured away from him, and she couldn't convince him otherwise.

'We will, all in good time. Be patient for a bit longer, Lizzie, please.' He threw himself down on the shabby horsehair couch.

'I think about you all day and of how nice it is to come home to you like this.' His manner was taut; she could feel his excitement simmering beneath the surface.

She found his gaze could make her breathe more quickly. 'I can't take my eyes off you, Lizzie. You're beautiful.'

She found him reaching out to her more often. 'I just want to touch you, tell myself you're real.' His finger moving up her arm made her shiver with anticipation. He pulled her down beside him on the couch and kissed her. He touched her breast. It made her cling to him.

It was so easy to be carried away with love but the room was filling with the scent of fish.

'Come on,' she said, breaking free from his arms. 'We must eat first.' She hooked the bloaters out on to the plates and set them on the table.

They always ate first. Usually they were too hungry to think of anything but food. But then, later, the evening was their own.

Joey made up the fire with the flotsam she'd picked up on the beach during the afternoon. It didn't matter that the room filled with the scent of burning tar, or worse, burning rubber. The warmth spread to the furthest corner where they had the bed.

As soon as she put her tea cup down, he was leading her over to it, as he did every evening, unless they were going out. It was the time of day she loved best, lying in the firelight with Joey holding her close.

Over the months they had been here, Lizzie had found Joey looking at her when she dressed or undressed in a way he never had before. At the gatehouse they'd all walked about half dressed or undressed, looking for clothes to put on. Although there had been curtains to divide the boys' side of the bedroom from the girls', none of them had taken much notice or felt the need for privacy. But now Joey would stop what he was doing to watch her.

They'd spent weeks petting heavily. Kissing, cuddling and curling up to sleep like young puppies. The first time he'd made love to her, it had seemed an easy and natural progression, all part of growing up. Seamus had made no secret of what he'd wanted of Maisie. It seemed a very normal part of life. The outcome seemed a normal progression too. It was always happening to Maisie. There'd been animals all round them on the farm.

At first she'd been frightened. 'What if we have . . .'

'Won't happen,' Joey said confidently. 'I know what to do. I've heard men in the office talking about it. You can get these things in the chemists.'

'I've never heard . . .' she worried.

'Trust me,' Joey said. 'I'm head over heels in love with you, Lizzie.'

She knew she loved him too. Otherwise Joey's fingers, trembling as he undressed her, wouldn't bring such delight.

'Aren't we supposed to wait 'til we're married?'

Joey had grinned in his lopsided fashion. 'The girls in the office think it's very naughty not to. But, Lizzie, we'd have to wait years and years.'

'It's nice.' She snuggled closer.

'When we're old enough, we'll get married,' he said contentedly. 'Of course we will. But being married won't make that much difference to us. We've always been together, always will be.'

It seemed to Lizzie that no girl could be loved more than she was.

Another year went by and Joey was beginning to feel better about everything. His savings were growing faster now he had the little enterprise started with Bill.

Last night he'd told Lizzie they could afford to rent a house all for themselves. Her face had lit up with smiles.

'It would be wonderful not to have to face Mr Redway at every turn. He's always in the lavatory when I go.'

'An unfurnished house,' Joey said. 'We'll go out and buy our own furniture. That way we'll get everything smart, just as we want it.'

Lizzie was over the moon. 'You're doing that well?'

'I've been saving up. It's the only way for us.'

He'd brought a newspaper home and now they went down the columns of houses to rent, picking out one or two.

'You look at them tomorrow afternoon, Lizzie. See if there is one you like.' It made him feel good to think he was providing more comfort for her. She'd been wonderful, she deserved the best.

He was getting bored with his duties as office boy, one of which was pushing round a trolley with the tea urn at mid-morning. Accompanied by one of the kitchen staff, they filled cups and saucers and placed one on the end of each desk in the main office hall.

Greg Mortimer liked coffee in the mornings, and liked it in a pot so he could pour it himself. Joey set a tray for him and laid out four biscuits on a plate. If any remained when he collected the tray later, he slipped them in his pocket.

It had made him boil with frustration – the monotony, the time he had to spend at work, and that so far he'd been able to do so little to hurt Greg. But now at long last he was taking Mortimer money and it was whetting his appetite for more.

Like all his other employees Joey addressed Greg respectfully as Mr Mortimer. Behind his back he was referred to as the Golden Boy, or Tutenkhamen the Second. Said to have been born not with a silver spoon in his mouth, but a gold one.

Arriving at his office door one morning, Joey knocked and released the catch, opening it a fraction before turning back to the trolley to pick up his coffee tray. He heard Greg's voice say: 'I'm tired of hearing about Bill Purley, he's always up to something he shouldn't be. Sack him. He's been warned before.'

Joey stopped dead in his tracks. He felt winded, as though

he'd been kicked in the stomach. He thought he heard the word 'police', and his mind fluttered with panic.

He felt paralysed with terror, quite unable to show himself in that room. Afraid he'd hear them say: 'Sack Joey O'Malley too. He's in it up to his neck.'

'What's the matter with you?' The woman from the kitchen who helped him was staring at him.

Joey took a long shuddering breath and made himself push the door wider. The china rattled as he set the tray down on the desk. He could see Mr Gleeson glowering at him.

He'd almost returned to the safety of the corridor when Greg barked: 'Boy, bring another cup.'

Joey turned. He knew he was staring as though he hadn't understood a word.

'No, I'll have tea, please,' Mr Gleeson said, and when Joey still didn't move, added: 'Bring my tea here.'

He got back to the trolley but was straining to hear what they were saying now. He thought he heard his own name. His hands shook so much he half filled the saucer as well as the cup.

He was stiff with tension. He had to keep a grip on himself even though it looked as though his newfound prosperity had been blown sky high. He tried to look at the names on the file folders in front of Mr Gleeson when he took his tea in. He was no longer capable of seeing anything. He felt a nervous wreck.

He'd been so sure he'd covered his tracks. He couldn't see how they could possibly have found out. He went back to the mail room, his private bolt hole. He closed the door though it made it airless and dark, because the only window opened into the hall instead of outside.

He knew his panic must show on his face. There was an internal phone on the wall so that he might be summoned to do tasks elsewhere. He expected every minute to be summoned back to Mr Gleeson and be told he had the sack too.

He drank his own tea, and tried to pull himself together. He had to take the mail round the factory. He felt better walking about and doing familiar tasks. He helped himself to

253

butterscotch praline. It was his favourite, but for once it didn't please him.

Returning to the mail room, he could hear his intercom buzzing before he opened the door. When he heard the secretary's voice say: 'Mr Gleeson would like to see you in his office', the blood was pounding instantly in his head again.

He asked: 'Now?'

'Yes, right away.'

His feet felt like lead. He'd written off his job, written off the chance of getting his own back on Greg Mortimer. Malice and hatred were bubbling through him.

He tapped softly and died a thousand deaths as he waited. In the end he had to knock harder to be heard.

'Come in.' Joey opened the door six inches and slid inside. Mr Gleeson looked at him over his glasses and put his pen down.

'O'Malley – yes.'

Joey held his breath. It took him a few moments to get the gist of what was being said to him.

'Coped well with the mail and being general office boy for over two years. Made a success of it. Offer you the job of junior clerk here in the personnel department.'

Relief was winging through him, it was not at all what he'd expected. Another instant and shock bells were ringing again in his head – not the personnel department! He had to go where the money was.

'Well, what do you say?'

'Thank you, sir, it's very kind . . . I'm quite overcome.'

'Well then . . .'

'I'm grateful really, it's not that, but to be honest I was hoping for the accounts department.' The words were coming out now in a rush. 'I was good at sums at school and it's always been my ambition to be an accounts clerk.'

Was he laying it on too thick?

'There's no vacancy in accounts for you at the moment.'

Joey gulped. 'I don't mind waiting, sir.'

'You're turning down an increase in pay.' Gleeson's eyes

twinkled behind the spectacles, as though that would tempt him. 'You'd get five shillings more.'

'I'd still prefer to wait, sir. Accounting is what I really want.'

Gleeson smiled. 'I like to see a boy who's keen. Much better than drifting in this life – to know what you do want. I'll put you down for the next vacancy in accounts.'

Joey found himself out in the corridor again, his head in a whirl. He'd not only survived but ensured that when he moved it would be of advantage to him. He couldn't believe it! He was in a lather of sweat and quite incapable of doing anything else for the rest of the afternoon.

'I've lost my job,' Bill railed that evening when Joey called at his house. 'It's all right for you, they haven't even noticed you're up to no good.'

'I take good care they don't. Taking the van home at night! Honestly, Bill, you should have told me you'd had three warnings. And fiddling the mileage!'

'I had to do extra miles to sell the stuff you got for me.'

'You must have known there was a limit to what you could get away with. You should have taken more care. They could have looked further into what you were doing, and then you'd be far worse off. You got their backs up.'

'Do you know what got their backs up, Joey? Greg Mortimer saw us at seven o'clock last night in Hamilton Square. And what was I doing there? Giving you a driving lesson, that's what.'

Joey was horrified. 'You didn't tell them?'

''Course I didn't, but it's no good your going on at me. It's not all my fault.'

He could feel his heart hammering away again. 'He didn't recognise me?' He wanted to kick himself. He'd jeopardised everything to save a pound or two on lessons. He'd thought in a big town like Birkenhead nobody would know him. Of course the toffee adverts made the van stick out like a sore thumb.

'No, you've got the luck of the devil.'

'He always calls me "Boy" anyway. Perhaps it's just as well.' Relief was trickling through him. He'd thought all was lost this afternoon. 'Sorry, Bill.'

'He said I was treating a company vehicle as though it was my private property. He took the number, that's how he knew it was me. I told him I was working late but I'd already handed in my sheets for the day, all made up, so he didn't believe that.'

'Calm down, Bill. You've got your cards and that's that. Just be thankful they won't be taking it any further. It could have been a whole lot worse.'

'It's the end for our little earner too. Just when I'm going to need the money.'

'Not necessarily,' Joey said slowly. 'I've been turning it over in my mind for a long time. We were working hard for that money. Much too hard. You were spending too much time doing Evans's work.'

'Well, I had to, I told you. Anyway, it was good money.' Bill was looking at him warily.

'I think I know a better way.'

'Well, I'm open to suggestions, aren't I? I've got no job now.'

'It's come at quite a good time. Evans's have two old vans for sale. We've got enough money now to buy one.'

'I haven't! Good God, we haven't made that much.'

'What have you spent your share on?'

'Nothing.'

'Come off it.'

'Once in a while I've gone out and had a good time. A few beers and that. Nothing else.'

'I've saved mine and I have enough,' Joey said. He was careful to keep the contempt he felt from his face. 'You can work for me if it's a job you want.'

'You're just a kid, you're talking through your hat.'

'I'm not, I mean it. I'll pay you what Evans's did, and all your running costs. You can do as much mileage as you want. Think of it, Bill, you'll be on easy street. You'll spend all day working for me. I might even give you a bonus if we do all right. After all, I'm not going to have the same overheads as Evans's, am I?'

'You won't be able to keep the van stocked.' Bill was looking at him pityingly. 'I won't be able to drive in and fetch the stuff any more.'

'I know that,' Joey said. 'It's been a stumbling block for a long time. I've finally thought of a way. I'm going to have to learn to drive, though.'

'You can already.'

Joey sniffed as he considered. 'I've got to have a licence.'

'Unlucky for you they brought the test in,' Bill sniggered.

'Am I good enough to pass?'

'You seem all right to me.'

'Then I'll apply for a test.'

'You aren't seventeen yet.'

'I need to drive now. I'll say I'm a year older. Lots of people did that to join up in the war.'

'Joey, you've got to buy the van yet, and they sell by tender, so there's no guarantee you'll get it.'

Joey smiled. He knew exactly how he'd fix that.

'I'm still the office boy, remember? I'll steam the envelopes open as they come in and fix my tender just a bit higher. Don't want to pay too much, do I?'

'Aren't you the clever one? But it's going to look a bit suspicious, isn't it? You wanting a van? They know you're only sixteen.'

'It'll have to be a false name and address. Do you know anyone who'll go in and pick it up?'

'I suppose I could ask my Dad.'

'Good. Will you?'

'If you manage to get it. There's the bigger problem of how you'll keep it stocked. You can't just drive in and ask the stockman to load it up either. It's all pie in the sky, Joey, and you know it.'

'You leave that end to me,' he retorted. 'It'll all be up and working in a couple of weeks. Wait and see.'

257

Lizzie turned eagerly into Onslow Road with her friend Irene. It was further to walk home from the Lyceum in the centre of New Ferry, but close to the river. Once it had been possible to catch the ferry over to Liverpool from here, but a steamer had run into the end of the pier years ago demolishing part of it and the service had been stopped. Now, only the boarded up ticket office remained, growing shabbier year by year. The once smart New Ferry Hotel now relied on local custom in the bar. Many of the shops in the parade were boarded up too, because trade had gone. The district had become a quiet and shabby backwater.

Now that they could afford to rent a whole unfurnished house, she felt they were doing very well. Joey had let her choose this respectable Edwardian terraced house of shiny red brick. It was bigger than the gatehouse, but not over large.

Lizzie felt a surge of pride as she put the key in the lock. 'This is our house.'

'You are lucky,' Irene breathed. She was a skinny girl with protuberant brown eyes and frizzy hair. 'You've got it lovely.'

Lizzie had polished the brass work on the door until it shone. She'd chosen the new fawn lino that spread up the hall and looked very smart.

'Come in.' She took Irene into the parlour first to admire the new three-piece suite in green velvet.

'We've only just finished doing this room, only had the suite for a week.' Lizzie looked round with satisfaction. It looked settled and fashionable with the new mirror over the mantelpiece and the aspidistra on the windowsill. She'd been dying to show it off.

'Oh, Lizzie! I love your curtains. It's all lovely.'

'It's been hard work.' She laughed excitedly.

'It hasn't taken you long.'

'We've been at it every weekend for ages. Papering and painting and getting everything together.'

'Not on hire purchase?' Irene's face screwed up with horror. 'You didn't dare?'

'No, it's all paid for. Joey doesn't hold with HP.'

'You're lucky having a husband with such a good job.'

'Yes,' Lizzie agreed warily. She'd had to tell a few fibs at work to explain things. She'd told Irene she was eighteen and Joey twenty and that they'd been married a year. She'd bought herself a wedding ring in Woolworth's. It stopped a lot of questions from their new neighbours.

'Lucky to have a husband at all, it's more than I've got. Golly, he's doing well for himself.'

Lizzie tried to smile. She knew the mercurial rise in Joey's income had not come about honestly, but that it would look suspicious if she didn't show pride in it. She loved Joey and felt a tremendous loyalty to him.

She knew everything he did revolved around his love for her, but at times it seemed he wanted to possess her. She was beginning to wonder if this was normal loving.

'Not many could afford all this. You've a much better place than my sister and she's been married for five years.'

'Come and see the kitchen.' Lizzie was especially proud of having a kitchen to herself. She had a gas cooker she was learning to use. She lit it and put the new kettle on to boil. From the new cream enamel kitchen cabinet she took the sandwiches she'd made before going to work.

'Have you got a bathroom?' Irene wanted to know.

'Yes, upstairs. All mod cons and two bedrooms.'

'Can I go and have a peep?'

'Of course, go on up while I make the tea and put a match to the fire in the living-room.'

Lizzie meant to impress Irene. She'd spread a clean cloth on the table in readiness this morning, and now she set it out with scones and sandwiches just like Mrs Bender used to.

She was taking in the tea pot when she heard Joey's key in the lock. It stopped her in her tracks.

'Is something the matter?' she asked as he came in. Her stomach was churning, afraid that there must be to bring him home in his lunch hour. Now they were further from the bus stop, he'd only be able to stay fifteen minutes or so. She was constantly aware that some dreadful calamity might overtake him.

'No. Just thought I'd come home to see you.' He was smiling as he kissed her. Lizzie wanted to ask why, but she was aware of Irene coming downstairs again. She introduced them, feeling confused. Joey had never come home in his lunch hour before.

She ushered Irene into the living-room, sat her down by the fire which was burning up nicely. Handed her a plate and a sandwich.

She turned to Joey. 'Do you want a sandwich?' She'd packed his lunch for him to take to work as usual and was afraid there wouldn't be enough here to satisfy three of them.

'I'll just have tea and a piece of scone.'

He smiled at her lovingly. He appeared to be listening to Irene's praise of the bathroom, but Lizzie could feel his eyes watching her.

Irene said brightly: 'I'm an usherette now. Has Lizzie told you? It's a smashing job. I sell the ice cream in the interval too.'

Lizzie blanched. She knew what was coming. She'd meant to broach the subject that evening when she had Joey to herself.

'There's another vacancy coming up next month. Lizzie's going to ask for it, aren't you, Liz?'

That threw her into a tizzy. She knew she was speaking too quickly. 'Well, it's different for me. You see, I don't want to leave Joey alone every evening, do I?' This wasn't at all how she'd planned to handle it.

Joey's strange eyes looked into hers. They had a new intensity.

'Take it,' he said, 'if you want to.'

She'd expected him to be hurt and angry, but there was no rancour in his voice.

'I'll be busy too. There are things I'd like to do in the evenings. It might be easier if we're both busy.'

It almost took her breath away, though she had spent a few

260

evenings without him recently. It was an about-face for Joey. He'd been very much against it once. She'd expected to have to fight him before she could take it.

Irene asked breathlessly: 'Oh, what are you going to do in the evenings?'

'I want to learn to drive for a start, so I can get a little car when we've saved up a bit.'

'Lizzie, do you hear that? You are lucky!'

A few minutes later, he stood up, wrapped his arms round Lizzie in a bear hug and kissed her. 'See you tonight, love.' He raised his hand in farewell to Irene and was gone.

'Well, I think that's dead romantic,' Irene enthused.

Lizzie felt a niggling anger. Was Joey checking up on what she did? On her friends?

He'd said last night: 'What do you want to ask her here for? This is our place.' All the pleasure she'd felt in showing her new home to Irene was gone.

'He came all the way home just to be with you for a few minutes. He made me feel quite the gooseberry. Even a film star couldn't have more love than that. You don't know how lucky you are.'

Lizzie knew he was jealous of everybody else she knew, even of Irene. Joey believed she belonged to him body and soul.

She was the reason he'd do anything to get money. She was the reason he hated the Mortimers so much and wanted revenge. He thought the richer he was the more she'd love him.

She was beginning to feel she couldn't cope with Joey's feelings. She felt trapped by his love.

Chapter Sixteen

8 May 1936

Joey wheeled the tea urn into the kitchen and made himself a fresh cup. By the time he'd taken tea round the office, he didn't fancy what was left in the urn. He pinched two biscuits from the tin reserved for Greg Mortimer and headed back to the mail room.

This was built under the main staircase, so at one end the ceiling came down to within inches of the floor, making it a claustrophobic place. He was well aware he spent more time here than the job justified, but this was where he had privacy.

An over-large table took up most of the space. He always kept a heap of letters and papers on it waiting to be sorted. Then, if one of the bosses happened to come in, it looked as though he had plenty to do.

He slumped into the only chair, tipped it backwards and put his feet up on the table to make himself comfortable. This was where he worked out his plans to take more money from the company. He'd been mulling over new ways to get goods out of the building for a long time. There were all sorts of things, especially in the office, that he might be able to sell.

The possibilities of this had become clear last winter when he'd been asked to work late one night during stocktaking. He'd been reluctant at first, until he'd found that Evans's was a different place when the workforce went home. He realised immediately that this would suit his purpose better.

He'd been told he wouldn't be expected to count stock, only write down figures on clipboards. In practice, it turned out he was required to hump cartons and boxes round, dust down shelves and make tea for the stockmen.

He'd been coming back with the big teapot along the dark passage from the canteen when he saw a ghostlike shadow flitting ahead of him. He could even hear the clink of metal as though he were in chains.

Joey had a hearty contempt for nervous men, but the mugs were rattling on his tray. It had been pitch dark since half-past five and he'd thought only the four stockmen were in the building with him, and they were all wearing khaki drill coats. He lunged for the next light switch and called: 'Who's there?' The light failed to work.

'Hello?' The grey-haired ghost was waiting for him now. Joey knew he was dragging his steps, still half convinced it was a supernatural being.

At fifteen yards he knew it was human. A man wearing a dark grey pullover and grey slacks. He spoke. 'You one of the stockmen then?'

'Yes,' Joey said weakly. 'Who are you?'

'Night watchman. Elija Jones.' He had a great bunch of keys fastened to his belt that jingled as he moved. Joey breathed more easily. Why had he not thought of a watchman?

'You got a cup of tea for me there?'

'Yes, sure, if you've got a cup.'

'Hang on, I'll fetch my mug.'

Under the brighter light of the boiler room Joey thought he still looked ghostlike. He was short and thin to the point of emaciation, with a grey lined face. He took short even steps so that he seemed to float along. Joey watched him take an enamel mug from a canvas haversack hanging on a nail.

'What's that then?' he asked when the man came back, nodding towards a string contraption hanging across the corner of the boiler room.

'It's me hammock, I bring it with me. Got to get some rest. Good place there, nice and warm always.'

'How many watchmen are there?'

'How many does it take? There's only me. Well, I work five nights, Tommy Lowther does the other two.'

By the time they'd reached the stockroom, it had occurred to Joey that it would pay him to make a friend of the night watchman. The stockmen knew him. They all put down their clipboards and fell on the tea.

'Still doing the two then, Eli?'

'Sure. Got to, haven't I? I've got seven kids to feed and clothe.'

'Pity you didn't start sooner, you might have had fewer kids. Should stop you getting any more, though.'

'Eli's moonlighting,' one of them explained to Joey. 'He works for Cammell Laird's in the day and comes here at night. That's right, isn't it, Eli?'

'How do you manage without sleep?' Joey asked, appalled at the thought.

They all sniggered. 'He sleeps here, of course.'

'There's not too much going on at night.'

'You're doing too much,' Joey said, running his eyes over Eli's frail figure and lined face. 'It'll kill you if you keep on.'

'Here, don't you be saying anything to that Mr Gleeson or anyone in the office. I don't want them giving me the sack.'

''Course I won't,' Joey assured him. Surely this gave him some sort of a hold?

'It's not as if I don't do the job properly. I bring my alarm clock. Every two hours, I wake up and walk round the whole place.'

'I bet,' one of the stockmen said. 'Bet you settle down at ten and sleep like a baby. You'd have to, to keep going. How many years you been doing this now?'

'Nearly nine.'

'Bet the youngest is over nine, Eli?'

'There's never been anything wrong. I've always given satisfaction.'

'Bet you set your alarm for six o'clock in the morning. That would give you just enough time to make a cup of tea and have a wash before you go off.'

'Do you always sleep in the boiler room?' Joey asked, trying to make it appear an innocent question.

'Now I do. Used to use the first aid room. A good couch there with pillow and red blankets, but Sister got nasty though I made sure I left everything as I found it. Now I bring my own hammock and just borrow a blanket.'

Stocktaking started again and Eli took a walk round. He was back quite soon and spent the next hour talking to whoever would listen. Joey felt the gang would have finished sooner if Eli had left them alone. He set about being as friendly as he could.

By seven o'clock the gang was hungry. When they estimated the job would take at least until ten, Joey suggested he go out and get fish and chips. He was hungry too.

'Do you want some, Eli?'

'Yes, be a bit of a treat for once. Bring me a pennorth of chips and a twopenny fish. I'll have to let you out. The yard gate's padlocked.'

'How am I going to get in again, if the place is all locked up?'

'I'll hang about, listen for you.'

'You won't hear me outside at the gate.'

'You'll have to lend him the keys, Eli,' the stockman said.

'Not supposed to let them out of my possession,' he grunted. 'Not 'til I hand them over to Miss Peacock in the morning.'

'Joey's all right,' the most junior stockman said. Joey had had a pint with him down at the Dog and Whistle the week before. 'We don't want him stuck outside with our chips going cold.'

'I'll look after the keys, Eli.'

'Here then, and see you do.' Eli slipped two keys off the ring that jangled at his belt. 'This one's to the door on the loading bay and this to the yard gate. Lock up behind you as you go out.'

The keys were cold against his palm but his cheeks were burning with excitement. He had to stop himself breaking into a run as he headed to the cloakroom first. He took two half used tablets of soap and made impressions of both keys before balancing the soap carefully on top of his lunch paper inside his haversack. Chance had brought him a wonderful opportunity.

He had keys made from the impressions and tested them. He could get in and out of the factory at will, but was unable to get from the factory to the office.

This was part of the same building, taking up one wing of the ground floor, and there were two connecting doors.

Joey made a point of trying them first thing in the morning and found they were kept locked until Eli handed his keys over to the office staff when they came in.

The office could also be reached directly from the street through the main entrance, and through a side door which was used by junior staff.

Another opportunity to work out of hours came shortly afterwards. The office was being redecorated, and the painters were in for two weeks, working in the evenings and at weekends. Joey was asked to come in an hour earlier in the mornings, to get the furniture back in place so that staff could get straight on with their work when they came in.

The cleaners also used the side door and their forewoman had the key. Joey arrived earlier and earlier until one morning he was waiting at the door for her. He watched her unlock it using a Yale key. She put her key ring in her coat pocket and hung that behind the kitchen door. He had to hover nearby for ages until all the women were in, had hung their coats in the kitchen and had started work.

Then, with his heart in his throat, he sorted through the coats swinging on the door. The shapeless green tweed was now the lowest on the peg. His fingers closed on the key ring. There were only two keys on it and the other was not a Yale, so he knew which he needed.

The only soap on the sink was of the kitchen variety, and on the hard side. He was still trying to press the key in evenly when he heard footsteps coming back. He shoved everything into his jacket pocket just as she was coming round the door.

267

His mouth was suddenly dry. God help him if he was caught doing this.

'What you up to then?'

Joey was afraid he looked as guilty as he felt. His cheeks were burning. He had to turn his back on her. He saw a cup on the drainboard.

'Just getting a drink of water,' he said, filling it. 'Haven't you made tea this morning?'

'Yer cheeky bugger. It's hardly worth you coming in if you're going to hang about in here.'

The woman was feeling through the pile of coats. For an awful moment he thought she was checking whether the key was still in there. Then she took a packet of cigarettes from a black coat pocket, put one in her mouth and lit it from the pilot light on the stove.

Joey drank the cup of water and fled to the mail room. He didn't dare breathe until he'd got the door closed and his back against it. When his hands stopped shaking, he made sure the impression was the best he could make, hid the soap and polished the key. He knew he had to return it to the coat pocket before the cleaners left.

He could feel his heart pounding as he went quickly to the kitchen. He opened the door, and the room was deserted. He leaned round and slid the key ring into the pocket of the green coat.

Seconds later, he was striding up the hall, hauling Miss Peacock's file cabinets back against the wall, putting up her curtains, telling himself he could relax. It had been easier than he'd expected, and now he could get into the office too and no one need be any the wiser.

Joey watched the local papers in which Evans's was likely to advertise the vans for sale. It was there the following Friday. 'For sale by tender, two delivery vans in good condition, first registered in 1930.'

He read the instructions carefully. Tenders were to be sealed inside a separate envelope together with ten percent of the cash. For his plan to work, he had to have one of the vans, but he didn't mean to pay over the odds.

He kept a closer watch on the incoming mail over the next week as he sorted it, removing the envelopes he guessed contained tenders.

At work, the only place he could steam an envelope open was the kitchen and during the day he was never alone there long enough. He couldn't risk being seen. He decided to take the letters home and bring them back in time for the next day's delivery.

It meant he had two envelopes to cope with for each tender. The first time he managed to open and re-close them without leaving visible traces. The second, he had to add more glue but thought they'd pass. The third time, the flap creased up when he tried to stick it back. It looked as if it had been prised open and re-sealed.

Lizzie had been dead against him touching them at all.

'I do wish you'd stop all this,' she protested. 'We're doing all right, Joey, we're having a good time, aren't we? If you get caught, you could go to prison. That would break us up good and proper.'

'What am I going to do now?' He stared at the envelope in horror.

'A new envelope,' she suggested coldly.

'But this one's been typed.'

'Get there early and type it then. Surely you can do that?'

'Perhaps.' He'd never tried a typewriter.

'You'll have to,' she said. 'Or be found out.'

Joey was still trying to smooth out the creases. He'd burn both the cheque and the letter except this one had been handed in and signed for.

He bought paper and envelopes the next day, and an hour after everybody had gone home, he went back to the office. He knew his key would turn in the lock, he'd tried it surreptitiously one day when he'd come in late.

He carried a typewriter into the mail room because there he could shut himself out of Eli's sight.

He found he could type with two fingers, but it took a lot of concentration. Having addressed the envelopes, he started typing his own tender. It took him longer than he'd expected. He was afraid Eli would catch him at it, and kept stopping to open the door and listen for him, afraid he'd hear the clacking typewriter. He laid his coat along the bottom of the door in the hope it might deaden the noise. It became too dark to see what he was doing. He used the torch he'd brought to shine on the typewriter, but his heart was in his throat.

It was a relief to finish and put the typewriter back in its rightful place. He was having a drink of water at the kitchen sink when he heard Eli doing his round. He stepped back behind the door and held his breath. Eli came almost close enough to touch, shone a torch round the kitchen before moving on.

Joey felt exhausted but knew Eli would head back to his hammock in the boiler room and he was safe for the moment.

He decided he'd have a good look round before going home. He crept to Miss Peacock's alcove and tried the door to Greg's office. It was locked.

He straightened up in dismay, remembering now seeing him lock it one day when he was going home early. He tried Matthew Mortimer's office and that was locked too. He found all the managers' offices were locked. He wanted to swear with frustration.

He'd seen them being cleaned in the mornings and the doors standing wide open. He remembered too the other key he'd seen on the cleaner's key ring and wanted to kick himself. That had to be some sort of a master key that opened them all. He should have made an impression of that too.

The secretaries didn't lock their offices, they didn't lock their desks either. Joey went carefully through most of their drawers. He found little to interest him.

He would have preferred to go through Greg Mortimer's drawers. He'd wanted to go into Matthew Mortimer's office to take a look at the safe. He found it was impossible.

Hell! He was engulfed by a wave of fury that he'd been

stupid enough to miss the chance when he had it.

Joey bought a van in the name of Daniel Hopkins by tendering five pounds more than any of the others and Bill sent his dad in with a bundle of pound notes to pick it up.

Joey was pleased. He felt he was making progress. All he needed now was to pass his driving test and he could put his new plan into action.

He had a date to take his test, but it was still two weeks ahead. He decided he couldn't wait that long. His luck would have to be really out if he was stopped while driving it over the next couple of weeks.

He told Bill that he'd stock the van for him that night and leave it outside his house. Bill agreed to start selling the stuff the next morning.

Joey had checked that Eli would be working tonight. He'd taken some of the latest sales literature from the office and put it in the van, together with the usual bills and receipts that would make Bill appear to be part of Evans's sales force.

He had the van waiting outside his own front door. He'd leave it until later, when Eli would be thinking of settling down for the night.

He planned a relaxed evening at home alone, glad that Lizzie was not there to ask awkward questions. Up until now he'd told her everything. It had helped to talk things through. He'd wanted to involve her and have her opinions and ideas.

But Lizzie had lost her nerve. He knew she was worried about what he got up to. She nagged at him and kept saying the risks were enormous. He was afraid she wouldn't keep her mouth shut if anything went wrong. She was making him nervous and adding to the danger at the same time. Reluctantly, he'd decided the less she knew the better.

Joey didn't feel relaxed. He was on edge, plain nervous as the clock ticked round. At nine o'clock he made the sandwiches they usually had before going to bed. It was some comfort to think it would all be over by the time he sat down to eat them. He thought of scribbling a note telling Lizzie to go to bed and not to worry, in case it took longer than he expected and he wasn't able to collect her. He started but tore it up. Everything would go according to plan. He didn't want her to know anything out of the ordinary had taken place.

Then he made up the fire and pulled on a navy blue polo necked jersey. He had butterflies in his stomach by the time he was driving along the New Chester Road. He stopped to buy fish and chips for two. Eli was the one component of his plan he had still to cope with. He was hoping to give him to understand that loading the van in the middle of the night was part of Joey's job. Eli hadn't seemed all that bright.

By the time he came to unlock the yard gate he felt on tenterhooks. He drove through and locked it behind him. He'd forgotten about the security lights in the yard; he'd have preferred less light. He backed up to the loading bay and opened the van doors.

He didn't need his key to get inside. The door opened and Eli, looking tired and frail, came out.

'Nobody told me you were coming,' he grumbled. 'What you doing here at this time of night?'

Joey stood on the running board to reach the hot parcels of chips in the front of the van and passed the fragrant scent under Eli's nose.

'Brought us in some supper. Where shall we have it?'

'Well . . .' Somewhat mollified Eli led the way into the boiling shop, sat down on an old form and started to tuck in. 'That won't be all you've come for, will it?'

Joey didn't have much appetite. 'I've come to load the van,' he said.

'What with?'

'Toffee, of course.' He tried to make it sound a bit of a fag.

Eli's eyes were studying him intently. 'Now?'

'Got a nerve expecting me to work at night, haven't they?'

'They never load at night. Come off it.'

'In future they will be. Things have changed. They'll be different from now on.'

'Nobody's told me.'

'They must have forgotten.' Joey slid another chip nonchalantly into his mouth. This wasn't going as well as he'd hoped.

'They never forget that sort of thing.' There was a more decisive tone to Eli's voice. 'Where's your papers?'

'What papers?'

'The usual papers, of course. You've got to have authorisation, lad. So many trays of Devon toffee, so many nut and raisin.'

'Well, I haven't,' Joey said, trying to stay calm. He must keep his wits about him.

Eli, exasperated now, had forgotten his chips. 'You can't just take what you want. I'll have to phone Mr Stickler, he makes out . . .'

'No,' Joey said firmly. He'd have to put his back-up plan into operation.

'You're not going to say anything to anybody. Or I'll have something to say to Mr Gleeson about you moonlighting.'

'What's this, blackmail?' Eli's lined face was twisting with resentment.

'No, of course not. I was hoping we'd be mates.'

'Mates? How can we be mates? You're up to no good.'

'Mates because I'm going to pay you, Eli. I'll pay you the same as Evans's pay you, so you'll have three wages coming in. That can't be bad.'

'How long will that last? We'll both get the sack when they find out.'

'They aren't going to find out, not unless you tell them. You're going to get into that hammock now, and settle down just as usual.' He nodded towards the corner where it was already hung up, a red blanket thrown across it. 'You've not seen me, everything has been quiet. That's all you have to say if they ask.'

'They're bound to miss it sooner or later.'

'It'll be later if at all. Even if they do realise something's gone, they'll think it happened in the daytime.'

'No, you won't get away with it.'

273

'We will. I know we will. But if it comes to the worst and they find out, just keep your mouth shut. I will. Tell them you must have slept through it all. Better to be thought an incompetent watchman than a crooked one. That'll be the time to tell Gleeson you work in the day, then he'll believe you sleep soundly at night.'

'I suffer from insomnia,' Eli said indignantly.

'I certainly wouldn't tell them that! You'll not be wanting to work double shifts for ever, will you?'

'No.'

'You'll be doing a lot less for the money I pay you, and it'll give you a chance to get a bit behind you. How old are you, Eli?'

'Fifty-two,' he said grudgingly. 'What's that got to do with it?'

Joey would have put him at least a decade older than that. 'Can't be good for a man of your age.' He shook his head. 'You should be taking it easier at your time of life. What do you do at Laird's then?'

'I'm a draughtsman.'

'Got a good trade there.'

'The pay isn't all that good.'

'I pay on the dot.' Joey took pound notes from his pocket and handed them over. 'Now all you have to do is put your head down for the night. You'll see nothing, you'll do nothing, and most of all you'll say nothing. Okay? I'll be back next week sometime. Good night.'

Eli trailed up to the stockroom behind him. Joey turned on him. 'Good night, Eli. It's better that you don't know. Honest it is. Good night.'

He heard the soft clink of keys as the man went away. All Joey had to do then was to load up. He'd discussed with Bill what was needed. He'd said plenty of Everton toffee and Devon cream fudge and as wide a variety as possible. He pushed the hand-truck along the shelves in the stockrooms, piling it high. He had to take it down to the van three times and thought it damned hard work all on his own. He was careful to put the truck back exactly where he'd found it and to lock up after him.

As he drove away he wanted to sing. He'd done it. He thought he could go on doing it. He left the van outside Bill's house and put the keys through his front door as arranged. Then he walked briskly to the Lyceum, and was in good time to meet Lizzie. He felt like a walk home and hoped she did. What he'd accomplished tonight was putting a real spring in his step.

Joey was pleased with the way things went over the next few months. He had to pay Bill a good wage, and because he handled the money and knew just how much Joey was making, he had to hand over bonuses too. He also had to pay Eli, but at last money was coming in fast and he felt he was really kicking Greg Mortimer.

'I'm in the money,' Joey crowed, slamming a fistful of pound notes down beside Lizzie's plate. They were just finishing breakfast one Saturday morning. 'I've really come up in the world in the two years we've been here.'

'If you're caught you could go down even faster.'

'Come on, Lizzie, I want to buy you a present. What would you like?'

'I've got everything I need.' He saw her shiver.

'Don't be silly. What about going out for a slap up meal? At a posh hotel. The Adelphi in Liverpool if you like.'

'No, Joey. What's the point of putting yourself in lumber for a meal out?'

'Come on, Lizzie,' he wheedled.

'If it's so important for you to have money, don't fritter it away. You've got things to spend it on, I'm sure.'

'Yes,' he beamed. 'I've got my master plan. I want . . .'

'I don't want to know.' She flounced off to the kitchen and he heard water rushing into the sink.

Joey told himself he had to stop trying to involve Lizzie. He'd been thinking of her more as an extension of himself than another person.

She'd been a useful sounding board for his plans to start with. Perhaps it was a bit too grandiose, to think of setting up his own factory and making toffee too? He could pick up a lot of gear for nothing, and already he had the beginnings of a sales team. If he manufactured similar stuff, even on a small scale, it would be harder to prove where it came from if ever anything did go wrong. But would it be too much trouble?

He'd thought it another stroke of luck when Bill explained to him that Evans's sold their toffee direct to small retailers only on Merseyside itself. In other parts of the country it was sold through wholesalers.

It meant Bill Purley could establish a new round for himself. He chose to go out beyond Chester, didn't even have to do much extra mileage.

The van still carried advertisements for Evans's Toffee on its sides. Everything Bill handled was exactly the same as when he'd represented the firm, except that Joey had had new receipts made out giving the manager's name as P.B. Connell.

It seemed a reasonable precaution to take because if any of his customers had reason to write in, Joey would be alerted by the name and remove the letter when he was sorting the post.

It was all working so smoothly that he had considered hiring another salesman to set up a further round. Bill had recommended Manchester. The difficult part was finding the right man. Joey was trying to decide whether it would be feasible to leave the office and do it himself. He was full of plans. The hard part was deciding which would bring in the most money for the least risk.

Nowadays he made a point of chatting up the stockmen as he took the mail round. He wanted to know if there were any anxieties about stock levels or if any emergency stocktaking was about to take place. It was comforting to find there was not.

Joey believed nobody had noticed that the stock was disappearing. He hoped they wouldn't for a long time. Even if they did, any lead to incriminate him would have to come from Eli. And he was no longer worried about Eli. He thought he would turn out to be as loyal as Bill.

He was growing more careful now. He always parked the van in a side street outside, and came in first to check that only Eli was inside.

The one niggle he had was that Bill occasionally had to accept payment by cheque. Bill did his best to discourage this because cheques had to be made out to Archibald Alfred Evans Ltd, to maintain his front, and then they couldn't cash them.

He brought Joey three cheques in one day which peeved him sufficiently to get his mind moving on another idea.

Why shouldn't he open an account in the name of say Alan Anthony Evans, and get an ink pad and rubber stamp with A.A. Evans on it, to make sure there was no mention of Archibald Alfred on the cheques they received? He'd use an entirely different bank, of course, and preferably one without a branch too near the factory.

Suddenly the whole horizon seemed to open up. Big cheques from the wholesalers flooded into the accounts department all the time. Many of them were made out to A.A. Evans. If he opened an account, some of them could be diverted to that and it would involve him in very little physical work. No wages to pay to anyone else either. Nobody else need know.

With careful thought and planning it ought to be easy. Joey tingled at the simplicity of it all.

Book Four

1937

Chapter Seventeen

5 April 1937

Matthew Mortimer snored softly, his mouth not quite closed.

Hannah pulled her pillow further away so she could study his face in the grey morning light. She decided he was looking older. His monk's rim of hair was turning grey. The dome within was pale because he always wore either a topee or a hat, but the harsh sun of Egypt was leaving its mark on his face. His skin had had an almost permanent tan these last fourteen years. There were deeper lines round his eyes and mouth.

Matt had gone to Egypt in 1923 and spent a whole year there. He came home for a few months now and again, but Egypt always drew him back. When the work cataloguing Howard Carter's find finally finished, Matt found further work at other sites.

None of them had seen much of him recently and the years were going by ever faster. Sometimes Hannah thought of them as empty years; even wasted years. Yet she'd managed to find peace in the small events of living alone. Last night, that had been shattered when Matt had arrived home for a month's leave.

He'd left his suitcases piled up in the hall, though she'd told him only Edna lived in now and she was cooking supper for them. Hannah wasn't used to hearing his resonant voice ring and echo through the house. He was walking up and down like a caged tiger. On the doorstep, he'd given her one dutiful peck on her cheek. He seemed a stranger.

'You've told Greg that you were expecting me home?'

'No. I didn't know myself until yesterday.' She'd been resentful that he hadn't given her more notice.

'I'd better ring him. Let him know I'll be in the office tomorrow. What's his number?'

Hannah found it for him and left him to it. She went to stare through the sitting-room window at the tulips now in full flower, trying to make excuses for his behaviour. He was tired after the journey. Disorientated after travelling by air.

He came to the door, his face like thunder. 'A woman answered saying I'd got the wrong number and that she's never heard of Greg.'

'That's the number he gave me, I've spoken to him on it.'

'You can't have.'

'It must be about six months ago. He must have moved again. He doesn't tell me everything.'

'He doesn't tell you anything! Why does he keep moving?'

'You know Greg, never stays on one track for long. Always chasing off after something new.' Eunice had been right about his marriage to Dulcie Wentworth. It hadn't lasted a year, though Hannah had heard it was Dulcie who had left him not the other way round.

'He's still running the business,' Matt growled.

Hannah sighed. Hugo said he was still drawing his salary but doubted he was doing much else.

'But he hasn't bought a house?'

'No, he rents.'

'But why? Father gave him the money to buy.'

'He said he preferred to rent when I asked him. Anyway, you'll get him this morning at the office. You can ask him yourself.'

'I wish he'd settle down. You said he had another girlfriend?'

'According to Hugo, he's had a whole succession since I said that. Since he and Dulcie have never got round to a divorce, he doesn't introduce them to me, or the rest of the family come to that. Your mother's always on about the same thing.'

'You've seen her then?'

'No. I saw Hugo last week and we talked about Greg.' Hannah paused. 'He took me out for dinner.'

Matt grunted. 'At least you speak to one of my relatives. What else did he say?'

'He asked about you.' He always asked about Matt. She'd sensed last time that he was asking about her relationship with Matt, though he'd put his question in general terms.

It had taken last night to bring home to her just how much distance there was between her and Matt. He'd never been a great lover. It had been a perfunctory business, seeing they'd been apart for two years. Merely going through the motions. She wondered if he had another woman out there.

She thought of Hugo with much more warmth. As the years went by they were seeing more of each other. She had come to rely on him for help with daily difficulties; she even confided in him. She went as his partner to formal dinners and acted as hostess for him at Ince when Eunice wasn't about.

She knew he confided in her. He talked at length about his investments and his gifts to charity. She thought she knew roughly what he was worth. He saw his great fortune as a responsibility and something requiring time and effort on his part. He feared he'd done Matt a disservice and believed now he must think much more carefully before handing large sums down to others and changing their lives. He was rather austere in his personal needs and spent little on himself.

But Hannah also knew they didn't confide fully in each other. They talked of Matt, but she kept her feelings about him and the state of their marriage under wraps, never allowing him the slightest hint.

He was, after all, Matt's father. At first she'd thought it would upset him to know things were not right between them. Now she wasn't so sure.

There was another thing they didn't talk about – their feelings for each other. Hannah saw his smile of welcome if she called unexpectedly, heard the lift in his voice when she phoned. But it seemed he expected nothing more of their relationship. He seemed to be holding it steady, not allowing feelings to go deeper.

For her own part, she thought it too late. Hugo had only to touch her to make cold shivers run up her spine. The very hairs on her arms could pull erect with the thrill of being close to him. But Hugo treated her as a father-in-law should. He was very correct. It seemed that was how he wanted it.

Matt's breathing was growing more shallow. He turned over on to his side and his eyes flickered open.

'Hannah?' But the lids were down again. She thought he was drifting off.

'Hannah.' He seemed suddenly wide awake. 'I want to hear all the news. Bring me up to date.'

'I've told you all I know,' she said. 'I don't see as much of your family now.'

'What about Dorothy?'

'I saw her at Ince last Christmas. She's keeping well.' Her manner had been particularly unfriendly.

Hugo had whispered that Dorothy was not overjoyed to find she was pregnant yet again. Even less pleased when she found later she must expect twins. But she couldn't say that to Matt. Any mention of Dorothy's pregnancy could betray the envy she felt and catapult him into a worse temper.

When Matt was away Dorothy ignored her. She'd never accepted any of Hannah's invitations. Hannah would have liked to be on better terms, if only to see more of her growing family. Henrietta was now sixteen years old, Cecilia fourteen, Honor five and Patience three. The little girls were prettily blonde like their mother; always in the charge of a nanny and always beautifully turned out. Lovely children, but rather spoiled, just as Dorothy had been.

'She must be near her time now,' Matt pondered. 'Have you heard?'

'Any minute.'

'I'd like to see her, but we can hardly ask her to travel this far now. How's Franklin?'

'Haven't seen him since Christmas either.'

The alarm clock started to jangle. She reached over to switch it off.

'Our tea is late coming.'

'I don't have morning tea brought up. Now there's only Edna living in, I told her not to bother. She'll have breakfast on the table in half an hour.'

He flung back the covers and stood up. 'What are things coming to?'

Hannah sighed. Matt was a total stranger. This time his homecoming seemed a disruption in her life.

She had learned to drive in the intervening years and now had a car of her own, a Morris Cowley two-seater with a canvas hood and a dickey seat at the back. Matt borrowed it to drive down to Evans's, leaving her without transport.

It was mid-morning when the phone rang.

'Hannah?' Matt sounded tense. 'Dorothy had her babies last night. Twin boys, all are well. I'm going to drive up to see them. Had you better come with me?'

'Yes.' The Mortimers always flocked to see new members as soon as possible after their birth. She only ever went to Dorothy's house on family occasions.

'Mother's coming to stay at Ince for a few days. She wants to see the new arrivals. I've invited her and Dad for dinner tomorrow.'

'Yes, Matt, all right. Will you ask Greg too?'

'Greg's not here.' There was fury in his voice. 'He's taken a few days off. They tell me he isn't expected back 'til next week.'

'Well . . . He has to take a holiday sometime.'

'He always takes them at the most inconvenient times.'

'He didn't know you were coming home, Matt.'

'He knew about Dorothy. You'd think he'd want to be here.'

'Is everything all right at the factory?'

'I think so. I'll pick you up in an hour.'

Franklin had cotton mills in Rochdale and Oldham and lived in a sizeable house out in the country between the two towns. He had another house near the beach in Formby where Dorothy took the children for the summer months.

Matt was morose on the journey, grumbling about Greg, speculating about where he'd gone.

When they arrived, Hannah was relieved to find Franklin in a convivial mood. He met them in the hall and after a hearty welcome took them straight upstairs to see Dorothy.

She lay propped up on pillows under pink satin coverlets and appeared to be holding court. Hugo was already there, perched on a slippery satin couch, the four daughters of the house surrounding him.

'Congratulations. Sons at last.' Hannah kissed Dorothy's cheek. She seemed anything but pleased. Already she was developing a discontented droop to her mouth.

Hannah thought the bedroom vast and rather grand. There were eight large vases filled with fresh flowers. The bouquet she had insisted they stop and buy on the way up lay unheeded on the pink satin eiderdown.

Hannah had never heard Dorothy say she was content with her marriage, but she seemed to have everything she could possibly wish for. Franklin Flower danced attendance on her and seemed to be a faithful and loving husband.

'Where are the new babies? I can't wait to see them.'

Henrietta led her and Matt up to the nursery. The nanny hovered. She wore a badge on her apron to show she was fully trained. Each infant was asleep in a frilled bassinet, a pink crumpled face topped with straight dark hair.

'Identical twins,' Henrietta whispered. 'Mummy thinks they look like Daddy.'

Hannah felt the pull of attraction. She longed to pick them up and hug them.

'They're lovely.' She'd been determined not to brood on why she had been denied even one child to bring up, when Dorothy, who seemed not over-keen on motherhood, had been blessed with six within her marriage.

'Yes, lovely,' Matt agreed, making hastily for the door again.

Down in Dorothy's room, Franklin, in festive mood, was opening champagne.

'Let's drink to Dorothy and my two new sons. Good health to them all.'

Feeling cheered, Hannah raised her glass. She hoped Matt would be cheered too.

'I can't describe how I feel.' Franklin's eyes glistened with emotion as he swirled the wine in his glass. 'Very indebted to Dorothy. We're a real family now.'

'You already were a family.' Hannah was afraid she was letting her envy show again. 'Four lovely daughters.'

'But twin sons this time. Six now.' Franklin was filled with pride. 'The greatest satisfaction of my life.'

Hannah looked up to find Hugo's seafarer's eyes on her. 'What brings you satisfaction, Hannah?'

She didn't know how to answer. She could hardly say in front of the whole family: 'Your friendship.' She tried to think. Her disappointments came to mind easily enough, but she couldn't mention those either.

'My home, I suppose.' She knew she was giving the stock answers for a childless woman. 'My marriage to Matt.' Any satisfaction she'd had from that had long since dissipated, but she felt the family would expect it. Hugo's eyebrows went up, telling her he had not. Matt continued to quaff his champagne, looking sour.

Hannah was seeing much more of the family now Matt was home on leave. It seemed that almost every day brought some occasion. Hugo and Eunice came to Oakridge for dinner. Matt said he'd invited them only because it was expected of him; he seemed more irritable than ever when they arrived.

Hannah looked round her dining table once they were seated and noticed Hugo's usual air of good humour was absent. Only Eunice was in high spirits.

'I am so thrilled! Twin boys. How fortunate Dorothy is, to

287

be blessed in this way,' she gushed. 'Absolutely delightful, and rather like their father, I think.'

'Like Franklin? Can't see the likeness myself,' Matt muttered.

'His dark colouring. They've got such beautiful fingers, so tiny.'

Hannah guessed both Hugo and Matt would soon have had enough of this. She found it painful for another reason.

Eunice was wearing shiny satin again and showing too much of her over-plump shoulders. 'Hugo, you must settle something on them.'

'I've said I'll think about it.' He sounded testy.

'To have so much money and not to secure their future . . . It's ridiculous.'

'I've told you, Eunice, having a lot of money won't necessarily make them happy.'

'You're giving it all away. You ought to look after your family first. Tell him, Matt, that he really must settle something on the twins.'

In order to help Hugo, Hannah said: 'I thought Franklin had enough to see to that?'

'Of course he has.' Eunice was losing her patience. 'But he's going to have a big family. Hugo should look after his own.'

'When I have, in the past, it hasn't brought the recipient much pleasure,' he said tetchily.

'Nonsense!' Eunice pushed her plate away, for once finding the argument more important than food. 'Nobody can have too much money.'

'With hindsight, Eunice, what I've given Matt is already too much,' he said gravely.

'Now you're being silly!'

Hugo pushed his thick silver hair off his forehead. 'Tell her, Matt. It would have been better if I'd left you to get on with your own life. You've never taken much interest in the business I gave you. You could have had a job with the British Museum from the beginning. Got in on the ground floor, made a real career for yourself in archaeology. You'd have stood on your own feet and enjoyed life more.'

'He's had that too,' Eunice said. 'Haven't you, Matt?'

Hannah had never seen him look so embarrassed and disconcerted. She knew Hugo was speaking the truth.

'Not quite,' Matt said soberly. 'I wasted years in Evans's. I wasn't out in the field working when all the wonderful finds were being made. Yes, I managed to get work in cataloguing and restoration, but I missed the big opportunities.'

Hannah couldn't take her eyes off him. Money had never interested him. He bought everything he needed and didn't stint himself, but his needs were few. He didn't care for fancy food and fine wine. Clothes he replaced when they grew shabby, fashion was not for him. Like his father, he had an austere streak. Now, as he was growing older, it was becoming stronger.

'Matt hasn't achieved what he might have done.' Hugo sounded regretful. 'And it was my fault. On top of that he feels guilty because he hasn't achieved great things in business either. He feels he's disappointed me. That right, Matt?'

Matt's cutlery crashed down on his plate. 'I suppose so,' he admitted.

'Everybody's different,' Eunice snapped, peevish too now. 'Matt's always had this enthusiasm for ancient relics, but Greg's very pleased with what you gave him. He's happy to make a big success of Evans's.'

Matt's lips were straightening into a line of displeasure. Hannah was afraid Greg wasn't the great success Eunice believed him to be.

Nobody in the family was able to contact Greg until he returned to his desk at Evans's on the following Monday. Matt came home in a furious temper that lunch time and told her Greg had been to Epsom for the Derby. Hannah knew relations between them were strained as a result.

It surprised her when a few days later Greg invited the family to his house for dinner. He had had a home of his own

289

for more than a decade now, but Hannah could count on one hand the invitations he'd issued. He'd moved away from Birkenhead and had rented houses in Heswall and West Kirby. This time he'd chosen a house in Hoylake with windows looking straight out over the Irish Sea.

Matt didn't really want to go. It took him longer than usual to bathe and change in readiness. They were late arriving. Greg wore the smartest dinner jacket Hannah had seen in a long time, but he wasn't in a good mood.

'Had trouble finding your place,' Matt greeted him. 'Don't know why. We should have known it would be the biggest in the district.'

Hugo and Eunice were already in the sumptuous forty-foot-long drawing-room, standing by separate windows and looking out to sea. If Greg had a current girlfriend, he had not invited her to meet his family.

As Hugo kissed her cheek in greeting, Hannah asked: 'Everything all right?'

'No,' he whispered. 'Eunice hasn't stopped prompting me about money. I wish she'd let it drop. And you?'

'Can't believe we're invited. Matt's hardly on speaking terms with Greg.'

Hugo grinned. 'You look very smart tonight.' She was wearing a new dinner dress in dark red. It came high at the neck in front and had long sleeves, but left her back bare.

'Such a lovely house,' Eunice was saying. 'You've got good taste, Greg.'

Hannah took in the Aubusson carpet, the marble fireplace, the prisms of colour sparking off matching chandeliers. It was far grander than Oakridge. Grander even than Ince Hall.

'Do you rent it furnished?' Hugo wanted to know. 'Or is all this yours?'

'It's mine.' A manservant was bringing drinks on a silver tray. 'Try a Manhattan cocktail, Grandpa, or Bennett can mix you a Sidecar.'

'I'd prefer straight whisky if you don't mind, Greg, can't do with these deadly mixtures.'

Hannah found the dining table a revelation. Even Eunice didn't have baskets carved from ice to hold curls of butter.

'Who makes these for you?' There was envy in her voice.

'I have a French chef.'

'Good God!' Matt said. 'This is quite a place for a bachelor.'

'How many staff do you have living in?' Hannah asked faintly.

'I have a housekeeper and my valet.'

The table was set with antique silver and crystal, with a bowl of white carnations and gypsophila in the centre. Festooned round it and down the white starched cloth were garlands and trails of green smilax. Everything sparkled in subdued candlelight.

'I just love it,' Eunice said. 'Delightful. You've got wonderful taste and quite a talent for entertaining.'

'Quite a talent for spending,' Hugo said.

'It shows he enjoys money,' Eunice snapped. 'You and Matt don't.'

Hannah smiled. When Eunice left Hugo at Ince, he didn't display his wealth but seemed rather to play it down and move unnoticed amongst others.

'It shows conspicuous consumption.'

'Grandpa, you enjoyed money when you were young, didn't you? You used to say you got great pleasure from being a millionaire at twenty-two.'

Hugo smiled. 'That did give me a lift.'

'Everything in your life gives you a lift,' Eunice said spitefully. 'Everything you've ever wanted has fallen straight into your lap.'

'That's not true.' He was frowning at his plate.

'Name one thing?'

Hugo chewed his duck slowly. 'I couldn't persuade Churchill he was wrong. He returned us to the prewar gold standard in 1925.'

'Having friends in high places gives you real satisfaction.'

'I've been courted by politicians. I've given to their cause so they show gratitude and hope I'll give more. But as for

291

accepting my advice . . . No, not often, even though as a businessman I knew I was right.'

'But that didn't affect you personally.'

'Indeed it did. It led fairly rapidly to the General Strike, a long coal stoppage, and reduced the profitability of my businesses. Everybody else's businesses too, including yours. We're still feeling the effect.'

'But that is such a general . . .'

'It's given me no pleasure to watch the decline of the British Empire either.'

'Surely you don't feel you can affect such things?'

'Of course we can. We are all responsible. Every one of us has obligations.'

'For lesser mortals, our obligations are nearer home.' Eunice crashed her knife and fork down on her plate.

'What do you mean by that?' Hugo's tone was still one of quiet reason.

'Obligations to our families. The rest of us put those first and foremost.'

'Are you saying that I don't?'

Hannah could see a heightened colour in Hugo's cheeks now. The discord was making them all uneasy.

'You're dragging your feet about settling something on the twins. And poor Greg too. He's in need of a little more.'

The silence dragged. Hannah knew Eunice had touched Hugo's raw nerve. She watched his gaze swing to Greg.

'Did I not give you enough?' His voice was cold.

Greg seemed not to know where to look. He muttered: 'It was quite a long time ago . . .'

'That, Greg, is an advantage. You've had the interest all these years. You asked for it then. You were twenty, about to get married and in need of a home of your own.'

'You know that fell through, Grandpa.'

'And several subsequent engagements and a marriage have come to nothing. But each time you managed to console yourself with a spending spree. You wore the first Oxford bags I ever saw and you bought yourself a double breasted dinner jacket as soon as the Prince of Wales started wearing them.'

Greg stared back at him with his mouth slightly open. He looked affronted.

'You bought yourself a sporty Chrysler Roadster – quite an expensive toy – and you've had a new car every year since. What was that one with the Egyptian mascot on the bonnet? The Sun God Ra with an asp on the forehead signalling power?'

'The Stutz Black Hawk Speedster,' Greg said reluctantly.

'I suppose you thought the mascot would please your father?'

'Don't be silly,' Matt said.

'Greg's been silly. He must have found other ways of spending money, because even this would not account for what I gave him.'

Hannah watched Greg's face turn brick red. 'What's the point of having money if I don't spend it and enjoy it?'

'None at all, but I'd hoped you'd have enough sense to spend first on things that would secure your own future. You said you wanted a business of your own. You certainly need a roof over your head. But instead you rent a house and manage your father's business. A French chef, for goodness' sake!'

Matt was growing more angry. 'I rely on Greg to run Evans's. You know I have to, if I'm out of the country.'

'I'm disappointed in that too,' Hugo said quietly.

The banquet came to a halt. Cutlery was laid down on plates only half cleared. Greg sat turned to stone and did not ring for his housekeeper to return.

'If Evans's was making the profit it should, you wouldn't need to ask me for money.'

Greg blustered: 'Times have been hard since the war. For everyone.'

'That's why you should take more interest in what the politicians are doing. They pass new laws which change

293

conditions and your business has to change with them.'

Hugo sat back in his chair, looking balefully round the table.

'Much of my satisfaction has come from earning my own fortune. I've had a wonderful life. If wealth had been handed to me as a child that satisfaction would have been denied me. I don't want to deny it to my relatives, but neither do I want them to go to the lengths I had to in order to get a little capital to start up. That was the reason I gave you money. You've wasted it.'

His anger erupted again. 'I've seen at first hand how the offspring of millionaires squander their lives. Young men who've had every wish fulfilled almost before they think of it. Young men with money burning holes in their pockets.

'They use money as you've used it, Greg. Trying to buy life's thrills, believing them to be found in wild parties with wilder women, unlimited alcohol, gambling and betting.

'They've no need to prove themselves; no need to work; no need to apply themselves to anything but pleasure. I've seen many end up dissolute and useless.

'It isn't wise to hand on too many of this world's goods to the next generation. It can ruin them. It damps down ambition and removes the hunger for work. Money brings power to those who earn it but to those to whom it is given, it can bring disaster.

'So, Greg, as I see it, you've squandered a small fortune. You're thirty-four. If you aren't capable of earning your own living now, you never will be. What's it gone on? High living? Fast women? Slow horses? I see no reason to underwrite that sort of life for you.'

Hugo got up from the table, refilled his glass from the bottle on the sideboard. 'Dorothy's children are a different matter. Another generation. They may prove more rewarding.' He went out, closing the door behind him.

Nobody spoke for five minutes. Then Greg rang for the pudding to be brought in, a fantastic creation of spun sugar with whipped cream and fresh pineapple. The rest of the family showed interest. Hannah felt she couldn't take another mouthful.

'Excuse me,' she said. Dropping her starched napkin on the table, she went to find Hugo.

He was stretched out on an armchair by the drawing-room fire. It was a warm evening and the room was rather too hot.

'Children can be a disappointment, Hannah,' he said without looking up. 'They don't always turn out as you'd like them to.'

'Every parent knows children are a mixed blessing. That they bring both joy and sorrow.'

'In my case disappointment and sorrow. First Matt and now Greg. They might be Mortimers, but there's too much Schofield in them. And that's my fault.

'I had such high hopes of Greg. He used to love following me round factories. Kept telling me he was going to be just like me when he grew up. But lusting after luxuries and getting them became his first aim. Not understanding business.'

He sighed and rubbed his beard thoughtfully. 'What is the matter with me, Hannah?'

'Nothing.'

'What I really enjoy is making more and more money. Stupid, isn't it? I still watch my investments like a hawk. Yet I have no use for the money.'

'You give huge sums to charity, Hugo.'

'Yes, I give it away,' he said slowly. 'Yet when Greg asks for more, it sticks in my craw.'

'Might have been better if he'd asked himself, instead of getting Eunice to do it for him.'

'He should pull Evans's round and make it more profitable. If he'd just put his mind to it . . .'

'Perhaps he doesn't know how?'

'Of course he knows. I explained it often enough.'

Hannah thought Matt's leave would never end. She began to dread the family gatherings. All they seemed to do was bicker when they came face to face.

In the middle of one, Greg mentioned he'd like to take another few days off to go to Ascot. It caused an eruption.

Matt's face turned crimson. 'I thought you were supposed to be running the business? You're never at your desk.'

Greg was doing his best to appear relaxed. 'I thought while you were home, Dad, it would be a good time to take some holiday. If anything should come up, you're on hand to deal with it now.'

'So much needs to be done. We need to get our heads together and get on with it.'

'I'll do what's necessary.' Greg's lips were tightening. 'All in good time.'

'You'll never get round to doing anything!' Matt said through clenched teeth.

'If you don't like the way I'm managing Evans's, you can stay home and do it yourself,' Greg flared back at him.

Hannah knew it was the last thing he wanted to do. Matt backed down.

'Under the circumstances,' Hugo said wryly, 'I think you'd be wise to miss Ascot this year, Greg.'

Eunice held a family lunch every Sunday at Ince Hall. During one, she said: 'It's a shame Dorothy's lying in and missing all this. It would be lovely to have her here. The family isn't complete without her.'

Hannah surmised Hugo, too, was tiring of the present state of affairs when he suggested: 'Why don't you go up and see her, stay with her for a few days?' Eunice had already been several times, but always returned on the same day.

'She's going to invite us all before Matt goes back.'

His leave was almost over before Dorothy recovered sufficiently. They were all invited to see how well the twins had advanced in their first month of life, have dinner and then stay the night because of the distance.

Matt wanted to go to a lecture that evening. 'Do you suppose she'd mind if I didn't go?'

'Of course you must go,' Hannah said sharply. 'It's

a farewell party for you too.'

As soon as she was in the hall Hannah sensed a different atmosphere. Franklin looked peevish and not at all pleased to see them. Even his moustache drooped more.

Dorothy came downstairs to kiss each in turn, wearing a red crêpe dress that seemed a little tight for her. Hannah noticed she kept tugging at it. She also noticed Franklin and Dorothy neither looked at nor spoke to each other. The air was stiff with tension.

Greg arrived two minutes behind them. 'You're getting fat, Dot,' he said, patting her rump.

'It's the first time I've worn a dinner dress since,' Dorothy said crossly. 'Having babies is ruinous to the figure.'

'You'll soon get those few pounds off,' Hannah tried to soothe her. 'Can we see the twins before we change?'

The nanny didn't approve of her playing with little Patience when she was on the point of being put to bed. The babies were already asleep, tight bundles but noticeably larger.

'Please don't touch them,' the nanny said, when she saw Hannah hover over them. Hannah would have loved to give them a cuddle. 'I've had a lot of trouble getting them off to sleep tonight.'

'Twins are such a lot of work,' Dorothy complained. 'And the nursemaid's left without giving notice. It's very difficult to get girls to live in these days. I have to spend such a lot of my time in here, helping out. Feeding them and that sort of thing.'

Hannah knew such a state of affairs was unlikely to suit Dorothy. 'I expect you'll find somebody soon. The babies are beautiful.' She couldn't resist adding: 'You're very fortunate to have them.'

Dorothy's style of entertaining was very like her grandmother's. A cocktail each was waiting on the dressing table in their room. Matt drank his in a couple of gulps. He hurriedly changed into his dinner jacket, and rushed down to get another drink.

Hannah followed more slowly. Franklin had little to say to

anyone. She was glad to see Hugo and Eunice, who had been changing when they arrived.

The food was excellent, but the evening seemed long. Franklin became more withdrawn as time went by. He seemed morose, sunk in misery. Dorothy was aggressive.

Hugo tried to brighten things up. 'Wonderful to have a family of this size, Franklin. You really do have something to celebrate. I'd have given my back teeth to manage this. So would Matt.'

It didn't help.

Dorothy's look of discontent was more familiar; tonight she proved she could be almost as waspish as her grandmother.

'I don't think you realise just how much work babies make, Hannah. If you did, you certainly wouldn't want them. There's no let up.'

Hannah was glad when it was time to go to bed. Franklin had gone to work before any of them were up for breakfast the next morning.

Chapter Eighteen

12 May 1937

Matt had returned to Egypt two weeks ago and Hannah was relieved to be settling back into a peaceful routine without him. She was tidying up the rockery in front of the dining-room window when she heard the phone ring. A moment later Edna was calling her in.

'Hannah?' Franklin's voice was charged with emotion.

'Yes, what is it, Franklin?' Mid-morning was an unusual time to hear from him. 'The twins are well, I hope?'

'Yes, it's Dorothy. Hannah, she's gone!'

'Gone where?' She was kicking herself then for being such a crass idiot.

'Gone away. She's left me. She says she isn't coming back.'

It took her so long to reply, Franklin's voice came again: 'Hannah, are you there?'

'Yes, do you know where she's gone?'

'She's gone off with another man. Run away with him. I can't believe it.'

Hannah went cold then hot. She was shocked, but knowing Dorothy, had no difficulty believing it.

'What about the children?'

'They're here, she hasn't taken them. But she's taken Gladys the new housemaid with her, and it's left us short staffed. The nurserymaid left a month or so ago, and we haven't been able to get a replacement. Nanny's finding it hard to manage on her own, and with Dorothy gone it's a lot of responsibility.'

'I'll help you find somebody,' Hannah soothed.

'It's practically impossible these days.'

'You could borrow Edna as a temporary measure. She's a good all round help.'

'Could I?' She heard the relief in his voice.

'Have you rung Eunice? She'll need to know. Warn her in case of questions from the press. They're both in London.'

Hannah was missing Hugo's company, but he'd said he'd not stay much more than a week. He had business matters to see to.

'I know, I tried to, but she was out at one of her Committees.' Franklin sounded despondent. 'She'll be upset.'

'Franklin, we're all upset. Did you . . .?'

'Yes, I spoke to Hugo. He suggested I ask you; said you'd be the best person to help with the children. Do you mind?'

'I'll be glad to, Franklin. I'll come right away.'

Hannah put the phone down and sat staring into space, warming towards Hugo because he'd remembered how she felt about children. Her first reaction had been to go up and see how she could help, taking Edna with her. But of course she'd have to ask the maid and if she was going to stay, she'd need time to pack.

It occurred to her that Hugo would know what she really wanted and would expect her to ask for it.

Perhaps Franklin would allow her to bring the twins here instead? Might even prefer it. She could see to their well-being more easily than he could. He had to see to his business as well as the girls. She felt fluttery with anticipation as she reached again for the phone.

'Take them to Oakridge? I don't know . . . Without the nanny?'

'You'll need her to look after the girls, Franklin.'

He sounded as though he was beyond making decisions, but he didn't object. It would take her an hour or so to drive up there and meantime he could be thinking about it. She told Edna to put her hat and coat on and come with her.

Franklin's housekeeper spoke in shocked whispers as though

the household had been bereaved.

Franklin was even more distraught than Hannah had supposed. She couldn't mention Dorothy's name without causing his eyes to shine with unshed tears. He couldn't sit down; couldn't even keep still when he spoke to her.

She'd never felt close to Franklin. She'd thought him blinkered not to see Dorothy for what she was. Foolish to think of marrying any girl of her age. Now she felt a rush of sympathy. He'd loved Dorothy and she knew how painful it was to be rejected by someone you love. She'd been through it herself.

'My housekeeper had the nerve to tell me Dorothy had been packing for a week,' he complained. 'She might have warned me.'

'Probably didn't realise she was keeping it from you.' Hannah was trying to make him see reason.

'So she said, even so . . . Dorothy waited 'til I went to work yesterday. She let him bring his car to the door and had everybody helping to carry her things out. She's no shame!'

'Who is he, do you know?'

'Yes, it's Duncan Grieve. I know his father quite well, he owns Teddington Mill. We've been going over to play bridge at their place quite often. Dorothy didn't play, of course, she used to sit and watch. She met Duncan there. Hannah, he's years younger than me.'

Poor Franklin, she thought. This morning he'd pass for sixty. His shoulders were bowed, his prominent teeth biting on his lip.

'But he's the same age as Dorothy?' Hannah counted up the years. She'd be about thirty-one or so.

'Perhaps a year or two older.'

Hannah kept a firm hold on her tongue. There was nothing she could say to comfort him. Franklin had always been too set in his ways for Dorothy. He was only a few years younger than Matt.

'Do you think she'll come back to me?'

Hannah did not, but thought it wiser not to say so. Franklin had the look of a man who feels his whole life has collapsed about him.

'Do you want her back, after this?'

'Yes, of course. How can I manage without her? And the children? The poor children. The twins are not sleeping through the night. They're difficult to feed.'

'Let me take them home with me. I'll be able to give them all the attention they need. I'll love having them, Franklin. I'll keep them safe for as long as you like.'

He was nodding his agreement, sunk in his own misery. 'They're too young to know what's happening to them.'

'What about the girls? Do you want . . .?'

'They are some consolation to me, some company. Besides, the older ones are settled at school. It wouldn't help them to be taken away. Nanny can manage if she doesn't have the twins to see to.'

'It won't be long before Patience starts school too,' Hannah said cheerfully.

'They're upset, of course. Poor children, they're missing their mother too.'

Hannah could not help but be moved by his agony, but she knew his children would fare better than Elizabeth had. At least they still had a father who cared.

'Such a scandal. It's all over town. I can hardly bear to go to the mill. Everybody's talking about it.'

'You must, Franklin. Don't put it off. It'll be even harder if . . . Will they come back here to live?'

She knew she'd shocked him. 'After all this fuss?'

'If he has a mill here . . .'

'No, no, it belongs to his father. Duncan worked for him. He has nothing.'

'Then how will they live?' Hannah bit her lip. She knew without going any further.

'Her grandfather, Sir Hugo, has seen to that.' His voice was bitter. 'I asked him not to give Dorothy more money. I never liked the idea of her having her own. Thanks to him, she can afford to keep Duncan Grieve in comfort for the rest of his life.'

Hannah winced. Now she was seeing what Franklin was really like. Set in his ways, wanting his wife to be completely dependent on him.

'I wish Hugo hadn't interfered. He knew Dorothy would want for nothing. He's got far too much money and all he ever thinks about is making more. He thinks it can buy anything.'

Hannah rushed to support him. 'Sir Hugo is well known for his philanthropy.'

'Sir Hugo! That's another thing. He bought himself that knighthood. Eunice didn't like being plain Mrs.'

'No, Franklin, it was awarded for services to the community.'

Hannah had heard Eunice say she considered the knighthood conferred on her husband to be very much inferior to the baronetcy her father had inherited.

'He's always been hand in glove with Lloyd George. It's well known he's sold honours. Ten thousand is what he asked for a knighthood. Disgusting thing to do.'

'If Hugo was buying an honour he'd have gone for a peerage,' Hannah said sharply. 'We all heard peerages were going for a hundred thousand. You said yourself he has more money than he knows how to spend.'

Franklin was staring at her tight-lipped. 'Eunice should never have married him, he's really not one of us.' She knew Franklin was pointing out that they came from the class of traditional nineteenth-century wealth and privilege, and Hugo did not.

'I'm sorry. This isn't the time to argue about such things. Hugo will do all he can to help, I'm sure. He'll be upset too.'

'Upset because it'll reflect on him. He won't welcome the scandal either.'

'No.' Hannah sighed, remembering how she and Matt had tried to spare him this all those years ago. This time, there was nothing anybody could do about it.

But she drove home in high excitement. Behind her on the

back seat she could hear the twins whimpering softly and Edna making clucking noises to them. She felt ashamed to be finding pleasure in their company when Franklin had been so upset.

The scandal was splashed on the front pages of the national newspapers the next morning. There were photographs of Sir Hugo and Lady Mortimer and photographs of Dorothy and Franklin, some taken at the time of their wedding. Hannah knew Franklin would be horrified to see them.

From where Hannah sat in her small sitting-room she could see the big twin pram swaying slightly as the babies settled down for their morning nap. When the weather was fine, she put them out in the garden under the trees.

A week had gone by. The news about Dorothy had resulted in a lot of telephone calls and had brought Hugo and Eunice back to Ince Hall from their London home in Albany. They had come together to Oakridge to discuss the problem.

'Have you heard from Matt?' It was always Eunice's first question. It made Hannah realise he wrote even less often to his mother. He was a methodical man who wrote to Hannah on the first of every month.

'He had a good journey back, but says the heat is awful at this time of the year. He's at Knossos now on Crete. There's still a lot of work to be done there. He's enjoying it.'

She poured coffee for Hugo. He was pulling a face about Matt.

'He'll have to know about Dorothy. Such bad news.' Eunice dabbed at her eyes with a fragment of lace. 'I blame this Duncan Grieve. He must have talked her into it. He must have some hold over her. He's an evil man. How could she have fallen into his clutches?'

'I didn't know he was a Member of Parliament,' Hannah replied. 'Franklin said he had nothing but what his father paid him.'

'Bringing disgrace on the Mortimer name. I can't bear to open the newspapers these days.'

'You don't have to,' Hugo said. 'Anyway, her name's Flower, has been for years.'

'Every paper points out you're her grandfather. They're very hard on her again this morning, saying she's abandoned her children.'

'She has,' Hannah said, and couldn't help the note of satisfaction creeping into her voice. Having the twins had brought new purpose to her life.

She even liked to hear them cry; they were bringing this warren of a house to life. At the turn of the century an army of servants had been employed to run it. Soon she would have only two daily women.

She couldn't let Eunice know Edna had given in her notice. She was going to get married, and her husband-to-be was a policeman who had been allocated a police house in the suburbs of Liverpool. Already, most of Hannah's own day was spent looking after the babies and she was loving it.

Eunice was staring disdainfully at the playpen in the corner of the room. 'A bit young for that, aren't they?'

'It's a safe place to put them down,' Hannah faltered. 'There's two, you see.'

'I'll take them home.' Eunice got up, sucking in her breath painfully as her weight went on her bunions. 'To make sure they're properly looked after.'

She limped to the pram just outside the french window. 'I can do so much more for them.'

'No.' Hannah jerked to her feet in alarm. 'They are being looked after properly, you can see they are.'

'Just a peep at them in their pram,' Eunice sniffed. 'You've no experience of children, Hannah. And neither has that girl you've got to help you. I've had Matt, and I virtually brought Dorothy up after her mother died.'

'Not much of a recommendation,' Hugo grunted. 'Be too much for you now, Eunice.'

'Of course they won't! I'll get a trained nanny.'

'You'll want to go back to London soon and Albany isn't ideal for babies.'

305

Once he'd owned a house in Cadogan Square, but when it became difficult to get live-in staff, that had become too much for Eunice too. It had been easier to take rooms in Albany. It meant they could no longer have guests to stay while they were in London, but that didn't seem too great a price to pay.

'Far too much for you, Eunice. The babies will be better off here with Hannah. Anyway, you can't possibly take them without Franklin's permission. And he wouldn't want them to go to London, would he? He'd never see them there. Too far.'

Hannah felt a wave of gratitude but Hugo's eyes wouldn't meet hers.

'Having them here has made all the difference to me, Eunice. I've always wanted children of my own. I feel alive . . .'

Eunice was staring at her aggressively. Hannah was afraid she meant to take them.

'There's no question of our taking them away, Hannah,' Hugo said gently.

She felt relief stealing over her. Outside in the garden the pram began to shake and she heard an infant's cry. She ran out to bring the babies in.

Piers was the stronger, slightly bigger with a slow wide smile. Paul's limbs seemed always to be kicking and punching, he needed less sleep and cried more. Hannah hugged them both, delighting in the scent of baby powder and warm milk.

It made her think about Hugo when he'd gone. Usually he treated her with warmth and friendliness. Yet occasionally she sensed him withdraw from her. She felt it was deliberate, that he wanted to keep his distance.

She didn't like it, it was hurtful when it happened, but Hugo would turn up again on her doorstep a few days later and it wouldn't be mentioned. They'd have a cup of tea and a laugh, and she'd be sure once again that he was the closest friend she had.

She decided to thank him. Let him know how grateful she was and how much she was enjoying having the twins in her house. She went out to the hall and reached for the phone. It rang before her fingers closed on it, making her jump. 'Hello?'

'Hannah? It's Clarissa.' She sounded slightly breathless.

It took her a moment to reply. Her mind was still on Hugo. 'Clarissa! How nice to hear from you.'

'I just had to let you know, Peggy O'Malley is home for a few days. Quite grown up now.'

'She's the older girl who went to Crewe?'

'Yes, and she's heard from Lizzie and Joey. I saw her walking with the younger O'Malleys into Pen-y-Clip. She was wearing a very smart cardigan and when I admired it, said they had sent it for her birthday.'

Hannah was gasping. In her life, months passed when nothing happened, now things seemed to be moving faster.

'They are together then?'

'Yes, and in Birkenhead. I asked about Lizzie and Peggy said she had a good job. That they both had good jobs and were enjoying themselves.'

'Did you get the address?'

'She was defensive the moment I asked. If she knows, she wasn't saying. I did try, Hannah, I know that's what you want. I couldn't get it out of her.'

'That'll be Joey's idea. Probably told her to keep it quiet. He's determined I won't find Lizzie, and cleverer than I thought at stopping any leak.'

'Peggy thinks they're doing very well for themselves.'

'If only we knew where they were.'

Hannah tried to think. Since Dorothy had run off so publicly with another man, it was surely pointless to try to hide her earlier lapse. Her reputation was already in shreds, there was no reason now to hide Lizzie's existence. Hannah could invite her openly to the house. Now, there was no reason why the rest of the family should ignore her .

'You've no need to worry about her, Hannah. She's all right.'

'By O'Malley standards I expect she is. Clarissa, have you heard about Dorothy?'

'Read all about it in the papers. A full-blown scandal this time, and him a Member of Parliament. After all we did for her . . .'

Hannah suddenly felt as though she was choking. 'Yes, we put Lizzie through all that. Deprived her of love, care, a decent education, everything. And all for nothing. That's what it adds up to.'

'You mustn't blame yourself, Hannah.'

'I can't help it.'

'Matt and Dorothy herself are far more to blame.'

'Oh, I know, but I would like to find her. She deserves better than she's had. Come and stay with me for a few days, Clarissa. I've got Dorothy's twins here, you'll love them. Lizzie's half-brothers.'

'I'd love to, but it's summer again and Leo's busy time. In the autumn perhaps. I could help you look for Lizzie.'

'I've tried, but it's not that easy. Not like Pen-y-Clip where everybody knows everybody else. I'll tell Hugo about her. He'll know what to do.'

For once, Hugo was deliberately letting his mind dwell on Hannah. To do so gave him pleasure and blotted out the chaos Dorothy was causing. The phone never stopped ringing. Journalists kept intruding. Even Beaverbrook who claimed friendship telephoned, but since he owned the *Express*, Hugo was wary of speaking to him. He felt hounded.

Eunice complained that neighbours and strangers approached her, asking if details they'd heard, usually scandalous details, were true. He was tired of telling her to speak to no one.

There had been a new radiance about Hannah this morning, making her achingly beautiful. Hugo was afraid what he felt must be imprinted on his face, and could not understand why it was not obvious to Eunice. But her mind was on Dorothy. She felt betrayed by her and could not stop lamenting.

He'd instructed his housekeeper to answer all calls and say

he was busy elsewhere. She came to the dining-room while they were eating lunch.

'Mrs Hannah Mortimer says she'd like a word with you, sir,' she told him.

His hand jerked because he'd been thinking of her, and he leapt to his feet more quickly than he should have done.

Eunice's voice followed him querulously: 'Why don't you ring her back when we've finished eating?'

Hannah's voice was soft. 'Hugo? I wanted to thank you. I'm so grateful for your help.'

He felt mesmerised. 'What help?'

'Eunice wanting to take Piers and Paul. You insisted they stay with me.'

'Quite right too. They'd tire her out.'

'Something else has come up. I'd like to know what you think. Have your advice.'

'I'm flattered. What about?'

'I can't explain over the phone. It's a long and complicated story. Could you come back to Oakridge? Alone, please, Hugo.'

He took a deep breath to steady himself.

'Are you free this evening? Could you come round for a drink?'

'Of course, Hannah. Six o'clock all right?'

'Yes, fine. See you then.'

He put the phone down very slowly, hardly able to believe it. There was nothing he wanted to do more, but he'd have to keep himself on a tight rein.

Chapter Nineteen

15 May 1937

Hugo nosed his old Buick into the drive of Oakridge. He'd grown attached to the car over the many years he'd owned it. He bought new cars to be chauffeured round in. If he was driving himself, he preferred to use the Buick.

By the time he was on the steps the front door was opening. It pleased him that she'd been watching for his arrival.

'Hello, Hannah.'

He followed her through the large square hall to the small sitting-room at the back. Her figure was still girlish in a blue dress that was slender to mid-thigh and then rippled and swirled about her legs in the latest style.

She'd lit a fire because the evening was cool and overcast. It was little more than a comforting glow in the grate.

He studied her now as she busied herself getting him some whisky. He'd always found her high cheek bones and large straight nose attractive and the passing years had left them unchanged.

He could just see the first silver threads coming in her dark hair, but she wore it shorter and loose about her shoulders these days and that made her seem young.

'What is it you want to tell me?' He'd been pondering on that since she'd phoned.

'Rather a confession, Hugo. Something Matt wanted to keep from you.' Her dark eyes shot a nervous glance at him.

'You don't have to tell me.'

'I do, because I want you on my side.'

Hugo said nothing. He couldn't tell her he'd be on her side no matter what she did, that he'd always champion her against the rest of the world.

She was rushing on: 'We were trying to protect Dorothy's reputation.'

'Waste of time,' he grunted.

'She's blown it to smithereens now, but . . .' Hannah's eyes wouldn't leave his, she was suddenly serious. 'She had a baby you don't know about, when she was seventeen. We pretended to take her to Switzerland for her health.'

He stiffened with surprise and tried to cast his mind back. He had thought . . .

'You were very tense when you got back.'

Hannah was searching his face as though for signs of condemnation.

'It was a girl, I named her Elizabeth. Matt wouldn't let me keep her. I should have done more for the child than I did. She was brought up at Yarrow.'

'What better place? Good country air. You have a friend there, haven't you?'

'Yes, but I couldn't ask her . . . I put too much responsibility on her anyway. Elizabeth was brought up by one of her farm workers. She ran away when she was fourteen and about to start work.'

'At fourteen?'

'Yes, she came here to Birkenhead. She's with one of the family who brought her up. He's the office boy at Evans's, and he's letting it be known that she wants no contact with us.'

'What do you want?'

'I'd like to offer her a home. I feel I must do something for her. Would Matt be too shocked if he were to find her here, do you think?'

'Why should he? No point in worrying about Dorothy's reputation now.'

'But what about Eunice? She has very strict and straight ideas . . .'

312

'Don't worry about Eunice. How old is this girl?'

'Seventeen. Just the age Dorothy was when . . .'

'She could help you look after the twins. They're her half-brothers after all. Only right she should get to know them.'

'That's what I thought.'

'But if she doesn't want any contact, if she doesn't want to come, you can't force her.'

'But I can't even talk to her! This Joey O'Malley is determined to hide her away from me.'

Hugo knew what she wanted of him before he said: 'How do you think I can help?'

'Hugo, you know how to get anything you want. Couldn't you arrange for Joey O'Malley to be watched? A private detective would soon find out where he was living.'

He wanted to do anything she asked. Her eyes were so eager, so full of concern.

'I could.' He sighed heavily. 'But you've said they know where you are. She could arrive on the doorstep any time she wanted to. Lift the phone, write a letter. If she doesn't, it's because she doesn't want to.'

'She's still only seventeen.'

'But she's survived without anybody's help since she was fourteen. She's got more guts than the average Mortimer to do that, and she's bound to find it easier as she gets older. I'm not sure it's wise to interfere now.'

Hugo heard the tap on the door and saw the woman put her head round. 'I've got them off, Mrs Mortimer. They both took a full feed.'

'Thank you, Edna, you go for your evening off now. I'll listen for them.'

While Hannah refilled their glasses, she told him that Edna was leaving to get married, and she'd need Elizabeth's help.

He caught at her wrist as she turned and made her face him.

'Hannah, my dear. I feel quite strongly that we shouldn't interfere in other people's lives. Everybody has the right to go their own way. Whenever I have intervened it's proved a

313

disaster. Matt for instance. Greg and Dorothy too. Can't you accept that help with the babies will have to come from somebody else?'

He could see the disappointment on her face, it pulled at his sympathies.

'I have something important to tell you, too.' He stood and put his glass on the mantelpiece, feeling the warmth of the fire on his back.

'Franklin told me Dorothy's departure was not as sudden as he first made out. He'd known about Duncan Grieve for some weeks.'

'Poor Franklin.'

'Dorothy told him the twins were not his. That's why he allowed you to take them out of his house.'

'That's why he feels differently about the little girls?'

'Yes. Franklin was in a terrible state when I saw him. He admitted things had been fraught between him and Dorothy throughout her pregnancy, and grew worse once the twins were born.

'"I hate children," she'd screamed at him. "Especially babies. They cry day and night, there's no quietening them. I'm sick to death of attending to them. This house is overflowing with children, I can't stand it."

'He believed it was her conscience, that she felt guilty. "Nobody need know," he'd tried to comfort. "They'll be brought up as though they're mine."

'But Dorothy was beside herself, there was no soothing her. "Just as well since their real father doesn't want anything to do with them. You always wanted children, especially sons."'

Hugo sighed. 'Franklin said it came as a shock to find Dorothy had gone, although she'd threatened it.

'He'd told her he'd accept the twins as his, but of course he meant if she were to stay too. He didn't want to be landed with bringing up another man's children.

'It seems they're in need of a permanent home, Hannah. That's why I think it's better if you have them.'

314

'I've more to thank you for than I thought. I'm so pleased, Hugo. I'd hate to part from them now.'

'Am I forgiven? For not wanting to trace Elizabeth? For limiting your family to two?'

If Hannah had had a radiance about her that morning, she was vibrant now. She came closer and put her lips against his cheek. It was a kiss of gratitude he knew, and not meant to inflame his feelings. His arms went round her as though of their own accord. He hugged her to him with an abandonment he hadn't intended. The feel of her, the scent of her in his nostrils inflamed him further.

Hannah was almost as tall as he was. Her dark eyes were level with his and filled with understanding. He put his lips against hers, tasting them gently at first. As his arms tightened round her, he knew Hannah would recognise this as a lover's kiss.

She hid her face against his shoulder but still she held him close.

'We're laying all our secrets bare tonight, Hannah,' he whispered in her hair. 'I've loved you for years. Did you know?'

She seemed to cling closer but didn't lift her head.

'Are you shocked?'

'No.' He could barely hear her whisper. 'Sometimes I felt you did.'

'We needn't mention this again if you don't want to. I'll understand. I didn't mean to tell you; didn't mean to embarrass you.'

When she raised her face to his again her smile had a new brilliance.

'Oh, Hugo!' she gasped. 'The last thing I am is embarrassed.' Then her lips were pressing against his.

He felt a surge of love for her. She was showing him she felt love for him too. All he'd felt for her and kept in check over the years exploded.

He hadn't meant to let it flare into raw passion so quickly, he blamed the whisky for robbing him of his normal inhibitions.

315

She took him upstairs to her bedroom. Matt had always stood between them, kept them apart. He felt Matt's presence here, but even that couldn't cool him.

Hannah had a quick bath and dressed herself again. She was alive and tingling as she went down to the vast kitchen. In the Aga, she checked the contents of the lone terracotta dish. Edna would already have eaten her share of the steak and mushroom casserole before going out. What remained was intended for Hannah's dinner. It was simmering nicely, not overcooked, and there would be plenty for Hugo too.

Excitement was coursing through her. She couldn't believe he had said he loved her. Her cheeks felt flushed.

She scrubbed some more new potatoes. Looked out the apple pie and opened a bottle of Bordeaux. Tonight she had something to celebrate.

Hugo came to sit at the end of her kitchen table, his hair still damp from his bath.

'I've wasted so many years,' he said, getting up again to help himself to a glass of wine. 'I was so envious of what Matt had.' Already he seemed thoroughly at ease with her. 'And now I feel doubly guilty. Matt hasn't much to thank me for. What am I to do about him?'

'Nothing. He doesn't want me, doesn't need me. You could say he's deserted me, though he spends his time with antiquities instead of another woman.'

'Meaning, anything to fill a vacuum?'

She laughed and shook her head. 'Hugo, we've been friends for a long time and shared a lot.'

'This isn't friendship.' She heard the break in his voice.

'It's both, Hugo, friendship and love.'

'If you had been anyone other than my daughter-in-law, I'd have told you I loved you years ago. Would you have welcomed that?'

Hannah smiled. 'For most of those years, you've been the most important person in my life. I thought I wanted more from you than you could give.'

'Never, my love.'

'I had the same problem. You're my father-in-law. I couldn't see beyond that. I've had very little apart from you. No children, effectively no husband, my friends estranged. I play tennis and chat to people at the club, I garden and have cups of coffee with the neighbours, but my life has been flat.' She looked at him through her lashes. 'Now I have a lover.'

'All the same, guilt . . . I just had to tell you, Hannah. I couldn't bottle it up any longer.'

'I'm so glad you have. Glad I have the babies.' She sighed with contentment. 'Things are coming right for me at last.'

'What a fool I've been,' he breathed.

Nick felt better as soon as he headed his car towards Birch Hill Farm. The hours he spent in the factory dragged, those he spent on the farm flew. He'd been coming here for some time now. In the evenings after work if they were busy and almost every weekend.

This year, he'd arranged his holiday from Evans's to coincide with the hay harvest and spent all his time at the farm. He was paid for the hours he worked, though he'd have willingly done it for nothing. Birch Hill was the complete antidote to Evans's and helped him survive the hours he had to be there.

Occasionally, like this evening, he was going specially to take Marion out. The Young Farmers' Club was holding a dance in the village hall and she wanted to go. He'd been looking forward to it all day. He felt easy with Marion.

His Austin Seven rocked from bump to pot hole as he went down the lane to the farm yard. He thought of the Dodges as good friends. The supper dishes had not been cleared from the table when he arrived. The family were lingering over second cups of tea.

'Our Marion's upstairs changing,' her father greeted him. 'Lorna, run up and tell her Nick's arrived. Sit yourself down, Nick, and have a cup of tea while you wait.'

He got on well with Marion's mother too. Jess Dodge was a large capable woman in her late forties who did a good deal of the work at Birch Hill Farm. Marion had inherited her perennial good humour from her mother. From the beginning Jess had referred to Nick as Marion's boyfriend.

'Was it the cow that attracted your attention over the fence that day or our Marion?' she'd teased him one night.

With Marion's brown eyes looking at him expectantly, Nick knew it wasn't the moment to say that his first impression had been that she was a boy.

'Both,' he said, trying to sound enthusiastic. He'd started taking Marion to the cinema. 'And what would I do on Saturday nights if I didn't have Marion?'

He was fond of her; she had an attractive giggle that bubbled out all the time, she encouraged him to come to Birch Hill and suggested things they could do together. He'd liked that, it was nice to be wanted.

At first, he'd thought he could fall in love with Marion. He wanted a real girlfriend and eventually he wanted to get married.

He'd tried very hard to warm up what he felt for her, but had come to the conclusion he couldn't. Love had to come from the heart not the head. Her looks were not the sort that attracted him. Even the kindest would describe Marion as hefty.

'She's been up there ages painting her face,' her father said.

Nick smiled. That was the last thing Marion did. Her looks owed little to artifice, she was a wholesome country girl through and through. There was something unusually ponderous about her father's manner, though.

'I've been thinking,' he said seriously. He could spin his wooden wheelchair round on a sixpence, and did so now to come down the table to where Nick sat. 'Mother says I'd better spell it out, so that you know.'

'Know what?' Nick asked, expecting it to be some aspect of farm work he wanted to clarify.

'We'd welcome you here full-time, you know.'

'Living here, he means,' Jess put in. They were both looking at him expectantly.

'We'd very much welcome you into the family. If you and Marion decided . . . You know what I mean.'

Suddenly, Nick's toes were curling up in an agony of embarrassment. He gulped at his tea.

'We'd all get on very well together. You know we like you. You'd have a free hand to run the place. Well, you and Marion . . .'

'Yes, but I'm not . . .' Nick knew his face was scarlet, he didn't know how to cope with this.

'We've willed the place to Marion. We want you to know that. We've got a bit put by we can leave to our Lorna.'

'It's very kind of you to tell . . .' Nick didn't know where to look, nor what to say.

'Eh, you're embarrassing the lad, Neville. Here we are, rushing him on faster than he wants to go.'

'It's a bit tricky talking of things like this, but we wanted you to know how things stood.'

'It needed to be said, to clear the air.'

Nick tried to pull himself together. 'Perhaps Marion has other ideas? She could do better than me.'

'Nonsense,' Jess said wholeheartedly. 'You'd be good for her.' That seemed to make it a whole lot worse.

'You know I can't sell the place,' her father went on. Nick knew it had been on the market for more than the year he'd been coming here. 'But it gives us a living of sorts. Not much money in farming, with the depression and that.'

'It's a comfortable living,' Nick said with a shiver. He was sure he could make more from it than the Dodges. He'd like to try pigs and perhaps turkeys at Christmas time. Of course, Neville and Jess were still quite young, they'd be here for decades yet, but he thought he could get on with them. Little Lorna was a sweet kid. To spend all his time here instead of going in to Evans's was very tempting.

'A family of girls. We can't manage without a man about

the place. It's too much for Mother. It would be the best thing for us all.'

Upstairs they heard a door close. Marion's father spun his chair round and shot away from Nick as though afraid of being caught doing something he shouldn't.

Marion was coming down. She came into the doorway, tall and statuesque in her dance dress. Her bare shoulders seemed unfamiliar, rising above the blue taffeta. Handsome they certainly were, with the strength and grace of a young mare. She broke the heavy silence.

'I'm ready at last, Nick.' Everybody seemed awkward; he'd never felt like this with her before.

He knew then he couldn't take up the offer. There was no fire in what he felt for Marion. He'd kissed her once or twice in the hope of kindling it, but it wasn't there.

He wondered as he led her out to his car whether she knew just what her father had offered? Whether it was her idea or that of her parents?

He went cold again at the thought that Marion might have asked them to do it.

He knew he must tell her quite clearly how he felt. She'd always treated him with honesty, he must do likewise. Perhaps she did hope as he'd once hoped. It was only right to tell her she was wasting her time.

His car was tiny and they were both big, overfilling the small seats. He was conscious of his arm pressing into her as he changed gear. It was the first time he'd known her wear perfume.

Outside the hall in the village, even before he'd switched off the engine, he could hear piano, saxophone and drums blasting out in strict tempo: 'If You Were the Only Girl in the World'.

Marion hurried inside. She knew everybody, they were neighbours and friends who'd known her all her life. She introduced him to a lot of people. There was Carol, a girl she knew from school, showing off a new engagement ring and a husband-to-be. It made Nick cringe anew to see Marion take such an interest in the ring and their future plans. Another man asked: 'Would your boyfriend mind if I asked you to dance?'

'No.' He made himself smile. 'Marion doesn't see me as a permanent fixture. She'll welcome a change.'

She came back to flop on the chair next to his, and as soon as the trio started up again, she said: 'Good, a barn dance. Come on, Nick,' and was pulling him on to the floor that had been sprinkled with french chalk.

He knew from her flushed and shiny cheeks that she was enjoying herself and hints such as he'd made would just not do.

He didn't enjoy the dance, couldn't take his mind off what he must say. There seemed no way of doing it that didn't deliver hurt and the last thing he wanted was to hurt her.

On the way home, as they bounced together down the lane to the farm, he knew he couldn't put it off any longer.

'Marion,' he said, switching off the engine, 'you've been a good friend to me, I'm just sorry we couldn't make it more. I'd have liked us to be in the same position as Carol and John.'

She was opening her mouth, but he daren't give her a chance to speak until he'd spelled it out. It would be more embarrassing for both of them if she said she loved him.

'Once I hoped you'd fall in love with me, but you're right to hang on. Marion, love, you can find a much better husband than I'll ever make. The men were lining up for you in there.'

He kissed her. A peck on her cheek such as a fond aunt might give. Her eyes looked at him levelly through the near dark. She was giving nothing away, but he thought he'd done what was necessary.

'Yes, well . . . So you think Mr Right will soon be along for me and Miss Right for you?' Her giggle bubbled out as usual. 'Hope they hurry up.' She got out of his car. 'Good night, Nick, thanks for taking me. See you tomorrow.'

His forehead was damp with sweat. He wanted to get away as quickly as he could after that, but his car wouldn't start. The kitchen door slammed behind Marion, and he was left in the yard. He cranked and cranked on the starting handle, until the perspiration was running down his back. He wished he could love her, it would have solved so much. Marion deserved a husband who loved her.

At last the engine fired and he could go.

Nick was a bit apprehensive about going to Birch Hill the next morning but he had to because he knew they were relying on his help. Apart from the odd conspiratorial glance in his direction, nothing had changed. He was glad, and he continued to go.

Another year went by, and the older Dodges seemed to have accepted that he and Marion were never going to marry. He was no wiser now as to whether she had hoped for it. She'd never given him any sign, just continued in her normal friendly, giggling manner.

Last month the Dodges had heard of a prospective buyer and were trying not to be too hopeful in case nothing came of it. Two representatives had visited the farm and said they were very interested, having recently bought other land in the neighbourhood. Nick knew Neville was quite excited.

'Not a private buyer. Birch Hill will no longer be a family farm. It's a company called Capital Farms. They treat farming as a commercial enterprise, have land all over the place, and they're buying more. Employ a lot of people.'

Before this had come up, Nick had persuaded Neville to let him try sowing wheat in the autumn instead of the spring. And since, if sold, the farm would be taken over with standing crops, he'd taken a day off from Evans's to prepare the land for it. He was following the pair of heavy horses up the field concentrating on keeping the furrows straight when he saw the big car come bumping down the lane and into the yard.

Two men got out and went into the house, and a little later came out with Jess and Marion and changed into Wellington boots. He could see the men taking notes on clipboards as they toured the fields and outbuildings. They didn't look like farmers.

When he saw them coming across to speak to him he reined the horses in. They introduced themselves as representatives of a large corporate-owned farm. One of them, Edmond Stanton, even gave him a card.

'Mr and Mrs Dodge have accepted our offer. We're going to buy Birch Hill,' he said. He seemed only a few years older than Nick was, and carried himself with the confidence of a man who is achieving his ambitions. 'They tell us you're a good all round worker. We'll be glad to keep you on for weekend work. Most of our workers like to be off then. We've set Capital Farms up so men can work average hours if they want that. We use casual and part-time labour for busy periods and weekends. Would you be interested?'

'Yes,' Nick said. 'Very interested.'

'Of course, you won't necessarily spend all your time at Birch Hill. You'll move round a bit. It might be at some other farm nearby. Would that be a problem?'

'No, not at all.'

'We're taking on full-time staff too. If you want to change to that we'd be pleased to consider you. That way you could get promotion. Manage a group of farms.'

'Thank you.' Nick shook his hand and couldn't help but notice that he turned very quickly to Marion when she said something.

The following week, Neville Dodge said: 'It's all going through without problems.'

Nick was pleased for them. 'What's going to happen to you?'

'Got to leave the house, they want it for their own staff. Going to do it up, I believe. But we'll get another, no problem there.'

'I hope we won't lose touch,' Marion's mother said.

''Course we won't,' said Nick.

323

Chapter Twenty

Showing people to their seats in a warm dark cinema hardly seemed like work to Lizzie. She found the Lyceum a much more attractive place now she was there during the performances.

It became a place of escape, a place where dreams took on their own reality. A place filled with flickering silver light and sound. A place where stories unfolded constantly. Lizzie found it addictive.

The only reality was provided by the staff, and her fellow usherettes were all fascinated too. They laughed with the comedies, quaked at the murders, thrilled to the romances and wanted to sing along with the musicals.

Wearing her uniform dress of green serge, with its high neck and frogging of darker braid down the front, Lizzie felt part of the show.

It didn't matter that they couldn't watch continuously, because they worked through several performances of every film. By then Lizzie could recount the story line and had heard her friends discuss and assess the performances of the great Hollywood stars. Alice Faye, Claudette Colbert, Barbara Stanwyck and Charlie Chaplin were growing more familiar than her own neighbours.

On Thursdays and Saturdays there were matinee performances, but otherwise she didn't start work until evening. The first house began at five-thirty and the second at eight o'clock. It was all over by eleven. As the audience filed out to the sound of 'God Save the King', Lizzie felt she was returning to the everyday world.

It was a scramble then to change out of her uniform and check that no one remained behind to be locked in. Joey was usually waiting for her in the foyer.

'It's not safe for you to walk home at that time of night,' he said. 'The pubs are closing too and turning drunks out on the street. I'd rather fetcn you.'

Often he had the van parked outside. He'd found he could use it in the evenings and leave it outside Bill's house on his way to work in the mornings. That way, he had a shorter walk to the bus than from Onslow Road.

Over the winter months, when it was dark and cold, Lizzie liked being driven home. When the lighter summer nights came, she found after being confined in the smoky atmosphere of the picture palace that she needed fresh air and quite enjoyed the walk.

She was seeing less of Joey and feeling guilty that she didn't mind being apart from him. Sunday was the only day they had together. The early magic of their first days in Birkenhead was fading. Joey even found fault with the house in Onslow Road. The bedroom was cold, the intimacy of one-room living had gone.

One Friday night there had been problems with a projector and the performance finished later than usual. Lizzie went to the foyer humming one of the tunes Deanna Durbin had sung in the film, to find Joey not there. The cashier had cashed up and locked her booth.

'Not like your Joey to be so late,' she said, heading down the front steps of white marble.

'What you waiting for, Lizzie? Has he stood you up?' the girls joked as they set off home in ones and twos.

Lizzie was always anxious when Joey failed to appear when he said he would. He was reliable about keeping to time and she knew he'd be here if he possibly could. She was shivering and didn't dare think of a reason.

A policeman walked with measured gait along the edge of the pavement outside. She turned her back on him. She couldn't think of Joey and the police at the same moment.

The lights inside were being put out. The manager had already gone. John Arthur, the projectionist, came out locking up behind him. The last thing he had to do was to draw the iron grille across the bottom of the front steps and lock it into position for the night. Lizzie had to move out on to the pavement.

She knew he lived in the same direction as she did. She'd suggested to Joey one black snowy night that he might offer him a lift.

'No,' Joey had said. 'This is the only time we have together, we don't want him elbowing in.'

Now John Arthur said: 'I don't think you should wait here by yourself, Lizzie.'

Two youths staggered past singing raucously. The policeman had vanished.

'They've had a skinful. Look, I'm going your way, I'll see you to your door if you're worried.'

'Thanks. I'm not nervous, but I might as well start walking. Something must have happened. Joey's never this late.'

'Flat tyre or flat battery or something like that, I expect.'

Lizzie hoped desperately he was right. If Joey had been caught there was no point in her waiting. He never would come. Would he go to prison?

She took a grip on herself, made herself act as though all was well. 'Joey'll know I've started walking if I'm not here.'

They walked along the main road and then turned off into a quiet avenue of modern semi-detached houses. It was a balmy summer night and the lights were going off in the upstairs rooms. There was no traffic and nobody about. The moon was full, casting a silvery light over everything. Lizzie felt calmer as John talked about the film.

Then, from a long way away, she thought she could hear the engine of Joey's van. If it was, she'd let her imagination run away with her. She was relieved but nervous too about how Joey would react. His love was strong and real, it was silly to have doubts about it and yet . . .

Their footsteps rang on the pavement. John's voice droned

on though she no longer listened.

The van screeched into the road on two wheels, accelerated towards them then braked to a slithering halt alongside. Joey already had the window down and was leaning across the passenger seat. His eyes glittered angrily at her.

'Why didn't you wait? I'm only a few minutes late. I don't like you walking home, I've told you.' Lizzie shrank into herself. She knew he was growing more possessive and was easily worked up into a frenzy of jealous rage.

'I'd locked up.' John Arthur didn't appear to have noticed anything wrong. 'I persuaded her to start walking, didn't want to leave her standing there. Too many drunks about.'

'It's nothing to do with you.'

'Joey!'

She knew other people would find it hard to believe it was Joey's love that made him like this, but she didn't doubt it. He loved her so much it frightened her.

'I don't like you walking home with strange men.'

'John isn't strange, I know him, he's the projectionist.'

'With any man. Get in.' She could feel his love like a wall round her. Imprisoning her.

'I'm sorry, John. I'd better go.'

The van jerked forward almost before she was in and roared off in second gear.

'Don't you dare apologise for me,' Joey spat through clenched teeth.

'You were rude to him. He was only being kind, offering to see me home.'

'I don't like other men seeing you home. Lizzie, you're mine.'

'Oh, for goodness' sake!'

'I love you. I want to take care of you. It's not safe. Why didn't you wait?'

'Joey, I was afraid you'd been caught doing something you shouldn't, and you'd never come. You've never been this late before. I didn't know what to do. Anyway, we came this far without seeing another soul. I don't want you to meet me in future. I can't go through this again. I'll walk home.'

'With him?'

His love was suffocating her. Lizzie took a deep breath. 'Joey, there's no need to be jealous. It's you I love. Anyway, John Arthur is married with three children. He's not interested in me in that way.'

'How do you know? Look, Lizzie, we're on our feet now, you don't need to work. We've got plenty of money, haven't we? You can become a lady of leisure. Why don't you give your notice in tomorrow?'

'I don't want to!' She was tingling with anger.

The girls in the picture palace thought the greater the love a man had, the greater the security and bliss for the girl. But it didn't work like that. Joey was obsessional about her and she wanted to loosen his hold. The trouble was, she didn't know how to do it.

'Stay home and look after me. That can be your job now.'

Lizzie felt a rush of guilt as well as resentment. She had plenty of time to clean the house and prepare meals already. She enjoyed going out to the cinema in the evenings.

Nick Bender felt at a loose end. Lonely and a little down. Now Capital Farms had taken over Birch Hill, he found his weekend job much more impersonal. He did what he was told needed doing and that was that. Long drawn out meals round the kitchen table to discuss future plans for the farm were gone for ever. Friendship and companionship were not part of the bargain.

He saw much less of Marion, though she too was working for Capital Farms. He'd asked her to come to the cinema with him tonight. It had come as a shock as well as a disappointment to have his offer turned down.

'I've got a new boyfriend.' The giggle in her voice was more obvious than usual. 'Edmond Stanton, you know him, one of the managers. You said I ought to wait for Mr Right. Well, he's turned up at last.'

'I'm so pleased for you, Marion,' he said. But he was sorry for himself. He wanted Marion's company, but now she'd severed the link. It left him alone and bored, sitting in his lodgings on a Saturday night.

His discontent spilled over. He was fed up generally. He didn't like working at Evans's and he hadn't made any close friends with the people he worked with. Nothing provided him with solid satisfaction. He envied Jonathon and Hal who had been encouraged to go after what they wanted.

He knew he had to make changes in his life. He had to get out of Evans's, that was what he disliked most. After almost three years there, even Father couldn't say he hadn't tried hard enough.

The one certain way was to write to Edmond Stanton and ask for a full-time job with Capital Farms. It wasn't all that long since he'd offered it, but the fact that he was now enjoying Marion's company made it harder to ask.

He made himself do it while the bad mood was on him, he would post it straight away. Nick also knew he must go out tonight. Anywhere was better than moping here. He reached for the newspaper to see what was on at nearby cinemas.

He wasn't in the mood for Jeanette MacDonald and Nelson Eddy or Wallace Beery, but Noel Coward's *Cavalcade* was doing the rounds again and he hadn't seen it yet. He reached for his trilby, deciding to go.

It was showing at a cinema he'd never been to before, but he'd passed it often enough on his way to Birch Hill. A rather rundown place on the edge of town.

He crossed the foyer, bought his ticket and followed the couple ahead into the auditorium. He'd arrived during the interval, the second house had not yet started. A scratchy record of 'Alexander's Ragtime Band' was blaring out. Some cinemas had an organ and a resident organist but this was not one of them.

The lights were on but it was still a dim shadowy place. Small queues were forming to buy ice cream in front of the drawn curtains. Most of the seats were already occupied.

An usherette came towards him, and tore his ticket in half. There was something familiar about the way she walked.

'Just one seat?' There was something familiar about her voice too.

'Yes. You're full up tonight?'

She shook her ash blonde head. 'Plenty of singles left. There's one in the middle there.' She signalled with her unlit torch. He felt rooted to the floor.

'Is that all right? Or would you prefer to go nearer the screen?'

She looked up and met his eyes for the first time. It was the recognition on her face that confirmed what had seemed a wild surmise.

'Lizzie? It is Lizzie O'Malley?'

A delighted chuckle came fizzing out. 'Yes, Nick. It's me.'

He couldn't believe the difference a few years had made. He was counting them up, she'd be seventeen now.

He remembered her as a waif-like child in heavy boots and dresses a size too large that always looked as though they needed ironing.

Now she held her head high. Her slightly slanting blue eyes and generously full lips astonished him. She was beautiful.

Her O'Malley plaits had gone. She wore her hair shoulder-length and loose. It was blonde and had a slight wave.

The new thing about Lizzie was that she had shape. A really voluptuous figure that made his hands itch to reach out for her. Not at all what he would have expected. Her dark uniform, looking vaguely Cossack in style, came high at the neck, yet had it been cut daringly low her figure couldn't have promised more. There was something else about her that affected the senses. The way she moved, the way she carried herself. He felt intoxicated.

Surely she had to be more than seventeen? He couldn't believe this was the child who'd stirred his mother's sympathy. Nick felt as though he was choking.

He was looking at her from different angles until he caught a flash from those slanting eyes. She'd caught him assessing

331

her as though she were horseflesh. He felt the tug of attraction.

'Is that seat empty?' It was near the aisle a few rows further forward. He didn't want to put a lot of people between himself and her. 'I'll sit there.' He hastily threw his coat on to it. 'Lizzie, you have changed! I hardly knew you.'

'You've changed too.' She was laughing up at him in amazement. 'Fancy seeing you here, Nick. How are you?'

'Can't we go somewhere to talk?'

'I'm working. Not until we close.' Her lips still lifted slightly at the corners.

'I don't want to lose touch again. Can I take you home afterwards?'

'Well . . .'

'Lizzie, I want to talk to you. You rushed off to hide yourself last time. Where've you been?'

'I've got to go.'

'Come back when you can. Please.'

Nick couldn't concentrate on the film. Seeing Lizzie had jolted him back to life. He was tingling as he watched her showing latecomers to their seats. Turned round to see her standing by the door waiting for others to come in. Conscious of her presence all the time. It was, he decided, instant attraction, a new magnetism she'd developed in the last year or two. As he got up to go and talk to her, he was determined she would not disappear again.

'How long have you been working here?'

'A long time.' She was more guarded now; she was over the surprise of seeing him and she had a colleague within hearing. It was much darker now the film was on. He strained to see her face.

'I thought you were working for two old ladies. Living in. A housemaid or something.'

The other girl laughed. 'Lizzie's been here for years.'

'Joey O'Malley said you didn't want any contact with the Mortimers, or with me.'

He could feel Lizzie edging away, trying to get out of earshot of the other girl. He pushed open the swing door and took her out into the passage. The sound track echoed eerily in the distance.

'Lizzie, I've got to talk to you.'

'All right, after we close. It'll be about eleven.'

'Are you living with Joey?' She was nodding and not looking him in the eye again. He got the feeling something was wrong. 'I'll run you home.'

He felt her draw back. 'Does Joey meet you when you finish work?'

'Not any more. I'll see you in the foyer.'

Nick was back in his seat, trying to concentrate on England's history. The film wasn't what he'd expected either.

Lizzie was in a turmoil as she changed out of uniform. She'd sensed Nick's elation, his pleasure at seeing her again, and it had sharpened all her senses. One part of her was all eager anticipation, but he'd expect her to take him home and she was worried. Joey wouldn't like it and would probably make a fuss. She didn't want him to turn nasty in front of Nick.

She'd been trying to think of somewhere else she might ask him to take her. But late at night, nowhere else seemed logical. If she didn't ask him in, just sat and talked in his car, perhaps the men needn't come face to face?

She was glad she'd worn her good tweed coat and black velvet tam. She wanted to look her best for Nick. At the last minute she remembered the wedding ring of base metal she'd bought in Woolworth's. She pulled it off her finger, pushing it under a handkerchief in her pocket.

Under the bright light of the foyer Nick still had a few freckles as well as his boyish smile. In every other respect he was more of a man than Joey. Taller and more squarely built, he looked stronger and more robust. He took her arm in the proprietary manner she remembered.

'You said you'd go back to Yarrow but you never did.'

Lizzie shook her head.

'I don't suppose you ever meant to go?'

'No. How are they all?'

'Just the same. Joey has another sister, but I suppose he knows?'

'No. We've cut ourselves off rather.'

'No need to cut yourself off from me, Lizzie.'

There was no answer to that either. He was leading her to an Austin Seven Chummy. Opening the door and ushering her in.

'Joey says you're a manager now at Evans's, that you're getting on very well.'

'Not really.' He sighed. 'Not quite my niche, but I've got to earn my living like the rest. Are you happy working here?'

'Yes.' She smiled. 'What other news from Yarrow?'

'Lucy's training to be a nurse in Liverpool. Jonathon's practising as a vet, and Hal's a GP in Colwyn Bay. What made you hide yourself?'

'I haven't been hiding. I've been here all along, working at the Lyceum.'

'But I thought you wanted to find out about your family? They could have done so much for you, Lizzie.'

'Boarding school?' She nodded. 'Joey reckoned I was past school by then.'

'He did you no favour. You would have been better off than working in that cinema.' He kept turning to look at her; she felt mesmerised by him. Nick's eyes had not looked into hers like this in the old days.

'I asked him about you several times. He pretended you had a live-in job, that he saw little of you. And all this time you've been living with him?'

She was nodding again. Nick would be shocked if he found out they were living as man and wife. His sort didn't do that kind of thing.

'This is our road. I'd ask you in for a cup of tea, but Joey might be awkward . . .'

'Good lord! What's this doing here?' Nick pulled into the kerb behind Joey's van which was parked outside their house. It had been washed and polished and the advertisements for Evans's Toffee gleamed as freshly as ever under the street

334

lamp. 'Surely it doesn't belong . . .'

'Not to Evans's any longer. It belongs to Joey.' Lizzie leapt to his defence.

'What's he keep it like this for? These old vans are supposed to be re-sprayed. They're sold on that condition.' Nick was out of his car, trying to peer inside the van. There were security grilles on the oval windows in the back doors.

'Gracious, is it full of stock?'

Lizzie's mouth was suddenly dry. She was shaking. She realised that by bringing Nick here, she'd dropped Joey into the trouble she'd been hoping he'd avoid.

'I'll come in, Lizzie, and talk to him.' Nick was tight-lipped now.

'No, Nick, he'll be furious. You'll only have a row.'

'Better here than in the office. Better for him, I mean. Too many ears there. What's his game this time?'

'I don't know. Nothing. He's up to nothing.'

'He won't have changed that much.'

Joey's face came sleepily round the armchair as she led the way into the living-room. When he saw Nick behind her, he rubbed his eyes, stood up. Sleep left him.

'Look who I've brought in for a cup of tea. He came into the cinema. So nice to see him after all this time,' she said as brightly as she could.

Joey was staring at them in stunned silence. 'We see a good deal of each other,' he managed at last.

'You see a good deal of Lizzie too, though you go to great lengths to pretend you don't.' Nick's manner had stiffened.

'I told you Lizzie wanted to be left alone. That's right, isn't it, Lizzie? Tell him.'

It wasn't right at all, she'd never said such a thing. She should have pushed harder to see the Mortimers and pushed harder to see Nick. She'd been too willing to understand Joey's fears and do her best to resolve them. Too willing to believe they must always support each other. She knew now that Joey didn't always put her interests first.

'I thought we were friends,' Nick said.

335

'Some friend! You're on one side and I'm on the other.'

'And I'm pig in the middle,' Lizzie said. 'And I don't like it.'

'I still want to take you to see Mrs Mortimer. Will you come with me tomorrow?'

'I've told you, Lizzie, I'll help you do all that,' Joey blustered.

'Hannah was disappointed when you disappeared. Really she was. She very much wants to meet you.'

'She took her time about it. She could have done it any time while you were living at Yarrow.'

'You've taken your time too, Joey. You did promise,' Lizzie reminded him.

'She's a lovely person. You'll like her. You want to know all about your family, don't you?'

Lizzie was tempted. She felt she'd been patient long enough. She'd met Nick again by chance and there seemed no reason to pass up another opportunity. 'Yes. It's time we did, isn't it, Joey? We always meant to.'

'I wanted to do it my way,' he said coldly.

Lizzie took his arm. 'What better way than through Nick? We'll all go, Joey, if you want.'

'I'll come and fetch you tomorrow.'

Joey didn't answer.

'By the way, what's that Evans's van doing outside?'

'It's parked for the night.'

'I can see that but who does it belong to?'

'It belongs to Joey,' Lizzie said quickly, afraid he'd lie when she'd already told Nick.

'That right?'

'Yes. It's an old one.'

'You bought it when it came up for tender?'

Lizzie was growing more anxious, it sounded like an inquisition.

'No, bought it from somebody who did.'

'What do you want it for?'

'Got a part-time business going, with my friend. To while away the hours Lizzie spends in the pictures. He's a painter and decorator. Need it to carry step ladders, pasting table and stuff like that round.'

Lizzie never ceased to be amazed at the natural tone Joey could bring to whopping great lies.

'The Evans name should be covered, re-sprayed. It was sold on that condition.'

'Not to me,' Joey said easily. 'Not worth my bother.'

'Who did you buy it from?'

'Can't remember his name. It'll be on file in the office. You'll have to look there if you want to know.'

'Yes.' Nick was frowning.

'Evans's should be pleased to see it still on. Free advert, isn't it?'

Nick turned to Lizzie. 'I'll collect you about two tomorrow then?'

'Yes, thank you.'

'Better be going, it's getting late.'

Joey let him out and then joined Lizzie in the parlour window to see him go.

Before he got in his own car they watched him take another look in the van. It was past midnight now and the street lights had gone off.

'He'll see less than he did the first time,' Joey said grimly. She knew he was scared.

Then, with his own engine and headlights switched on, they watched Nick take a pen from his pocket. He was writing down the van registration and the number on their front door.

'They'll know where I live,' Joey fumed. 'Know where you live. You've blown it sky high. We'll have to move.'

'Joey!'

'What do you want to bring him here for? Snooping around. He's suspicious, like a dog sniffing out a rat. You led him straight in, Lizzie. Thank you very much.'

'How did I know the van would be here? Usually it's up at Bill Purley's.'

Joey's face was scarlet with rage. 'You don't bring anyone

337

to our house. Never again, do you hear? I don't like other people here. Not anyone. And it's safer for me that way. You go on about me being caught, but you're the one putting me in danger. It was a stupid thing to do. And I don't want you getting involved with the Mortimers.'

'But, Joey, you always said . . .'

'It's them against us, isn't it?' His eyes glittered angrily, seeming even less like a pair. 'I'm trying to take away what they have and give it to you. What do you want to make friends with them for? They didn't want to know you when you were a child and needed them.'

'Joey, I'm not a child now.' Lizzie had long since realised she and Joey were no longer pulling in the same direction. She didn't want to go where he was taking her. 'I want to hear what this Mrs Mortimer says. What's the harm in that?'

'Who's to know what you'll come out with when you get talking?' Joey was totally exasperated with her, she knew. 'You're always going on about being afraid for me. Well, now I'm afraid you'll tell them something they shouldn't know. It makes it more dangerous for me. Surely you understand that?'

Lizzie paused. She understood only too well. She went closer, put her arms out to him. 'I want you to forget about getting your revenge on the Mortimers. I want you to stop stealing from them before it's too late.'

His face was like stone. He stepped backwards away from her.

'I'll be happy as we are now.' She tried to slide her arms round his neck. 'So will you. We both need a more peaceful . . .'

Joey pushed her away angrily. Lizzie gulped, it had never happened before. Any approach she'd made had been eagerly received.

'Don't be so ridiculous. Wasn't this always our aim? Nothing has changed, Lizzie, but you. We came here to get our revenge.'

'No, Joey. We wanted to be together.' Lizzie turned to him

338

again. Touched him. He shook her off roughly and strode upstairs without her.

Lizzie rested her forehead against the cold glass of the parlour window. She felt empty, she'd had nothing to eat since four o'clock. Hollow almost and drained of energy and hope.

She went slowly to the kitchen. Joey had made ham sandwiches in readiness for her return. They waited, piled on one plate with another turned over them. She saw it as an act of love. Usually they ate them in front of the dying fire.

She put on the kettle to make tea, feeling torn in two between Joey and Nick.

She'd been so pleased to see Nick and talk to him, but once he'd seen that van he'd acted like a policeman and got Joey's back up.

And Joey's reaction had made her see how wrong he was. She anguished over his cover up story fabricated on the spur of the moment. The worse part was, Joey said it was all for her. She was upset and hurt by his accusations.

Lizzie set cups and saucers on a tray, and took it upstairs. She pushed open their bedroom door, it was in darkness. Joey was a still mound on the bed.

'Joey? We haven't had our tea and sandwiches. I've brought them up.'

She put on the light. He grunted, tossed over so he faced the wall and pulled the blankets over his head.

'Joey? I'll pour you a cup. Please, Joey!'

'Don't want any. Leave me alone, can't you?'

Lizzie bit into a sandwich. It tasted like dust in her mouth, almost choking her.

She started throwing off her clothes and then slid under the blankets to him. Put her arms round him. Made him turn back to face her.

'Joey,' she whispered, 'we've never ever quarrelled like this before.' She rained anxious kisses on his face. 'Not ever in our lives.'

He held her away from him. 'He's turning you against me.'

She knew it was jealousy on top of everything else. Jealousy at its most virulent.

'No, it's not Nick.' How could she say it was anybody who came near her? 'I hate us being like this.'

Joey was shuddering, his breath coming in great pent up gasps, his chest heaving with emotion. Her own face was wet with tears when he started to return her kisses.

Joey was at his wildest. His lovemaking had never been so violent, so frenzied, so uncontrolled. The ecstasy came but was short-lived. Her own feelings were a tumult of raw anguish.

'I love you, Lizzie. I'll give you anything. Would you like a new coat? You can have it.'

'No,' she whispered. 'I've plenty of clothes now.'

'A gold bracelet? Or some pearls? I want to give you everything.'

'No, Joey.'

'A ring, that's it. An engagement ring. I should have thought of it sooner. Real diamonds.'

'What I really want,' Lizzie said, 'is for you to realise you needn't be jealous of anyone.'

'I do,' he said. 'When I'm thinking clearly, I do.'

'I want us to be like other people. I want us both to be happy.'

'We will be from now on, I promise. We'll get that ring too.'

Lizzie felt a glimmer of hope. Perhaps it was possible to turn it all round? 'If you stop stealing. If you give up all ideas of revenge. You've got to stop, Joey, before you get in real trouble. And you have to accept you're doing it for yourself and not for me. It isn't what I want.'

She felt him stiffen and knew immediately she was expecting too much.

'We'll do it my way.' He sounded confident again. 'Give up work, Lizzie. You're going to be busy looking for a better house. Bigger, newer, out in the suburbs, away from here.'

Lizzie felt the tears wet on her face again as Joey fell asleep in her arms. She could still feel the rift between them like a physical no man's land. It was widening and she could see no way to bridge it. She felt resentful and angry and wondered if she'd ever feel quite the same about Joey again.

Chapter Twenty-one

18 May 1937

Nick spent a restless night. He woke early and though Sunday was his morning for a lie in, he couldn't stay in bed. Seeing Lizzie O'Malley had shaken him up. He couldn't wait to see her again.

Last time, Hannah had been disappointed because Lizzie had disappeared before they could meet. He didn't want to raise her hopes again if they were to be dashed. He couldn't make up his mind about the best way to bring them together.

He knew Hannah would be more than welcoming. Should he just walk in with Lizzie? Would she even come with him when it came to the point? He didn't trust Joey not to whisk her off somewhere else.

He rang Hannah as soon as he thought she might be out of bed. Last time he'd got Lizzie to her door, Hannah had not been home. He had to make sure she would be this time.

'Can I come and see you this afternoon?' he asked.

'Of course, Nick. Is something the matter?'

'No. You weren't planning to go out?'

'No, Hugo will probably come for lunch. He likes to see the twins. Do come too.'

'Thank you, but no. There's somewhere else I have to go first.'

'Tea then?'

'You won't mind if I'm early?' he asked cautiously.

'Come when you're ready, Nick.'

He was restless all morning too. Couldn't even settle to the

Sunday papers. He was back in Onslow Road earlier than the time he'd set. If Joey was persuading Lizzie to be out, he planned to get there before they went.

Lizzie opened the door to him. She seemed more anxious than she'd been last night. She was wearing an apron over a blue dress.

'We aren't quite ready, Nick. I was just washing up after dinner.'

'No hurry, I'm a bit early.'

In the living-room, the scents of Sunday lunch lingered in the air. Joey gave him an aggressive look before taking pudding plates out to the kitchen. Even in the office Nick had found his strange eyes and cunning face disturbing. Here, in his home, Joey affected him more.

Nick followed him to the kitchen door. He was surprised to find the house well furnished, even smart. He hadn't noticed last night. He'd been too intent on trying to fathom out what Joey was up to. He'd failed, but was aware for the first time of a wall between Joey and Lizzie.

'You're determined to go then?' Joey sounded surly.

'Yes, I've told you.'

'I think you're making a big mistake. You're going to ruin everything if you aren't careful.'

'Come with me then. I want you to.'

'I don't know . . .'

'You don't mind if Joey comes too, do you, Nick?'

He minded a lot. 'No,' he had to say while Joey eyed him suspiciously. 'Of course not.'

He had to get her to Hannah. He was sure Hannah would persuade her to stay at Oakridge. Perhaps it would have been better to discuss it with her first? He wasn't sure about Hugo being there as well. Would he want Lizzie there all the time? And taking Joey would only complicate matters.

Lizzie was untying her apron at last. The slim blue dress emphasised her shapely figure. She had pale fair skin with the faintest of apple pink cheeks. He couldn't take his eyes off her.

344

'I'll just get my hat and coat. Joey, do come with us, please.'

Nick sensed they'd had a row. He'd never known them less than easy with each other. It wasn't hard to guess it was about going to Oakridge. Joey clearly didn't want to come, but he didn't want to allow Lizzie out of his sight either.

'If you're sure you want me?' he said grudgingly.

Lizzie sat in the front of the car with Nick, but turned sideways in the seat so she could include Joey in all she said.

'Bit cramped in the back here,' Joey complained. 'I'm jammed in.'

'Yes, it's really just a two seater,' Nick agreed. 'They call that a parcel shelf or a bench for children.'

'Austin Seven, is it?' Joey sounded disdainful.

'Yes, the early models were called Chummies, because the occupants had to be on good terms to squeeze into such a small car.'

When he changed gear Nick felt the lever move against Lizzie's leg. Joey wouldn't like that.

'You don't like my new car, Joey?'

'You've had this for years.'

'No, I bought it second hand, a couple of months ago. I had one like it, a 1926 model, for three years but it was starting to give trouble. This is newer, 1933.'

'The ride's very bouncy.'

Nick thought he was envious. 'Yes, and it rolls terribly on corners, quite hard to control sometimes. Not always easy to cope with it. The brakes aren't all that good, either.'

'What made you buy the same sort again?'

'I've got used to it. It's a very popular model.'

'Only because it's the cheapest car on the market.' Joey sniffed.

Then, as the car turned into the drive, he was gasping. 'Is this it? Where the Mortimers live?'

'Yes, you've been here before. I brought you.'

'On our first day.' Lizzie nodded. 'Everything was so strange then, we hardly took it in.'

Joey whistled through his teeth as he got out. 'This is Greg Mortimer's home?'

'Not now, he has a place of his own. This belongs to his father. His step-mother is my mother's friend.' Nick went to the front door and hammered on the knocker, aware that Joey stared round him in silent wonder.

'I've brought somebody to see you,' he said to Hannah when she opened it. 'This is Elizabeth.' He pulled her forward. 'Our paths crossed again. I know you want to meet her.'

Hannah made a sound somewhere between a gurgle of astonishment and a triumphant laugh.

'At last . . . I've so wanted to see . . . How you've grown! You're really Elizabeth? What a wonderful surprise.'

Nick knew he'd done the right thing for Lizzie as he watched Hannah's arms enfold her in a hug of welcome.

'Let me look at you.' Excited dark eyes surveyed Lizzie's face from no more than a foot away.

'Oh, you're so pretty!' The arms tightened in another hug. 'I'm thrilled you've come at last. Nick, you naughty boy! Why didn't you tell me what you were up to?'

He could see Lizzie was puzzled. Her slanting eyes were seeking a resemblance in the other, but Hannah was as dark as she was fair, a large woman where Lizzie was dainty.

'Are you my mother?' she blurted out awkwardly.

'No, no.'

Nick's heart jerked with sympathy even before he heard Hannah's gasp of shock. Her mouth was sagging open, her dark eyes bewildered, her pleasure gone.

Only then did he remember overhearing his mother speak of another child born out of wedlock. Lizzie looked older than her years. Perhaps she was thinking . . . He kicked himself for not preparing Hannah for this, but she was recovering quickly.

'No. See what a mess you're getting us into, Nick. Come on in.' Her laughter sounded a little flustered.

Lizzie's stomach was churning, she wished she hadn't eaten so much dinner. The hall was very grand. A fine carved staircase with a mahogany handrail curved up to a wide landing. The vast stained glass windows sent shafts of coloured light to dapple the parquet floor.

She couldn't take her eyes off Hannah. Her startled dark eyes had searched Lizzie's with the same fever she herself felt. Lizzie recognised the same need in her. She'd wanted to find her roots. This large handsome woman had wanted to find her. Half dazed, she bumped into Joey.

He was staring up in amazement at a stuffed stag's head over a door. 'What horns,' he marvelled.

Nick was introducing him. Poor Joey looked even more out of his depth than she was. It was all a bit grand for them.

Lizzie had never seen a fireplace in a hall; it was vast and had dog irons. The date 1904 was carved into the oak surround. There seemed to be lots of rooms opening off the hall. She found her tongue again.

'Nick said you might be. My mother, I mean.' She still didn't understand who this large woman was, except she was Clarissa Bender's friend.

'I was a kid at the time, Hannah. I didn't mean mischief.' Nick was full of apologies. 'Mother used to talk about you. I really did think . . .'

Hannah's dark eyes were smiling at her, but they were glistening with tears too. Lizzie felt her throat constrict as the bands of tension tightened within her.

'I'm your mother's step-mother. I suppose that makes me your step-grandmother.' Her laughter died. 'How complicated it all must seem.'

'My mother, is she here?' Lizzie was half choking. She felt fluttery. How often had she and Joey surmised about her relatives? She'd come to believe they only existed in fantasy.

'Dorothy? I'm afraid not. She's run off, deserted her other children. You have four half-sisters and two half-brothers.'

Surprise flooded through her, then delight. 'Six? I'm not the only one?'

'Your half-brothers are here. Only babies still.'

Lizzie clapped her hand to her mouth. 'Oh!' Her voice was

347

almost a squeal. 'Can I see them now?'

Hannah led the way into a cretonne-filled sitting-room. It seemed more homely than the other parts of the house and was made more so by the playpen in the corner and much evidence of rattles and bibs lying about. A large twin pram was just outside the french door to the garden.

A determined-looking man with a small grey beard and thick silvery hair rose heavily from an armchair as they entered. He was clutching a whimpering baby to his shoulder with one hand. He offered Lizzie the other.

'Would you believe, Hugo,' Hannah's voice seemed an octave higher, 'Nick's brought Elizabeth to see us?'

Lizzie felt herself being drawn forward. 'This is your great-grandfather, Sir Hugo Mortimer.'

'I'm Lizzie,' she managed. 'I don't feel right answering to Elizabeth.'

His handshake was firm and friendly. He kissed her on both cheeks too. His beard felt like sandpaper. 'You've got the Mortimer hair . . .'

'Schofield,' Hannah corrected. 'Those white-blonde curls are definitely Schofield. From your great-grandmother's side.'

'She's got the Mortimer face though.'

'Yes.' Hannah smiled. 'There's no doubt you're a Mortimer. I was just telling her about Dorothy, Hugo.'

'Turned out to be a bit of a black sheep.'

'I can't believe I have real relatives.' Lizzie felt overwhelmed by a heart-warming bliss. Her laugh sounded a little wild. 'I seem to have spent so long without any.'

She could see Hannah was finding it impossible to control her feelings. Her dark eyes had been aflame with pleasure, now they were glistening again. Already ties were being formed. Lizzie turned to her and was pulled close. The next moment she was sobbing against her shoulder. Hannah had opened the floodgates.

Nick pushed his handkerchief into her hand. Even her great-grandfather seemed touched by such a display of emotion and was patting her shoulder.

Only Joey stood stony-faced, untouched by it all.

'This is your half-brother Piers.' Hugo tried to cheer her out of her tears. 'His twin Paul is out in the pram asleep. This one should be too.'

'I'm so thrilled.' Lizzie mopped her face and took the child from him. 'Half-brothers! How marvellous.'

'You were a twin too. But your sister was stillborn.'

'I was? I had Joey instead.' She turned to include him in her watery smile. 'He's been like a twin to me. We always said we were. How strange.' She flushed then, remembering that they weren't acting like twins any longer.

'So where is my mother now? I'd love to meet her.'

'What a strange family you must think us.' Hannah and Hugo were trying to explain together that the one person she wouldn't be able to meet was Dorothy.

Lizzie felt warm fingers close on hers and lead her into a formal dining-room. The bare mahogany table dominated the room, but Hannah was pointing out the portrait over the fireplace.

'This is your mother.' Lizzie studied the girl wearing a diaphanous white gown.

'Yes, she is like me.' That gave her a surge of pleasure. 'Except . . .' Surely her mother hadn't been as petulant and sulky as she looked?

'She was about fifteen when this was painted.'

'It's lovely to find her at last. I didn't seem to belong anywhere 'til now.'

Hannah's mouth was twisting with pain and regret. 'I've always felt very guilty about leaving you with Maisie O'Malley.'

'You shouldn't be,' Lizzie said. 'I've not been unhappy. I had Joey, you see, and we had some good times. You did what you thought was best.'

'Don't blame yourself, Hannah,' Hugo said, as he led the way back to the small sitting-room.

He turned back to Lizzie with a chuckle. 'Hannah didn't even tell me you existed until recently. We were all to think the best of Dorothy. You come from the wrong side of the blanket, if you know what that means.'

Lizzie nodded.

'I'm afraid you suffered because of that, but Dorothy's ruined her own reputation now. We couldn't protect her from this even if we wanted to.'

'I wanted to keep you, Lizzie, and bring you up myself, but Matt wouldn't let me. He was afraid everybody would know you were Dorothy's child.'

She had to ask: 'Who is Matt?'

'Lizzie,' Hannah said, 'you must tell us all about yourself. You have a job?'

'Yes, I'm an usherette at the Lyceum.' She could see from their faces that they didn't think much of that. 'It's smashing, not like work at all.' She couldn't stop her enthusiasm bubbling out. 'I get to see all the films and the girls are good fun.'

'Where's the Lyceum?'

'In New Ferry,' Nick said. 'A bit of a flea-pit.'

'Hannah,' Hugo said quietly, 'you say you need help with these babies. It might be a good idea for Lizzie to get to know her own family.'

Hannah laughed. 'I can't even think straight now. Of course, I'd like very much for you to come here.'

'You mean, to help with the babies?' Lizzie turned it over in her mind. 'I'd like that, I'm used to babies. Had plenty of practice, haven't I, Joey? Aunt Maisie had a new baby every couple of years. Most days I only work in the evening, so I'd have plenty of spare time to spend here.'

'No, Lizzie,' Joey protested. 'I don't want you rushing up here every day. It would be too much for you. Wear you out.'

She hesitated, knowing he wasn't worried about how much she did. What he hated was the thought of her coming here.

'Joey, you did say you wanted me to give up the Lyceum . . .' She turned to explain: 'It's evening work, you see. We're never at home together.'

'Not to come here and do other work.' Joey's face had lost

all its colour. It seemed thinner, more foxy. 'I want you to stay home and look after me and the house.'

'But I need more to do than that. I'd be on my own all day.'

'Then keep your job on,' he retorted angrily. 'If that's what you want. You're settled at the Lyceum, you like it.'

That made Lizzie catch her breath. Joey had turned round completely. He meant to stop her coming here at any price.

'Lizzie,' Hannah said, 'you need a proper home. I'd like you to think of Oakridge . . .'

'You mean live here?' Lizzie asked, looking round. 'In this house with you?'

Joey was gaping at her in horror. 'No, Lizzie. You decided you didn't want a live-in job. It would be the same for you as it is for our Peggy in Crewe, you wouldn't want that.'

Hannah looked appalled. 'I didn't mean as a servant. Of course I didn't. You're family, we need to get to know each other. I want you to come and live here. Just give a hand with the babies when you feel like it.'

'They're beautiful. I'd love to help with them, but . . .' Lizzie felt she was being torn in two.

'I wouldn't interfere with your private affairs. You must come and go as you please and feel free to bring your friends here. I'd want you to look upon it as your home.'

All her life Lizzie had wanted to find her family. Joey had persuaded her to come to Birkenhead promising he'd help her. She hadn't needed his help, she could have done it on her own.

Joey hadn't always played fair with her. When Nick told him Clarissa was planning to send her to boarding school, he'd kept that to himself. He'd let her go on believing she'd be sent to work as a scullery maid in a boarding house in Crewe.

And he'd gone back on his promise to help find her family. He'd deliberately kept her away from Nick and made her promise not to approach Hannah.

Joey didn't consider her needs, only his own. He said he loved and needed her, but it was a selfish love. Last night he'd been very hurtful. She'd never seen him like that before.

She couldn't allow him to prevent her seeing her family any longer. Because Joey wanted it, she'd already been living in the same town for nearly four years without any contact.

But Joey's present wretchedness was tearing her in two. He grunted out: 'Lizzie's got a proper home with me. I want her to stay.' She felt sick with indecision.

Hugo was trying to help: 'Stop worrying about what everybody else wants, Lizzie. It must be what you want yourself. And there's no reason to make any decision on the spur of the moment. Go home and think about it.'

'You're really my great-grandfather? I've heard of you. Seen your picture in the paper.' But she knew he was wrong, she'd have to make up her mind now. If she went home with Joey, he'd be at her until she promised never to set foot in Oakridge again.

'Joey, I would like to come here and see more of Hannah and the babies.' Lizzie was in a fever but knew she had to be firm.

'No!'

She wished now she had not persuaded him to come here with her. Both she and Joey were laying bare their feelings in public. It was more difficult and an added embarrassment.

'Perhaps if I give a week's notice at the Lyceum so they can get someone else, and then come here during the day? While you're at work. We'd have the evenings together like we used to. That way, we'd both have what we want.'

'It's not what I want.' Joey was getting angry. He wasn't prepared to give an inch. Everything had to be exactly what he wanted. He was behaving as though he owned her, body and soul.

'It needn't make any difference to—'

'It'll make all the difference in the world,' Joey raged. 'Come home with me, now.' He didn't say: 'and stay away from here', but it was there clearly in his voice.

'Where's the harm in getting to know my half-brothers?'

'Don't do it Lizzie. Please don't do it. I don't want you to.' Joey's voice was an intense whisper. 'You promised you wouldn't stay here.'

That made the perspiration break out on her forehead. She knew they were all holding their breath. She felt locked in mortal combat with Joey.

'I'd like to spend some time . . . We'll talk about it later, when we . . .'

Joey backed against the door. He had the look of a fox at bay. 'I knew this would happen. They've turned you against me. All right. Have it your way. You don't want me any more.'

He stamped out to the hall. Lizzie rushed after him. 'Of course I want you, Joey.'

'You're leaving me.' Joey's odd eyes glared into hers.

'Would you rather I did? Do you want me to stay here?' He'd caught her on the raw and her voice was cold. Perhaps it sounded too much like a threat. She'd been trying to do what was best for them all.

'Stay here then. Stay for good.'

Lizzie glimpsed tears in Joey's eyes as he turned from her and slammed through the front door. The crash echoed round the large house.

Lizzie froze. Nick came out to the hall; took her arm, led her back.

'I'm sorry . . .'

She should never have let this happen. Ought to have known he'd be obstinate and upset. What was she to do now? She couldn't part from Joey like this.

Arguing with him here in front of everybody had distorted her perspective, made her lose sight of what she valued most. She couldn't believe Joey had meant to leave her like this. She was in agony.

'Don't worry, Lizzie.' Though he comforted, Nick's eyes seemed to reflect the horror she felt. 'Joey will come round.'

353

'Why don't you stay with Hannah for a few days?' Hugo suggested. 'It's the sensible thing. Give things time to cool down.'

'Yes, please do. You can decide later whether you want to stay permanently.' Flushed and embarrassed, Hannah was doing her best to make her feel welcome. 'Come upstairs. Come and see which bedroom you'd like to have.'

The landing seemed vast as she crossed it. Hannah was throwing open a door.

'This was your mother's room when she lived here.' Hannah was opening the window to let in some fresh air. It was a large bright room furnished with a single oak bedstead, two big wardrobes and a large doll's house.

Lizzie's stomach was churning. She and Joey had rarely quarrelled, and never like this before. She wanted to go after him. Make her peace. Joey meant too much to her to open up a rift like this.

'Dorothy used this room all through her childhood. Would you like to see the others before you decide? The guest room is ready to use, this is dusty.'

Lizzie couldn't keep her mind on what Hannah was saying. Joey's face was imprinted before her eyes. He'd looked so bitter, so hurt. 'No, I'd like this one, but where do the babies sleep?'

'Their nursery is on the top floor.'

'Will I be able to hear them from here? If they cry in the night?'

'No, Edna sleeps up there at the moment. She's leaving to get married soon.'

'Perhaps when she's gone . . .' Lizzie sought for words. She felt quite shaken. Poor Joey, she knew he'd be feeling just as bad as she was. She couldn't think of anything else.

'That's not why I want you here.' Hannah sank down on the bed looking distressed.

'No, but I need some reason . . . I want to be some help to you.'

'We'll see. I have advertised for a nanny and a nursemaid

but it doesn't look hopeful. You'd like to sleep here for the time being?'

Lizzie nodded. She couldn't throw off the feeling of doom. 'To think my mother slept in this bed.'

'She took most of her things away with her when she married, but of course she'd grown out of the doll's house. She was fond of it when she was a child.'

'It's magnificent.' Lizzie knew she sounded drained of feeling.

'Let's get you some bed linen then.' Hannah went out on the landing to open the airing cupboard. She loaded linen sheets and wool blankets with blue stripes along the edges into Lizzie's arms.

Then she stripped the dust sheets off the flock mattress and unfolded something from the airing cupboard on top.

'What's that?'

'A goose feather bed.'

'I've never seen one before.'

'Very comfortable.' Hannah shook up the feathers. 'Dorothy used it. Clarissa Bender gave us several. She made them. The feathers came from Yarrow. That should make you feel more at home.'

Lizzie was pulling a pillow case on to a warm pillow. She didn't feel at all at ease here, she half wished she hadn't agreed to stay.

'This should have been your home.' Hannah was frowning. 'You should have been brought up here.'

'But I wasn't,' Lizzie said. 'I was brought up with Joey and now I feel terrible because he thinks I've abandoned him.'

Hannah sighed too. 'You can go back to see him and explain, make up your quarrel. You mustn't feel guilty. Put it right out of your mind. Guilt can wear you down, stop you enjoying things now. I know, I've felt that way myself. Perhaps it's one of the reasons I want you here. Better late than never.'

'I wasn't unhappy with the O'Malleys, not really.'

'That makes me feel better, but what seemed a solution then has brought its own problems. This trouble with Joey, for instance. You're a different person from what you would have been.'

'Would I have been better?'

'No, I didn't mean that, just different. Perhaps you're a stronger person because of it. But this is your rightful place Lizzie, and don't you forget it.

'I'm going down now to put the kettle on for tea,' she went on. 'Come down in ten minutes.'

Lizzie switched on the stainless steel and black vacuum cleaner Hannah had left with her for the carpet square, but felt more like throwing herself on the bed in despair. Tears were stinging her eyes, she mustn't let them come now.

The house seemed very strange. She went downstairs to hand round cups of tea and slices of sponge cake. She couldn't sit down and relax. Nick was the one familiar face. She knew that his eyes, filled with concern, followed her round the room, but Joey stayed on the edge of her mind.

'Does the business world suit you?' Hugo was asking Nick. 'I take it you've had plenty of time to find out what it's all about?'

Lizzie knew Nick was uncomfortable too. 'I should have by now, I suppose. I've worked in every department in the factory and most in the office, but I don't feel settled. Not part of the team.'

'You're telling me you don't enjoy it.' Hugo's eyes twinkled.

'Greg has been very kind. You all have.'

'That's not what I'm asking.'

Lizzie handed round the cake again. Hannah smiled encouragement, but it didn't help.

Nick went on: 'I know I'm moved to give me experience and I need that if I'm ever to manage the business, but . . .'

'Your heart isn't in it?'

'Not exactly that. I do try.' He flushed. 'Perhaps not.'

Hannah asked: 'Did Greg work his way round every department?'

Nick shook his head. 'Didn't need to.'

Hugo smiled at him. 'You won't learn anything of

356

importance at Evans's. It isn't being run as it should, I'm sure profits could be much higher. It's done no more than tick over for years; neither Matt nor Greg is sufficiently interested.

'If you really want to learn about business I'll fix you up in an efficient company, where you'll learn the right way of doing things.'

Lizzie saw the quickening of interest on Nick's face, followed swiftly by a flush of embarrassment. 'Would that mean working in London?'

'Yes, or Birmingham. That's where my businesses are now.'

'Thank you, sir.' Nick was scarlet in the face. 'I'm all right really.'

'I'm not sure about that,' Hugo said seriously. 'How old are you?'

'Twenty-two.'

'Should be steaming along at your age. If you want to make something of yourself, achieve anything, you must be interested in what you're doing. Get out if you don't like it. Take no notice of what your parents want for you. You must decide.'

Nick said awkwardly: 'Has Hannah told you I've been working on a farm in my spare time? I've been offered full-time work if I want it.'

'That's exactly what your father wanted you to avoid,' Hannah reminded him. 'He'll be cross. You're not going to take it?'

'I don't know. Still trying to make up my mind.'

'Coming here was his father's idea,' Hannah explained to Lizzie.

Hugo barked back, 'So you told me. Nick, your father would have done better to let you have your head. We elders interfere too much in the lives of others.'

'You're doing it now,' Hannah pointed out.

'You told me I should,' he countered.

'I didn't mean quite like this.'

Lizzie saw Hannah flush. 'You must think us a pair of old busybodies, Nick.'

'All we can say to excuse it,' Hugo put in, 'is that we have your interests at heart.' The silence lengthened uncomfortably.

'Another cup of tea, Hugo?' Hannah asked brightly.

He began to speak at the same moment: 'Now Lizzie's here, she'll give you something else to think about. Perhaps you'll like Birkenhead better?'

Lizzie didn't think that eased Nick's embarrassment. She got up to clear the tea things away. He followed her to the kitchen.

'Can I run you back to collect your clothes?' he offered awkwardly from the door. 'There'll be things you'll need.'

Lizzie had been thinking about that and had decided to put it off until tomorrow, when Joey would be at work. She didn't want to make matters worse by arguing with him again, but she'd have a suitcase to carry, and it was a long walk up to the main road to where she could catch a bus.

'Shall I take you now?' he pressed, and she knew he wanted an excuse to get away from Hugo. 'Will there be room on the back seat for your things?'

'Oh yes, thank you. I'll only need one case.' Joey would probably be home now. She'd make him understand she only meant to stay a few days with Hannah and tell him she was sorry they'd parted on such bad terms.

But she was afraid he'd still be cross with her, and he wouldn't like her bringing Nick again. She hoped it wouldn't mean another confrontation.

Lizzie was filled with dread that they'd find the van parked outside the house again. Joey could easily have called at Bill's on his way back and driven it down. It was a relief to turn into Onslow Road and find it wasn't there. Perhaps Joey hadn't come home yet? Nick pulled up outside the house.

'I won't be long,' she said awkwardly. 'I'll just throw a few things in a case.' She couldn't invite Nick up to their bedroom to help, she daren't let him see their double bed.

'Better if I wait in the car,' Nick said. 'Don't want to upset

Joey again.' Lizzie's heart leapt with relief. She let herself in with her key.

'Joey?' she called from the hall. Some sixth sense told her he was here. She reached the living-room door before he started to get to his feet. His face was grey, he looked ill.

'I've come to get some clothes, Joey.' His mouth hardened.

'I'm only staying with Hannah for a little while.' She wanted to put her arms round him and beg forgiveness. She went closer, put her hand on his shoulder. Impatiently he shook it off and stepped back.

'You'd better get them and go.' He was coldly sullen. He turned his back on her and slumped on to the easy chair again.

'Please, Joey,' she implored. 'Don't be so angry.' She knew she hadn't given him enough time to recover.

Lizzie felt tears prickle her eyes again. She blinked them back, angry herself now, and ran upstairs to open her wardrobe. She slid a dress and a skirt from the rail. Scooped a pullover and a blouse from a shelf. Then she was dragging underwear from a drawer and ramming it into her suitcase. Tossing shoes and a hat on top. She wanted to be quick, take very little. When she slid the case downstairs, Joey was leaning on the newel post.

'Will I see you again?' His face was stiff with resentment.

'Of course, Joey. I'm going to give a week's notice at the Lyceum. The following week I'll come round and make your tea, we'll have a talk. What night would be best? What night will you be staying in?'

'Tuesday?'

'All right, I'll come a week on Tuesday.'

As Nick braked at the bottom of Onslow Road, she said: 'Joey's terribly upset.'

'If anyone has reason to be upset, it's you, Lizzie. Joey's being a pig. We're going to forget him now. I'll cheer you up.'

Nick helped her carry her things up to Dorothy's old bedroom

359

and hang her clothes in the wardrobe.

'Come out for a walk,' he suggested. 'You can unpack all this later.'

This was a changed Nick. He'd been friendly at Yarrow, but never like this. He hardly took his eyes off her. It made Lizzie's heart beat faster.

He took her arm as they strolled down the Oakridge drive. His touch, the movement of his hip against hers, was exciting. They wandered through part of Prenton and then down the old Roman road.

Nick's brown hair was lifting in the evening breeze. She felt drawn to him, grateful for his help and for his company. The events of the afternoon had left her feeling buffeted. She thought Nick had found it difficult too.

'When I first came to Birkenhead, I used to walk down here almost every evening. It's a good place to get away from the town though it's on its doorstep. I bet this part hasn't changed in centuries.'

'The road hasn't been made up, no traffic,' Lizzie agreed, striving to seem her normal self. She felt aroused. It was an effort not to stroke the hand he'd put on her arm. Living with Joey had heightened the sensual side of her nature. She wondered if Nick had ever . . .?

'I like to get away from the streets.' He told her about Birch Hill Farm and all the time he'd spent there.

'You need the country that much?'

'Don't you?' His brown eyes were sweeping over her again. She sensed he was aroused too.

'I like it here as well. I love the river and the shops and the pace of life.'

Nick grimaced. 'Hugo was right. I feel shut in and tied down working in that factory, but I have to earn a living. Three years ago, I was articled to my uncle in London. I'd be a solicitor by now if I'd stayed.'

'Would you have liked that better?'

'With hindsight, possibly. There was less hustle and noise in the office, but the city streets stretched for miles, it was impossible to get out of them there.' Nick's hand tightened on her arm and brought her to a halt.

'Listen. We used to hear the larks at Yarrow. Here there's only the cry of gulls and the chirp of house sparrows. Where I lodge, all I hear is the traffic and the clattering that comes from Laird's.'

'Nick, I can see two blackbirds and that's a thrush over there. There's plenty of trees, and the flowers in the gardens are lovely.'

'I'm hard to please, Lizzie. I want open fields with cattle grazing in them.'

'There's green fields all round you here, Nick. You're homesick, that's your trouble.'

'No, not homesick. It's Hugo's fault. He's trying to straighten me out, and that's driving things home to me. I'm a round peg in a square hole in that office, that's my trouble.'

'What are you going to do?'

'I think I can get a full-time farming job with Capital Farms.'

Lizzie laughed. 'Even Joey turned that down. A tied cottage and thirty shillings a week at the end of it? It wouldn't be much of a life for you. Think of Seamus O'Malley, you don't want to end up like him.'

'It wouldn't be quite like that. Capital Farms is run like any other business. Not much money now but there'd be the possibility of promotion. Perhaps a decent job in the long run. I think I'd enjoy it.'

Lizzie shivered. 'You could go home and help your father. He could employ one less man.'

'He doesn't want that. He thinks he'd raise my expectations. The farm will be Jonathon's, you see.

'Aren't I rotten company? I meant to cheer you up. You were so upset – about Joey – and here I am sounding off about nothing. My prospects are better than his, I should be grateful for that.'

'I wish I could help. You know, there's lots of things here you'd enjoy. Joey and I went over to the Isle of Man on a boat,

361

a round trip. It was lovely, like a cruise. Have you even been out on the river? And there's so much life about the town. There's usually a hurdy-gurdy playing in Grange Road. And in Hamilton Square, by the underground, there's a man who plays the concertina.'

'He's doing it for pennies, Lizzie. He can't get a job because of the depression.'

'He plays smashing tunes, they make me want to dance. Your problem, Nick, is you never think of anything but work.'

He was smiling at her. 'I'm too serious, too stick in the mud?'

'You work all day at Evans's, then work again on that farm in what's supposed to be your spare time. You need to live a bit. Try to enjoy yourself more.'

'You'll be good for me. I'd like to go on the river. Will you come with me?'

'Next weekend,' she promised. 'We'll take the ferry over to Liverpool, then catch the boat to New Brighton. It's nice there too, donkeys on the beach and a funfair.'

'Good, it's a deal then.'

'You haven't given the place a chance.'

'You're right, Lizzie, I haven't. You and Joey, you're far more at home here than I am. He knows everybody in that factory and office and I see him chatting first with one and then another as he goes round. They seem to like him. Joey's found his level. I expect he's wheeling and dealing just as he always did. Enjoying himself.'

Lizzie shivered again. That was too close for comfort.

'You're getting cold. We're standing about instead of walking.' The sun had gone down now and as night came it was getting cooler.

She slid her hand into his and thought she felt him shiver too.

'It's not that I'm cold,' he whispered, and suddenly his lips were against her cheek. Her heart was hammering with anticipation. It seemed an age before his lips found hers and she felt his arms tighten round her in a long kiss. His touch

362

was like velvet, gentle and sensual. Her fingers were in his hair.

'I think,' he said shakily, 'I'll be more content now I've found you again.'

There was nobody about. She'd lived with Joey so long she expected Nick to pull her down among the tall ferns against the wall, rip half her clothes off and make love to her.

His arms tightened again in a friendly hug before he put her firmly from him. 'I'm rushing ahead far too fast.' He sounded breathless. 'Mustn't knock you off your feet.'

Lizzie was shuddering with disappointment she daren't let him see. Joey had awakened feelings in her, changed her for ever.

'Lizzie,' his voice was still shaky, 'we've known each other all our lives. Dad thought of you as a tiresome kid, but we always liked each other, didn't we?'

'Yes, but you seemed almost grown up then. I used to tag around behind you.'

'You've grown up faster, you seem to have caught me up. You're the duckling turned into a swan, do you know? You're stunning now. Really beautiful. Hannah is very taken with you.'

'And you?' she whispered. She could feel the blood pounding in her head.

'I think I'm falling in love with you.' Nick was gazing down at her. She could see love in his eyes.

'No, that's not quite true,' he whispered. 'I'm already in love with you, Lizzie. I'm so glad I found you again. You're what I want.'

Chapter Twenty-two

20 May 1937

As he caught sight of Greg Mortimer coming up the corridor towards him, Joey felt the hairs on the back of his neck stand erect with the strength of his loathing.

'Good morning.' Greg passed with a nod, his blond head held arrogantly erect.

'Good morning, sir.' Joey was careful not to show the convulsive hatred he felt. Ever since Lizzie had gone, he'd thought of little else but how he was going to make the Mortimers pay for what they'd done. All the Mortimers, he blamed the whole family now.

The need to do something had become urgent. Only the greater need for caution had held him back until now. He was determined to bankrupt Greg Mortimer if it was the last thing he did.

He couldn't help turning round to study Greg's back. Taller and with broader shoulders, he looked everything Joey would have liked to be himself. Confident, successful and rich.

Today he was ready to take his plans a step further. He always had qualms when he was doing something he should not, but thought it unlikely he'd find himself in difficulties today. He told himself he was a fool to feel keyed up like this.

In the mail room, the morning post was piled high on the table. Slowly, he started to sort it. He'd thought it worthwhile to come in and do it. He didn't like anybody else nosing round in here.

Then, with the letters in order, he set off delivering them

round the office and factory. He walked more slowly than usual, in case anyone should notice, and was careful to look miserable and say as little as possible.

He always felt tense when he went to the stockroom the morning after. Last night, he'd refilled Bill's van and he had to find out if they'd missed what he'd taken. If there was going to be trouble, he had to know about it as soon as possible.

He went in, tossed a couple of letters in their tray. 'How's things?' he asked. It pleased him to see two of the three stockmen were drinking tea.

'So-so,' one yawned in reply. Joey relaxed. All seemed well, he had nothing to worry about here.

It was time to put his plan into action. He went to a cloakroom and appraised his appearance in the mirror. He didn't look sick, but on the other hand he didn't look the picture of blooming health. At a washbowl he rinsed very hot water round his mouth several times then set off to the first aid post.

'I've just been sick,' he told the starchy Sister. 'Been vomiting my guts out. I don't feel at all well.' She rammed a thermometer in his mouth and took his pulse rate.

'Temperature's up a bit,' she said. He was sure his pulse must be too, he was nervous. 'How are your bowels?'

'Creasing me,' he groaned. 'Got the trots too.'

'You'd better go home. You'll probably be all right by tomorrow.'

'Yes,' Joey said, trying to look as though his stomach was heaving again. He meant to be all right by tomorrow. He watched her fill in a form.

'Take this to Mr Gleeson's secretary, so they know you've gone off.'

'Yes,' he mumbled. That part had been easier than he'd expected, but all he wanted to do now was to get away.

Outside in the street he felt a sense of freedom. He spent far too much of his time cooped up in that office. He took the bus home.

His house always felt cold when he opened the door these

days. One glance at the fawn lino stretching up the hall made him feel the icy chill of loss. Everywhere was evidence of Lizzie's presence. She'd chosen the lino and made the curtains. She was here all round him and yet she was not.

The living-room grate was full of cold ash. His breakfast dishes were still on the table. Anger was rising in his throat as he rushed upstairs to change. His bed was unmade. He pulled half-heartedly at the sheets to straighten them.

The worst part was that Lizzie had betrayed him to Nick Bender. He no longer felt safe in this house because the Mortimers knew where to find him. He had to find another and move, just in case things blew up.

From his wardrobe, he took out the clothes he'd prepared. He meant to be ultra careful, leave nothing to chance. He wasn't going inside any bank until he'd changed his appearance.

He'd bought himself a white belted mackintosh and a wide-brimmed trilby with a feather in the hatband. He'd never worn anything like it before, mainly because he hadn't been able to afford it. Immediately, he looked more prosperous.

He had to hide his eyes. Dog's eyes, his mother had called them, and he'd always hated them. They made him so easy to identify.

Spectacles of any sort helped to give his face balance. He'd bought a pair of horn-rimmed reading glasses from Woolworth's in the lowest possible magnification. Then he'd painted the lenses with varnish to tint them slightly. He couldn't see very well through them, but he was pleased with the change in his appearance. He carried a brief case and bought a copy of *The Times* to put under his arm to complete the picture.

He had the wind up again by the time he was on the bus going into town. Just before going into action was always his worst moment. In a tight corner, when he had no time to think of the consequences, he seemed to sail through without the nail biting.

To make his plan work he had to open several bank

accounts. For the first, Joey chose Martin's bank in Birkenhead because Evans's banked at the Westminster.

Before going inside he put on his spectacles. They felt heavy across the bridge of his nose. He was really on edge now.

'I'd like to open a current account,' he told the counter clerk, and was given a form to fill in. He stated that his name was Alan Anthony Evans and he signed it A. A. Evans. He gave a false address and occupation. He'd brought enough pound notes to open all the accounts with cash.

He kept a firm hold on his tongue and said as little as possible. At Evans's, some said he still had a Welsh accent though he was doing his best to lose it. He didn't want to stand out in any way.

The whole thing proved very easy. He felt more at ease now he knew exactly what to expect.

He headed straight for the National Bank and did it again, this time in the name of Paul Ogden Pendlebury. It would give him somewhere to move his money. Somewhere that had no connection with the business. He'd heard that some criminals went to prison and came out to find their money still intact. It would pay him to look after his very carefully.

He'd already worked out several other names and addresses and he went to several other banks. He opened another account signing A. A. Evans a second time. This time he stated that his given names were Adrian Ainsworth. He was careful to write the name on the inside of each cheque book as soon as he received it. It wouldn't do to get confused between them. When he'd been round most of the Birkenhead banks, he went over to Liverpool and opened a few more accounts there.

Joey knew he was growing more ambitious. Now that he had some Mortimer money coming his way, he wanted more and he wanted it faster. He kept his eyes and ears open as he went about his work, looking for new ideas and new ways to get it.

He needed a master key before he could move through the office at night and get to any valuables. He knew the cleaners had one. Several times he'd come to work half an hour early in the hope of getting it from the green tweed coat again.

The first time he'd found the forewoman still wearing her coat. Next time he'd found the kitchen full of women drinking tea and smoking cigarettes, their work completed. Then he'd found the green coat missing, though the woman was swinging a polisher about in the hall.

It was a wet morning and she'd worn a mac. He ran his fingers through all the garments hanging behind the door but failed to locate the keys. The problem had defeated him for weeks. He was beginning to feel frustrated.

He knew Gleeson, Stickler and Greg Mortimer locked their offices before leaving the building, so they must each have a master key, but he couldn't think of any way to get his hands on theirs.

Eli certainly had it on one of the great bunches of keys he fastened to his belt, but Joey didn't want to ask for it. He'd be telling Eli more than it was good for him to know.

He spent a long time trying to work out some scheme to trick Eli into lending him his keys. And all the time, he carried a piece of soap round in his pocket to take an impression as soon as he could get his hands on it.

The day was warm. Inside Evans's the pot pourri of strong flavourings was more sickly than usual. Joey held his breath as he strode through the door of the loading bay and then towards the communicating door to the office. This was kept unlocked during working hours and was much the safest route when he knew he was twenty minutes late returning from his dinner break.

He put bounce in his step as he headed for the mail room. He needed to look as though he was returning from an errand. He had his white mac turned inside out over his arm to cover his brief case and trilby. It was a major drawback having to bring his bank disguise to the mail room, but he hadn't time to take it home again and it would be safer than hanging in the cloakroom.

It took his breath away to find Mr Gleeson already in the mail room sifting through the mail he kept on the table.

'O'Malley,' he said authoritatively, 'where've you been?'

'To the Post Office, sir.' Joey slid his mac down in the corner where the stairs came low, and returned to the table doing his best to smile.

'At this time of day?'

'Urgent letter. Catch the early post, sir.' Joey hoped Gleeson wasn't going to ask who had sent him.

'I asked Miss Peacock to find you before lunch.' Joey swallowed hard. He'd nipped off a little early because he'd wanted to go into town and pay some cheques in.

'What I wanted to tell you was that there's a vacancy for you in the accounts department.' Gleeson was looking at him so hard, it was making Joey nervous. 'You've been very patient.'

Joey did his best to appear pleased. Really he was pleased, it would bring him new opportunities.

'Bring you new opportunities.' Gleeson's words echoed his thoughts, startling him. 'Start next Monday. Five shillings a week increase.'

'Thank you, sir. Thank you very much.' He gulped. 'I'm very pleased.' But he wasn't over pleased at the thought of moving to accounts. He'd have to learn a new job when he wanted to concentrate on his own affairs.

As soon as Gleeson had gone, Joey collapsed on his chair and mopped his forehead. It was hanging around waiting for buses that took up the time. If he was to get round the banks without taking whole days off or being late, he needed transport. He'd asked Bill to pay in the cheques that he'd had to accept in payment, but it wasn't good for him to know Joey was getting cheques from other sources. Everything would be easier if he had a car and he wouldn't need to borrow the van in the evenings.

He thought about it carefully. He didn't want anything

flashy to attract attention. He deliberately chose an Austin Seven like Nick's, except that it had the saloon body instead of the canvas top. Nick had said it was the car of the people and there were more of them on the streets than any other make. Gleeson had one too.

He bought it second hand from an advertisement in the newspaper and paid for it with a cheque written on the account of P. O. Pendlebury.

He couldn't boast to his fellow workers about owning a car, they'd all know he couldn't afford one on the wage Evans's paid him. He was careful to park it in a side street out of sight of the factory. He didn't use it every day, so he could still be seen hanging around the bus stop with the others and pretend he relied on that for transport.

Joey sighed as he surveyed the ledgers and the piles of empty wage packets on his desk. He had so much writing to do now, he was growing a seg on his middle finger. He threw down his pen to rub some life back into his hand.

Every week he had to write the name of every employee on a wage packet, together with his payroll number and the amount he was due for the hours he'd slaved here.

He'd thought going to the accounts department would be a good move, but it had its drawbacks.

He didn't like desk work, it suited him better to do fetching and carrying. He missed the freedom to walk about the factory and office. Being pinned to this desk made the day seem twice as long and he got all the rotten jobs. He had to make out the wage packets but he wasn't allowed near when the pound notes were being put inside.

He was nearer the money but still not near enough. If he was making up the payroll and working out what everybody earned, for instance, then a few ghosts might be inserted and their wages drawn by him. But he hadn't got within yards of the payroll so far.

He'd discovered that the money was drawn out of the bank on Thursday afternoons, and the job of filling the wage

371

packets started behind the closed doors of Mr Draper's office immediately afterwards.

He'd seen the money being carried in; that was a job in itself and took three men. It came in leather bags because they needed silver and copper as well as notes to make up each individual screw. When he'd been on the tea trolley, he'd seen the senior clerks sitting round a large table filling the packets. They hadn't let him in though, one of them always came to the door to get their tea.

He knew the job took up part of Friday too, because none of them got to sign for their wages before midday. For weeks he'd hung around on Thursday nights instead of rushing off with the rest of the office staff. After many fruitless patrols he'd discovered where the money was kept overnight. He saw it being carried to a safe in Matthew Mortimer's office.

He'd tried to get a closer look at the safe but the office was kept locked all the time. Joey sighed restlessly. Would he be able to take the money and get away with it? The idea had been going round in his head since he'd first been given the wage packets. The payroll was an amount well worth taking, but unless he could get a master key as well as the key to the safe, it wouldn't be possible.

Joey leaned back in his chair and allowed himself one small grunt of satisfaction. His new job allowed him to handle cheques as they came in.

He'd initiated Colin, a fair-haired lad who looked as though butter wouldn't melt in his mouth, into his old job. Now he dumped all the mail for the accounts department on Joey's desk twice a day. In his new job Joey had to open all the envelopes that were not addressed personally to one of the staff. Many contained cheques which he had to pin to the letters accompanying them, place in a folder and take up to Mr Stickler for his perusal. Later, he collected them again to sort amongst the clerks around him.

Now he had bank accounts into which he could pay company cheques, he'd thought it would be simple to keep a few back for himself. But he missed the privacy of the mail room. That was the greatest drawback of all.

He was overlooked from behind by two rows of desks, and there were others on both sides. He could never be sure that he wasn't being watched by somebody and he had to be careful not to look furtive or suspicious. He kept a shaving mirror in his drawer so he wouldn't have to turn round too often.

Joey stole a glance at Stanley Bream whom he had superseded as office boy. He now occupied the next desk on Joey's left. All his attention was on his work at the moment, one hand pushing heavy brown hair back from his forehead while his pen scratched on the page. But he'd given Joey a nasty fright yesterday.

He'd kept back two cheques with their letters before taking the rest up to Mr Stickler's office. He'd started on another job when Stanley Bream jolted his elbow and said: 'Can I borrow your blotting paper for a minute?'

Suddenly the blood was pounding in his head. He'd hidden the two cheques beneath his blotting paper. Now he anchored them to his desk with his elbow. If Stanley did see them, he'd have to pass it off as an oversight, but he'd lose this chance and it would be remembered later if anything was found to be missing.

He could see the nib of his pen shaking as his mind cleared. 'I've a spare piece I can give you.'

He rummaged in his drawer and produced it. Clerks were issued with only one piece of blotting paper at a time but Joey had filched a second piece when he had helped himself to extra nibs. He congratulated himself on his foresight. He was saved for the moment.

'Gosh, thanks. I say, do you shave when you get to work? What's that mirror for?'

Joey slammed the drawer shut. He could feel the blood running into his cheeks.

'I like to squeeze my spots in the dinner hour,' he said nastily. He had very few spots but Stanley was a bad case of acne. He had been a bit offhand since then.

Joey knew he shouldn't have rubbed Stanley up the wrong way. It never did to make enemies. He also knew pilfering incoming cheques was not something he'd be able to get away with indefinitely. Customers were bound to say they'd already paid when the company sent a reminder. And if lots of customers complained, there'd be a hue and cry and it could be traced back to him. He'd only be able to do it once in a while.

He was drooping over his desk the following morning, too tired to keep his mind on his work after being up half the night loading Bill's van again. Bill was selling so much he needed to restock it more often than once a week now. Joey watched idly as Greg Mortimer strode through the desks in the hall en route to his office.

Once in the alcove outside, Joey saw him take the bunch of keys from his pocket and unlock his door, pushing it ajar.

Miss Peacock, his secretary, looking more drab than usual in a dress of gun metal grey, spoke to him and he turned back to her desk.

Stickler was loping towards the alcove and engaged Greg in conversation next. Joey straightened up in his chair. The key he wanted to get his hands on was still hanging in the lock. He watched, hardly able to breathe, as Greg Mortimer followed Stickler back to his office and the door closed behind them both.

Only Miss Peacock stood between him and the master key. He was willing her to leave her desk. Joey could feel the heat running up his face. He daren't be seen watching like a hawk. He picked up his pen, lowered his head, but followed her every movement with rapt attention.

The phone on her desk rang and she seemed to talk into it for ages. Would he be able to take them while she was sitting only two yards from the door? He was rising slowly to his feet. He needed something to justify leaving his desk. He had nothing, had already taken the morning cheques to Stickler's office.

While he watched, she put the phone back on its hook and

got to her feet. She was taking her handbag from a desk drawer. Miraculously she was going to powder her nose. Would she notice the keys? It seemed impossible that she would not.

Joey was stiff with tension as he covered the few yards. He knew he was in full view of more than a dozen clerks working at their desks, but most seemed to have their heads bent over their ledgers. He could also hear the familiar clatter of the tea urn on its trolley working its way round, but he had to risk it. He might never get another chance like this.

He snatched the key ring from the lock and slid into Greg's office where he couldn't be seen from the hall.

The key he wanted was the one that had been in the lock. The soap tablet he'd had ready for weeks had dried out in his pocket and was hard. He pressed in the key with all his might. He mustn't lose this one chance in a million.

So far so good, but Greg Mortimer would also have a key to the safe and he had to have an impression of that too. It must be on this ring, but there were at least a dozen other keys, large and small.

The clink of tea cups told him the trolley was coming closer and he'd only have a few moments. He was acutely aware that the door was ajar. He turned his back to it and kept the keys close to his body to hide them while he looked. How would he know which one was the safe key? He was wasting precious time. His mind felt blank. Then he saw the name Chubb stamped on one and felt excitement boil through him. That had to be it!

The sound of approaching footsteps in the corridor was making him feverish. He turned his soap over and embedded the key deeply into it. Then he was picking vainly at it with his finger nail, but couldn't loosen it again. He was sweating as he snatched a paper clip from the desk to lever it free. Out at last. He was gasping for breath as he shoved the soap in his pocket.

He put the keys on the desk. He daren't risk being seen putting them back in the keyhole. The keys he'd copied stood out from the rest, dull and smeared on one side. He was wiping them desperately on his sleeve and telling himself he shouldn't have used toilet soap because he could still smell it. He mustn't leave any clues to help Greg Mortimer guess what had happened. The door he'd left ajar creaked fully open.

'What you doing, skulking in here?' It was the woman with the tea urn. He knew her well, they'd done the teas together until recently. Joey was thankful it wasn't Greg himself.

'Just trying this room for size.' He smiled with what he hoped looked like envy. 'I feel it in my bones, I'm going to get rapid promotion. But when I'm the boss, I'll get a bigger, more comfortable chair.' He sat down on it and swung it right round on the swivel.

'Get off with you,' she said, as she put Greg's coffee tray on his desk. He saw the flakes of dried soap on the red carpet and rubbed them in with his foot. He followed her out, keeping close behind, feeling exultant as he went out to the corridor. Greg was just coming out of Stickler's office. The glance he gave Joey was frosty.

'Just taken your coffee in, Mr Mortimer,' he dared. Greg wasn't the sort to notice he'd become a clerk. 'Don't let it get cold.'

He wanted to laugh. He felt triumphant.

Joey took the precaution of going up to the north end of Birkenhead, a district he'd never been in before, to have his keys made up. He didn't want to be known in any shop that cut keys, it wouldn't do to go to the same one twice. Some looked at soap impressions with suspicion and said half jokingly: 'Going to rob a bank, are you, lad?'

'Wish I could,' he'd grinned. 'These are for me granny's house. She's ninety and turned a bit funny in the head. Locked me mam out last week, she did, and wouldn't let her in. Had to borrow a ladder and climb through the bedroom window. She wants a set of keys for herself after that.'

That night, by the time he was positioning the hand truck exactly where he'd found it, Joey was feeling dead dog tired. After working all day, the physical effort of loading boxes of toffee on to Bill's van late at night always finished him off.

But he had to know if his two new keys would work, and wanted to try before he went home. He went quietly down to the basement boiler room where Eli slept. It was conveniently distant from the route he had to take between the stockrooms and the loading bay, and the unavoidable clatter the metal hand truck made did not break Eli's sleep.

He peeped round the door and the heat that had built up during the day felt like a wall. Eli was a half seen mound in his hammock. Joey could hear him snoring softly. He had to make sure and didn't want to meet him doing one of the security rounds he spoke of.

Joey tiptoed away, locking up carefully behind him. He got into the van, drove it out to the street and parked it round the corner. The street was empty. He let himself back into the office through the side door.

It always seemed ghostly at night with every typewriter under its rexine cover. The silence seemed eerie. One look round the empty desks brought his heart to his mouth.

He pulled on the wool gloves he used to keep his fingers warm on winter mornings. The master key got him inside Greg's office. He felt a surge of power. He could do anything he set his mind to. But the desk was locked and so was the file cabinet. He was no nearer Greg's personal belongings.

He tried the key in Matthew Mortimer's door and it opened that too. He felt another surge of power when the other key opened the safe. This was what he'd set out to do after all. Inside it smelled of money but it was almost empty, just a few papers, a file, and some cheque books.

Joey shuffled through the cheque books. It seemed Archibald Evans ran several accounts too, but all were with the same local branch of the Westminster.

Suddenly his hand was shaking. With these he could draw money directly out of Evans's accounts. Pay it into the accounts he'd opened. It seemed so simple, the very idea frightened him.

Here was another way to take money from Greg Mortimer.

Large sums this time and without the work of moving boxes of toffee. To make it even easier, a running balance had been kept in the front of each cheque book, telling him how much there was in each account. Thousands and thousands. There was real wealth here.

He could feel his heart hammering. He mustn't be greedy and make it too obvious. The cheques were numbered, of course, and the balances looked to be in Mr Stickler's writing. He'd be likely to notice straight away and would be on to it like mustard as soon as they were cashed.

But the entries had not all been written by the same hand. That must make it easier for Joey to use a cheque without it being noticed straight away.

He looked again and found that two cheques, each for a hundred pounds, had been drawn in Greg Mortimer's name on the contingency account. Joey wished he knew what a contingency account was used for.

Greg Mortimer's would be the safest signature to forge on the cheque because he'd be entitled to sign cheques on all the accounts.

Joey turned it round in his mind. If he wrote Greg Mortimer's name on the balance in front, would Stickler be likely to question it? He didn't think so.

Dare he? Joey was in a lather of nerves. He decided he'd try one cheque to start with. It was too good a chance to miss.

Chapter Twenty-three

22 May 1937

Joey knew it was possible for him to take the wages now, but he needed to plan carefully and decide on the best time to do it.

He had noticed that when the last day of the month fell on a Friday, the money for the monthly paid staff was in the safe overnight too. That set the date for him. The next time it would occur would be the last Thursday in June. If he was going to take the payroll, he might as well do it when he could have both the monthly and the weekly pay.

He hoped the dates would coincide with a race meeting somewhere, and that Greg would take himself off. That would be the ideal.

Joey didn't want to be here when the loss was discovered. The police would be called in. Everyone would be questioned. He'd be a nervous wreck if he had to sit at his desk through all that. He was due for two weeks' holiday, so he immediately applied for the last week in June and the first in July.

Every year a boarding house in Blackpool was advertised on the office notice board, because it was owned by Miss Peacock's sister. He'd heard other clerks say it was all right, that they'd enjoyed their holiday.

'Nothing to do with me.' Miss Peacock's flint grey eyes surveyed him haughtily when he asked her about it. 'You'll have to write off and make your booking direct.'

He booked his two weeks as soon as he got back to his desk, and made sure everybody in the office and factory knew how much he was looking forward to it.

He meant to go. It would do him good to have a change and a rest from this place. He'd send half a dozen postcards back here, telling them what a good time he was having and how wonderful the boarding house was. He'd come home on Thursday night to do the job and go straight back to Blackpool afterwards.

If he wasn't around the office for a few days before and after it happened, hopefully he wouldn't be suspected of doing it. Even if he was, he'd make sure he had an alibi. He'd arrange it so he wasn't missed at the boarding house. He'd be there at supper and again at breakfast. He'd take his car but keep it out of sight and tell everybody he'd come by train. They'd find out he couldn't get there and back by public transport in the time.

He had an uncomfortable feeling in the pit of his stomach whenever he thought of it. But it would be safe enough. He was going to take the wages without help from anyone. Strictly on his own. Much the safest way. He'd told nobody of his plans and he wouldn't have to share the proceeds.

Just before he went on holiday, he'd step up all his other schemes. He would take all the cheques coming in the mail from the big wholesalers, and put them in his own accounts. And he meant to make several more trips to the safe to get at those cheque books, so he could draw on Evans's accounts at the same time.

He was going to take every cent of Greg Mortimer's he could get his hands on. If his plans worked out, he'd have the revenge he craved.

He would ditch his job. He was sick of spending every minute of the day at his desk and he'd be able to manage without his pittance of a wage if he played his cards right.

But he'd have to give notice and work the week required because it would pin suspicion on him if he suddenly disappeared at the same time the wages went.

All he had to decide on now was the right moment to put his plans into action. He would need to be very careful to get his timing right.

To take the maximum amount from Greg Mortimer, he wanted to start taking cheques as soon as possible. But to start too soon would increase the risk of its being discovered before he got away on holiday.

Joey was wondering if he dare risk starting three weeks before, he knew he'd feel safer with two. Stickler, the accountant, never took very long to find anything amiss. When he noticed this, he'd be through the department with a fine-tooth comb and Joey wanted to be away before that happened.

He decided he'd definitely go full steam ahead for the last two weeks. Perhaps he'd risk starting a few days earlier if everything was quiet.

When a month before Joey's holiday Stickler went off sick with gall bladder trouble, and the news was he'd be undergoing an operation that would keep him off work for a couple of months, Joey decided to go into action immediately. It meant he could get away with much more than he'd expected to in the beginning.

Nick climbed the stairs at his lodgings, and in the privacy of his own room re-read the second letter he'd had from Edmond Stanton. It made him sigh with indecision.

He'd made up his mind he wanted Lizzie, nobody else would do. If she felt the same, he wanted them to be married. Nothing was going to stand in his way over this.

The trouble was, it had made him dither again about his job. It was ten days since he'd had Edmond Stanton's first letter. He'd offered immediate full-time general labouring work on a farm out on the Cheshire plain near Beeston, or on another in East Anglia. Both were too far away to see much of Lizzie, so he'd said no.

He'd wanted to have more time to spend with her so he'd written back to resign from his part-time job. Even so, Stanton had now written that he expected an under manager's post to come up shortly and that he'd be prepared to consider Nick for that.

It left him in an undecided state. It didn't make it any easier to have Hannah and Hugo discussing his future with such kindly intent. He'd found it difficult to tell Hannah he was thinking of throwing up the job she'd found for him. He'd only hinted it might be a possibility, but he hadn't made up his mind one way or the other.

He was hopeful about the under manager's job, but it wasn't a firm offer yet and he didn't know what it entailed or when it would come. He was afraid Evans's might pay better anyway, and if he was to marry Lizzie he had to have a job.

Hugo felt he had to spend some days in London to oversee his businesses, but he begrudged the time he spent away from Hannah. He'd come home a day earlier than he'd intended. He found London a lonely place now.

All the way up on the train, the rain had lashed against the carriage windows. There was nothing to see but lowering skies and fields lost in mist. He'd let his mind dwell on Hannah. He was afraid he was being selfish. What he was doing could make things more difficult for her.

When he reached Woodside, he took a taxi. He'd told nobody he was coming, made no arrangements at Ince. He hadn't even told Hannah.

Her face lit up when she saw him. He heard pleasure in his voice, her welcome warmed him. She drew him into the cretonne-filled sitting-room. The babies were there, and Edna, who began gathering them and their equipment up to remove them to the nursery.

'I've come for a cup of tea,' he said. 'I think I need cheering up.'

'Come to the fire.' Hannah poked it into a blaze that brightened the room on this dark afternoon. Her dark eyes comforted him.

'What's the matter, Hugo?'

He caught her hand between his two cold ones. 'You know I love you,' he said gently. It wasn't a question, he'd told her often. 'I want you to know you've made me very happy over these last months.'

'Hugo, you make me happy too.' He could see it in her face. She shone with love. 'I've never felt like this before, not ever. For years I didn't dare think of it as love, but I felt it. To hear you say it, well, it's wonderful.'

He sighed and hesitated. 'One thing does make me sad.'

'About me?'

'Yes. You're so much younger. When I'm dead and gone . . .'

'Oh, Hugo, for heaven's sake!' She was smiling up at him when he wanted her to be serious.

'It will happen, love. The big disadvantage of being an old man's darling. I'll love you always, watch over you from up there.'

'You aren't going just yet,' she laughed.

'No, but I've always tried to look to the future. To foresee those things that will affect my businesses. This will come, nothing is more certain, and it won't be easy for you.'

'Don't talk about it.'

'I want to, Hannah. I'd like you to be prepared.'

'Hugo, don't make it sound as though you're going next week!'

'My father died very suddenly. He was younger than I am now. Who can say when it will happen? I want you to know when it does that you gave me what I wanted most in life.'

'But you're giving me what I most want too.'

'Perhaps.' He tried to be more gentle with her. 'It may come as a shock when I go. I hate to think of leaving you. That I won't be here to comfort you, to tell you I love you.'

'Hugo, it won't come for years yet, why should it? You're healthy. Anybody would think you were really ancient.'

'I'm on borrowed time already. None of us can live for ever.'

'Has something happened?' She was serious at last.

'Sometimes I have a feeling,' he said slowly. 'A foreboding.' He felt her shiver. 'Just your imagination,' she said.

★ ★ ★

383

Joey's stomach was churning the next morning. The time had come to step up all his activities. When the morning post came to his desk, he slid every letter that had an accompanying cheque into his drawer.

He meant to spend his dinner hour paying them, and others he'd collected, into his accounts. Joey was very glad he had the car, he needed it now. He left the office a few minutes ahead of the crowd, and drove off before anyone he knew was likely to see him.

He parked in a quiet backwater close to Grange Road, where he made out his paying-in slips and ate his sandwiches. He put on his mackintosh and trilby before leaving the car. Now he'd done this a few times, he thought of it as a pleasant break away from his desk.

He felt different in his disguise. Reasonably safe, though the spectacles bothered him a little. When he wore them, anything at a distance looked fuzzy. He put them on just before he pushed open the swing door to the bank.

The customers and the black and white stone floor were a little hazy. He tried to put confidence in his step as he went up to the mahogany counter. As he waited, he checked his paying-in slips. He could read them well enough.

The cashier was stamping them. Joey pushed across another cheque, to withdraw money to keep himself in funds and to pay Bill and Eli. He felt he was making progress to have money like this in his pocket.

On his left he heard another cashier say: 'Good afternoon, Mr Draper.'

Joey was overwhelmed with sudden panic. He swung round before he could stop himself. And then because the customer's image was blurred, he'd been about to lift his spectacles. He just managed to stop that in time. Draper had been speaking to Miss Peacock when he left the office. Now he was no more than six yards up the counter.

Joey had never given a thought to the possibility of being seen in here by someone who knew him.

Quickly, he turned his back but his heart was hammering

and he couldn't get his breath. Every moment he expected to feel a hand on his shoulder. He had to fight the urge to turn and run.

Slowly, so slowly the clerk was counting out the bank notes for him. He had to bite on his tongue to stop himself shouting: 'Hurry up.' He pulled his trilby down over his forehead.

At last the notes were pushed across the counter towards him. His fingers felt stiff and clumsy, he couldn't pick them up. He only just managed to stop one fluttering to the floor.

'Thank you,' Joey knew he should not have spoken. His voice could be recognised too.

'Good day, Mr Evans,' the clerk said clearly. That made him cringe too. He reached the door, took off his spectacles and almost ran back to his car.

He stripped off his disguise and put it out of sight. Then sat, clinging to the steering wheel, in a cold sweat. He'd meant to visit other banks, he'd a dozen cheques to pay in and money he'd meant to move. He couldn't do it now. He'd have to put it off. He felt thoroughly shaken up.

Even worse, he didn't know whether Draper had recognised him. He'd have to go back to his desk and see what happened.

Joey was in time to see Draper go to his office without a glance in his direction. Time seemed to stand still. Halfway through the afternoon Draper came back into the hall and seemed to be coming towards him. Joey closed his eyes, thinking his end was near. But Draper put some papers on Stanley Bream's desk and stood talking to him.

It was only when he returned to his own office that Joey began to breathe normally again.

The days were passing too quickly for Lizzie. She spent most of them mooning round Oakridge trying to make up her mind what to do. She was afraid Hannah must think her very strange.

It was Tuesday, the day she'd told Joey she'd go home to spend the evening with him, and she was dreading it. Home!

It seemed she still counted Onslow Road as home.

She'd known, from the moment Nick had told her he loved her, that she couldn't go back to live with Joey. The break had to be permanent. Taking the decision didn't make it any easier, she didn't know how she was going to tell him.

Lizzie spent the morning helping Hannah cook steak and mushroom pies and was given one, with the other ingredients she'd need to make a meal for herself and Joey.

She went down to Onslow Road early in the afternoon, and let herself in. Dirty dishes were piled in the sink, and the living-room was dusty and untidy. Lizzie swallowed the pang of pity she felt. She'd been afraid Joey wouldn't look after himself. The house looked as though he hadn't lifted a finger from the day she'd left.

Upstairs, one glance at the rumpled double bed hardened her resolve. It was Nick she loved and wanted. She could never come back to live with Joey. Not the way he would want her to live.

She was glad she'd come while Joey was still at work. It gave her time to strip the bed and put on clean sheets. Time to wash them and the clothes he'd left lying on the floor and peg them on the line in the yard.

She packed some more of her things and left the case behind the front-room door where he wouldn't see it.

She had the table set and the pie warming in the oven when she heard his key turn in the lock. He came to the kitchen door and stared at her, tight lipped and sullen. 'I didn't think you'd come.'

'I said I would. We need to talk.'

She saw hope flare in his strange eyes and it scared her. She mustn't give him hope.

'You've cleaned the place up. It's not the same without you. I'm glad you're back.'

'No, Joey, I came to tell you how sorry . . .'

'What's the good of that?' Hope was dying, she was kindling anger in its place. 'I want you here.'

'In front of everybody at Oakridge . . . We couldn't talk.'

He straightened up, alert now. 'You are staying aren't you? You are staying now?'

'No, Joey.' She felt terrible. 'I came to make it up. I can't stand being at sixes and sevens with you.'

'For God's sake.' He was on red alert now. 'You could make it up by saying you'll stay. It's as simple as that.'

Lizzie was silent. She'd known he'd see it as desertion. She could not stay.

'Why not? What have I done to deserve this?'

'Nothing, Joey. It's not that . . .'

His thin face was flushed with rage. 'You'll come back. We belong together. What have you got in common with the Mortimers?'

'Nick says . . .'

'Nothing in common with him either. It might take time for you to see it, but you'll come back.'

'No, Joey.' Her voice croaked with agony.

'All right, we've had a hard time recently. I know I've not been easy to live with. But I'll try harder. I'll change. I'll show you I'm better than Nick. I'll make us richer than the Mortimers. I'll get you back.'

She snatched her coat and ran from the house without even getting the meal on the table. She forgot the case she'd meant to take with her. There was no talking to Joey in his present mood. She'd done more harm than good by trying.

Another week went by but Lizzie felt no better. She found it harrowing just to think about it.

Now baby Paul gurgled contentedly on her knee. She gave him a little hug before popping the last spoonful of dinner in his mouth. 'All gone. Ready for your pudding now?'

As she reached for the second bowl she found Hannah's eyes watching her from across the room. She was feeding Piers.

'You are happy with us, Lizzie?'

'Yes, yes I am.' She tried to smile. She would be, if she hadn't had to hurt Joey to do it. 'I'm settling in.' But changes

387

were taking place too quickly for that.

'I'm glad you've decided to stay with me. I like having you here. And you're so good with the babies.'

'I enjoy them, and it's lovely to think they're my half-brothers. But you don't really need my help.' Hannah had employed a nursemaid to replace Edna. 'Nancy's here every day but Sunday.'

'There's plenty to do with twins. Plenty for us all to do. I don't know how mothers manage on their own. And Nick seems happier now you're here. I think you're settling each other down. He seems very taken with you, Lizzie.'

Nick was on Lizzie's conscience too. She was still trying to find the courage to tell him she'd been living with Joey as his wife. She wanted Nick to think well of her. At the cinema, the girls had said men didn't marry fast women and she'd been more than fast.

She kept the spoonfuls of rice pudding coming, and Paul kept opening his mouth for them like a baby sparrow.

Lizzie shook herself. She had made the right decision. Of course she was happy here but she did seem more moody. One minute she'd be bursting with happiness because Nick said he loved her. The next, after he'd gone home, she'd be hurting inside, thinking of Joey alone, in a messy unmade bed.

Although she loved Nick, it wasn't easy to break the cords that bound her to Joey. She still hadn't, quite.

Paul was dozing in her arms. Lizzie got up to put him outside in the pram while Hannah carried Piers out to settle him at the other end.

'I'll set the table,' Lizzie said, going into the dining-room. Nick and Hugo were expected for Sunday lunch. Hannah came to twist the napkins into fancy shapes and make sure everything sparkled.

Already delicious scents were coming from the kitchen. Hannah had found a cook who came in for a few hours each day. Lizzie thought it a very comfortable life. She was beginning to feel more at home here, though occasionally she missed the little house where she'd been sole housewife.

Nick arrived five minutes before Hugo. Lizzie danced to the door to let him in. He kissed her in the big hall when he stopped to leave his hat on the table. He didn't seem to care that Hannah was crossing at that moment with flowers she'd picked for the table.

He was in a buoyant mood. Lizzie sensed a new excitement in him. He kept them amused throughout the meal.

They were having coffee afterwards when Hugo said: 'Nick, what's this Lizzie's been telling me, about you being offered a job in farming?'

'Yes, I have,' he admitted, looking embarrassed. 'I've decided against it.'

'Why?' Lizzie asked. 'I thought you were tempted?'

'Don't try to please your parents,' Hugo urged. 'If you want any satisfaction in this life, you must follow your own inclinations.'

'You're putting off the decision,' Hannah told him severely. 'In a year or two you'll be dissatisfied again. Grasp the nettle now.'

'My offer still stands if you want to train with a more efficient company in London. But you must decide where your natural abilities and interests lie.'

'Thank you, sir. I'm very grateful, but . . .'

'His father won't like it, Hugo,' Hannah said. 'If you encourage him to take up farming after all.'

'It's not that.' Nick seemed covered with confusion, his good humour gone. He seemed unable to look at any of them. 'I hardly know what to say.'

'There's no need to say anything,' Hugo told him. 'You must make up your own mind. If you do decide on a business career, you know where I am.'

'Don't think I'm not grateful . . . Perhaps I'm getting used to Evans's?'

'Nick, all I want is to help you make your own choices and settle down.'

'Lizzie is doing that.' Hannah smiled, her dark eyes twinkling.

Nick stood up. He seemed desperate to escape again.

'We won't be back for tea, Hannah. I'm taking Lizzie up on Thurstaston Common to walk our dinner off. Then we'll probably go into West Kirby.'

Lizzie couldn't understand what had got into Nick. She would have expected him to know exactly what he wanted, and make every effort to get it.

'We'll be back in time to baby-sit for you this evening,' he said.

It was a blustery day with fitful sunshine, and cooler than it had been of late. Lizzie was stepping out briskly.

'Hang on a minute,' said Nick. 'When we get to the top I want us to have a talk.' That sent the blood rushing to her cheeks. She sensed Nick was going to propose, and though she wanted that badly, it also meant she had to tell him. She didn't want secrets of any sort between them.

He was spreading his mackintosh on the moorland heather in the lee of a large rock. It sheltered them from the brisk breeze blowing straight off the Irish Sea.

From here they could see for miles. The Manx ferry was coming into the channel to enter the Mersey and behind it a cargo ship. They could see across the Dee to the Welsh hills. Below them, she could see roads winding, and houses like toys spread along them.

She sat down beside him, knowing what would happen next if she were with Joey. But Nick was different, he would hold back. He would not expect love like that until she had his wedding band on her finger. He didn't know she ached for him. Ached too because Joey was always there between them.

Nick's golden brown eyes were serious. 'Am I taking the fences too fast for you, Lizzie? I know I'm going at breakneck speed.'

'No,' she choked.

'Marry me, Lizzie?'

She couldn't meet his gaze. Nick was offering her everything. She felt heady with enchantment.

'I mean, why wait if we've both made up our minds? You do love me, don't you?'

'You know I do. I love you very much.' She closed her eyes and took a deep breath. She must tell him now, but the words she'd been rehearsing were gone.

'Then we are engaged? I've bought you a ring, it's been burning a hole in my pocket all afternoon.' He took out a small leather box and opened it.

'Do you like it? Three diamonds in a row.'

Lizzie could see only the fire of them flashing in the sunlight. Tears were glazing her eyes. What a coward she was!

'If you don't like it, we can take it back and choose something else.'

She blinked hard and the ring came into focus. 'It's beautiful, Nick.' She smiled up at him but Joey's face danced before her eyes.

'Here then, let's get it on your finger. Does it fit?'

'Yes.' It was almost a sob. She wanted to bury her face in the rough tweed of his jacket.

'I love you, Lizzie. I'll try and make you happy.' His smile lit up his face.

She should have told him, she'd had the right opportunity. Even now she could say: 'There's something I want you to know before we tell anyone.' Somehow she couldn't make the words come.

'Let's not wait too long to get married. I'd like it to be soon, Lizzie.' Nick lay down and put his hands behind his head. 'I'm earning enough at Evans's.'

Lizzie sat up straighter. 'Is that why you've changed your mind about wanting a farming job?'

Nick looked self-conscious. 'A bit embarrassing with Hugo, wasn't it? He probably thinks I'm a complete buffoon, telling him I want a job in farming one minute and then changing my mind when I have it offered.'

'I think you should still take it. Grab it, Nick. It's what you want, isn't it?'

'I've decided to stay with Evans's. You know farm labouring

doesn't pay much and I can't ask you to live on fresh air.'

She laughed. 'I've lived on fresh air before now, Nick. Nobody's better at it than I am. I can do it again.'

He was frowning. 'There's no house offered with the job. If I'd gone to agricultural college it might have been different.'

'Nick, I still think you should take it.'

'I'll be content here if I have you.'

Lizzie sucked on a stem of grass. 'You'd do that for me? Carry on working at Evans's?' Nick was being so honest with her, so generous. She could see love in his eyes which wouldn't leave her face.

'I'd do anything for you.'

Lizzie swallowed. She had to explain about Joey. If she was to be happy, Nick had to know. She couldn't let him marry her in ignorance or Joey would be a ghost between them always.

She forced the words out: 'Nick – before we met up again – there was Joey.'

'I know,' he said gently.

'I loved him.'

'I know.' He put a finger on her lips. She pushed it away. He didn't know she'd been a wife to Joey in everything but name for the last two years. She opened her mouth again, but he was already going on.

'Do you think I don't know how close you were? I know you found it painful, leaving him like that, but you did leave him. Let's forget Joey, he's behind you now.'

His lips were on hers again. Lizzie knew she hadn't made him understand. It was almost as though he didn't want to. She felt full of love for him.

Nick felt he was treading on air as he took Lizzie back to Oakridge. Her slanting blue eyes were shining and her fair hair was wind-tossed because he'd taken her hat off up on the common.

Hannah and Hugo were having a drink in the sitting-room when they went in.

'We've something to tell you,' Nick announced proudly. Lizzie went forward looking shy. She held out her left hand to show off her ring.

Hugo leapt to his feet to kiss her, and Nick felt his hand being shaken warmly. Hannah laughed with delight and made a big fuss. She found a bottle of champagne which she gave him to open. The cork came out with a swoosh and champagne spilled over. He watched Lizzie, her cheeks flushed with excitement. They drank to their future and he knew she was as thrilled as he was.

'We must phone your mother.' Hannah seemed almost as delighted as Nick was himself. 'Clarissa will be pleased for you.'

Nick wasn't sure. He was afraid she might have preferred Marion Dodge.

Hannah's brown eyes were shining with affection for them both as she picked up the phone and asked to be connected with Yarrow Hall Farm. Then she pushed it into his hand.

He felt at a loss for words because they were all listening. 'I'm engaged to be married, Mother. Who to? Lizzie O'Malley.'

There was a silence, then Clarissa said: 'You've rather taken my breath away. I am pleased, Nick, just surprised.' All the time Lizzie's blue eyes were sparkling at him over her glass.

Hannah took the handset from him. 'Clarissa, he didn't lead up to that very gracefully. What a shock for you! You must come and see them both. Why don't you pack a bag and come in the next day or so? You know I'd love to see you.'

He could hear the tones of his mother's voice, distorted by the wire. She sounded quite excited too.

Clarissa came to stay a few days later. Nick happened to be at Oakridge the evening she arrived.

He was uneasy. He knew he was looking for the disapproval he always seemed to get from his parents, in her words, in her face, in her manner. For once there was no sign of it.

'Lizzie, I'm so pleased for you.' She'd taken the girl into

her arms. 'Welcome to the family. It's lovely that Nick's chosen someone we already know so well.'

Seeing his mother with Lizzie, he realised Clarissa had always been fond of her. He need have no worries on that score.

He'd seen Lizzie almost every evening since the engagement. Sometimes he'd taken her for a walk and sometimes to the cinema. Hannah had invited him to come to Oakridge whenever he wanted, and he was always included in a meal if he happened to be there. At last he was happy with the way his own affairs were going.

Today Nick sat at his desk and wrestled with the figures before him. He couldn't stop his eyes straying to Joey O'Malley. He was sprawling over his desk, fifteen yards in front. Joey didn't seem to be concentrating on his work either. He was restless, opening and closing the drawers of his desk.

Nick had worked in sales, personnel and buying for several months each. He'd been in the accounts department now for a month but felt he hardly knew what he was doing.

His personal affairs had tended to push thoughts of work to the back of his mind. Mr Stickler the manager was supposed to be showing him how the department ran, but he'd gone off sick three days after Nick had moved here. With Mr Draper his second in command busy with the wages, and the senior clerk on compassionate leave, Nick felt he'd been left to cope with his job too soon.

He'd asked questions of the other clerks, tried to feel his way round, done his best to keep the books up to date, not really knowing whether what he did was right or not. He had a feeling that something was wrong.

There were very few cheques coming in. He couldn't understand why they'd suddenly stopped. He'd checked last year's records and they'd come in at a steady pace all the year round. But in the last two weeks they'd been drying up. For the last three days there hadn't been any at all in the mail. He didn't understand it.

The clerks said: 'Just a fluke,' and seemed glad they had

less work to do. 'We'll be inundated next week, you'll see. It happens like this sometimes.' As far as Nick could see, it never had before.

Joey too said: 'Just a fluke.'

Nick knew Joey too well to trust him. He'd always been in a fever to get rich. He'd been totally obsessed with the idea and Nick knew he wasn't above helping himself to what didn't belong to him. He'd seen him do it with his own eyes at Yarrow.

Quite deliberately he pushed his suspicions of Joey to the back of his mind. He had to. He knew how Lizzie felt about him. For her sake he'd tried to like him, made an effort to seek out his better points. But he knew he'd never trust him.

He owed it to Lizzie to keep his suspicions to himself. She'd never forgive him if he wrongly blamed Joey.

Yet something was dreadfully wrong with the figures he had to work with. Production figures were high, the toffee was going out, but nobody was paying for it. If fraud it was, then it was massive fraud and that was another reason he didn't believe it could be Joey. He was a small-time thief. More likely to be someone in a more senior position. He mentally checked through the staff and failed to come up with a name, but then he hardly knew them.

Nick opened the books on his desk. He was even more worried now. There was only one way he was going to get this off his mind. He would have to tell Greg and let him sort it out.

He gathered all his ledgers together and went over to the alcove. Miss Peacock was missing from her desk. He tapped on Greg's door before pushing it open.

Greg was drinking his morning coffee, standing in a patch of pale sunlight by his window. His body was thickening with over-eating. Already there were lines of indulgence marring his handsome face.

'Hello, Nick, I think we're going to have a fine day. The mist is lifting nicely.'

'Yes. Can I have a word?'

'Is it important?' Greg came back to his desk to put his empty cup on the tray. 'I was just going out.'

'Well, yes, it is.' Nick frowned in concentration. 'There's something funny going on with the accounts. I can't see that we're going to make any profit this year. There's no money coming in. Let me show you.'

He started to lay out his ledgers in front of Greg's leather swivel chair.

'I haven't much time now.' Greg remained standing, easing his sleeve up to consult his Rolex Oyster. 'Traffic can soon build up.'

His blue eyes looked into Nick's as he smiled. 'Business seems to be in a bit of a trough. We didn't do so well last year or the year before. Bring your books back on Tuesday, Nick, and we'll go into it then.'

'Next Tuesday?'

'Yes, I'm taking a few days off. Having a long weekend.'

'Oh!' Nick had heard Greg went to almost every race meeting in the country. 'I don't think it's just a business trough.'

'What do you mean?' Greg was frowning.

'It could be fraud,' he said reluctantly. He hadn't meant to spell it out like this. Really, he'd wanted a second opinion first. Perhaps he was doing something wrong?

'Surely not, Nick? You're not imagining it? I do wish old Stickler would come back. I think he's swinging the lead a bit now. How long has he been off?'

'About three weeks. But he won't be back yet. He only had his operation the other day.'

'You're doing very well, Nick, to cope like this.'

Nick nodded resentfully, afraid he wasn't coping at all. Greg wouldn't listen to him, he was acting as though he was afraid he'd miss the first race. 'Is there racing at Newbury today?'

'Tomorrow at Epsom.' Greg gave him a look which told him to mind his own business. He was putting on his smart new mackintosh.

Nick closed his ledgers and gathered them together. If Greg attached more importance to racing than listening to fears of his company being defrauded, then so be it.

Chapter Twenty-four

3 June 1937

Nick stood in the bows of the *Royal Iris* with an arm round Lizzie's waist. It was a grey blustery day and he was enjoying the way the deck heaved beneath their feet as the ferry tossed in the choppy water.

'I love the smell of the river.' She sniffed appreciatively. 'Tar and ozone and seaweed and rope.' Lizzie's ash blonde curls swirled in the breeze, tickling his chin.

'And hot oil,' he said. 'From the engines.'

Her hand grasped the rail and the three diamonds he'd given her glinted in the pale daylight. She was right, there was a zest to life here that the countryside did not have.

He'd seen more of Merseyside and had more fun in the last few weeks than in all the preceding years. He knew it was Lizzie's company that was making all the difference.

He didn't want to miss anything on this trip downriver, and kept turning from the trees and houses on the Wallasey bank to watch the docks slide past on the Liverpool side. They seemed miles apart now in the estuary.

The Mersey seagulls swooped and called over the muddy water. They were approaching New Brighton. The engines were cut at precisely the right moment to allow the tide to swing the ferry gently against the end of the pier.

They were drawn with the holiday crowd towards the promenade. It was all so new and different, Nick couldn't believe he hadn't even been here before in three whole years.

'I've been here with Joey, several times. He always wanted to go round the fun fair.'

He took Lizzie's arm and led her determinedly in the opposite direction, along the promenade.

'You'll not want to see it again then.' But he wondered if he'd done the right thing. There was rain in the wind now and some of the funfair was undercover.

Nick had decided the only possible way he could cope with Joey O'Malley was to put him right out of his mind. The things he wanted to say about him would upset Lizzie. Nick was certain he was pilfering at Evans's. It hadn't been possible to see inside the van parked outside his house, but he was almost sure it had been stocked with toffee.

He knew if it had been anyone else he'd have mentioned it to Greg Mortimer. He knew he probably still should. What tied his hands was knowing how Lizzie would feel if Joey fell foul of the law. He'd decided he would do nothing and say nothing about Joey's deeds.

That was why he didn't want her to talk about Joey. She'd shied off in the past when he'd mentioned his suspicions.

The rain began lashing down. He hurried her away from the promenade, across the road where it was more sheltered. They took cover in the foyer of the Winter Garden Theatre with a crowd of other day trippers. The matinee of a pierrot show was about to start.

'Would you like to see it?' he asked. 'It's one way of staying dry.'

'Yes, please.' She relaxed for a moment and smiled. 'Joey never asked what I wanted to do. He always decided everything.'

Nick said: 'I envied what you and Joey had as children. I was always on my own.'

'We looked after each other then. Recently he's grown pig-headed and there's no changing his mind. He's got a will of iron. He can make people do things, takes them over. I think he took me over.'

'He's taken us both over.'

'Perhaps I gave in to him too much?'

The show started and it was good. Lizzie laughed a lot and

400

he liked that. When he came out with the catchy tunes still jingling in his head, the pavements were still wet so it had rained quite heavily.

It was clearing up as they walked further along the promenade in a wind that had grown sharper. Nick saw a small cafe and took her inside for some tea.

'I expect you're tired of hearing me go on about Joey?' She seemed more determined, more serious than usual. 'I'd like you to understand about him.'

'I do, Lizzie.' He put out a hand to cover hers on the table cloth. He was afraid she was trying to excuse something Joey had done.

'This bond between us . . . I wish I could explain it. I didn't know 'til recently I was a twin, but I've wondered since if what I feel for Joey is what I'd have felt for my twin? If she'd lived, I mean.'

Nick unbent enough to say: 'When you were small, I think Joey really believed you were twins. He told everybody so.'

'Because we were close in age.' She nodded.

'Joey lived in fantasy land.'

'So he did, I'd forgotten that.'

Lizzie had the sort of looks that turned heads. He felt people were watching them now.

'Still, he dropped the twins idea as soon as you grew up.'

'Yes.' He saw her blinking hard. She helped herself to another cake and went on quickly: 'But he didn't drop the fantasy. He's grown quite strange. He frightened me sometimes.'

'In what way? He didn't hit . . .?'

'No, no, not that. But he has a strange way of showing . . . It hardly seemed like affection . . .'

Nick stifled a twinge of jealousy. He knew it was love she meant, not affection, that she was trying to tell him something more about their relationship.

'That's what made it so hard. But his is not a generous love like yours. It's not out-going. He's so intense, so possessive, so horribly jealous. His is a sort of obsessional Heathcliff love, all twisted and warped. He's changed so much.'

It was dry when they came out on the prom again. Lizzie wanted to go down on the beach. It was dull and overcast, but huddling against her in the lea of the wind it didn't matter. It was high water now. They watched the tankers and the merchant ships coming into the mouth of the Mersey. The distant bank was lost in haze, its tiny buildings and chimneys barely visible.

'It's you I want to marry, Nick,' she said. 'You seem so normal, so uncomplicated. I do love you.' He pulled her closer.

But something in her manner led him to believe she hadn't said all she'd meant to about Joey. She was holding something back and it still bothered her.

'Let's set the day,' he said suddenly. 'When?'

'Christmas?'

'Sooner than that! Why wait?'

She laughed up at him and cuddled closer. 'How soon?'

'What about the beginning of September? That should give Hannah enough time to arrange things.'

'That's barely two months off.' She was excited and laughed again. 'We'll have to find somewhere to live.'

'I'll start on that straight away. What do you say?'

'Oh, yes,' she breathed. 'Yes Nick, that's what I want.'

A few days later, Hugo lay back in his tub letting the warm water swish over his chest. His feet were propped against the end of the bath, one under each brass tap; aged feet, pale, bony and misshapen. He remembered them as they had been, strong and tanned. They offended him now. He slid them under the water out of sight.

His bathroom had grown old with him, the polished mahogany dulled with a covering of steam, a dado of Victorian picture tiles edging the white ones halfway up the wall. The bath was big, that was what he liked about it. He'd stopped Eunice ripping out the fitments when she was doing up her own bathroom.

'Why live in the past?' she'd taunted him. 'Don't you ever want anything new?'

'Not in my part of the house.' He loved his bedroom at Ince and wanted to keep it just as it was. It was in the oldest part of the house, dating from about 1820, and was large, some thirty feet square, with two big windows. He loved to lie in bed and study the ceiling which was wonderfully moulded with swathes of fruit and flowers.

It had been intended as a double room, of course, and had a dressing alcove on each side. One had already been converted to a bathroom before he'd bought the house, and as the bath had seemed incredibly old and shabby, he'd refitted this bath then.

But keeping the house largely unaltered was not living in the past. Hugo felt he'd always looked ahead, in the way a chess player must look ahead, but his future no longer seemed to stretch all that far. All the same, his present had opened up. He was living gloriously again and with more abandon than he ever had in his youth.

Hannah said he didn't seem old to her. She treated him as though he was a full-blooded lover. He hadn't felt like this since the first year of his marriage. It was ridiculous that once again he should have such appetites. He thought of Hannah's half smile of anticipation and loved her for it.

He felt more alive, more energetic, and very happy. The years were falling from him; the aches and pains he'd once had were banished. Except for his indigestion. There were times when that was still troublesome.

As soon as he was with Hannah he forgot his weaknesses. He mentioned none of this to her. He wasn't going to give in to old age and indigestion.

Eunice had been very touchy since he'd insisted the twins stay with Hannah. He'd had to rush up to Rochdale and speak to Franklin before she thought of doing it. He'd told Franklin they'd be too great a strain for Eunice at her age and he personally didn't want them at Ince. He'd convinced him that the best thing for everybody was that they should stay with Hannah. Franklin didn't really care where they went.

Last month the newspapers had been full of scandal about the King and Mrs Simpson. Hugo had felt sympathy for the King. He was in love too and knew only too well how strong its hold could be.

The affairs of royalty interested Eunice more than they did him. She couldn't wait to get back to London to be nearer the action, where she had friends who were in the know. He'd been glad to see her go. The arrangement suited him well. He had freedom and Hannah was nearby.

Hugo towelled himself dry and dressed carefully in a new pale grey suit. He was taking Hannah to the Royal Court in Liverpool to see *Chu Chin Chow*. Already he could feel the tingle of anticipation that the thought of spending an evening with her brought.

He was going out and about much more. This week he'd already taken Hannah to the Argyll in Birkenhead for the music hall, and to the cinema to see Ginger Rogers in *Top Hat*. They'd had dinner out twice. He'd played in the garden with the babies and gone walking with Hannah as she pushed the pram. He'd had several meals at her house.

Last week had been hot and she'd persuaded him to go with her and Lizzie to the new open air baths in New Ferry. She had ideas about teaching the babies to swim, but they'd cried when she'd immersed them. They'd swum a few widths together while Lizzie looked after the infants and then they'd all spent too long sunbathing in the gardens that surrounded the huge pool.

Fool that he was, Hugo had thought his grey and ancient skin could be improved by a light tan. He should have known better. Hannah never seemed put off. Her eyes when they looked at him were filled with affection. His shoulders had been sore afterwards and the next day he'd felt utterly exhausted as he sat at his desk.

From the work point of view, it had been a relatively light week, though he did a lot of reading to keep up to date. He'd been to only one board meeting, had one session with his accountant and another with his stockbroker.

He felt unaccountably weary as he went out to his car. The Buick had grown old and the spare parts difficult to get. He'd replaced it with an SS1 Jaguar saloon. It was new and he drove slowly. He didn't feel quite at ease in it yet, the controls were stiff and felt different. As he pulled in to the drive at Oakridge he felt a pain prodding at his chest, though mercifully it went after a few deep breaths.

Hannah opened the door to him, clipping her fox fur in place over her blue costume.

'You're early, Hugo.' She smiled, kissing his cheek. 'We've time for a glass of sherry first if you'd like one.'

Just to see Hannah in her smart little hat covered in a froth of net cheered him up.

'I'd prefer a spot of brandy,' he said, wanting to keep his indigestion at bay so he could give himself up to the pleasures of being with her.

'Hello, Grandpa, is this enough brandy?' The girl swooped a kiss on to his cheek when she brought the glass.

He chuckled. 'It's at least a double, thank you.' Then he almost disgraced himself by calling her Dorothy, such were the handicaps of age.

Lizzie was prettier than Dorothy had been and so clearly delighted with everything Hannah tried to do for her. A sweet girl.

He was out on the drive again with Hannah when she said: 'Hugo, a new car! I'd love to drive it. May I try?'

'Of course.' He was glad to push the keys into her hand. He couldn't describe the pleasure it gave him to see her settle into the driving seat. He pointed out those controls whose function he could remember.

'It's so much easier to get over to Liverpool since they've opened the Mersey Tunnel,' she said enthusiastically.

Hannah seemed to manage the car with more ease than he had. He couldn't take his eyes off her face. Her beauty had not faded over the years. She was elegant, and looked strong and capable and sensible.

He bought chocolates, wanting to shower her with presents, but ate only one himself. He'd felt a little off colour, but now he was with her all other considerations were pushed out of his mind.

Hannah was watching the stage with rapt attention. He derived greater pleasure from watching her in the semi-darkness. The footlights cast enough of a glow into her face for him to see her constantly changing expression. Her eyes widened with suspense. The smile lines tightened round her eyes when she was amused. And she would open her mouth wide in unaffected laughter. When the last curtain call came, she was all sparkling eyes and animation. For him she had wide smiles of affection.

'Wasn't it good? I did enjoy it. Wonderful.' She held tightly on to his arm as they moved slowly in the crush to get out of the theatre.

He'd seen the musical before and thought it would appeal to Hannah. He'd enjoyed it more this time with her.

'Would you mind driving home?' he asked, and as she seemed happy to do so, sat quietly with his eyes closed throughout the journey. He felt spent, as though the excitement had been too much for him. The journey gave him a chance to pull himself together.

For a change, he'd asked his housekeeper to leave a cold supper for two before she went off for the evening. It was easier to bring Hannah home here. Having Lizzie living in Oakridge constrained them both when it came to making love. Goodness knows what she must think of her family!

He opened a bottle of champagne to have with the cold salmon set out on the dining table. Hannah liked champagne and he wanted her to think they had something to celebrate. He managed only one glass because its fizzy gas seemed to fill his stomach. He poured himself a glass of brandy instead.

He could relax with Hannah, there was no need to make conversation. If they were silent it was a companionable silence. As she nibbled on a bread roll, he said something he never had before: 'I wish I'd had the luck to marry you instead of Eunice.'

When her dark eyes met his they were full of love. 'I was hardly the right age when you were looking for a bride.'

'You weren't even born.'

'You would have had to be more patient, a long-term bachelor.'

'All the same, you'd have made all the difference to my life.'

She smiled. 'In twenty-two years, I haven't made much difference to Matt's.'

'It just shows you don't suit him any more than Eunice suits me. Why did I wait so long, waste so much time? We could have had years and years of this.'

She reached for his hand. 'We have it now, Hugo. Isn't that the main thing?'

'It's everything,' he said. 'Everything, love.'

He looked into Hannah's luminous eyes. She was smiling gently at him.

'You've never told me what went wrong between you and Eunice? Sometimes I feel . . . I'm taking something that should be hers. I'm doing wrong. I've a bad conscience about that.'

He felt a quiver of anger. Hannah was the most generous person he knew.

'Believe me, you're taking nothing she wants.'

'She'd be hurt if she knew. She is your wife.'

He shook his head. 'She's always been jealous of you. She goes out of her way to be unpleasant to you. I think she sensed years ago that I found you attractive. She never cared about any of the others.'

The dark gaze held his for a long time. Then she said quietly: 'She must have loved you once.'

'It was my money she loved.' He could hear the hurt in his own voice. Even after all these years, it still cut deep enough to draw blood. He'd trained himself never to think about it.

He felt Hannah squeeze his hand. 'You don't have to tell

me,' she whispered. 'Shouldn't have asked.'

He took a deep breath. 'I want to. Can't have you feeling guilty for loving me. It's the greatest gift I've ever had.'

He knew she was waiting. He sat back, tried to keep calm. It made him angry even now. Already it was boiling up in his throat. Eunice had been so young, so beautiful, that first year of their marriage. He'd felt so full of love for her.

'Perhaps I'm too hot-blooded. Perhaps I have too ardent a nature.'

'You're loving and gentle.'

'I was much younger then. Perhaps I wanted too much from her.'

'If she loved you, she'd have wanted to give you everything.' Hannah's voice trembled. 'Just as I do now.'

He held on to her hand. 'I thought she was wonderful then.' He'd only had to look at her to feel a tautening, a headiness, a crying need to make love to her. 'If she touched me, my skin would crawl with longing.'

Hugo stopped and took a great jagged breath. 'I feel that way now about you.' Hannah had exactly the same effect on him. He stole a look at her face. Her dark eyes were regarding him with grave understanding. He felt his hand being squeezed. It was more than he could bear. He had to free it from hers, or he'd be crushing her to him and he had to tell her first.

'After the first few months, I found it harder to kindle any response from her, but she was growing heavy with Matt.

'"Goodness, you're never satisfied," she complained one night when I tried to rouse her. "Surely you don't expect me to go through this almost every night?"'

He heard Hannah's swift intake of breath.

'It was rather like a cold shower. The heady rapture I'd been feeling was gone.' He shivered, reliving something of the rejection he'd felt.

'"I've had enough," she said. "I'm not in the mood. Not now there's a child on the way. I can't, Hugo. Not any more."

'I found when I came home from work the next day that

she'd moved her things to another room and I now had our marital bed to myself.

'I was as patient as I could be. It wasn't easy, but I thought everything would be back to normal once the baby was born.'

'And after Matt arrived?'

'She was never like you. Never generous with her love. There was no passion in her, but I came to accept that.'

Hugo sighed as he remembered the night of their first wedding anniversary. Eunice had arranged a special celebratory dinner, inviting some of her cousins as well as her parents.

'I had no relatives I wanted to invite. My father had died while I was in Africa.

'She knew how things were between me and her father. We'd seen very little of each other. I told her she must stand between us. But they'd come to see Matt when he was born, I couldn't bar their entry then. We exchanged nothing but a few pleasantries. I assumed he didn't want to get on closer terms with me.'

Hugo could see Eunice now, singing for them after dinner. She was wearing a dress of lavender satin, all frills and flounces. He'd been delighted to think she was her old self again, laughing with the cousin who was playing for her. Matt was six weeks old.

'That night I undressed for bed and went into her room. I had tried once or twice before and she'd sent me away, saying her doctor didn't advise it until the infant reached six weeks of age. Now it seemed the time was right. I slid into her bed.

'She was in a happy mood. It had been a pleasant evening. She let me kiss her and hold her in my arms.' It hadn't taken much to get him sizzling. He'd been starved of sex. 'The wonderful thing was that she was returning my kisses and running her fingers up my back.' He'd felt flooded with ecstasy. 'I thought I was right, things were back where they'd been at the beginning of our marriage.'

He'd been intoxicated. Heady and shivering with delight. Unfastening her lawn nightdress with shaking fingers.

409

'"Hugo," she whispered, "I want you to do something for me."

'"Yes, love." I didn't want to talk, I wanted to make love. I thought she was of like mind and at last I was receiving encouragement.

'"Will you promise?" she wheedled.

'"Yes." I gave it gladly. "You know you can have anything you want."

'She pushed me away from her, and suddenly I was shuddering. I felt rejected. Her satin eiderdown slid to the floor.

'She said: "I want you to help Daddy."

'She knew how I felt about him. Any mention of his name made me prickle with antagonism. Anger and frustration were choking me. But it seemed I had to jump through certain hoops before I could have my marital rights.

'"Mummy's absolutely desperate. You must help. I know you can."

'I reached for her again, but she pushed my hands away. I was fighting to stay calm and reasonable and said: "Possibly I could help someone else in his position, but your father, no. I can't help him."

'"You mean you don't want to?"

'"It's not that, Eunice." How could I explain that the distrust and dislike I felt for Sir Cecil would immediately cause sparks to fly? I collapsed back against her scented pillows.

'"He refers to me as 'that little whipper-snapper you married". Do you think he'd accept any advice I might give?'

'"You're successful . . ."

'"And he isn't, and that makes it all the harder. I know he'd hate telling me all the details I'd need to know. His income and his losses. It would be embarrassing for both of us."

'"But it's not advice he's asking for," Eunice said impatiently. "He says he's done everything possible to put his creditors off. It's money he needs."

'That did it. I felt ice in the pit of my stomach. "I can't give him money. Not in the amounts he'd need."

'"He said fifty thousand would solve everything."

'"Good God!" I'd kept a tight rein on my temper, but that made it flare up out of control.

'"If I gave him fifty thousand it would ruin my own business! I can't possibly afford it, not now, when I'm trying to expand. It would be throwing good money after bad in any case. He's no idea how to look after his affairs."

'"Don't be silly, he's been doing it all his life."

'"All the more reason why he shouldn't be in this mess now. If I gave him fifty thousand, he'd want more, if not this year then next."

'Eunice hadn't drawn her curtains. The room was bathed in silvery moonlight, enough to allow me to see us both reflected in her cheval glass. She looked beguiling. I felt fraught as I tried to explain.

'"In two years I aim to double the income my capital produces. He would use it to pay interest on loans he should never have taken out. In two years he'll let it drain away and have nothing.

'"The answer is no, Eunice. It's not in my interest and it's not in yours. If you want to live in comfort, I cannot pay your father's debts. He'll spend my fortune for me if I let him. Isn't this what he was trying to do before we married? He lives far above his income. He always has."

'"He's had bad luck with his horses."

'"The horses are an extravagant indulgence. He had the good luck to inherit a fortune from his father. Where's it gone?"

'"He said even ten thousand . . ."

'"Nothing, Eunice. I can't forgive him for trying to defraud me. Why should I help a trickster? I made it plain that I was marrying you, not your family. I've cut off all business connections with your father. I had to."

'"He said that made things worse for him."

'"He's quite right there. I was providing him with income.

411

I can't become involved in his affairs. He could run me into the ground too."

"'But, Hugo,' her tone was sugary, "Mother's afraid he might go bankrupt. You know how to save him. You can't refuse.'

"'He knows, and I know, those stables cost a fortune to run. He should have sold them years ago. We both know one house is essential, two a luxury. His best plan is to hire a competent accountant to work out what assets remain and to sell them off to pay his debts. He'll have to live more simply. I don't doubt it could be done and something salvaged. But knowing him, it won't. I don't propose to give him anything.'

'I'd told her how I saw the matter and thought that had settled it. I'd expected to be allowed to resume. She'd interrupted our love making and made impossible demands, and I'd resented that. Perhaps I did reach out abruptly to pull her closer. I'd been so starved of her I was intoxicated again in an instant.

"'Just a minute, Hugo,' she said coldly, fighting to get free from my arms. "If you're refusing to help my family, I'm refusing to let you do this. You're using my body.'

"'Not tonight, you mean?' I was furious with her by this time and neither of us was in the mood for making love by then. I should have known better.

"'Not until you help him. Just ten thousand would put him on.'

'That made me pull away. I couldn't believe she meant it, but she was stiff with determination.

'Eunice was a small slight woman then. I was much stronger. I dragged her towards me, tore at her nightdress, determined she'd not deny me what was rightfully mine.

'Her lips curled in scorn. "I might have known you'd take me by force.'

'I felt as though she'd doused me in cold water. It brought me to a shuddering halt. I got out of her bed and slammed the door as I left her room.'

Chapter Twenty-five

7 June 1937

Hugo didn't know how long he'd been sitting at the dining-room table with Hannah clinging to his hand.

'I've never tried to put it into words before. You're the first person I've wanted to tell.'

He knew the telling of it had charged the atmosphere. He felt tight with tension.

'You could have divorced her,' Hannah whispered.

'Not so easy then. I mulled it over for a long time, couldn't make up my mind.'

'Why not? You'd have been free of her.'

'It would have meant giving her half the fortune I'd worked so hard to earn. It would have been giving the Schofields what they'd wanted in the first place. They'd set out to trick me and they'd succeeded.' It had eaten into him that he'd been fool enough to fall for that.

'But staying together all those years. It's hard to believe . . .'

'Divorce was something of a disgrace then. Eunice said she didn't want one, divorcees were not accepted in society. I was a good meal ticket, that was what she wanted.'

'She'd have had the meal ticket in any case. I do see she had you where she wanted you. She couldn't lose.'

'I've always known when to cut my losses in business. When it's been necessary I've gritted my teeth and got on with it. Yet on a personal level I wasn't able to bring myself to divorce her.

'When I'd cooled sufficiently to see Eunice as she really was, my business was hungry for capital. I couldn't bring myself to spend it on a divorce settlement.

'As I saw it, Hannah, becoming wealthy was a matter of balancing the greed of wanting more capital with the fear of losing what I already had. I couldn't cut myself off from what I already had. It was a foolish decision.'

'But later on?'

'The more I had, the more I stood to lose. By the time I didn't care about that, Eunice and I were spending more time apart, so I didn't feel so strongly about being free. I had nobody else, you see.

'When Sir Cecil went bankrupt the following year, she blamed me.'

'You were trapped in a marriage of hatred.'

'It was more an empty shell. A neutral relationship. I can't believe now that money meant so much to me. It didn't buy what I wanted most. After a time, I didn't want what it would buy.'

Hannah seemed to rouse herself. 'You have to be very rich to know that. You went your separate ways but stayed married?'

'I suppose so. I told Eunice there'd be no divorce. To be fair, once I became successful and there was more kudos in being my wife, she became a sort of figure-head. When I needed to do any entertaining, she organised it and gave a performance. She always appeared to have my interests at heart. Always appeared affectionate.'

'But in private?' Hannah had her hand pressed against her mouth. He knew she was trying to imagine how he'd felt about his wife.

'We haven't much in common. She had the Schofield way with money. I gave her a large allowance and made it clear I wouldn't add to it. The years passed quickly enough.'

'But you said you wanted more children? You understood about . . .'

'At one time, Matt seemed to be holding us together. We tried to have another child. Eunice wanted one badly, so she let me try hard. All fairly cold-blooded by then. Love had died.

414

'It's a terrible confession, isn't it, Hannah? The story of my life. Fêted as the most successful man in British business, yet a total failure on a personal level.'

'Not any longer, Hugo.'

'I have you now.' He put an arm round her shoulders and pulled her closer.

'Everything has suddenly come right for me too. I have you, and I have the twins and Lizzie. I've never been so utterly content with my lot. Who would have thought it, Hugo?'

He picked up the bottle and Hannah's glass. Put an arm round her waist to draw her to the stairs. Felt the comfort of her arm round him.

He took her to his bedroom. To undo the buttons on her silk blouse tightened the tension he felt. His heart was racing as he ran his hands over her smooth shoulders.

All Hannah's underwear seemed gossamer fine, enhancing her large figure. Though well covered, she was not over fleshed; her breasts were generous and her abdomen firm, the way a woman should be once past the first flush of youth.

He was carried away, as he always was. The touch of her hands on his bare skin was almost more than he could bear. Passion came so easily when he was with her. He gave himself up to it, hearing her whispers of love.

The pain, when it came, sliced like a knife through his chest. Every gasp for air seemed to push the blade deeper into his flesh. From showering love on Hannah's glorious body, wild with delight, aware only of the softness of her flesh, he was reduced in an instant to helplessness. He felt her body continue to move against his for a moment. She slowed.

'Hugo?'

The pain cut again. He collapsed on top of her, no longer able to support his own weight on his arms.

'Hugo!' He knew he'd knocked the wind out of her and that she'd never be able to breathe with his weight crushing her like this. He could feel her struggling, trying to pull herself out from under him. She rolled him off, over on to his back.

'Hugo, what's happened? Are you all right?' Her frightened face hovered six inches above his own, terrible concern showing in her eyes. Yet he couldn't answer, could only gasp in agony and shame.

He had felt something like this before. Four or five times over the last month, pain had ripped through his chest, knotting his heart and his hands as well as his stomach. Bad enough to double him up. At the same time, his chest had felt as though it was locked inside a metal cage which wouldn't expand to let him breathe.

A good belch would relieve all the symptoms, so he knew it was indigestion. He'd been liverish for years, but this was worse than anything he'd ever suffered before. It made him cut down on wine and drink more brandy instead. He ate smaller helpings of the wonderful steak and kidney pudding Hannah produced for him.

Normally he wouldn't have dreamt of belching in front of Hannah. It was too obvious a sign of infirmity and old age. But tonight he had to try. The pain had never been so bad. For the first time, the belch wouldn't come and the pain was getting worse. His mind crawled with fear that it might be something more serious than indigestion, and anger that it had happened now while he was with Hannah. He wanted to breathe deeply but that made the pain worse too.

He became aware of Hannah's naked body scrambling out from under the covers. He heard pure desperation in her sobs as she rushed round the bed to the phone on his side.

He heard her voice ask for an ambulance and tried to tell her it wasn't necessary, that he'd be perfectly all right in a few moments.

She was throwing her clothes on. As she fastened the last button on her brown silk blouse, she bent over him.

'Hugo?'

He found he was able to croak: 'Lucky it's my bed I'm in,' and tried to smile.

He knew Hannah was heartened and thought it signalled recovery.

She asked: 'What about you? Wouldn't it seem more normal if you were wearing something? I'd laugh, Hugo, if I wasn't so worried.'

She'd found his pyjama trousers and was putting them on for him. He tried to lift himself, but the pain jarred through him again.

He knew the ambulance had come. Felt the terrible insecurity of being carried downstairs on a stretcher. Staring up at the ornate plaster ceiling in the hall.

Blackness came and went. He was hardly aware of what was happening. He knew that Hannah held on to his hand and that she was talking to him. He found it soothing, but didn't know what she said.

'Hannah, love,' he murmured. He kept drifting away.

Hannah shivered as she held on to Hugo's hand, willing him to live. She knew he was drifting in and out of consciousness. They'd put an oxygen mask over his face now. It was hissing softly from the cylinder on the other side of the bed.

'Will he be all right?' she demanded of the doctor. He'd shaken his head doubtfully. 'Hard to say. Too soon. He's not a young man.'

'He's got to be all right,' she'd burst out.

'His heart . . . Has this happened to him before? Did he have any warning?'

'No.' She was vehement. 'Absolutely not. He's been very well these last few months. Said he'd never felt better.'

The doctor was shaking his head. 'We'll do our best . . .'

A nurse came and went every fifteen minutes, taking his pulse. He stirred uneasily on the bed and she knew he was on the edge of consciousness.

'Hugo,' she whispered. 'Darling, get better. You know how much I need you You've made me so happy these last few months. I couldn't bear it if you left me now. You've everything to live for.'

She stared at him but his eyes were closed, he gave no sign that he heard her. Tears were stinging her own eyes. She couldn't believe what was happening.

'I do love you, Hugo. You must get better.'

His hand was growing colder. She felt as though ice crystals were forming in her own body. She was stiff and tense and utterly terrified for him.

The nurse was inside the screens again. Bending over Hugo, writing on his charts. Something in her manner made Hannah feel colder still.

She knew his life was ebbing away when the nurse returned with the doctor. He turned off the oxygen. Hugo's face looked waxen and he breathed stertorously now.

She sat without moving for another hour while his noisy breathing grew slower. She kept telling him over and over how much she loved him. He didn't speak to her again.

Lizzie woke with a start, aware of a throbbing engine outside on the drive. For a moment she couldn't think where she was. The bedroom, clearly lit with serene moonlight, was unfamiliar. The silver clock on her bedside table told her it was two-thirty.

Outside, a car door slammed. Anxiety niggled in the pit of her stomach. Normally if she was woken in the night it was by the twins in the adjoining room. She slid out of bed and went to the door. They were small still mounds in their cots and she could hear their even breathing.

She came back to her own open window. It was a soft summer night. Below was the roof of a taxi and Hannah was paying it off. She'd said she'd be home before midnight.

Lizzie's first thought was that she'd had a better time than expected, but Hannah looked crushed. The tyres crunched as the taxi drove round the circular flower bed and out into the road. Hannah made no move to come in, but stood staring after it.

Had something terrible happened, or had she just forgotten her key? Lizzie was opening her mouth to call down when she heard an unmistakable sob. It sent panic fluttering through her. She grabbed for her dressing gown, a present from Joey,

418

and ran downstairs. The heavy front door creaked as she opened it.

'Hannah? Is something the matter?'

Lizzie was shocked when she saw her face, ravished with anguish and running with tears. The jaunty little hat swathed in net perched over one eye looked incongruous now. Lizzie ran out to throw her arms round her, to comfort and bring her in.

'Hannah! What's happened?' The step was icy to her bare feet. She couldn't stand on it. She was hustling Hannah inside.

'It's Hugo. Heart attack. He's dead.'

Lizzie felt her heart turn over with shock and regret that she hadn't had time to know him better. But pity for Hannah was stronger. She drew her into the kitchen. Opened the dampers on the Aga to make it burn up because Hannah's hands felt frozen. Put the kettle on for tea.

Under the electric light, Hannah's agony was even more apparent. Her eyes were red and swollen. She slumped on to a chair at the table and seemed unable to tell Lizzie exactly what had happened. She mumbled and corrected herself and gave two conflicting accounts. Lizzie thought her hardly coherent and put an arm across her shoulders to comfort her. It brought further torrents of tears.

After some hot tea, she said: 'I've got to pull myself together.'

'Go to bed, Hannah, you'll be better in the morning.'

'No.' She seemed agitated. 'I've got to tell people. Greg and Eunice. And then there's Matt. And Dorothy . . . she ought to know, she was fond of her grandfather.'

Lizzie poured her a second cup, but Hannah blew her nose and said she was going to the bathroom to wash her face. She was away long enough for Lizzie to feel worried. She even went upstairs to make sure Hannah was all right.

'I'm just coming, Lizzie,' Hannah said in answer to her call, and seemed more in control of herself when she came out. She went to the phone in the hall and gave Eunice's number to the operator. Lizzie hovered, wanting to show support. It rang for a long time before it was picked up.

'Very bad news, Eunice. So sorry to tell you, I'm afraid it's Hugo.'

Lizzie heard Eunice's voice on the line, querulous at being woken.

'We'd been to the Royal Court in Liverpool. We'd gone back to Ince and were having a late supper when he had this terrible pain. So bad he went straight up to bed. He asked me to bring him some brandy. I waited a little while to see if he wanted anything else, but when I went up he seemed worse so I rang for an ambulance. Yes, he died in Clatterbridge Hospital shortly after getting there.'

Lizzie stood open-mouthed. Hannah's account of what had happened was clear and concise now. She'd been so shocked and grief-stricken and had gone to such lengths to pull herself together, Lizzie was suspicious. Was that really the whole story? She was too tired to think properly. She told herself she was being silly.

Hannah was trying to find out if she could reach Matt by telephone in Crete and getting into a panic because she was making no progress.

'A telegram?' Lizzie suggested. In the end she had to send one.

Hannah was white with exhaustion. 'I don't know what to do about Dorothy.'

'It'll be soon enough in the morning.'

'Won't be any easier. None of us knows her address. Oh, and I've forgotten Greg.'

That done, Hannah stood up. She seemed suddenly much older. 'I keep thinking I'll wake up and find it's all a bad dream.'

At her bedroom door, she paused to pat Lizzie's hand. 'Glad you were here, Lizzie. You've been a help.'

Lizzie was afraid that wasn't the truth either. She'd not been able to comfort her. Hannah's loss was too great for that.

In the days that followed, Eunice returned to Ince to organise a big funeral, with all the pomp and ceremony that befitted a man of Hugo's status. The papers were filled with accounts of his death. They recalled his past exploits, listed his gifts to charity, and assessed his probable wealth to several wildly different levels.

Lizzie looked ahead across the bleak days to the funeral, wanting it over. Nothing could seem normal while that hung over them. Hannah spent most of her time nursing one or other of the twins, finding some comfort in them. She was past crying now, but locked in misery, as though she had nothing more to live for. She hardly left the house for fear of being photographed.

A date was discussed for the funeral, but when they heard from Matt it was delayed another two days to allow him to get home.

Lizzie was worried because she was installed in his house and was afraid he wouldn't like it. Eunice sent her car to meet him at Speke aerodrome. As it happened Lizzie opened the door to him at Oakridge while the chauffeur was unloading his suitcases on to the step.

Matthew Mortimer, her grandfather, was not at all as she'd imagined. He was not a younger edition of Hugo. If anything he seemed older. His skin was lined and dry, sunburned to a dark mahogany shade.

'Mr Mortimer,' she said as he came up the steps. 'I'm Lizzie.'

'Good evening,' he said. 'Bring my suitcases upstairs, will you?'

Hannah was behind her in the hall. Matt pecked her cheek mechanically.

'No, no, Matt. Lizzie isn't the maid. She's Dorothy's . . . I wrote and told you.'

'Oh!' He turned to survey her then, with a cool unwelcoming stare. 'I suppose it doesn't matter now. What a mess everything's in.'

Hannah stood looking nonplussed, then reverted to domestic matters. 'Have you had dinner?'

'Yes,' Matt said. 'But I'd like a cup of tea.'

'I'll make it,' Lizzie offered, eager to get away from him. She dragged his suitcases in off the step, but left them just inside the front door.

The next morning, Lizzie went down to breakfast in her dressing gown. She was dreading the funeral and could hardly eat. She'd never been to one before and had no idea what to expect.

Matt didn't have much to say. He opened a newspaper and read. Hannah didn't appear at all.

Lizzie went back to her room and dressed herself in her new black outfit. It didn't suit her, but when she'd gone out to buy it, she'd seen nothing in black that did. The sales assistant had assured her that the pillbox hat with its glossy black feather was the latest thing. It seemed to cast a grey shadow on her face, making her look washed out and ill. She was nervous because she knew she'd be meeting other members of the Mortimer family.

'If Lady Mortimer seems off-hand, don't let it upset you,' Hannah warned quietly. 'I don't. She's never very kind to me.'

They gathered in the hall to wait for the car Eunice was sending to fetch them to Ince Hall. It was a grey overcast morning and the light coming through the stained glass windows seemed washed out too.

Lizzie thought they all looked as ill at ease as she felt. Matt, looking drawn and old, had brought his newspaper to read. He sat near the empty fireplace. Greg had driven over to join them. He strode restlessly backwards and forwards, his yellow hair seeming brighter against his sombre suit and black tie.

He stopped in front of his father's chair and asked: 'How much do you reckon he'll leave?'

Hannah sat quietly resigned with her hands in her lap, her black gloves already on. They were all silent on the journey

422

and arrived to find the funeral cortège already assembling on the drive. A long row of cars, all large, all highly polished, all black.

Lizzie followed the family inside. She was sure her heart was thumping loud enough to be heard. This wasn't how she'd imagined herself meeting her great-grandmother: standing in a line of people waiting to offer their condolences.

Eunice reminded Lizzie of pictures of Queen Victoria, plump and short, seeming to be draped entirely in black crêpe and wearing a big black hat with the veil thrown back from her face.

Lizzie watched Matthew hug her and whisper his sympathy. She couldn't believe he was her grandfather; she felt nothing for him. The old lady offered a plump lined cheek to be kissed by each of her family in turn. She had several chins and her flesh fell in deep mournful folds. Then Hannah was drawing Lizzie forward.

'Eunice, this is Elizabeth, Dorothy's eldest daughter. A great-grand-daughter you haven't met before.'

The large black hat was inclined in her direction for a moment. No cheek was offered for a kiss. Not even a hand to be shaken. Eunice was already turning to greet people who had followed them in, giving no sign that she understood who Lizzie was.

'I'm going upstairs to see Father. Pay my last respects,' Matt said. 'Are you coming?'

'No, thank you.' Hannah's voice was strangled. Lizzie clung to her, afraid she'd be asked to go too. Matt gave them a rather pitying look and strode off with Greg.

Lizzie felt spurned and out of place waiting in this grand room with so many people dressed in black. She thought the men looked like penguins and the women like crows. She knew nobody but Hannah and was careful to stay close to her. Nobody came to speak to her, but very few spoke to Hannah either.

Lizzie looked up the forty feet of Eunice's drawing-room that still managed to look over-full of furniture and nick-

423

nacks. Everywhere she turned there was something to take the eye: pictures, cut glass, silver, fine china and family photographs. It reminded her of a museum but today she couldn't concentrate on such things.

They were near a window overlooking the front entrance. Cars were continuing to arrive. A woman alighted from a taxi and started to climb the front steps. Beside her, Lizzie was aware of Hannah straightening up and feeling for her hand.

Lizzie's heart was pounding harder than ever. She guessed even before Hannah whispered: 'This is your mother.'

People were turning to look at the woman who was now in the doorway. Lizzie felt a stirring of interest round the room. Hannah was easing her closer. Her mother was dressed from head to foot in black and a black veil billowed round her face, but behind it the blue eyes were defiant. She flounced up to Eunice and kissed her cheek in greeting. Eunice turned her back on her in deliberate insult.

'Grandpapa would want me to come,' said Dorothy coolly, and a ripple seemed to go round the room. 'I'll go upstairs to see him and make my farewells.'

'Dorothy.' Hannah touched her arm as she made to pass. 'How are you?'

'I'm fine, thank you, Hannah.' She put so much conviction into her voice, Lizzie couldn't doubt it. 'How are my children?'

'Here's one of them you haven't seen for a long time.' Hannah was pulling her forward. 'Elizabeth. We call her Lizzie.'

'Hello . . .' Lizzie's mouth was dry, she felt stiff with tension. Should she call her 'Mother'? How many countless times had she imagined this meeting? Her mother would be twice as excited to see her as Hannah had been. She'd say she'd missed her and that she loved her.

Lizzie put out her hand, hardly knowing what she was doing.

Two black-gloved hands flew to the veiled face in shocked surprise. In an instant Dorothy had turned to weave through people towards the door, but not before Lizzie had seen her

424

brilliant blue eyes glaze with tears.

Hannah was squeezing her hand. 'She's upset. We took her too much by surprise.'

Lizzie tried to rid herself of the lump in her throat. She wouldn't have recognised her own mother, she was nothing to her. A complete stranger. 'She doesn't want to know me now.'

'She's in a turmoil, overcome by emotion,' Hannah whispered.

'Look, here's someone else you'll want to meet. In the same boat as yourself. Her other daughters – Henrietta and Cecilia, Honor and Patience, and their father, Franklin Flower.'

Lizzie was blinking furiously, trying to hold back the tears that threatened.

Half-sisters. She'd tried to imagine what they'd be like. They were tearful too.

'I don't know why Dorothy had to come.' Franklin was agitated, half whispering. 'She must have known we'd be here. She must know that seeing her would upset the girls.'

Lizzie kissed each of the four girls in turn. They too seemed strangers; she was much closer to the O'Malley children. She knew she was expected to feel pity for them, but seeing them against this background it was hard.

'At least you still have a father to look after you,' she said, and was immediately sorry. It made her sound heartless and unfeeling.

She was still on tenterhooks as she watched six stalwart pall bearers tackling the bend in the stairs. The coffin of polished oak with handsome brass handles turned the corner and came smoothly down to be loaded into the hearse. She couldn't bear to think of Hugo inside it.

Outside the village church, wreaths and flowers lined the walls for fifty yards. Lilies and gladioli behind cellophane. Lizzie felt worse, inside the church was full to overflowing with mourners. A bishop had come from Chester to assist the vicar. He extolled Hugo's fine character and generosity at length. The music swelled mournfully, making the tears harder to control. Voices were raised, but many missed the first notes of 'Rock of Ages, Cleft for Me'.

Hannah wept openly with no veil to hide behind. Matt blew his nose hard as they went out into the cool morning air.

It wasn't over yet. Lizzie knew she'd have to get back into the car and go back to Ince Hall.

It wasn't quite so bad this time. There was sherry that burned her already dry tongue. She craved water instead, but couldn't bring herself to ask for it. There was food she couldn't touch, though it engrossed most of the others.

Franklin Flower and the girls were becoming less tongue-tied now. A nanny took the two younger ones away. The older ones were asking about Lizzie's life at Yarrow. She hardly knew how to answer them. It seemed impossible not to give them further reason to turn against their mother.

Dorothy was here, moving amongst the mourners, veil thrown back now. Lizzie could see the resemblance that stamped them mother and daughter, and that was painful too. She felt haunted by her. She wanted this gathering to disperse so she could go home.

She heard someone say to Hannah: 'Sir Hugo left this for you.' He pushed an envelope into her hand. She saw Hannah freeze. The colour drained from her face and she slid it quickly into her handbag without a second glace. 'I shall read the will in the library in fifteen minutes. He asked me not to give it to you then in front of the family.'

He went round spreading his message. Heads were nodding, whispers going round the room: 'This is why Dorothy's come, of course. She wants to hear the will.'

Lizzie's spirits sank further. She was afraid she'd be left alone to face the polite conversation of strangers. But Hannah had recovered. Her hand was on Lizzie's arm, steering her towards the library.

'All the family,' she said. 'Mr Wilcox, the family solicitor, mentioned you 'specially.'

Lizzie felt bewildered by it all. She was in another vast room with bookcases all along one wall. She perched uncomfortably beside Hannah on a Victorian horsehair sofa.

They were all streaming in: Matt and Greg, Dorothy and her estranged husband Franklin Flower and the girls, to sit about the room. She felt uncomfortably hot as she waited again. It seemed to be a day for waiting about. Never had one passed so slowly.

Eunice, her great-grandmother, sat with the solicitor at a polished round table. She patted her dry eyes with a black-bordered handkerchief. At last Mr Wilcox opened a folder and began. Lizzie was aware that the tension in the room was heightening.

He read out a long preamble. Lizzie only half listened. It seemed to be telling them that Hugo Mortimer did not believe in inherited wealth and that he had already made provision for some members of his family.

They were all sitting up straighter in their seats as the solicitor came to the part they wanted to hear.

'For my wife Eunice, the use of our home, Ince Hall, with all fittings and fixtures, pictures, furniture and motor cars. Also the remainder of the lease at Albany and all furnishings there for her lifetime.'

Lizzie was aware of the shock waves this was causing.

'I have already made adequate provision for upkeep of these properties and a sufficient income from . . .'

They all heard the strangled grunt Eunice gave, but the solicitor read on, quoting trusts set up many years earlier.

'On her death, the above properties and trusts to be handed on for the use of my only son Matthew Charles Mortimer for his lifetime, and hence to my grandson Gregory John Mortimer and hence to his issue.

'Also to my only son Matthew Charles Mortimer, my personal effects, wrist watches, fountain pens, signet rings, cuff links, and such of my books as he might wish to take.

'For my grandson Gregory John Mortimer, my half hunter which he admired so much in his childhood and such of my books as he might wish to take.'

The man looked up and paused. Lizzie could feel the bitter

disappointment in those around her that Hugo had apparently meant all he'd said in the preamble. Greg seemed to be in a state of shock.

'To Hannah Mary Mortimer, my daughter-in-law, for whom I have not as yet made any provision . . .' Lizzie felt Hannah stiffen beside her '. . . the sum of two hundred and fifty thousand pounds.'

Her soft gasp of surprise was almost drowned by Eunice's snort of disgust. Dorothy's face was stiff with tension and paper-white.

'For Elizabeth Mercy Mortimer, also known as O'Malley...' Lizzie felt herself break —out in a sweat. It had not occurred to her that Hugo would leave her anything '. . . for whom as yet I have made no provision, the sum of one hundred thousand pounds to be held in trust until she reaches the age of twenty-one. The income from such to be available to her immediately.'

She covered her face with her hands. She couldn't even envisage such a sum and certainly not what she might expect from it in income. She was only just in time to hear that Hannah had been appointed as one of her trustees. She was shaking with shock. She was rich! Rich beyond anything she'd ever imagined. Her life would be different, changed completely at one stroke.

Still the solicitor's voice droned on. Each of her half-sisters was to receive fifty thousand. The twins, Piers and Paul, one hundred thousand each.

Then followed a few small bequests to Hugo's butler, housekeeper, chauffeur and head gardener.

'The residue of my monies to go to the following charities.' The solicitor started to read out what seemed to be a long list.

'What about me?' a sharp voice interrupted. It was Dorothy, her face now ash-white and working with fury.

Lizzie was quaking. Those who had expected to receive money had not. Greg's bright blue eyes were staring at her in total affront. Hannah's hand was squeezing hers; she too must feel their envy and their hatred.

'I'm afraid, Mrs Flower, you are not a beneficiary under this will.'

'When was it made?' Eunice demanded, her face white and pinched.

'It's a new will,' the solicitor said. 'I received instructions to draw it up just over a month ago.'

'Grandpa told me . . .' Dorothy wailed.

'I understood I might expect . . .' Greg was protesting, his chin sagging with disappointment.

'As I understand it, Sir Hugo felt he'd already made adequate provision for you both. As is usually the case, his earlier wills are made null and void by this one.' He stood up to go. 'If there's nothing else . . .'

'Wait a minute! All those charities.' Greg's face was thunderstruck. 'What a waste! What a terrible waste. We'll contest it.'

'On what grounds?'

'We are close relatives, family. And he hasn't made adequate provision for our needs.'

'Those grounds might be reasonable for children who are still minors, or for elderly dependent relatives, but, forgive me, neither you nor Mrs Flower fall into those categories.'

Lizzie felt Greg's eyes burn into hers.

'You come worming your way into Hannah's household, worming your way into Hugo's affections! He felt sorry for you. I suppose you asked him for money?'

'No.' Lizzie was almost weeping again. 'No, I didn't expect, I didn't know . . .'

'No doubt you're crowing now! You've got what you want. You've done me and Dorothy down.'

'Nonsense,' Hannah said briskly. 'Hugo had a perfect right to leave his money to whomever he wished.'

'Dorothy, I would have thought you'd be pleased he's remembered Lizzie. He told me he felt he had to make himself responsible for her welfare because you were not doing so.'

'But why give her a hundred thousand? My other daughters

have been left only fifty thousand. I don't understand it.'

Franklin Flower grimaced. 'I asked Hugo not to leave my daughters anything more. I told him I preferred to provide for their needs myself. The twins and Elizabeth have a greater need. They can't expect money from any other source.'

'I've never been so humiliated in my life!' Dorothy's voice was a cry from the heart. 'I thought Grandpa loved me. I thought you did.'

'Dorothy, you've abandoned your husband and children.' Eunice was at her most self-righteous. 'Such things are inexcusable. You've let us all down. Disgraced the Mortimer name. You don't deserve more money. You'd only spend it on keeping your fancy men.'

'And you, what have you done to deserve a quarter of a million?' Eunice had switched her gaze to Hannah, her face full of malevolence. 'I've always known you were up to no good.'

Dorothy hadn't finished. 'You aren't going to starve, Grandma, but he hasn't left you anything extra. What have you done to deserve that? It must have been something very bad too.'

Lizzie was horrorstruck as she realised the Mortimers could be as bitterly quarrelsome as the O'Malleys.

She could see that what little colour Eunice had was draining from her face. The next moment she'd slumped over in her chair.

'She's fainted,' Hannah said weakly, and had them all seeking the smelling salts Eunice kept in her handbag. She'd come round by the time Lizzie found them, and Hannah put her to lie on the horsehair sofa.

'Come on, Lizzie,' Hannah said with dignity. 'We'll go home.'

Chapter Twenty-six

Joey felt jittery. He was finding it nerve-racking to sit still at his desk for eight hours each day. He kept telling himself all was going well. For over two weeks he'd been taking every cheque that came in and helping himself to generous amounts from most of the accounts Evans's ran. Nobody appeared to have noticed. No questions were being asked.

His fellow clerks had commented that their work was reduced, but they seemed to be in no hurry to bring it to Mr Draper's attention.

Joey told himself he was uneasy because Lizzie had left him. She was on his mind when he should have been thinking of other things. He had even greater reason to get even with the Mortimers now.

Thursday came, it seemed an ordinary day. He'd been sitting at his desk working on the wage packets for half an hour when the news came that Sir Hugo Mortimer had been taken ill during the night and had died in hospital.

Everybody knew Sir Hugo was Greg Mortimer's grandfather, and they stopped work to whisper. Joey felt a bow wave of speculation go round the office about how much Greg would inherit now.

Joey tried to think through what it would mean for his plan. Greg wouldn't be coming to the office for the next few days, that was certain, and all to the good. Bereavement would surely take his mind off the affairs of A. A. Evans and that was even better. And the wages would still have to be paid.

He decided it was another bonus for him. He tried to reckon up how much he'd taken so far and it ran into

431

thousands. He'd had a good run of luck to get away with it this far, and it looked as though his luck was holding.

On the following Tuesday, it came as something of a shock to find both Greg and Matthew Mortimer in the office and holding conferences behind closed doors.

Gleeson was called in, everybody looked serious and shocked. He told himself Hugo Mortimer's death was the cause, but the atmosphere in the office seemed tense. His fellow clerks were edgy too.

It took all his nerve to stay at his desk. Eight more working days to get through before he could go off on holiday. His nails were bitten down to the quick.

Nick sat at his office desk staring into space. He still hadn't recovered from the funeral. Hugo's death had come as a shock. He'd gone to the church, as had many others from Evans's, and had not been able to find a seat. Many had not even been able to get inside. He'd tried to go to the graveside, but it had proved impossible in the crush.

He shivered. Lizzie had looked so forlorn in black. He hadn't been able to get near her and she hadn't even noticed he was there. He'd wanted to offer her comfort, but he hadn't seen her since. There was no phone at his lodgings and he hadn't wanted to intrude on the family last night. He decided he'd ring her in his lunch hour today.

It had pleased him this morning to open his newspaper and see her in a photograph captioned 'Mortimer Family's Grief'. A row of women in mourning, and there she was, between Hannah and Dorothy, where she belonged.

He shuffled through the papers on his desk, feeling somehow less secure. Hugo had offered him help and encouragement. Recently Nick had seen quite a lot of him at Oakridge. He'd miss him too.

He felt in his pocket and took out the letter Edmond Stanton had sent him, headed 'Capital Farms Limited'. It was no good denying it. This was exactly the job he wanted. He'd have jumped at this chance if it hadn't been for Lizzie.

He could just afford to keep a wife on what Evans's paid him; anything less would mean putting off the wedding for a time.

He looked round him at clerks writing in ledgers. Two rows in front Joey O'Malley was biting the end of his pen and wasting time too. Nick sighed. More than anything else he wanted Lizzie. He could put up with this if he had her.

He saw Matthew Mortimer stride up the hall towards his office. He looked bleak and withdrawn, his mouth in a straight line. Greg followed him in a few minutes later, looking totally bereft, even ill, and slammed into his own office.

Greg had said he'd see Nick to discuss the problems he'd thought were caused by fraud. In the intervening days he'd become more certain he was right, and it was continuing. He had the evidence ready in a neat pile on the edge of his desk. It seemed a good moment. He was on his feet, ready to go up, when he saw Matthew Mortimer go into Greg's office.

Edmond Stanton's letter caught Nick's attention again. He was very tempted. But he'd be expected to move about the country. They had a lot of arable land in Essex. He didn't think he could bear to leave Lizzie once they were married. The prospect of that made him hot with anticipation.

An hour went by and Greg seemed busier than usual. His father was with him and senior managers were going in and out. Nick decided he had to tell him what was on his mind and went up to the desk in the alcove to talk to Miss Peacock.

Her grey dress was as drab as ever, but today she had a patch of crimson on each cheek. She seemed harassed, with piles of correspondence on her desk, and said quickly: 'I don't think he'll have time for you today. With his father here, he has more important things to think about.'

Nick felt a rush of impotent rage.

'For him, nothing can be more important than this. I tried to tell him about it last week. It's now urgent. It's his problem and he's got to know about it. Ask him when I can see him, and it won't wait 'til tomorrow.'

When he turned round, Matthew Mortimer had come into

433

the alcove and was standing behind him with a face like thunder.

'You'd better come in now,' he said, tight-lipped. 'It's Nick Bender, isn't it?'

Lizzie felt quite flurried when Matt telephoned to say he and Greg were coming home for lunch because there was something they wanted to thrash out in private. It didn't please her. Matt had a way of looking at her as though she wasn't welcome in his house, and she felt Hannah needed peace after the shock she'd suffered.

Lizzie went out to the garden to let Hannah know and found her sitting quietly in a leafy corner well away from the house, reading a letter. She looked so tranquil and Lizzie didn't like disturbing her.

But Hannah stood up immediately and walked back to the house in her usual unflurried way. She went to the kitchen.

'We'd better have the chops we were going to have for dinner tonight,' she told her cook. 'They'll be here in half an hour. Doesn't give us much time to arrange anything else. We can think again about dinner this afternoon.'

Hannah pushed her dark hair off her forehead and went to spread the cloth on the dining-room table.

It pleased Lizzie to find she was getting over her shock so quickly. There was a calmness about her, as though she was accepting Hugo's death.

When she heard the front door slam and heavy footsteps in the hall, Lizzie was feeding Piers his lunch in the garden. Nancy was with her feeding Paul.

'What's the matter, Matt?' she heard Hannah ask. It was a warm day and the french doors to the sitting-room were open behind her.

'It's the business. In deep trouble. We may not be able to save it.'

'Greg, it can't be that bad?' Hannah's shocked voice asked.

'It's no good asking him! It's Greg's fault. He's not been giving it his attention. Too busy gadding off to race meetings.'

In the silence that followed Hannah's voice carried clearly. 'Yours too, Matt, you're never here. It's your business. You should have looked after it.'

'I didn't want it in the first place.' Matt sounded angry. 'My interests lie elsewhere. Greg wanted to be a businessman and was so sure he knew what he was doing.'

Lizzie heard them go into the dining-room and shuddered. Nancy's eyes were like saucers. Clearly she'd heard that too.

Hannah came to the french doors. 'Lizzie, lunch is ready.'

'I could have mine in the kitchen with Nancy. You'll want to talk business.'

'No,' she said. 'There's no reason why you shouldn't be with us.'

At the door, Lizzie met Matt's cold questioning glance. 'Hannah?' He seemed affronted.

She said firmly: 'Lizzie is family and she lives here.' Matt's lips straightened into a harder line. Greg seemed angry and even more hostile.

Lizzie wasn't hungry but she sat down. They all started on the soup in silence. The chops had come in before Matt spoke.

'I think you'd better try and sell the business,' he said, addressing Greg coldly. 'If not, close it.'

'Close it? Don't be silly, Dad!' Greg was highly indignant.

'I don't understand what you've been doing. If my father could run a dozen businesses at once and make each earn its way, I can't understand why you failed to manage one.'

'Grandpa didn't involve himself,' Greg blustered. 'Hardly went near them. He had a knack of keeping managers on their toes.'

'Pity he didn't keep *you* on your toes. You've run Evans's straight into the ground. There isn't much of value to sell.' Angrily, Matt dabbed at his mouth with his napkin.

'There's been no new investment for twenty years. The buildings are old and the machinery out of date. We've been making the same old toffee for a hundred years. Tastes change. We should have branched out into boiled sweets or

435

even chocolate. You made no effort to extend the range. We have too many employees doing too little. You've made no attempt to maintain efficiency.'

'Dad, you ran it yourself for twenty years and did none of those things. It's no good blaming me.'

'What I do blame you for is helping yourself to company money. You know damn well it isn't your personal property.'

'I thought of it as a loan. I was going to replace it. I meant to.'

'No doubt when one of your horses came up? You've no judgement, Greg. You can't even pick a good horse. Taking company funds for yourself . . . have you no sense? It's a criminal matter.'

'For God's sake, Father! You're not . . .'

'Of course not. We can't have that sort of publicity. But Evans's is short of cash and that makes everything more difficult.'

'I'm quite willing to help, Matt,' Hannah said softly.

He swung on her abruptly. 'Better not. Too many other problems. There could be fraud too. Your Nick Bender reckons there is.'

Lizzie went cold and then hot. Nick must have told them about Joey. She wished he had not, but Nick would see it as his duty. It made her feel more guilty. Nick wouldn't have seen that van if she hadn't taken him home.

'It's not all my fault. Be fair, Father. If there's fraud as well . . .'

'You didn't notice. How could you be expected to? You were always away at the races.'

'Nobody else noticed either.'

'What you did, hid what was happening from the rest of the staff. Did anybody question what you took?'

Lizzie swallowed at the wrong moment and almost choked on a piece of potato. She knew she was drawing everybody's attention by coughing. It had to be Joey! Hadn't he vowed he'd do it?

436

'I certainly blame you for not seeing it sooner. You wouldn't even listen when Bender tried to tell you.'

'Don't you know who's doing it?' Hannah asked.

'Greg knows nothing. We'll need to sift through everything to find out exactly what's missing. We aren't sure about anything yet.'

Lizzie froze in panic. Joey would be caught! Hadn't she feared this all along?

'We'll catch the culprit,' Greg said easily.

'Even that might not save Evans's. With Father leaving me nothing . . .

'Fortunately, you'll be all right, Hannah. I'm afraid I might be bankrupted. This house might have to go. At least you can afford to put another roof over our heads.'

'It can't be that bad?' she breathed.

'What about me?' Greg demanded. 'I'll lose my job and have nothing.'

'You have your own money. Father gave you enough to set yourself up.'

'But I didn't! You wanted me to help you at Evans's. If only Grandpa were still alive, he could have baled us out.'

'If he'd wanted to.'

'All that money wasted on charities! A fraction of it would be all we'd need.'

Matt sighed. 'Start sacking staff. There's far too many of them sitting round all day. Can't afford their wages any longer. But quietly, we don't want all this to come out. Employees will panic if they think we can't pay their wages, and if there's any publicity the business will be harder to sell.'

Nobody was even pretending to eat now. The chops had hardly been touched.

'Clogs to clogs in three generations. Isn't that what they say?' Matt asked, sitting up straight in his chair. 'We Mortimers are running true to form.'

Lizzie didn't know what to do with herself.

'The whole thing's a shambles,' he went on. 'I wish I could go back to Crete.'

'There you go again.' Greg's voice grated with indignation. 'Leaving all the dirty work to me. Then you blame me when things aren't to your liking.'

'I think it would be better if you stayed here and sorted things out,' Hannah said quietly.

Nick was hunched over his desk at Evans's and couldn't stop his eyes from straying to Joey O'Malley's back fifteen yards in front of him. Joey wasn't concentrating on his work either. He was restless, opening and closing the drawers of his desk, and looked absolutely stiff with tension.

He wasn't the only one. Everybody knew Matt was reviewing the business. He'd had several long and heated sessions with Greg. Occasionally, they heard raised voices. Miss Peacock typed furiously. She'd not been given so much work for a long time.

Managers were going into Greg's office and coming out an hour later with stiff, serious faces. Nothing was being said to the rest of the staff but Nick could feel the tension spiralling round the office. He'd swear there was fear too. Everybody was waiting. There was a feeling of approaching disaster.

Matt Mortimer had listened to what he had to say, and studied the figures as he'd pointed them out without saying a word.

While he'd done so, Nick had studied the man's fringe of hair. It was growing thinner, almost non-existent now across the front. He knew Matt was shocked. His eyes were strained, he looked haggard and bewildered by what Nick was telling him. He made no comment at all, just dismissed him afterwards. Nick knew his suspicions were well founded. It made him fearful too. He felt the atmosphere was growing heavier and darker. He felt they were all waiting for the storm to break.

Hugo's death had altered everything. Nick felt he couldn't impose on Hannah at a time like this and had stayed away. Matt had come home and the household seemed very different. Matt wasn't very welcoming where Nick was concerned.

He'd had to make arrangements to meet Lizzie elsewhere.

Nick sighed. Hugo's death had changed things for her too.

'It's silly,' Lizzie had laughed uneasily, 'but I can't think how I'll ever spend so much money.'

Nick was wary. 'Even Dad would consider you very rich.'

'Richer than him?'

'Lizzie, Yarrow Hall Farm isn't worth anything like as much as you'll have. I'm glad I proposed before I knew about it. At least you know I'm not marrying you for your money.' He loved her, ached for her.

'I could buy a farm.'

'It's your money, Lizzie. I don't want you to spend it on me.'

'Once we're married it'll be *our* money. It's only sensible to spend it on something you want so much. We'll have to wait three years, though, 'til I'm twenty-one. It'll buy a big farm and there'll be plenty left over for anything I could want.'

'Lizzie!' He was overcome by her generosity, wanting to hug her for that. 'All the same, the money hasn't made things any easier.'

'Of course it has!'

'It's changed you already, Lizzie.'

She laughed. 'It hasn't changed me at all.'

'You can do anything you want now.'

'I still want to marry you. It hasn't changed that. It won't.'

Lizzie's blue eyes sparkled up at him. She said: 'You need to think again. About what you really want.'

'No, Lizzie, I know exactly what I want. I want us to be married. I do love you.'

'I didn't mean that.' Her laugh died. 'I want you to think again about the job with Capital Farms. I know you don't like working at Evans's, that you only decided to stay on so we could get married. I thought you were wrong then, but now – well, you won't have to support me.'

Nick shivered. He'd told Edmond Stanton he'd be interested in the under manager's job, but had heard no more from him.

'That makes me uneasy too. You don't need me as much any more.'

'I do, Nick.' Lizzie was serious. She twisted his ring on her finger. 'Money won't buy what you give me. Hugo was right. People have very strange ideas about money. You have.'

That made him smile. 'Only because I've never had enough.'

Lizzie turned to him again. 'Hannah told me to list the things I want, because the interest is going to be paid as soon as the will is proved. I can hardly think of anything. She says I won't be spending a fraction of my income, but then neither will she.

'She says I must take driving lessons and buy myself a car, and she's planning a holiday for us all. She'd like to take me to Italy, but it wouldn't suit the twins . . .

'I've been in a flat spin ever since I heard the will read. Never in my wildest dreams had I ever thought . . .'

Nick sighed. 'In a way, I wish he hadn't given you so much. It changes everything.'

He ought to be glad for her. Poor Lizzie had gone without so much. All Hugo had done was to make sure she'd never go without again.

'Let's go up on Thurstaston Common again,' Lizzie suggested.

'It'll be cold up there.' Nick looked up at the sky. It was grey and overcast, a chilly evening for June.

'We'll have it to ourselves then. We've got to talk.'

She wasn't happy with the way things were going, and blamed herself. She'd agreed to marry Nick but had left unfinished what she'd been trying to tell him. She had to make him understand.

They had no difficulty finding the same huge rock where Nick had spread his mackintosh on the heather. Lizzie leaned against it. The breeze was fluttering at her hair. She felt wind-tossed and invigorated by the climb. Nick looked tense as he watched a solitary car travelling along the road below into West Kirby.

She spread out her own coat. She'd brought an old one

specially, wanting to feel Nick's arms round her.

'What's the matter with us, Lizzie?'

'Two things, and we've got to sort them out.' She turned his ring gently on her finger. 'First, you won't let me tell you the truth about me and Joey.'

He looked at her warily. 'Go on then.'

'We were lovers.' Nick was staring up at the scudding grey clouds, his expression didn't change. 'Do you understand? For two years we lived as if we were married.'

He met her gaze at last. 'I got the idea the first time round,' he said miserably. 'Why do you have to keep on about it? I'd rather forget. It would be better if you did.'

'Oh, Nick! Why didn't you say? It's been bothering me. I couldn't keep that a secret from you. I wanted it said out loud.'

His soft brown eyes were watching her. 'Does it make you feel better now you have?'

Lizzie shook her head. She didn't know. 'Do you mind?'

'I suppose I accepted it. I guessed, Lizzie. Seeing you together.'

'I love you,' she said. 'I'm glad it's out in the open. I feel Joey like a ghost between us. Keeping us apart.'

'He always has been. You were always close to Joey.'

'Not any more. It's you I love, Nick.'

He put his arms round her then. His kisses were passionate. She wanted him to make love to her and scotch Joey once and for all.

But Nick never quite let himself go. He felt it was the gentlemanly thing to keep control, even after what she'd told him. She didn't dare ask him in words, though it was what she wanted. Bad enough to be a girl with a past like hers.

'Joey has changed me,' was the nearest she got to it. After all, she didn't want Nick to think she was a loose woman.

'Even now you can't forget him.' He seemed sad.

She said quietly: 'I'd like you to try to understand.'

'I do, Lizzie. It was bound to happen, living the way you did.'

441

'It did feel like Joey and me against the world.'

'But you were so young.'

'Fifteen.'

'You were just a kid.'

'So was he. Childhood is briefer in the gatehouse. Always has been.'

'I suppose I knew that too. I'm jealous of Joey. Always have been.'

'Don't be. I shall put all that behind me now.'

'It's not just that, Lizzie. Joey's on my mind as much as yours. He's got both of us wrapped round his little finger. He worries me. I'm sure he's up to something at work. He denies it, of course, but he's such a wily fellow.'

Lizzie was so appalled she couldn't move.

'I haven't seen a cheque in the post for the last ten days. I don't know what good they are to him, because they'll be made out to the company and mostly they'll be crossed. He swears it's just a fluke, but I don't know . . .'

Horror was knifing through her. Lizzie knew without a doubt that Joey was the cause. Hadn't he sworn to bankrupt the Mortimers? Hadn't he said he would do it for her?

Nick was frowning in concentration. 'That time I ran you home and I saw that van with the toffee adverts outside his house . . . He was up to something then, wasn't he?'

Lizzie could feel sweat breaking out on her forehead.

'You know Joey, he's always up to something. Always was, even back at Yarrow.'

'But what is he up to now? Did he let you in on his plans?'

'No!' she choked. 'No.' She couldn't direct that sort of attention on Joey. She couldn't betray him in that way too.

But Nick already knew.

Chapter Twenty-seven

14 June 1937

Lizzie tossed in her bed as a whimper penetrated her sleep. It grew fainter and stopped. It was Piers. She could now recognise each baby from his cry. She settled back.

Moments later it came again, louder, more insistent. She got up, pushed her feet into her slippers and ran to the adjoining room.

'Poor Piers, what's the matter then?' She swept him up in her arms and over to the window. When she drew back the curtains, she was surprised to find it was morning and the sun was already up.

Suddenly, and without warning, her stomach was churning. She couldn't believe it was threatening to expel its contents until she felt the acid of vomit rising in her throat. Dumping Piers hurriedly back in his cot, she ran for the bathroom. His wails of protest followed her but her own need was urgent.

She was retching over the bowl, on and on, but nothing would come up. Her stomach was empty. She felt ghastly. As she reached for a tumbler of water, she saw her face reflected in the mirror: paper-white, with sweat standing up in beads across her cheeks and a look of absolute desperation in her eyes.

As soon as she'd drunk the water the feeling of nausea left her. She stood with her forehead pressed against the cool tiles, taking deep breaths, trying to calm her thudding heart.

For the last two weeks, she hadn't allowed herself to think such a calamity was happening to her. It had been a shadow in the back of her mind, too awful to contemplate.

Piers was wailing at the top of his voice now. She splashed cold water on her face, steadied herself against the washbowl for a moment and prepared herself to return.

She'd been worried about this happening when Joey had first started loving her. But he'd been taking precautions, she knew, and he was reliable about that sort of thing. After a year she'd ceased to worry. Time seemed to be proving Joey was right, it was perfectly safe as he'd said.

Until now. Why, oh why, did it have to happen now?

Piers' cries stopped abruptly and she could hear Hannah crooning to him. Oh God, it didn't bear thinking about. Here she was engaged to Nick and wanting to marry him.

She dragged herself to the nursery door. Hannah was changing Piers' nappy.

'You all right, Lizzie?'

'Yes.'

The walls were solid in this house. She'd kept her wits about her and flushed the lavatory to drown any noise, so Hannah couldn't have heard her retching.

She couldn't talk about it. Not yet. After all, she couldn't be sure.

'You look a bit washed out.'

She pulled herself together. 'Still half asleep.'

Of course she was sure, she'd heard Maisie complain often enough about the first symptoms. Heard her deliberating whether or not . . . What else could be causing her to feel like this?

Paul had been wakened by the noise and his round blue eyes were staring up at her from his pillow. He opened his mouth to demand attention and she lifted him. Glad to have something to occupy her hands.

Hannah's dark eyes followed her across the nursery. 'They're such a comfort to me. Hugo has gone, but I still have the babies. I do feel so fortunate. They are lovely.'

Lizzie flung the wet nappy into the bucket and reached for a clean one for Paul. The trouble was she hadn't accepted it yet. She wasn't on an even keel about it, and worse, she hadn't decided what she was going to do.

She didn't want to do anything, change anything, but . . .

'You can't imagine how desperately frustrating it is to yearn for a baby and be unable to have one. I think it warped my whole life.'

Lizzie buried her face in Paul's nightgown. She wanted to cry out in anger. She wanted to shout out that having a baby you don't want was a thousand times worse than being deprived of one when you do. Hannah had forgotten about that.

Hadn't Maisie railed against her lot when she found she'd fallen for another? And having Joey's baby now she'd left him was a million times worse. It was catastrophic. She didn't know what she could do.

'Funny, isn't it?' Hannah said. 'Now I'm too old to have my own, the twins are making me feel normal for the first time in my life.'

Lizzie wanted to weep. Just when she'd thought life was going her way. She didn't want to lose Nick, but she couldn't tell him this. She certainly couldn't expect him to be a father to Joey's child. No wonder she'd felt Joey between them every time Nick had kissed her – she'd been carrying his child.

It had taken Nick to make her realise that she'd grown out of Joey. He had been part of her childhood. Now she was grown up she wanted Nick.

And how was he going to feel when she'd just accepted his ring and promised to marry him? When she'd talked of buying a farm with her money and of the idyllic life they would have together? Lizzie wanted to scream.

She loved Nick. How had she managed to do this to him?

'Now then, we've made them comfortable and given them a drink. They'll be happy to kick in their cots for a while 'til Nancy comes,' Hannah was saying as she smiled across the cots at her. 'I'm going to have a bath and get dressed.'

Lizzie did the same because it was part of the morning routine here. As the warm water washed over her, she knew she must make up her mind about what she was going to do.

She wanted to marry Nick, but she wanted to do her best for the coming child too.

She remembered her own childhood and Joey trying to console her by saying: 'Your father's a king.' Wanting to believe it, yet knowing it to be another fairy tale.

All her life she'd yearned to come face to face with her mother, knowing nothing of her but wanting to believe some catastrophe had parted them. Then meeting her so recently. Now, days later, that was still too painful to think about. Two black-gloved hands flying to her face. The veil had not hidden her shocked surprise, and most painful of all, she'd turned away, not even wanting to speak to Lizzie after all these years.

Lady Mortimer had been the same. Neither wanted to acknowledge her presence. They were treating strangers with more friendliness. That had cut to the quick.

She now knew her own mother to be selfish, thoughtless and downright cruel. All her life she'd railed against what had been done to her. She had to believe that to be truly contented a child needed to feel loved by both parents and be brought up by them. For her child nothing less could be justified. She could not do to her child what her mother had done to her.

That would mean marrying Joey. How often had they already agreed they would? During their childhood he'd been all in all to her. He could be again. The bond seemed unbreakable.

A gulf had opened up between them recently and they'd quarrelled, but it was because he stole and pilfered and wanted revenge on her family.

Now Hugo had left her all this money, Joey must see revenge was no longer appropriate. Hugo and Hannah had done their best to atone. She and Joey would have all the money they needed, and he would have no reason to steal anything. She might be happy with Joey again. Perhaps fate intended them to stay together?

It was the longest bath she'd ever taken.

By the time she was drying herself Lizzie had made up her

mind. She would go back to Joey.

She felt a little better now she'd made the decision. Joey would be pleased to have her back, he'd be thrilled about the baby. For herself she felt numb. She dared not examine her own feelings. It would be selfish to follow her own wishes. She felt bad about what she was going to do to Nick, bad about what she was going to do to Hannah after all her kindness.

As she sat opposite Lizzie at the breakfast table, eating a boiled egg, Hannah said: 'I mustn't dawdle too much. It's my morning for the tennis club.'

Lizzie knew that for years she'd been playing tennis on Wednesday mornings. She'd already tried to persuade Lizzie to go with her.

'What are you going to do?'

Lizzie tried to find the words to tell her. They wouldn't come. She was going to pack her suitcase and go back to Joey. She shivered. She'd made a complete mess of things.

After breakfast she took some writing paper up to her bedroom and wrote to Nick. It was the hardest letter she'd ever written.

She folded it into a large manila envelope and wrote his name on the front. Then she slid the ring he'd given her from her finger and put it back in its leather box.

She almost changed her mind when it was time to seal it in the envelope with her letter. Turning her back on Nick was even harder than rejecting Joey. She loved and wanted Nick. All her instincts were to cling to him.

She told herself her duty was to the coming baby. Hadn't she rated duty to a child very highly when she had been that child? She'd felt very strongly that her own mother should have done more for her. Dorothy was responsible for her position now eighteen years later. Dorothy's action had caused her to be bound so closely to Joey.

She found writing to Hannah no easier. All the time she was doing it, she could hear Nancy in the nursery next door, talking to the babies as she got them ready for an outing.

She'd moved to this bedroom, intended for a live-in nanny, so she could attend to the babies if they needed anything in the night.

She heard Hannah's footstep on the landing. She was going straight into the nursery. Guiltily Lizzie pushed her letters out of sight and went in too. Hannah was kissing the babies goodbye, and telling Nancy when she'd be back. On impulse, Lizzie kissed her too.

She heard Hannah drive off and waited again until she heard Nancy carry the babies downstairs one by one to the big twin pram. From the window, she watched her push it out down the drive and into the road.

Then at last she took down the two new suitcases she'd bought in preparation for the holiday Hannah had proposed and started to pack her possessions. When she'd almost finished, she went downstairs and telephoned for a taxi to come to the house.

Methodically, she carried her suitcases down to the hall and propped the two letters on the mantelpiece there. When she heard the taxi on the drive outside, she went out and asked him to take her to Onslow Road.

She couldn't look back as the taxi pulled away. Daren't think of what she was doing. She had been happy at Oakridge, happy that she'd been accepted as belonging to the Mortimer family. She'd felt she'd found herself here and now she was turning her back on those she loved.

She had to blink hard to keep the tears back. New Ferry looked painfully familiar. It made her think of happier times with Joey. She forced herself to think she would be happy with him again. As the taxi turned into Onslow Road, she was feeling in her bag for her purse and the key to the front door she'd never given up.

She didn't expect Joey to be home. She got out, watched her suitcases being unstrapped from the running board and put down on the pavement. It was only when she turned round that she noticed the aspidistra had gone from the sitting-room window and so had the curtains. Her heart seemed to turn over. The curtains had gone from every window. The shock left her gasping for breath.

'Wait, please wait!' she managed to get out before the taxi went.

She'd never even considered that Joey might have moved house. Yet she should have. Hadn't he been upset because she'd brought Nick here?

She put her face against the bay window with a hand each side to shut out the sunlight. The room was bare. Stripped of everything. It took three attempts to turn the key in the front door. The fawn lino stretched up the hall. There was nothing else there. The stairs had lost their turkey carpet runner.

She felt panic tearing at her. Joey had moved and she hadn't the slightest idea where he'd gone. He'd be careful not to let anyone know, she'd certainly never find out from the neighbours. He didn't trust anybody. Didn't trust her either. He hadn't given any thought to the fact that she might need to find him. The house felt chilly. She went back outside to the sun.

'Where to now?' the driver asked. Lizzie rested one foot on the running board and tried to think. Back to Oakridge? Would she be in time to get her suitcases inside and remove those letters before Hannah returned? She didn't want to go back, it would be twice as hard to leave next time, but where was she to go? She didn't have very much money, she couldn't afford a room for herself until she received the income from what Hugo had left her. She didn't know how long she'd have to wait for that.

And she'd still have to find Joey. She knew he'd do his best to cover his traces, that was the whole object of moving out of this house. He wouldn't have told anybody his new address.

She felt paralysed with shock, couldn't think what to do next. She glanced at her watch. Almost lunch time. Hannah had been telling Nancy when she'd be back. Lizzie tried to remember what she'd said, but she hadn't been concentrating. Sometimes Hannah had a sandwich at her club.

★ ★ ★

It came to her then that Joey would be at work. He must still be at Evans's. Nick would surely have mentioned it if he'd given up his job.

She gave the driver the address of the factory and got back inside. Now she was frightened. What if she couldn't find Joey? And the last person she wanted to see now was Nick who worked in this dour, mill-like building too. The taxi was pulling up outside before she felt ready. She looked up at it and shivered, then paid off the car because she might need her money for other things.

Desperation gave her the courage to walk in through the main door and ask the receptionist to let Joey know she was here.

Perhaps she'd timed it well? She knew she'd arrived just five minutes before he'd be due to break for lunch. She sat on the edge of the chair the girl had indicated, knowing now it would have been much more sensible to get in touch with Joey before she'd burned her boats at Oakridge.

She recognised his quick footfall before he turned the corner and felt a flood of relief that he was here. When he came in sight he had such a look of surprise on his face.

'Lizzie?' His strange eyes swept nervously from her to her suitcases.

'I've come back,' she whispered. He snatched up one, seized her arm and drew her towards the door.

'Let's get out of here.' He seemed even more nerve-racked than she was.

'You've moved. I couldn't find you. Couldn't think of any other way to get in touch.'

Lizzie found herself out on the pavement again, Joey's fingers biting into her arm as he hurried her along.

'I thought you'd be glad,' she said. 'I thought you'd want me to come back.'

'Of course I do.' His glance was desperate. He didn't look all that pleased. 'In here, we've got to talk. We'll have a cup of tea.'

Lizzie found herself in a small cafe. Joey urged her towards

450

a corner table covered with oil cloth and pushed the two suitcases as far underneath as he could get them. An urn hissed behind the counter as the girl served Joey. The windows were covered with steam. Lizzie was quaking. She'd never seen him so het up as this.

He came back with the tea. 'Nick said you were settling down well. That you liked being at Oakridge.'

'Yes.' Her mouth was dry, but the tea was scalding her tongue. 'I'm pregnant, Joey. I had to come back.'

It was never easy to know what Joey was thinking. His odd eyes stared at her, expressionless.

'It is yours.'

'How do you know it's mine? You and Nick, you got engaged.'

'Nick wouldn't until . . . He said this was our time for courtship and that's what we were going to do. We were going to build up to marriage and we'd do that quite soon. You know what a gentleman Nick can be. He wanted everything to be perfect for me. He never touched me.'

She heard Joey expel a long pent up breath. 'I'm glad you've come back. I always knew you would.'

Lizzie searched his face. There was no sign of pleasure on it.

The cafe was filling up. She saw two different men nod towards Joey and then look with interest at her. It seemed to be making him even more uneasy.

'Where are you living now then?'

'Shh. Come on, we can't stay here after all. It's filling up with people from Evans's.'

'Does it matter?' She tried to drink her tea, she was thirsty but it was still too hot.

'Of course it does.' Lizzie found herself outside weighed down with one case and being hurried along again. Up the next street, round the corner and down an alley.

'Where are we going?' She was puffing. Joey was looking round with such stealth. He waited until an old woman and a dog went round the corner out of sight and then he advanced on an Austin Seven, unlocked it and heaved her suitcases on to the child's seat at the back.

'You've got a car now, Joey?'

'Get in.' He took her up several more streets. She had no idea where she was when he pulled into the kerb and stopped.

'We should be all right here. We'll get married, Lizzie. As soon as possible. No point in pussy footing about now.'

She smiled with relief but he didn't seem to relish the idea, not really.

'Only if you really want to.'

'Of course I want to. Didn't I always say we would one day? Well, now there's some urgency, but I want you to promise not to go near the Mortimers again.'

'Why? Hannah was very kind . . .'

'Because you'll give away my new address. It was you who brought Nick back to Onslow Road. I wouldn't have moved if you hadn't done that. I don't want you to do it all over again.'

'All right,' she said. Joey was acting even more strangely. 'I'd hardly know what to say to them after this anyway.'

'How do I know Nick won't be coming round after you again?'

'He won't know where to come, will he?'

'Look, I'll take you now. You'll like it, Lizzie. It's in Bebington. A nice modern house. Got everything this time.'

'We had everything in Onslow Road.'

'I didn't feel safe, not after you brought him round.'

Lizzie shivered. She'd forgotten just how strange Joey had grown. She could see he'd gone well up market this time. The house was in an avenue with trees planted in the pavement. There were small gardens in front of the pebble dashed semis. Joey stopped before one of them.

'Open the gates for me, Lizzie.' She swung back the low wooden gates and Joey drove up on the drive and indicated the garage doors. Amazed, she opened those too, and Joey had the vehicle inside and was closing up again as fast as he could go.

'Aren't you going back to work?'

'Yes, but I don't want everybody knowing I've got a car.'

Lizzie blinked. 'Does it matter if they do?'

'Yes, it could. Come on inside.' He had the key in the lock when he saw a girl hurrying up the pavement. He almost pushed her inside.

'What's the matter?'

'That girl. She's a typist in Mr Gleeson's department. You stay out of sight.'

He was outside again looking for all the world like Sherlock Holmes, careful to keep behind the hedge but clearly watching where the girl went.

He came in, kicking the door shut in his temper. 'Looks as though she lives up the road. Could you believe such rotten luck?'

'For heaven's sake,' Lizzie said. 'What difference does it make?'

'I was hoping you could unpack and make things more comfortable this afternoon. I haven't had time yet.'

'Of course I will.'

'No, don't bother. We'll have to move again. I don't want anyone from Evans's knowing where I live.'

'For goodness' sake! She didn't even see you.'

'She soon will.'

Lizzie felt the tension tighten within her. Joey hadn't been as strange as this when she'd left him. 'You must be up to something . . . something big this time, that you have to hide.'

'What if I am? It shouldn't surprise you.'

'Who'd think to ask her about you?'

'If there's a hue and cry out for me, she might volunteer it. No, we've got to get somewhere safer.'

'Joey, you're obsessed about it.'

'I'm careful. That's what you want me to be, isn't it? Careful.'

'I want you to stop trying to swindle the Mortimers. Give it up, Joey. You won't have to do any more of that now. Give it up before you get caught.'

She told him about her inheritance. 'It's a gift from Hugo.

Family money. They don't owe me any more, Joey. We'll have so much we won't know what to do with it. I want you to promise you'll never steal anything again.'

'With that,' Joey breathed, 'I won't have to. And with what I've got already . . .'

'You'll put all this behind you? Turn over a new leaf?'

'Course I will. Be a pillar of society from now on.'

Joey was ten minutes late by the time he arrived back at Evans's. The familiar hush had settled over the office which meant the rest of the staff were already getting on with their work. He moved rapidly up the corridor, trying to put his feet down quietly and not draw attention to himself. Thankful he didn't meet anyone.

He slipped into the hall, taking in the back view of a dozen pairs of shoulders diligently bent over desks. He was gliding silently to his chair when he saw Mr Gleeson talking to a clerk on the front row. Joey was gripped with panic. He'd got his ledgers open on his desk by the time Gleeson stood over him.

'You're late, O'Malley.'

'Sorry, sir.'

'It's happening too often.'

'I'll try to be more punctual, sir.'

Joey held his breath. He was filled with dread now whenever a member of senior staff came near him. He was terrified they were going to mention the losses. Accuse him.

'See you do.'

He was going, thank God. Joey felt himself relax a little. He was a bag of nerves. Sitting at this desk hour after hour, day after day, was driving him mad. The clock was directly in his line of vision on the wall in front of him. Every time he lifted his head he saw it. The hands went round so slowly. Every morning he crossed another day off his calendar.

He hated every minute he had to spend here, but he'd been determined to sit it out. Up until this dinner time everything had depended on doing just that.

But now Lizzie was back. She'd done so much better than he had. In a few short weeks she'd netted a hundred thousand for herself and kept strictly within the law. A hundred thousand! He let his breath whistle through his teeth.

She was dead against his carrying on with his plan, though she'd no idea what it involved. He'd keep her in the dark from now on. He had to.

He wasn't doing too badly himself, but he'd be for the high jump if any of it ever came out. It would be foolish to stop now before he'd packed his bank accounts with cash.

If the worst came to the worst and he went down, they'd never find all his accounts. He'd still come out to a small fortune, because that was the way he'd planned it.

Nobody was on to him yet and with care they wouldn't be. He'd already done the hard work and set everything up. He'd get his hands on the wages if it was the last thing he did.

Today was Wednesday. He had two and a half more days to work this week. Then there was just next week, five full days before he started his holiday. Two weeks tomorrow and he'd have it all in the bag. He'd be a gentleman from then on.

For once Nick was engrossed in a job when one of the clerks came to his desk to say: 'You're wanted on the phone.'

There were two phones in the hall and the operator put personal calls for staff through to that manned by one of the clerks. Nick hurried across, expecting to hear Lizzie's voice because this was how she contacted him.

It was Hannah.

'Nick, something terrible has happened. Lizzie's disappeared.'

He stood staring at the blank wall, hardly taking it in.

'What do you mean?'

'She's gone away, packed her things.'

'She can't have! She said nothing about going last night.'

'She left me a letter. I went down to the club for a game of tennis and found it when I got back a few minutes ago.

Says she's going back to Joey.'

Nick turned round in consternation. Joey O'Malley was writing at his desk. He seemed to sense Nick's gaze and looked up. His odd eyes glinted wolfishly across the desks.

'He's here! He's been here all morning.'

'That's what she says.'

'But why? She was happy enough last night. I don't understand.' He had a cold feeling in his stomach.

'I don't either.' He heard the agony in Hannah's voice. It made him feel worse. 'She's left a letter here for you. Will you come round for it?'

'Yes, yes. When?'

'Any time you like.'

'I'll come now. It's almost lunch time.' He put the phone down and stared at the wall for a moment feeling totally gutted. He had a terrible urge to smash his fists into Joey O'Malley's face. He couldn't believe it, not when Joey had been at his desk all morning.

He looked at the office clock and tried to pull himself together. It needed another ten minutes to lunch, but there was no point in sitting down at his desk. Work was beyond him the way he felt now. He strode outside to his car and drove straight up to Prenton.

Hannah's face was ravaged with worry when she opened the door to him. He followed her into the square hall and she pointed out the manila envelope propped up on the mantelpiece.

'It's where she left it. I haven't touched it.'

Nick froze at the sight of it. He could see the square bulge inside, and knew she'd returned his ring. Hope died at that moment.

'Aren't you going to open it? Find out what she says?' Hannah's eyes were wide with suffering.

He snatched it down and collapsed on the baronial chair. The box with the ring fell into his hand. He rammed it straight into his pocket and unfolded her letter. Her writing danced before his eyes, making it hard to read.

Dearest Nick,

I hate having to write this because I know it's going to hurt you very much. I'm so very sorry to tell you I can't marry you after all.

I know you won't be able to understand, but I have to go back to Joey. Please, please, don't try to persuade me to come back. I can't.

I do love you, I meant all I said, and I shall think of you always. Please try to forgive me.

Love from Lizzie

He closed his eyes and leaned his head back against the uncomfortable carving. The letter cleared nothing up. She was still saying she loved him yet she was going back to Joey. It didn't make sense.

Hannah was pushing another letter into his hand. He saw it was in Lizzie's writing.

Dear Hannah,

You've been very kind to me and tried to make me welcome in your home. I've been happy here helping to look after my half-brothers. I'm truly grateful for all you did to make me feel part of the family.

I find after all I have to go back to Joey.

I'm afraid you'll think me very underhand that I didn't tell you this morning, but I couldn't find the courage. Also, I was afraid you'd try to persuade me otherwise and it has to be this way.

You'll think even worse of me because I've taken a note of Hugo's solicitor's address, so I can get in touch with him when he's had time to prove the will.

Please don't try to find me. I can't come back. Please forgive me.

Nick sighed. He felt sick. 'Where did I go wrong?' He pushed his letter over to Hannah.

'She does love you.'

457

'She can't do.' Nick felt rigid with a rage that was directed at Joey. 'If she's gone back to Joey, she must love him more. I know it.'

'It's not what she says.'

'I'll go and see her. I know where Joey lives. I'll go straight away while he's still in the office.'

'You must have something to eat first.'

'I'm not hungry.' But Hannah's hand on his arm was steering him into her kitchen.

'Just something left over from feeding the twins,' she said. 'You'll feel better if you do.' She made him eat cottage pie though it stuck in his throat.

He couldn't sit still, couldn't relax. Couldn't even look at Hannah's downcast face. Lizzie had asked him not to try and see her, but he had to. He wouldn't believe this, until he heard it from her own lips.

'Where did I go wrong?' he asked again. He refused to stay for a cup of tea and drove down to New Ferry at a breakneck speed.

He knew as soon as he turned into Onslow Road that the house was empty. The curtains had gone from the front windows. Anger boiled within him then. He'd been through all this before. Joey would be as obstinate as hell about giving his address. Well, this time Nick wasn't going to let him get away with it.

He drove back to work at an equally furious pace. Nick knew he was late. There was a settled silence in the hall that told him everybody else was back at their desks.

Joey's mouse brown head was bent low over his. There were ledgers open in front of him, but Nick could see his mind was miles away.

He strode right up to him and Joey looked up. There was perspiration on his forehead. Nick knew he'd seen Lizzie this lunch time. He could see it on his foxy face as clear as daylight.

'Where is she?'

'Who?'

'Don't let's go through all that again. I want to see Lizzie. I want your new address now.'

'I don't know what you're talking about.'

'Stand up.'

Joey didn't move. Nick yanked him to his feet by his tie. 'Tell me now,' he said through clenched teeth.

'Lizzie doesn't want to see you. Leave her alone, can't you?'

'Where are you living now?'

'Onslow Road.'

Nick hit him then, a hook under the chin that had him reeling across his desk and sent one of the ledgers skidding to the floor.

'Get up! You're going to tell me.'

Joey rocked back on to his chair. 'For God's sake! Can't somebody save me from this madman?' he gasped.

For the first time Nick realised the whole office had stopped work to watch. Somebody touched his arm. 'Take it easy, Nick.'

He shook himself free and strode hurriedly out of the office.

He sat in his car for twenty minutes until he'd cooled down. Then he didn't know where else to go but back to Hannah's house.

She was out in the garden in the sunshine with the babies. She asked her cook to bring out a pot of tea. He was gasping for a drink by the time it came.

'All employees have to give an address,' he said. 'I'll get Greg to have another go at him. Tell him he'll get the sack if he doesn't. He can demand that, surely?'

Hannah sighed. 'He might be getting the sack anyway. Don't say anything in the office, but Matt's talking of cutting the staff down.

'We'll be able to get Lizzie's address from the solicitor. She'll have to contact him before she can get the money. I'll tell him to insist on an address.'

'How long is that going to take?' To Nick, it felt like the

459

end of the world as he knew it. He wanted to get right away from Evans's. He couldn't bear to see Joey O'Malley every day and know Lizzie was with him.

There was no reason now why he shouldn't accept Capital Farms' offer. It was an escape route. He had to get right away from here.

Joey sank back on his chair, rubbing his chin.

'You all right?' Stanley Bream asked. 'Whatever made Nick Bender go for you like that?'

He shook his head, as though at a loss. Though Nick had socked him one, he'd managed to keep his lip buttoned and given nothing away.

Now he'd had time to think about it, he was pleased with the way things were going. He was another one up on the Mortimers. He'd taken their money and he'd got Lizzie back. And there was the baby, he mustn't forget that.

He'd been really upset when he'd heard Lizzie was engaged to Nick Bender. Lizzie was his. They must get married now, quickly.

But with the baby coming it was what she would want. He'd tell her it was because of that. Got to have everything right for Lizzie, now she was an heiress. There'd be more men sniffing round once they found out she was rich.

Marriage was the answer. He'd fix that up as priority number one. A hundred thousand! He still couldn't get over it. He'd done himself a bit of good making that baby.

Lizzie was one of the best anyway. She'd have been his choice even if she was still penniless. He'd certainly hit a lucky streak.

Could he arrange the wedding for a week on Saturday? They could have their honeymoon in Blackpool then. He took a piece of paper from his desk and started to draft a letter to the Belle Vue guest house, changing his booking from single accommodation to double.

He'd go in to Birkenhead in his dinner hour tomorrow and see if he could fix up the date with the register office. He could pay a few more cheques in while he was down that way. Had he thought of everything? There seemed to be a thousand and one new things to consider.

In a way, it didn't make it any easier, Lizzie coming back just at this time. She was a distraction and he had to keep all this a secret from her too, which wasn't so easy when he was living with her. She'd know when he went out at night. There'd be questions and he'd have to watch what he said.

He shivered in a sort of macabre ecstasy. It was a thrilling time all the same.

Chapter Twenty-Eight

21 June 1937

Hannah walked slowly up the garden to her favourite spot, settled herself on the wooden bench surrounded by high bushes and took out the letter Hugo's solicitor had given her.

In the strong sunlight his writing stood out boldly from the paper.

> I want you to know you have been the most important person in my life. From the moment I first saw you, I was a little in love. And my feelings grew stronger over 'the years. Knowing and loving you has brought my greatest happiness.

She read and re-read his words umpteen times. They were her greatest source of comfort now. She felt cossetted by them. It was a measure of Hugo's love that he'd thought of what she'd be feeling at this time.

Hannah lifted her face to the sun. Its warmth comforted her too. She was spending a lot of time in this corner of the garden now. Here she was closer to the next-door house than she was to her own and could not be seen from either. She liked the seclusion and the leafy greenery. It smelled fresh and earthy. She continued to read the letter, though she knew it almost by heart now.

> For years I tried to put you out of my mind, but I failed. I wronged Matt. I ask that you try, if you can, to make up for my wrongs. I couldn't reach him once he

grew up, and I know you find it difficult but please try. He has had far less satisfaction in his life than I've had in mine.

She was trying. She'd wronged Matt too. But she'd persuaded him to stay here now, and she'd try and keep him longer. Perhaps she could get closer to him.

She read again from Hugo's letter: 'I don't want you to grieve for me. I want you to be happy.'

She wanted to tell him: I can't feel happy without you. Not yet.

Nothing could stop her missing Hugo. Nothing could stop the tears pricking at her eyes. She longed to see him come striding round the bushes to join her as he sometimes used to. To grieve was normal, but his words eased her.

The best advice would be to tell you to forget me now, put what has happened behind you, but I can't. I want you to remember me and the joy we had, and to feel no regret.

She folded his letter back into the envelope. She had no regrets, quite the reverse. She would always remember him for his kindness. And she had the twins. He'd suggested she formally adopt them and it was all going through smoothly. They gave her something to cling to, and he'd given her so much love.

She heard heavy steps coming up the garden. A moment ago she'd been longing to hear this. She felt her heart quicken as somebody brushed against the bushes. But it was Matt who came in view and then slumped beside her on the bench. His face was creased with worry.

'Nancy said you were up here, hiding yourself away.' He sounded agitated.

'Has something happened?' Her breathing hadn't quite returned to normal.

'Things are worse than I thought. Much worse.'

464

'At the factory?'

'There's been wholesale theft. We've not been paid for half the toffee we've made this year. I've called in the police.'

'Matt!' She felt for his hand. 'It's hard, especially now, so soon after your father's . . .'

'It's desperate, and would be at any time. We've lost a tremendous amount of stock. The whole business is so pointless if it doesn't make a profit. All the work . . . Almost no cheques have come through the books in a month. And while Greg has been helping himself to company funds, somebody else has too.'

'Who?'

Matt sighed. 'That's for the police to find out.' His anger flared up again. 'To think Greg wouldn't even listen when Nick Bender tried to show him what was happening! If he'd checked through the books then and done something about it, we'd have stopped it by now.'

'It's still going on?'

'As far as I can see. What makes it even worse is it must be one of the staff.'

Joey felt balanced on a knife edge. The days had never seemed so long drawn out. Rumours were flying round the office, but the routine work ground on as usual. There was talk of losses and it was being said quite openly that Evans's would not make a profit this year. It gave him a real kick to think he'd done that to Greg Mortimer. He'd seen it as a personal success and crowed about it to Lizzie.

She'd been short with him. 'I've already told you, Greg's been taking money from the accounts for his own use, that's why Matt's very concerned about the business, why he's checking everything. He's thinking of selling.'

Joey had been reassured the first time, he was reassured again. It was good news if Greg was being blamed, but he couldn't help being worried about what else they would discover.

When he saw the factory manager going in to Matt

Mortimer's office with an armful of ledgers, and staying for a considerable time, Joey felt himself come out in a cold sweat. Was Greg getting the blame for every loss they turned up, or were they on to what he was doing? He had no way of knowing.

On Tuesday afternoon he heard an emergency stocktaking had started, and that scared him stiff. He thought it would take at least three days to complete and told himself he'd still be all right, he'd be away on holiday before they were finished, only to hear that extra men had been drafted in to speed the job up. He knew it couldn't be long before they had the complete picture. It would be touch and go whether he'd get away in time.

Today was Thursday. Only one more working day to get through. He kept telling himself he'd be all right, they wouldn't have enough time to pin it on him.

But he didn't know what they knew already. He couldn't work. He was no longer doing anything but move paper round his desk, and it was agonising to have to stay there.

He'd told Lizzie: 'We're going to get married next Saturday, the twenty-fourth of June, at ten o'clock, in the register office in Birkenhead.'

'Just like that?'

'Can't drag our feet, not now there's a baby coming.' He'd given her a wad of pound notes. 'Get yourself something nice to wear. Some things for the honeymoon too. Lizzie, it's time we both enjoyed ourselves.

'Yes, married on Saturday morning, then go straight to Blackpool.'

If he'd planned it this way from the beginning he couldn't have worked it out better.

He couldn't make up his mind whether or not to tell people in the office he was getting married. If he was on honeymoon it would be unthinkable for him to come back to take the wages, but he was not the sort to jaw about what he did. He'd trained himself to keep his lip buttoned, it was safer that way. Nobody must know Lizzie was a Mortimer.

That would put the spotlight on him.

He only broadcast things he wanted to be generally known, like his being in Blackpool when the theft took place. He decided to say nothing about his wedding. He didn't want people rubber necking at them.

On Monday he'd been a couple of hours late coming to work and told Mr Gleeson he'd overslept. He'd been up an hour earlier than usual and had taken Lizzie out to Neston to look at houses. He'd already picked out those he wanted to see and made the arrangements.

'Why Neston?' Lizzie asked. 'I've never even been there.'

He'd looked in Gleeson's files to pick a district in which none of the managers lived. It was too far from Evans's for the others to travel in on the bus every day. He'd never set foot in the town, so nobody would know him there.

'It's a nice place, a little market town. Away from the docks and the endless streets.'

'Too far,' Lizzie had protested.

'Healthier, and better for bringing up a family.'

He'd whisked her round three houses and persuaded her that the largest would suit them best. All the houses in the road had large gardens and were set well apart. He didn't want a place where the neighbours were always dropping in.

He went back to the agent, rented it in Lizzie's name, paid a month's rent and got the key. This time, nobody would find him. It was a nice house too, and away from the main roads.

'I'll have to take another day off work to move the furniture.'

'We can hire a van,' Lizzie said. 'That would be the easiest. Now you've got plenty of money, no point in killing ourselves.'

'I'll move us,' Joey said quietly. He had to. That way nobody could check through removal firms and find their new address. 'I'll get Bill to bring the van and give a hand.' It would be hard work and he was exhausted now.

'Wednesday,' he said, 'I'll tell them at work I'm not well.' He usually restocked Bill's van on Wednesday nights, so there wouldn't be too much left inside by then. 'At least you're here, Lizzie, to get the curtains up and the place straight.'

Yesterday, humping all the furniture he'd accumulated to the new house had been exhausting. It had taken several journeys and all the trouble of emptying the toffee out of the van first and putting it back afterwards.

They hadn't finished until six o'clock and Lizzie's face had been white with fatigue by then. Joey had run Bill home, fully intending to follow his usual routine. Go back and stock the van again that night.

Lizzie had a scratch supper of eggs and bacon ready when he got back and he'd nodded off in a chair, hadn't been able to stay awake any longer.

He hadn't given a thought to Evans's all day, but now when he did he was getting cold feet. Stocktaking must have told the Mortimers that huge amounts were disappearing. It would be common sense for them to keep a closer watch on what was left, and he'd no idea what had happened today because he hadn't been there.

To think of going in made him feel ill. He was too tired anyway. He'd decided to go to bed early instead. He'd tell Bill the game was over. Tell him to paint the toffee adverts off the van and sell it. It was too much like hard work anyway.

It hadn't been easy to face Gleeson again this morning. He'd been none too polite.

'Sick again? Have you brought a doctor's note?'

'No, sir. Couldn't leave the lavatory. Went between that and me bed all day. Couldn't get to the doctor, I was too bad.'

'You're taking too much time off, O'Malley. You'll have to bring a note next time. If you go on like this you'll get your cards. You're either late or you don't turn in at all. It won't do.'

Joey slumped on to his chair. The prospect of getting his cards seemed attractive. But a glance in the ledgers told him there'd been six big cheques in the mail yesterday that he'd missed. What if somebody noticed there were cheques when he wasn't here, but not when he was?

Joey felt his neck jerk involuntarily. It hurt, and he felt fuzzy. A glance at the clock told him he'd dozed off at hi desk. At least it had passed another twenty minutes. He rubbed his neck and along his jaw where Nick had belted him one. It still ached a bit, though the bruise was fading.

He was cat-napping like an old man. He still felt heavy with sleep, but edgy too. He wondered if it would be safe to come back tonight and take a couple more cheques from the safe. He was worried about doing it now because Matthew Mortimer seemed to be taking a big interest in the accounts. But if he chickened out of this too, he'd get less cash this week than he'd anticipated.

Having Lizzie in his bed meant less sleep too. He was overdoing things, had too many irons in the fire at the moment, but it wouldn't be for very much longer. He couldn't wait to get to Blackpool. All the difficulties bar one would be over by then, and he'd be sleeping like a baby.

Joey kept his head down over his ledgers and tried to cut out the sounds of the office around him. The whispered conversations, the distant clack of typewriters, the trill of the phone. He hated having to sit here day after day but it was going to be worth it. Only today and tomorrow. Surely nothing terrible could happen in that time?

Lizzie thought regretfully of the romantic notions she'd picked up about weddings at the Lyceum. As she watched Joey frown with concentration as he fastened his tie, she knew her wedding would have few of the trappings of romance.

'Are you ready, Joey? We don't want to be late.'

'We won't be.' His voice was impatient. 'Have you packed everything? My new swimming trunks? We'll be going straight off on honeymoon.'

'I do hope it'll be all right,' she worried. 'We're both under age. We're supposed to have permission from our parents to do this.'

'It'll be all right, I've fixed it.'

'I still think I should have asked Hannah. She's the nearest real relative . . .'

'No.' Joey bent to kiss her cheek. 'I don't want you to go

near any of the Mortimers again. Besides, we didn't have time to organise all that. I've seen to it, it'll be all right.'

'But I don't see how.' Lizzie was fitting the tiny hat of red feathers on her blonde curls. It had an eye veil of red net. She'd already dressed in the red costume of fine wool worsted and the cream lace blouse she'd chosen as her wedding outfit.

'You will. Come on, we'd better go.'

Lizzie sat beside him in the Austin Seven and reflected that despite his promise Joey hadn't changed for the better. She'd always resented the high handed way he settled her affairs without even asking her.

'I do love you, Lizzie,' he said. His mismatched eyes twinkled at her and for once he seemed more the Joey she knew.

Lizzie blinked hard. It didn't rid her of her misgivings. Joey was changing and not for the better. He'd been such a ball of tension since she'd come back, irritable and on edge.

'We'll need witnesses, Joey.'

'Yes, two. Eli Jones is coming. He's the night watchman at Evans's and a friend of mine. He's going to say his name is Seamus O'Malley and sign the form for me. Bill Purley is bringing his dad. He's going to pretend his name is James Mortimer and sign for you.'

Lizzie stiffened with displeasure. 'Joey! We can't do that.'

''Course we can. Who's to know? I would have said we were both twenty-one except it shows we aren't on our birth certificates. Good job you got your real one from Hannah.'

'It won't be legal.'

''Course it will, and who's to know? Can't see my dad questioning it even if he found out.'

Lizzie groaned. She'd wanted everything to be perfect today. Now she was going to be worried stiff about the questions the registrar would ask.

'Joey! What's the matter with you? You can't be straight about anything any more.'

She thought of Nick's honest face and longed for him

She'd always known where she stood with him.

She was having qualms about Joey. He no longer seemed to be normal. Why go to such lengths? He could have written to his father. Everything seemed unreal.

'In plenty of time,' Joey said, as he parked outside the town hall. 'Quarter to ten.'

Bill Purley was there with his father. She hardly knew what to say to them. The whole business was outrageous and unnecessary. Lizzie was smouldering with indignation.

'You haven't forgotten?' Joey asked Bill's father. 'Your name's James Mortimer. Okay?'

Lizzie swallowed hard. This was a horrible thing to do to her.

'Here's Eli,' Joey said, as a grey-haired man came round the corner. The next moment she was being ushered inside. She couldn't think of anything but the trouble Joey managed to get them into.

The small room seemed richly furnished, with flowers on the polished desk. Lizzie was terrified when she saw the details on the form she was required to sign. Her father's name, a fictitious James Mortimer. His address was fictitious too. Joey had given his occupation as school master.

Lizzie hesitated. What would happen if she refused to have anything to do with this? Joey was chatting with the registrar as though he hadn't a care in the world. With a shudder, she picked up the pen and signed.

The ceremony was very simple and over almost too quickly. Then she was signing the register and trying to hold back her tears. She was Lizzie O'Malley again and now she had a perfect right to the name.

The new wedding band glistened on her finger. Twenty-two carat this time, the real thing, not just a ring for pretence from Woolworth's.

On the way out of the building, she saw the next bride with a horde of guests in the waiting room. Out on the pavement and walking back to the car it all seemed unreal. All three men kissed her cheek.

'Pity the pubs aren't open yet,' Bill said. 'We could have had a drink on it.' Lizzie shuddered and slammed the car door shut.

'Straight to Blackpool now.' Joey rubbed his hands with satisfaction. 'It's all fitting in very well. I'm beginning to get the holiday feeling.'

'We needn't have been in such a hurry,' Lizzie mourned. 'We could have taken more time. Done it properly.'

'It's done,' he said impatiently. 'What difference does it make now?'

Lizzie told herself it was too late to have regrets. She'd had to do it for the coming baby. It was stupid to have second thoughts about Joey as a husband, though he'd been very strange since she'd come back. His behaviour had been so odd; he'd seemed to have urgent business to attend to all the time. He'd hardly been home.

She tried to throw off the feeling of gloom as Joey drove north. It was the first time she'd driven through the tunnel to Liverpool. It was the first time she'd ever done a long trip by car and she was enthralled. They drove out on the Preston road and the sun came out.

Joey stopped for lunch at a big hotel. 'It's our wedding breakfast. You have whatever you want.' They ordered smoked salmon followed by roast chicken, and suddenly everything looked brighter.

Blackpool seemed a long way, a different world. Lizzie was growing tired but the sight and scents of the sea and the busy promenade were a heady mixture.

Joey pushed a map into her hand and asked her to guide him to the boarding house. She managed it as they went round a second time. It was only a few minutes from the promenade.

'This is Brunton Street,' she said as they turned between long terraces of houses. 'And there's the Belle Vue.' It was a tall narrow house with bay windows. 'Stop, Joey, you've passed it.'

'I want to park the car,' he grunted.

'There's plenty of space right outside.'

'Don't want to be too close.'

'We aren't any longer.' Lizzie felt the first stirrings of alarm. 'We'll have to walk back with our cases. I would have thought the nearer the door the better.'

Joey said nothing. They were in another side street. It seemed little different to Brunton Street. He pulled into the kerb and stopped. Lizzie sat still in her seat. 'What are you doing this for, Joey?'

'It's safer here.'

'It would have been perfectly safe right outside.'

'All the same . . .'

'You don't want anybody to see it, do you? People who stay at boarding houses like that don't usually have cars.' He didn't answer.

Lizzie hauled her suitcase off the back seat and started to walk back. 'Nobody knows us here. What difference does it make if they do know you have a car? I don't understand why you go to all this trouble for nothing.' But she did. She had a sinking feeling in her stomach.

'You've got something else planned, haven't you?' Angrily, she dropped her case on the pavement and stopped. 'For God's sake, Joey! What's the matter with you?'

'Come on, Lizzie,' he said, picking up her case and carrying that too.

'It's too dangerous! Haven't I told you they know about the cheques?'

'They don't know it's me.'

'They will if they catch you at it. Anyway, there's no need. I'll have more than I know what to do with.'

'I said I was going to fix Greg Mortimer.'

'He's fixed himself,' she wailed. 'There's no need for you to do another thing.'

'I want to,' he said as they reached the door of the Belle Vue boarding house. 'I personally want to fix Greg Mortimer.'

'Miss Peacock?' He was unusually effusive to the owner. 'You aren't at all like your sister.'

473

Lizzie followed them upstairs, her head in a whirl.

'A pleasant room,' Joey said. Lizzie thought it nothing out of the ordinary. She had hung curtains in a much smarter bedroom back home in Neston. She went to the window. It was at the rear of the house and overlooked the back yard.

'Don't do anything else,' Lizzie said as soon as they were alone. 'Don't dare do anything else.'

'Just one last thing,' he insisted. 'I'm going back on Thursday night to do one last thing. Nobody will be expecting it. I'm going to help myself to the wages, the whole payroll. It'll be perfectly safe.'

'No, Joey! Whatever for? Soon we'll have all the money we can spend.'

'That makes it even safer. Don't you see, I'm going to have an unbreakable alibi? I'm in Blackpool on my honeymoon. It'll have the Mortimers running around like headless chickens. A real stab in the back.'

'The risk!' Lizzie groaned in horror and threw herself down on the bed. 'I won't let you do it.' She turned her face into the pillow.

The hardest thing, Joey felt, was to appear relaxed and in a holiday mood when inside he felt wound as tight as a watch spring.

He didn't want to go through another week like the last one. It had nearly finished him. He'd worked flat out moving house, still taking every cheque he could, still drawing money from Evans's accounts, and checking a hundred times over that he'd forgotten nothing.

Having Lizzie with him wound him tighter. She'd done nothing but nag since he'd told her about his plans for taking the wages. He'd never known her so determined to stop him doing anything.

'I feel it in my bones,' she said vehemently. 'You'll get caught.'

She wasn't even much fun. She was touchy about everything. Of course he wanted Lizzie very much, he loved her, but it would have suited him to be alone for these few days, as he'd planned in the first place.

He needed a rest. The last few months had taken a lot out of him, it was no use denying that. Regularly, for two nights a week, he'd spent only two or three hours in bed. He'd worked as usual all the following day.

Blackpool was a wonderful place and any other time he'd have thoroughly enjoyed himself. What he wanted to do now was lie on his bed and rest, get himself in good nick to do this one last job. Instead he had to get up for breakfast. Kippers or eggs and bacon were served between eight o'clock and nine, and after that they were expected to go out.

He made Lizzie do what all the holiday makers were doing. They went to the beach and walked for miles along it. They climbed to the top of the tower. They stayed out late at night dancing or watching a show.

They walked arm in arm along the prom, looking at the stalls with 'Kiss Me Quick' hats. He bought them ice cream and lovely salty mussels and winkles. The weather was breezy but dry and sunny most of the time. He couldn't have asked for more, except from Lizzie.

She couldn't see why he wanted his own money. But she hadn't got hers yet, and it seemed such a waste not to get the payroll when he'd gone to so much trouble to set the job up. The night when he must do it was drawing closer.

On Tuesday, he suggested they go fishing on one of the many boats plying for customers. It was a sunny morning but more blustery. He hadn't realised there would be a big swell once they were out of the harbour.

Lizzie saw the distant skyline come and go as the boat wallowed. She shuffled up the hard seat, trying to get more comfortable. Something was giving her back ache.

She realised now they hadn't chosen the right boat for this trip. She reckoned this one spent the winter trawling with nets, and the summer taking holiday makers out to fish with lines. It was thimble-sized, ancient and dirty, and in the swell it was going up and down like a lift.

Joey was hanging over the rail, engrossed in the silvery spin beneath the dark waves. He was catching mackerel by the dozen and thoroughly enjoying himself.

'We'll take some back to the Belle Vue and see if they'll cook them for our supper.' His strange eyes danced with pleasure.

Lizzie found the smell of fish overpowering even in the brisk wind which was plastering her hair against her face. The sun was shining straight into her eyes and glistening on the water, dazzlingly bright. She could feel a headache coming on.

They could have taken a shorter three-hour trip, but had elected to stay out for six hours. Lizzie looked at Blackpool, a thin line in the distance, and wished that they had not. The hours stretched ahead before they'd be back in the harbour.

'Come on, Lizzie, cheer up,' Joey said. His mousey hair was standing up in the wind. 'Come and have a go. We've hit a shoal, it's easy.'

All round her other holiday makers were pulling in their lines with squeals of triumph as they found mackerel glittering and squirming on the end.

Lizzie felt she couldn't sit still any longer. She went to the rail and threw the hand line and hooks she'd been given over the side.

'I don't feel very well,' she said.

Joey was sympathetic and got a drink of water for her from the wheel house. It didn't help much. Lizzie felt worse looking down at the water and although she too was catching fish, it didn't take her mind off her back ache which was getting worse.

The morning dragged on. Lizzie returned to her hard seat. Other people were noticing and came to tell her she didn't look well. Another woman said she felt sea sick and came to sit quietly beside her. Remedies were discussed, barley sugar sweets offered. Lizzie didn't think her problem was sea sickness.

She was having pains which came and went. And she had a terrible dragging feeling, like she sometimes had before a period, but this was worse. When she went to the single smelly lavatory, she found she was losing blood.

Joey was waiting for her outside, but she went straight to the rail and vomited over the side.

'You're sea sick,' he said, getting another drink of water for her. 'You're not the only one. There's a boy back there.'

A deck hand came round with a message. The wind was stiffening and the master had decided to return to shore earlier than had been arranged.

Lizzie groaned with relief. Joey came and buttoned his coat round her because she felt cold. 'You'll feel fine once we get on dry land,' he said.

'No, I think I must be losing the baby,' she whispered.

Joey went pale. He held her close. 'How do we stop it?' Lizzie had no idea.

'Are you sorry?' he whispered.

Lizzie couldn't think for the pains. What she really felt was frightened. 'Sorry it's happening now.' Two weeks ago she might have been pleased, but now she'd changed so many things for the sake of the baby she thought she felt sorry.

When the time came to get off the boat, she could hardly walk. The pains when they came doubled her up. She wasn't even able to stagger.

'I'd better take you straight to hospital, hadn't I?' Joey's face was paper-white now. He left her sitting on a seat while he went to ask where the hospital was.

She sat there alone for what seemed ages, afraid she might be sick again. Willing Joey to come back to her quickly. The next thing she knew he was helping her to her feet and there was a taxi waiting at the kerb.

Chapter Twenty-nine

29 June 1937

The front door of the Belle Vue stood open. As Joey pushed at the lobby door, the familiar notice, reminding him not to tread sand through the hall, caught his eye. He was past caring about wiping his feet.

The last two days had left him reeling. To think of Lizzie losing the baby brought a lump to his throat. He'd managed to get her to hospital in time, but the miscarriage had left her tearful and upset. Had upset him too.

It had left him feeling restless; unable to settle to anything. He couldn't get Lizzie's distress out of his mind. Couldn't think about his plans to steal the wages, though the night he was to do it was almost on him now. He needed more time to compose himself.

In the dining-room, he sat at the rickety table they'd been allotted, feeling very much alone. He was missing Lizzie's chatter. The table cloths were clean but they charged sixpence each for a week's use of the cruet.

He'd told everybody here about Lizzie's miscarriage. There were sympathetic smiles for him as they asked after her now. He made a point of telling them he'd be going in to see her tonight.

'Couldn't have happened at a worse time,' they commiserated, but as far as he was concerned, that wasn't true. He'd told Lizzie he wouldn't go tonight and now she didn't need to know any more about it. She had an unshakable alibi and that could improve his.

He smiled at Miss Lockwell at the next table, a sixtyish

spinster who'd come alone. She told him how delightful she'd found it sitting on the beach during the afternoon. The food wasn't bad, fish, chips and peas tonight, with rhubarb and custard to follow. Bread and butter, cup of tea.

He lingered over a second cup of tea until the dining-room was empty. Then he cornered Miss Peacock and told her he was on his way to see Lizzie again.

The hospital allowed evening visiting on Thursday nights, seven till half past. Lizzie had been given a wooden backrest and was sitting up against it, her ash blonde hair spread across the pillow. A little colour had come back to her cheeks.

'I might be able to come out tomorrow.' She was smiling.

'Got to see the doctor first. Sister wants to see you before you leave tonight. She'll tell you what time to telephone.'

'Just as easy to come in and see. I'll put your case in the car.' He'd already packed it. He'd half expected this.

'Will you bring my red frock?'

'All right,' he said, pleased he'd even chosen the right one. It brought him some comfort to think that by the time he was fetching her tomorrow, the job would be behind him. 'It'll be great to have you out of here. Don't like being on my own, Lizzie.'

He stood chatting for a few moments with the ward sister, trying to look as though he had nothing else on his mind. He wanted to make sure she'd remember him.

'Ring, or come by eleven and bring her clothes,' she said.

As Joey left the hospital, he felt he was on the starting line and itched to be on his way. He'd parked the car round the corner and filled it up with petrol earlier in the day, checked the tyres too. He got in. Twenty minutes to eight. He reckoned he could be in Birkenhead between ten and eleven. Eli would be down for the night by then.

He drove on mile after mile, the Austin Seven chugging along, eating up the road. It was a fine night with practically no traffic. The stars were bright and there was hardly any moon. Perfect for what he wanted. A glow shone up from the two instruments on the austere dashboard.

Suddenly Joey felt his head roll and the car swing from one side of the road to the other. Alarmed, he pulled himself upright on the steering wheel and braked to a stop. He'd almost fallen asleep. He was lucky there'd been no other traffic about. He hadn't been sleeping well and was desperate for his bed. He would have liked to close his eyes for half an hour but, though he could afford to, he had no way of being sure he'd wake up in time. It wouldn't do to sleep until day break, and the way he felt at the moment he could sleep for a week.

He got out of the car and walked back a couple of hundred yards. He was wearing his dark polo necked pullover and black gym shoes. The wind went right through it. Midsummer it might be, but it was cool here. He'd brought a dark jacket. He put it on before he got back behind the wheel. He drove on feeling more awake.

At last he was running through the tunnel to Birkenhead. He had the exact money ready to pay the toll so he didn't have to speak. He didn't want the toll collector to remember him.

He was drowsy again, there was something soporific about the chug of the engine and the car hardly rolled at all on the metalled main roads. His mind grew less easy as the time for action drew closer. When he saw the tall black bulk of Evans's factory, he felt strangely reluctant to go inside. Dread was building up into a hard ball in his stomach.

He parked the car, not too near, but nearer than when he was going in to work. There wasn't a soul on the streets now. He looked at his watch. It was a quarter to eleven. He'd made good time. It wouldn't take him long, less than half an hour and he'd be away again.

Joey pulled the bag he'd brought from the back seat and got out, closing the door with a soft click. Every Thursday he'd seen the weekly pay being carried into the office in two leather Gladstone bags, and the monthly pay filled another.

He'd bought two roomy rexine holdalls and crammed one inside the other. His bags were larger. He reached the side door used by the office staff. Put on his wool gloves and got out his keys and his torch. He'd done this lots of times. He'd gone up to Matthew Mortimer's office, opened the safe and helped himself to cheques. What was so different this time? He tried to tell himself it was almost routine to him now.

What was different was that he hadn't been sitting at his desk all day. What was really bothering him was the fear that his earlier thefts had been discovered and extra watchmen put on duty. Perhaps even the police were keeping watch.

When he'd left at five knowing all was well, it was less risky to return at eleven. And then he mostly had Eli to warn him first. This way he felt less safe. He told himself it was ridiculous to think of going back without the money after driving all this way.

He mustn't think of Lizzie. 'I feel it in my bones,' she'd said. 'You'll get caught.'

He'd been standing in the deep shadow cast by the building for five minutes. Nothing had stirred anywhere in the street, he was being foolish. Quickly, he inserted the key, turned it and let himself into the vestibule. It was as black as ink inside, but it always was.

It smelled familiar, sickly sweet, as though sugar stayed in the air. He locked the door behind him and crossed to the swing doors leading into the corridor. He'd pushed one half open when through the panel of wired glass set into it, he saw the powerful beam of a torch coming towards him.

His heart missed a beat. He let the door come slowly back against his hand. Eli was doing a security round at this time? The strength had gone from his legs, he felt unable to move. He had his face against the glass as the figure came level. Had he seen the door move?

It wasn't Eli! This man was taller and broader, the torch was sweeping along the walls. As it shone over the door he stepped hurriedly back from the glass. Would his face show white through that?

Joey was stiff with fear. Some sixth sense told him the man was going to push the swing doors and come into the vestibule. He stepped back against the wall and at the last moment

482

turned to face it. He felt the door open against his back and tried to flatten himself out against the wall. He saw the torch shine on the outer door. If the man stepped forward to check that the door to the street was locked, he'd be seen. Time was standing still, he no longer dared to breathe.

Then the light faded, the door swung back and forward and finally closed. Joey allowed himself to take a breath of relief. It had been a close thing. He'd been frightened the man would feel the door press against his body; he'd felt he was being squashed. When he'd recovered enough he quietly pushed the door to take a peep. The man was down the far end of the corridor and heading towards the factory.

Perhaps it was an omen and he should get away now? But after coming all this way, to get cold feet at this stage? Joey prided himself on being more of a man than that.

The Mortimers wouldn't move quickly. They never did. Perhaps it was only that Eli was sick? He thought it could be the watchman who worked at weekends. Eli should have been here. He wasn't on holiday. Or had they got extra men on because of the money in the safe?

They never had before, and anyway he had the place to himself again. Joey took a deep breath and, moving as stealthily as possible, went up the corridor and made for the stairs. Everywhere was in darkness. Everything was perfectly normal except now his heart was pounding away like a steam engine and his mouth was as dry as the bottom of a parrot's cage.

He reached the hall full of desks. It was almost like coming home to see his own. It seemed a long time since he'd sat there waiting away the hours. Matthew Mortimer's office was almost as familiar. How many times had he been in here before? Nothing had been moved. He locked himself in as he always did. If that man came back, he might check whether the door was locked. Joey had seen policemen doing it on their beat. They tried every shop door as they patrolled the street.

He took off his jacket and laid it on the floor against the door, so no streaks of torch light might betray his presence

483

from the corridor. He unzipped his bag, took out the one inside and put both in front of the safe.

Joey made himself stop and think. If he heard the key in the lock, he'd just have time to close the safe door, whip up his coat and hide behind the door. It was the only possible place to hide here. He moved the bags behind the desk where they couldn't be seen from the door.

His fingers were shaking as he opened the safe. It was filled to capacity, just as he'd known it would be. The filled wage packets were standing in a tray in numbered sequence. He'd seen them like this before when he collected his own screw. He tipped the tray into one of his bags. It made a phenomenal slithering crash that seemed to echo round the building. He stood listening but all he heard was his own pounding heart.

Get on with it, he urged himself. There were bundles of notes on another shelf. Much the easiest thing for him to handle. He pushed handfuls on top of the wage packets and rammed them down hard. Mostly, they were one pound notes, but there were also several bundles of fivers, great big lovely fivers.

There were hessian bags of silver. He needed his other holdall now. Small denominations and large ones. He pushed in as many as he could. There were bags of copper to make up the sum for each employee. It went against the grain to leave anything behind, but they would be too heavy for him to carry. Reluctantly he closed and locked the safe. Now all he had to do was to get back to his car and he'd be away.

He was pushing his arms into his jacket when he heard footsteps crossing the hall. Heavy boots were crunching towards him. No care was being taken to walk quietly.

The anxiety he'd been holding back flared into full-blown panic. He wanted to check that his bags couldn't be seen from the door if it was opened. In the nick of time he remembered the inch-wide gap under the door was uncovered and stopped himself shining his torch. The slightest glimmer of light would be enough to bring the man inside.

Joey could feel himself quaking. He stopped breathing as

the boots came into the alcove. They didn't stop. He thought the man had patrolled round Miss Peacock's desk and gone out down the hall again. Joey was leaning against the wall, gulping air in relief.

He waited until there was silence. This must be the safest moment to leave. When he picked up his bags the coins jingled in the wage packets. They were heavier than he'd expected. He'd left his key in the lock. Now he turned it gently. The click seemed frighteningly loud. He was sweating.

Miss Peacock's alcove was dark and silent. It was safe to go. He moved as quickly and quietly as his bags allowed. He knew every inch of the building like the back of his hand and could manage very well without any light.

He crossed the hall between the rows of desks, passing between that belonging to the lad with acne and his own. He wasn't looking forward to being back at it in another week, but he'd have to come. He'd give in his notice right away, say he'd got himself another job in Blackpool. He didn't want the law hounding him, and leaving like that would not be suspicious.

He opened the door into the corridor leading to the outside door. He reached the bend where the mail room had been fitted under the main stairs and stopped dead. A circle of yellow torch light shone down on heavy boots. Joey was sweating again. He couldn't go that way. The man was standing between him and the exit. He was also standing near the light switch. Any noise and he could reach up and flood the whole corridor with light.

Joey edged back round the corner and set off in the opposite direction. Thank God he knew his way round. He had a master key, he could get out through the factory.

The weight was dragging at his arms. He had to fight the impulse to jog because that increased the jangle from the wage packets. He mustn't make any noise, but he was in the grip of sheer and absolute terror by now. Things were not going as smoothly as he'd planned.

Through the communicating door and into the airless fug

redolent of the smell of sugar and toffee. His plimsolls were making a sticking sound as he walked, but he saw nothing and reached the door to the loading bay. The relief of being outside at last was enormous. He was taking great gulps of cool air, it was drying the sweat on his forehead.

He crossed the yard. It was easier to see, and nothing had changed since he'd come here regularly. Through the great iron gates to the street . . . He made himself lock up behind him instead of streaking away in blind panic.

He'd left his car on the other side of the building, he'd have to circle round to it. He set off, keeping to the far side of the street, going faster, not caring if the money did jangle a little now. He wouldn't really feel safe until he was out on the road a long way from here.

He came to the last corner and saw his Austin Seven lit up by the headlights of a car that had drawn into the kerb behind it.

Joey felt his knees turn to water as he realised it was a large black police car and there were two uniformed policemen inside it. He backed off, feeling desperate. This was more than he could stand in one night. Had the night watchman inside the building realised there was an intruder and called the police?

He was not too worried about the car. He'd taken the precaution of registering it in a false name with a false address. It could never be traced to him but he needed it now.

There were icicles in his stomach one moment and he was sweating the next. He couldn't think what to do for the best. Forget the car and go back by train? He didn't think there was one until morning, and he needed to be at the breakfast table at the Belle Vue to complete his alibi.

He backed off. It wouldn't do to be caught with these bags in his possession. They were so heavy they were making his arms ache and he could hardly move with them anyway. He had to hide them, but where? Brick walls rose eight feet on both sides of the road. It was all industrialisation down here. But he had passed a narrow alleyway not far back. It was darker. He went a few yards down it and propped the bags against the wall. They'd be all right there for an hour or so.

He felt too tired to think. He was dragging his feet with exhaustion. He wanted to scream with frustration. To get this close to success and then not have the money was more than he could bear. He went back to take another peep at the car.

Miraculously, the police car was pulling out from behind it. It drove to the end of the road, heading towards Evans's main entrance. In seconds he was inside his car, backing up to turn into the street along which he'd come. He leapt out when he drew level with the alley, leaving the engine running. The alley seemed pitch black now, and he had to feel around to retrieve his bags. He heaved them on the back seat and was away again within moments.

He wanted to sing with success. He laughed aloud. He'd done it. He turned out on the main road towards Chester. He couldn't risk going through the tunnel to Liverpool. It was too easy to stop traffic there.

This way it was further and he wasn't sure of the route, but it was safer. This way he couldn't be caught.

Fatigue had been banished. He was exhilarated, excited, and on top of the world. There was almost no traffic on the road now. Nothing could stop him. He increased his speed. The car would do up to fifty miles an hour, though there was sideways sway at top speed. He'd finally hit the Mortimers where it would hurt.

He'd almost reached New Ferry when he saw the headlights behind him. He couldn't be sure that it wasn't the police car. It was gaining on him, so he knew it was a more powerful vehicle. Renewed panic made him ram his foot down on the accelerator.

He wasn't beaten because he knew his way round New Ferry. He'd turn down towards the Great Eastern, go round by the new baths. He could lose this car in the short streets there and come back to the main road quite easily. The turning was coming up right ahead and the traffic lights were green. He glanced again in his mirror, with luck they'd turn red before the other car reached them and he'd gain enough time to get out of sight.

Joey swung on the steering wheel to turn into New Ferry Road. He was turning wide of the corner, and careering wider still on to the other side of the road.

The car wouldn't turn. He bumped up the pavement and headed straight into the plate glass window of the cake shop. The crash was deafening, the jerk painful. His head hit the windscreen. He knew the bags had jerked forward from the seat at the back and wage packets were hurtling round him. The last thing he was conscious of was the sound of tinkling glass and jangling coins.

Chapter Thirty

1 July 1937

Hannah fought off sleep. She could hear the phone ringing in the distance. Half comatosed she peered at the still figure beside her. 'Matt?'

She knew he was awake but he didn't answer. The bedside clock told her it was three-thirty. Fear tightened in her throat. Who could be ringing at this hour?

She slid out of bed and ran down to the hall to answer it. Matt kept saying they must put a phone upstairs but she hadn't got round to it.

'Hello?' All her worries about Lizzie came back. She was afraid something terrible must have happened to her.

She caught only one word: 'Police.' They were asking for Matt. Something about an accident and a break in at Evans's.

Matt was behind her by then. She handed him the phone. He'd taken time to put on dressing gown and slippers.

Lizzie had been on her mind since she'd gone so suddenly, but this didn't seem to involve her.

'He's dead?' Matt's voice was sharp, making her stomach muscles contract again.

'Yes, they sound like our wage packets. They were locked in the safe in my office at five-thirty yesterday afternoon. No sign of break in? I'll come straight away. About half an hour, I'll have to dress.'

'What's happened?'

Matt's face was stiff with outrage. 'Phone Greg. Tell him to meet me at Evans's. I want him there right away.'

'But what's happened?'

He was halfway up the stairs. 'As if we haven't enough trouble without this.'

Matt hadn't changed. His own worries always occupied him too much to think of resolving those of others.

Hannah asked the operator for Greg's number. She could hear it ringing, on and on.

'I'm trying to connect you,' the operator assured her at two-minute intervals. The parquet floor was cold to her bare feet. She stood on one, lifted the other behind her knee.

The operator's voice came again: 'I'm afraid there's no reply.'

'There is someone there. Probably asleep. Keep trying, please, it's urgent.'

At last the ringing stopped. A sleepy voice answered. It was Greg's housekeeper.

'Wake Mr Mortimer up,' said Hannah. 'I have to speak to him.'

Matt was clattering downstairs fully dressed as Greg came on the line. He snatched the phone from her.

'Someone's stolen the wages, but he crashed the getaway car and killed himself. No identification on him and it looks like a stolen car. Get yourself down there.'

Matt was wide awake now. 'You might as well go back to bed, Hannah.' He was struggling with the bolts on the front door. 'Don't put these on again or I won't be able to get back in.'

'Was it an employee?'

He shrugged. 'Could be. The safe is locked. If our money is gone, he must have used a key.'

Hannah went slowly upstairs, filled with dread that the thief might turn out to be Maisie O'Malley's son, the lad with the strange eyes.

The bed was warm but sleep wouldn't come. She was afraid Lizzie might be involved after all. She didn't understand why she'd gone, she'd been so certain Lizzie was happy here at Oakridge. Happy with Nick too.

* * *

490

The whole office was agog with the news that the wages had been stolen. Instead of getting on with their work, clerks stood about in groups wondering if they'd be paid today.

Nick slumped at his desk, his letter of resignation sealed in its envelope in front of him.

He was slow to start work too. He couldn't get Lizzie out of his mind. She'd been gone for ten days and he hadn't been able to fill the great gaping hole in his life. He'd read and re-read her letter and it didn't make sense. He loved Lizzie, and he'd been so certain she'd loved him.

She'd gone back to Joey and that hurt like hell. He could think of no good reason why she should change her mind. He'd never felt more lonely. He knew he had to face the fact she'd gone for good and he'd have to find consolation elsewhere.

He couldn't keep his eyes away from Joey's desk two rows in front. Cleared and polished, it had not been used over the last week because he was in Blackpool on holiday. He'd told everybody he was going and there was a postcard from him pinned to the notice board. Nick had taken it down to read but it hadn't mentioned Lizzie. Presumably she was with Joey, but he hated to think of their being together.

He'd written to Capital Farms, and he'd been for an interview. They'd offered him the under manager's job and he'd accepted it. There was now no reason to stay with Evans's. He'd promised his parents to give it a reasonable trial and three years more than fulfilled that. If nothing else, he could now do the job he wanted. But really what he wanted was for Lizzie to come back and tell him she'd made a mistake. That it was him she loved.

Nick looked round the hall. The loss of the wages was causing general unrest. It was almost ten o'clock and nobody was settling down to work, but that was no reason why his notice shouldn't go in. Nick got to his feet to go up to Greg's office. He'd leave it with Miss Peacock.

He was getting to his feet when Greg Mortimer slammed through the door behind him. They almost collided. Greg was moving faster than Nick had ever seen him move before, and didn't even acknowledge his presence. The theft was having an effect throughout the company. Nick saw him say something to Miss Peacock before whisking into Matt's office.

For once Miss Peacock did not blend into her surroundings. Her glasses had been discarded and her cheeks were scarlet. 'It was Joey O'Malley!' There was an hysterical note in her whisper. She looked ten years younger.

'What was?' Nick slid his letter into her tray.

'It was him they found dead in the car with the wage packets burst all over him.'

Nick felt sick with horror. Hadn't he known Joey was up to something all along?

'Mr Mortimer's just said so. He was asked to go down to identify the wage packets. They showed him the body too. Definitely Joey O'Malley.'

Nick felt worse. Surely Lizzie couldn't be involved?

Greg hadn't closed the door and Matt's harassed voice carried clearly: 'Did you ask when we could have our money back?'

'They said they'd release the evidence as soon as they could.'

'What evidence?' Matt sounded angry now. 'They can't bring a case, the man's already dead. Just as well he killed himself.'

'At least we can all be sure we'll be paid,' Leila Peacock said sotto voce.

'Bloody chaos,' Greg fumed. 'Do we withdraw more cash or do we wait to get the other back?'

'Tell everybody they'll have to wait,' Matt said crossly. 'We'll pay when we can. The money will come back. Cost us more if we have to start again from scratch.'

'This Joey O'Malley, he's not . . .?'

'Somebody Hannah knows. She asked me to take him on in the first place. Insisted. And all this time he's been robbing us blind.'

'Good God! But he wasn't here, you say?'

'On holiday in Blackpool. The police found ticket stubs in his pocket for the entrance to Blackpool Tower. Just building up an alibi, they thought.'

'Good job he killed himself then. Serve him right.'

'Send a memo to all departments about pay.'

Nick could hear them coming out. They paused in the doorway.

'Hannah asked you to employ this one too.' Greg's face showed displeasure as he nodded in Nick's direction.

'Nick Bender from Yarrow.' Matt frowned at him with equal resentment. 'Yes, I remember.'

It didn't seem the most auspicious moment for Nick to tell them he'd handed in his notice, but he did. He hadn't expected to be persuaded to stay, but he sensed relief that he was going.

'I'm sorry,' he said stiffly. 'I've put you to a lot of trouble to teach me the trade.' At least he'd never stolen anything from them.

'You don't need to work out a month's notice if you'd rather not,' Greg said with equal stiffness.

'Thank you,' Nick said. 'Then I'd like to leave now. I'll just collect a few personal belongings from my desk, and say goodbye.'

Matthew Mortimer actually smiled at that and shook his hand. He seemed not in the least put out at Nick's defection.

But Nick was more concerned about Lizzie. Whichever way he looked at it, she would need him now.

He wondered how much Hannah knew. Before leaving the office he picked up the phone and asked to be connected with her. He wanted her to know it had been Joey O'Malley who had stolen the wages.

'I think Lizzie must be still up in Blackpool.'

'Surely she wouldn't have anything to do with this?' Hannah sounded distraught. 'What has happened to her?'

'Perhaps she doesn't know what's happened to Joey? She could still be there waiting.'

493

'If only we knew where she was,' Hannah worried.

'I do know,' Nick said. 'At least, I know where Joey was staying in Blackpool. The address is on our notice board. The boarding house belongs to a relative of our Miss Peacock. Joey told everybody he was going there.'

'Shall we go up there and see if we can find her?' Hannah's voice lifted nervously at her own suggestion. 'Will you come with me? If Joey's dead . . . She'll have nowhere else to go. This is her home.'

'Yes, yes.'

'We'll take my car. I'll pick you up at the front door. Say in half an hour?'

Nick studied the notice board. There was even a map with instructions of how to find the boarding house.

Hannah thought Nick looked wretched as he sat hunched in the seat beside her saying little. She felt wretched herself.

'I can't see why Lizzie should go off with Joey like that.'

Nick was shaking his head. They'd been through all this countless times already. He looked very young and defenceless. The journey was longer than she'd anticipated.

'Are you getting tired, Hannah? Shall I drive for a bit?' She was glad to let him.

'A nice car to drive.' He smiled at her. 'Much better than my old Chummy.' He was driving faster. She wanted to get there and get it over.

The sight of the sea and the promenade thronged with holiday makers came at last. Nick turned the car down a side street.

'There it is. The Belle Vue, on your left.'

Nick parked. 'Let's hope we're lucky, after coming all this way.'

He was out of the car before she was and up the steps of the Belle Vue. The front door stood open. The inner lobby door, with its stained glass and a notice about not bringing sand inside, was closed.

Hannah rang the bell and went straight in. The woman

494

coming towards them might have been Greg's secretary. Except that her hair was lighter and brighter and she wore a brilliantly coloured floral blouse over a royal blue skirt.

'Miss Peacock?' she asked.

'We have no vacancies at the moment, I'm afraid.'

Hannah saw Nick smile. 'We were wondering if you could help us? We've come to see somebody we believe is staying here. The name's O'Malley.'

'Yes, that's right. Mr and Mrs O'Malley.'

Hannah gulped at that, but Nick didn't seem to turn a hair. It must upset him though. What was Lizzie thinking of, for goodness' sake!

'Are they in?'

'Funny you should come today. I'm a bit worried about him actually.' She pushed her rose-tinted spectacle frames further up her nose.

'About Mr O'Malley?'

'Yes, he didn't sleep in his bed last night, nor has he been in to any meal since. It's very strange, but he seems to have disappeared. All his things are still here though.'

'What about Mrs O'Malley?' It took an effort to say that.

'I'm worried about her too. She was supposed to be coming out of hospital today, but there's been no sign of her either.'

'She's in hospital? What's happened?' She heard the fear in Nick's voice, it showed on his face too.

'Very unfortunate. 'Specially to happen while she's on holiday, poor girl. She lost her baby. A miscarriage.'

Hannah found herself holding on to a coat hanging on the hall stand. She went cold with shock. At last the conundrum fell into place.

Poor Lizzie. A baby!

That it should happen to her too! She wanted to cry for Lizzie. She knew the emotional turmoil she'd gone through. She would so willingly have helped her. She'd been through it all herself, she'd helped Dorothy, but Lizzie had opted to manage on her own. No, not her own, she'd gone back to Joey. It was the only possible reason that made sense.

Nick was pushing his heavy brown hair back from his forehead and staring blankly in front of him.

'She was supposed to be coming out today, you said?' Hannah recovered first.

'Yes, Mr O'Malley was saying last night that he was going to collect her this morning. There's even a small case packed in their room.'

'Nick,' Hannah had to shake his arm, 'take the case and go to the hospital. See if Lizzie's still there.'

Miss Peacock was aggressive. 'You can't take their things away, not without paying their bill.'

'I'll pay it if you make it out,' Hannah said quietly. 'Show us to their room. I'm afraid Joey O'Malley won't be coming back. He was killed in an accident last night.'

As she climbed the stairs, Hannah felt as if she'd been kicked. She felt sick. Poor Lizzie! If she was pregnant that explained everything.

Stiff with apprehension, Lizzie felt she'd been standing at the hospital window for hours. The car park was below her. She'd expected to see Joey's Austin Seven turn into it an hour or more ago.

She'd watched every bus halt at the gates in case he had decided not to bring the car. He was so secretive about everything. Though buses disgorged passengers constantly, none proved to be Joey.

The miscarriage had shown her what a mess she'd made for herself. She'd wanted to marry Nick and here she was married to Joey. Everything she'd done for the last two weeks had been for the sake of the baby. Losing it now was another disaster.

On top of that she'd felt a vague unease since the hospital routine had woken her at five-thirty this morning. She'd tried to dismiss it from her mind but it wouldn't go. Joey had promised not to go back to Evans's to steal the wages, but she'd been afraid, so afraid that he would. Joey's promises were not to be trusted.

The doctors had come on a formal ward round at ten and pronounced her sufficiently recovered to be discharged.

It was dinner time. The heated trolley was being pushed into the ward. Lizzie had hoped to be back at the boarding house by now.

'Has my husband phoned yet?' she asked Sister who was dishing up.

'Not yet. You'll be able to have your dinner before you go.'

Lizzie looked at the boiled fish with distaste. She wasn't hungry. She was getting the jitters. How long would they keep her here if Joey didn't come? She had no clothes with her, only the nightdress and dressing gown she stood up in.

The meal was cleared away. Lizzie hovered at the window again and turned constantly to watch the hands of the clock. Two and a half hours overdue. This wasn't like Joey.

She remembered the time he'd been late coming to the Lyceum to pick her up. Nothing drastic had gone wrong that night. Perhaps she was imagining a disaster now?

But Joey knew how anxious she'd be. He had nothing else to do but come here. Gnawing doubt was growing into a certainty that something dreadful had happened to him. She had to do something.

She went to Sister's office. 'Can I make a phone call?' She'd ring the boarding house and ask for Joey. If he'd had his breakfast there she'd know he was all right.

'Perhaps you'd better find out what's keeping your husband. There's a public phone in the entrance hall. I'll get somebody to go down with you, show you the way.'

Lizzie felt she was going to the scaffold as she followed the probationer downstairs. She felt physically sick as she inserted her coins and waited to be connected.

She recognised Miss Peacock's effusive tones when she answered.

'It's Lizzie O'Malley,' she said. 'Is my husband there? He

promised to come and fetch me from hospital and he hasn't come.'

There was a few seconds' silence. She knew immediately something was wrong. Miss Peacock's voice when it came again was guarded, as though unwilling to speak to her.

'Er . . . we haven't seen him here . . . since last night.'

Lizzie was gasping for air, her worst fears realised. Joey had been caught!

'Do you know where he is?' She rested her head against the glass, avoided the eye of the probationer standing a few feet away.

The handset was still at her ear. 'Two people came here asking for you. A man and a woman. The man is on his way to pick you up now.'

That sent shock waves through her. She straightened up. The police must be looking for her too. She had known what Joey intended. Did that make her an accomplice?

Miss Peacock's voice came again. 'Do you want to speak to . . .?'

'Thank you,' she said hurriedly and slammed the phone back on its hook. The blood was pounding in her head. What was she to do now? She was miles from anyone she knew. She'd never felt so alone. She was distraught.

She heard the tap on the glass and assumed it was the nurse. She didn't even look up. Instead her nerveless fingers were gathering up the extra pennies she'd had ready.

Somebody pulled the door open and arms folded round her.

'Lizzie,' he said. 'Oh, Lizzie! Thank goodness I've found you.'

She'd been thinking of Nick, of how much she needed him, of how much she loved him, and at first she wasn't sure he was here in the flesh. She clung to him, finding comfort in the familiar rough Harris tweed of his jacket. Nick had come from nowhere when she needed him most.

'I've come to take you home,' he said softly against her hair. 'I've brought your clothes. Get dressed, Lizzie.'

She straightened up, rigid with fear. 'Joey? What's happened to Joey? Why hasn't he come?'

'We can't talk here. There's nowhere to sit.' Nick's eyes were overflowing with sympathy. She knew something terrible had happened.

She looked round the stone-floored hospital entrance and shivered. 'Joey's been caught, hasn't he? I've got to know.'

'Not caught,' he said gently. 'Worse than that.'

'What could be worse? Not . . .?'

'Come back to the ward.'

Her legs felt as though they were buckling under her. 'I've got to know.' But she knew already. She'd had this terrible feeling of foreboding all day. With Nick's arm round her waist, she was stumbling upstairs in the wake of the nurse.

She could feel horror washing over her in waves. At the ward door, she saw Nick take the nurse aside and tell her something. She watched the girl draw screens round her bed.

Nick put the case he'd brought on her locker. Lizzie knew her fingers were shaking as she opened it. The red dress she'd asked Joey to bring was neatly folded on top of her underclothes. It brought stinging tears to her eyes.

'Lizzie!' Nick sat on the bed and pulled her to sit beside him. He put his arm round her shoulders and drew her closer.

'He's dead, isn't he?' she whispered. Deep in her bones she was as certain as if Nick had told her already.

'I'm afraid he's been killed, Lizzie.' His voice was soft, hardly more than a murmur. She couldn't imagine the world without Joey. He'd been so important in her life.

'How?'

'An accident in his car. Last night. At New Ferry toll bar.' His voice went on unsteadily, telling her how Joey's car had smashed through the plate glass window of Gallagher's cake shop.

Lizzie felt light-headed. Nothing seemed real. 'I used to buy blackcurrant tarts there. They cost three halfpence each, so we didn't have them often. Joey loved them.'

She was weeping against Nick's shirt. 'What was he doing in New Ferry?'

'On his way back to you, I think. Nobody really knows how or why it happened.' She could hold back the torrent no longer. Great sobs were racking her. Nick held her tight.

His voice shook as he told her about the wage packets that had been found in the car with Joey. And about what had been happening at Evans's.

'I told him that car rolled on corners. That model was known for it. If only he'd listened.' She could see Nick was shaken to the core too.

'My poor Joey.'

On the front step of the Belle Vue, Lizzie paused. 'Why are we coming back here?'

'Hannah came with me. She's packing your things.' Nick hooked her arm through his in a comforting gesture. Her eyes felt hot and tight but there were icicles in her stomach. She didn't feel ready to face Hannah, not when she'd walked out of her house so suddenly without explanation.

But Hannah met her at the door to the sitting-room with outstretched arms. It was empty of holiday makers at this hour.

'Lizzie, love, you should have told me. You should have let me help you. We could have worked something out.'

Lizzie hugged her, then searched her face. She saw affection and understanding in her dark eyes, not the condemnation she'd expected.

'You're not the only one this has happened to.'

'I know, it happened to my mother too,' Lizzie choked.

'That was the problem, wasn't it?' Hannah asked. 'You understood how the baby would feel as she grew up?'

She nodded. 'I had to do it. Marrying Joey was the only way. I had to do the best for my baby.'

'It wasn't the best way for you, Lizzie,' Hannah said softly. 'You should have thought of your own needs too. There's never one simple answer.'

The room was overfilled with chairs, Lizzie found herself in one, with a cup of tea in her hand.

'I know because it happened to me too,' Hannah was telling her. 'My daughter was adopted but I don't know whether I made the best choice for her. I hope I did, and that she is happy. I know for me it was the most traumatic experience of my life. I know what you went through.'

'You must try to put it behind you now, Lizzie,' Nick said quietly.

Hannah drove home. Lizzie sat in the back with Nick. His arm was round her shoulders, pulling her against the warmth of his body. The terrible agitation had left her. She still felt weak, but she was better. She hadn't been able to stop Joey. He'd wanted to do things his way. He hadn't listened to her and now it was too late.

Softly, Nick began telling her that he was definitely going to work for Capital Farms now. She knew it was the right thing for him. The hum of the engine was soporific. She dozed on and off.

They were halfway home when Nick whispered: 'Both of you would have been better off with me.'

'It was Joey's baby.'

'That wouldn't have mattered to me.' His voice was tender. 'I'd have looked after you both. I love you, Lizzie, nothing else matters.'

'What a mess I made of everything.'

'When you can put it behind you, forget what's happened, I want you to marry me. It's what we planned, isn't it?'

He took the little leather box she recognised from his pocket. Opened it and took out the three stone diamond engagement ring.

He was lifting her left hand. His fingers encountered Joey's wedding band on her third finger.

'Joey and I were married on Saturday,' she choked. She saw the hurt in his eyes. His fingers closed round her wedding ring. She thought he was about to slide it from her finger. Instead he pushed it down, twisted it round twice.

'You've gone through so much, Lizzie. Losing the baby and now losing Joey. And it's all been so sudden. Wear Joey's ring. For as long as you want to.'

Lizzie swallowed hard. Nick was so kind and thoughtful. She offered her left hand to him again. 'I'm not sure Joey was right for me. Not the right husband. I've known him too long and too well. I'd rather it went now.' She felt the band of gold slipping away.

Nick put it in his pocket. 'We've both known him a long time. He's behind us now.'

Lizzie heard him snap the leather box shut. Felt it being pressed into her hand. 'Keep this until you're ready to wear it.'

She nodded and a smile trembled on her lips. She was quite certain Nick was right for her. It might take her a little time to get over what had happened but one day she would.

A Mersey Duet

Anne Baker

When Elsa Gripper dies in childbirth on Christmas Eve, 1912, her grief-stricken husband is unable to cope with his two newborn daughters, Lucy and Patsy, so the twins are separated.

Elsa's parents, who run a highly successful business, Mersey Antiques, take Lucy home and she grows up spoiled and pampered with no interest in the family firm. Patsy has a more down-to-earth upbringing, living with their father and other grandmother above the Railway Hotel. And through further tragedy she learns to be responsible from an early age. Then Patsy is invited to work at Mersey Antiques, which she hopes will bring her closer to Lucy. But it is to take a series of dramatic events before they are drawn together . . .

'A stirring tale of romance and passion, poverty and ambition . . . everything from seduction to murder, from forbidden love to revenge' *Liverpool Echo*

'Highly observant writing style . . . a compelling book that you just don't want to put down' *Southport Visitor*

0 7472 5320 X

HEADLINE

Merseyside Girls

Anne Baker

Nancy, Amy and Katie Siddons are three of the prettiest nurses south of the Mersey. They've been brought up to respect their elders and uphold family honour at all times. Then sweet, naïve Katie falls pregnant, bringing shame upon the family's name.

Alec Siddons, a local police constable, cannot and will not forgive his daughter for her immoral behaviour. But Katie isn't the only one with troubles ahead. Amy is in love with her cousin Paul, but owing to a family feud the mere mention of his name is forbidden in her father's presence; and Nancy is eager to wed her fiancé Stan before the Second World War takes him away.

With the outbreak of war, the three sisters offer each other comfort and support. Their mother, meanwhile, is battling with painful memories of the past, and their father lives in dread that his own dark secrets will be revealed. As the war takes its toll on the Merseyside girls they learn that few things in life are more precious than honesty, love and forgiveness.

0 7472 5040 5

HEADLINE